"I am a stray, Mr. Matthew
But I don't have any soft spo

Her eyes twinkled briefly, humor mixed with self-deprecation.

Fin struck him as a woman who would always find an out. But he believed in taking advantage, whenever it appeared.

He moved again, the distance between them a couple of breaths. Caleb could hear hers, feel his own shorten. Curious fingertips brushed the inside of her upper arm, a gentle caress that blazed through his senses.

"No soft spots? That's not true."

Bones melting, she gave his chest a shove. "Back off, Matthews."

By Selena Montgomery

DECEPTION
RECKLESS
SECRETS AND LIES
HIDDEN SINS

SELENA MONTGOMERY

Deception

AVON

An Imprint of HarperCollinsPublishers

This is a work of fiction. Names, characters, places, and incidents are products of the author's imagination or are used fictitiously and are not to be construed as real. Any resemblance to actual events, locales, organizations, or persons, living or dead, is entirely coincidental.

AVON BOOKS
An Imprint of HarperCollins*Publishers*
195 Broadway
New York, NY, 10007

Copyright © 2009 by Stacey Abrams
ISBN 978-0-06-137605-4
www.avonbooks.com

First Avon Books paperback printing: April 2009

Avon Trademark Reg. U.S. Pat. Off. and in Other Countries, Marca Registrada, Hecho en U.S.A.
HarperCollins® is a registered trademark of HarperCollins Publishers.

Printed in the U.S.A.

10 9 8 7 6 5 4 3

For Mom and Dad,
Andrea, Leslie, Richard,
Walter, Jeanine, Jorden,
Faith, and Nakia.
Muses all.

ACKNOWLEDGMENTS

With gratitude to Mirtha Estrada Oliveros, a voice of sanity; to Dr. Andrea Abrams, a constant friend and adviser; to Rev. Robert Abrams, for helping me aim straight; to Rev. Carolyn Abrams, for clearing the deck and my mind; to Lara Hodgson and Che Watkins, for clever touches; to Erika Tsang, for her patience; and to Marc Gerald, for the representation. And my fathomless gratitude for Leslie Abrams, whose eyes see what I cannot and whose heart holds more than I can imagine.

PROLOGUE

May 1991

"Ah, hell." Fin muttered the forbidden oath, but she figured that at this point, the minor infraction wouldn't matter much. Assuming she lived past the next few minutes.

"Hell?" Kell murmured in dry, sleepy response. "It's four in the morning. You'll see hell if you're lucky." She tucked her legs beneath her and propped her arms on her knees. In the adjoining twin bed, with its white eyelet canopy, Julia snored lightly and evenly. Too lightly. Too evenly. But Kell understood the pretense. If she'd had her way, she would have been pretending to be asleep too. No such luck.

Instead, she took a deep breath and plunged. "Mrs. F, I know what this looks like," she began in familiar refrain, "but if you'll just listen to Fin, I promise you she's got a good explanation." *I hope.*

Saying nothing, Eliza Faraday advanced into the

spacious bedroom, the sunny yellow walls having no effect on the stony look she shot at Kell. Suitably cowed, Kell scooted back against the headboard and prepared to watch the show.

The tableau told the story: mullioned windows that opened out onto a verandah conveniently located beside a massive oak tree; Findley Borders, one of the room's three inhabitants, leaning negligently against an ivory window frame, bare shoulders brushing the sheer curtains that covered the glass. Her tall, willowy form did not sport the pajamas or nightgown appropriate for an early Saturday morning. Instead, she wore a snug crimson top that hugged suspiciously ripe curves before disappearing into a jet-black skirt that could have doubled as a handkerchief. A runner's graceful legs flaunted a brief expanse of toned skin before meeting high-heeled black leather boots that began at midthigh.

At seventeen, the girl at the window resembled anything but. A woman's eyes had been expertly ringed with eyeliner, and the same practiced hand had slicked a berry red lipstick onto the wide, luxurious mouth. Black hair curled in wild profusion, framing a face that proudly announced a mélange of heritage.

Eliza studied Fin, noting the bold brown eyes' defiant stare and the nearly imperceptible tremble of the reddened lips. Beyond the gauzy sheers at the teenager's back, dawn crested, sunlight streaming over the wrought-iron fence that surrounded the acres of the Faraday Center for Children. A dawn that had arrived with one of her young charges on the other side of its protection.

It wasn't the first time, but heaven help them both, it had to be the last. She was getting too old for this.

"Julia, Kell. Outside, please." Eliza issued the edict in the cool, even voice the residents all knew as the Hard-day tone.

Julia, no longer feigning sleep, scrambled out of bed and dutifully tucked her feet into waiting slippers. A lavender nightgown settled around her diminutive form, and she shot Fin a look of pained sympathy. Fin caught the look, and her stubborn scowl softened. Defiantly, she sent back a saucy wink. Amused and concerned, Julia smiled encouragingly and scurried to the door.

More slowly, Kell flipped away the covers. At the grand old age of sixteen and two days, she already had her life's plan. Public defender, then Supreme Court justice. Fortunately for her, she already had her first client. Fin was making a habit of requiring alibis and defenses. Tonight's escapade was one more in an ever-increasing pattern of missed curfews, midnight rendez-vous, and blatant insolence. Sometimes, though, Kell worried that Fin would go too far out on the edge to return.

But Fin hadn't done so tonight. Unwilling to abandon her best friend, Kell swung out of bed and crossed to Mrs. F. Adopting her most placating voice, she entreated, "Can I say something?"

"No." Fin and Eliza replied in unison.

"Go on, Kell," Fin urged quietly. "I've got it."

"But Fin—"

"Out, Kell. Now." Eliza did not look away from Fin. But her voice gentled. "This is between Findley and me."

Julia opened the bedroom door. Kell hesitated, then turned and walked out with her. The door closed softly but didn't click.

From inside the room, Eliza instructed, "All the way, Kell. Go and wait in the sitting room."

The lock snapped against its plate, leaving the duo alone in the bedroom.

Fin felt a trill of fear, but she quashed the beginning of panic. In a week, she'd be eighteen, and in three weeks, she'd be done with high school. That's what she'd promised Mrs. F—a high school diploma. Maybe the diploma wouldn't have the gold stars that Kell's would, but that hadn't been the agreement. Graduation and no big trouble until then.

She'd held up her end of the bargain, unless Mrs. F considered gambling into the wee hours of the morning at a makeshift casino "big trouble." Given the glower aimed her way, she had the sinking suspicion the older woman did.

But to Fin's mind, as long as she hadn't come home in the rear of a cop car, she was in the clear. After all, what Mrs. F didn't know didn't count. And she had no clue that Fin had become a regular at the blackjack and poker tables installed in the Grove Warehouse's basement. Already her stash had doubled, and she'd nearly made the ten grand she wanted for her escape. Louis Pippin, the casino's manager, didn't like to lose too much at a time, but he'd let Fin keep coming back, knowing that hot girls were good for business.

Fin wasn't naïve, and she understood he'd soon press for more, but she expected to be gone long before it came time for that discussion.

Right now, though, Louis's interest in her other assets had to wait. She'd broken curfew and a dozen other center rules. Mrs. F was furious and, Fin understood, disappointed. She hadn't meant to stay out so late, but she'd had a run of good luck around 2:00 a.m. that now rested in the bottom of her purse.

Pride raced through her, but now wasn't the time for that either. Now she needed to show contrition and shame, with a dash of innocence. Still, she could feel the rebellion coursing through her along with the pride, and she was damned if she'd apologize for doing what she wanted. She wasn't a little girl. She was nearly a grown woman, a fact Mrs. F would have to accept.

An amateur in her predicament would have been tempted to speak first. To babble out a good lie about running out of gas or falling asleep. She'd already concocted the appropriate story, but she was no novice. When caught red-handed, don't blame the paint.

And don't talk first.

So the silence lengthened between them—the young girl who knew that womanhood waited just around the corner and the older woman terrified of what her ward would do in the meantime.

At last, Eliza sighed and rubbed tiredly at hazel eyes that had seen too much. "Findley, I'm scared for you."

Braced for scolding, the soft, despairing sentence caught Fin off-guard. Worse than a scolding, the sadness nicked at the heart she'd already begun to harden. Fin's ramrod posture slumped. Driven to placate, she stepped forward tentatively. "I'm sorry, Mrs. F. I didn't mean to worry you. But—"

"But you do. And you will." Eliza understood the impatience that tugged at her ward, the urgency of a life larger and grander than the confines of the center. Of all her children, Fin bore the deepest scars and the wildest dreams.

Kell had the better grades, the native intellect. Julia

possessed the guile and a deceptively quick mind. But Fin was the cleverest. Sharp-witted, sly-tongued Fin, who could charm a snake-oil salesman out of his coins.

Extending her hand, Eliza caught the firm chin, with its slight dimple. A striking face that would be stunning in a few more years. "Fin, I don't set these rules to hurt you. I want to protect you."

Taller than Eliza, Fin found herself looking down, desperate to explain what she hadn't quite figured out for herself. Each day, the frustration in her belly grew tighter, the impatience sharper. She didn't belong in Hallden, with its three stoplights: Atlanta, New York, Paris. Their brighter lights called to her in a way she couldn't resist. Couldn't put into words. "I know, but I don't need protecting. I can take care of myself."

"You're still a child, Fin. One that I've sworn to look after. I can't do that when you sneak out of windows and off to God knows where."

"I'm not a child, Mrs. F." Fin snapped out the denial. "We both know that. I might not be official yet, but I haven't been a kid in a long time."

"You're seventeen."

"Nearly eighteen. And age has nothing to do with it." Swinging away, she prowled the bedroom, her mind jumbled with the conflicts of impatience and obligation. "I'm bored! Bored with school, bored with Hallden and the folks who have nothing more important to do than gossip and whisper."

"When you go away to college—"

"We both know I'm not going to college." A sneer curled the glossy mouth. "That's Kell's thing. She's made for school. I'm not."

"What are you made for?"

She'd been trying to figure out the answer to that very question for a while. All she knew was that the thought of four more years listening to someone tell her about life was out of the question. With a restless shift of her shoulders, she tried to explain. "Something else. Excitement. Danger." Frustrated, she threw up her hands. "I don't know. Just more."

"More?"

"More than this. More than sleeping in a kid's bed beneath lace curtains, dreaming about the real world. I know the real world, Mrs. F. And this isn't it." She swung around, arms thrown wide. "The real world isn't pretty yellow paint and chores at five. It's got life. Ugly, dirty, real life."

Exactly what she'd tried to steer Fin away from. Folding her arms, Eliza chided, "And it will be there when you've gotten an education."

"I got all the education I needed when I was ten." Fin felt the nightmare swirl for a moment before practice deadened the memory of the night she'd grown up. The night her father had shot her mother. The night she'd become an orphan. "I brought myself here, Mrs. F. And now I'm ready to go."

Eliza inquired, her tone mordantly polite, "Go where? With what? A diploma and a duffel bag?"

No, Fin thought silently. *With a diploma, a duffel bag, and seven thousand five hundred and forty-two dollars.* "I promised you I'd graduate from high school, and I will. But I can't stay cooped up waiting for May. I've got to go. Live."

The rumors Eliza had heard frightened her into demanding, "Living? Is that what you call it? Spending your nights with trash? You're better than that, Findley."

"Am I?" Fin laughed then, the sound more adult than either of them expected. "My mom was a prostitute, and my dad was her cokehead pimp who killed her during a junkie high. I was five the first time I saw a john in their bed. Hell, for all I know, my dad wasn't really my father. No one's ever been exactly clear on that score. So why exactly do you think I'm better than they were?"

"Because I know you." Eliza closed the distance between them and urged Fin to sit on the edge of the room's third bed. The only one without the canopy. Even as a child, Fin had refused the trappings of fantasy.

Eliza recalled the gangly, too-old child that had arrived unaided on her doorstep. "I remember the little girl who knocked on my door and offered to clean my house if I'd let her live here. I know how strong you are, how determined. And how anxious you are to grow up. But I'm afraid that I've failed you, Findley. If you don't understand yet how special you are, then I've failed you."

Fin turned stricken eyes to meet Eliza's. "You haven't failed, Mrs. F."

"Then why do you sell yourself so short?" Eliza whispered, rubbing a patient thumb along a cheek shadowed by blush.

"I don't." Fin reached up, intending to push Eliza's hands away. Instead, she found herself clinging. "I know who and what I am."

Eliza shifted her grip to hold tight. "You haven't the foggiest idea."

Beneath the firm hold of hands that had tucked her into bed and zipped up her first dress, Fin instinctively turned her palms to link their fingers. Her throat closed over emotions she'd never known how to express. Now they crowded close, threatening tears.

"I'm not my mother or him. But I'm not you. I'm never going to be as good a person as you. You've given me more in eight years than they ever did. I won't forget that."

Hearing the good-bye that had come too early, Eliza resisted the urge to protest. She'd held on longer than she'd ever expected. Instead, she tightened her hold. "Make me a promise, Findley."

"What?" Fin asked warily. She didn't believe in much, but she kept her word. After all, her promise to graduate from high school had kept her bound to this place long after she'd been ready to go. Another promise might make her into a liar. "What do you want?"

Mrs. Faraday understood the stubborn loyalty and counted on it. It was the last protection she could offer. "If you're in trouble, any trouble, call me. I don't care when or where or why, you call and come home. Swear to me."

Love rose, pure and strong and humbled. "I'll call, Mrs. F. And one day, I will come home." She grinned crookedly. "Promise you'll let me in?"

"I promise."

CHAPTER 1

"One-fifty." Fin slid a stack of chips across black felt, the silver discs totaling $150,000. Shiny ebony coils, tamed at her nape by an elastic band, threatened to escape their confines. In the frigid air of the hotel suite, tendrils curved against a slash of cheekbone, the slope of a high, intelligent forehead. Absently, she brushed at the nuisance, her attention on the play of the hand.

Between her and the last two men at the table lay a queen of spades, a two of diamonds, and a nine of diamonds. And table stakes of fifteen million dollars. She'd already winnowed down the competition and collected most of the other players' money. Just two more to go. With a sleek smile, she nudged, "Bet's to you, Massimo."

"Grazie." The gorgeous Italian pushed in his chips, and the chandelier's light caught the platinum band on his wrist. A custom-made watch worth a small island. "I call."

"Calling, Massimo?" Don Harkleroad, an American

oil magnate, chuckled. "Since you don't seem to have the stones for it, why don't I sweeten the pot for supper? Here's your one-fifty and another one-fifty to keep it interesting."

"Where exactly do you plan to eat?" Fin teased as she gave over more of the glittery silver. At her elbow, mounds of silver, bronze, and gold chips had been growing for several hours, but she cared only for those left to be earned. "Call."

With a broad wink, Don leered amiably. "Depends on where you let me take you after I clean the lint out of your purse, sugar."

"She already has dinner plans," Massimo corrected, his slick baritone a contrast to Don's Southern twang. "When I win this game, Fin has agreed to join me for a midnight supper aboard the *Tesoro*." He met the required bet and inclined his head toward the dealer. "Call."

"We'll have to see about that," Don challenged as he called and signaled for the turn card.

The dealer snapped the fourth card onto the table. "Seven of diamonds."

Fin glanced at the dealer's addition but kept her attention focused on her opponents. Massimo Duarte was absurdly rich, outrageously handsome, and undeniably sexy. It was at his invitation that she'd been allowed to sit at the Regents table in Cannes, to play in a game that had a waiting list of the world's wealthiest men. Women were rarely granted an audience, and then typically as dulcet cheerleaders draped artfully around the room as scenery.

She'd wheedled an invitation by flirting shamefully with Massimo, wearing him down across two continents.

He'd finally given in and handed her a seat, which had provided her with one new fact about Massimo.

He was a lousy poker player.

His winnings had nearly evaporated, and he remained in the game based more on luck than skill. When the seven fell next to the flop, his winged ebony brows arched over dark eyes that danced with glee. Despite his drawn mouth and the somber expression he'd pasted on at the turn, the expressive eyes signaled satisfaction.

Fin figured Massimo was four cards into a possible diamond flush.

For his part, Don Harkleroad, a Mississippi mogul whose wealth came from a family diamond mine and a shrewd eye for mineral rights, played a more aggressive game. He had no obvious tells, no apparent weaknesses. And, if she wasn't mistaken, he held a pair he was trying to turn into trips.

Both studied her, doing as she had, trying to read the unreadable in the twitch of a mouth or the clench of a jaw. But they'd learn nothing from her she didn't intend to teach.

To string them out, Fin made a modest bet to follow. "Twenty-five." With reluctance, she pushed her chips into the pot.

"Cute." Snickering, Massimo shifted a hefty portion of his remaining chips to join her bet. "I raise two hundred."

"I've gotten bigger bites from a mosquito," derided Don. "Lady wants to play with the big boys, she'll have to risk some of those pretty coins she's been collecting. I'm raising y'all. Five hundred thousand."

A subtle flinch from Fin met his announcement. She pretended to hem, then gamely added her chips. "I call."

Not to be outdone, Massimo gritted his teeth. His allowance from his father would not be available for another few days. Already, he'd overspent. But he checked the dip of cleavage framed by black silk and thought of the woman known only as Fin sailing with him for a weekend on his yacht. Without silk or anything else. "Five dollars, five hundred thousand. It is only money." He shoved the chips into the center, the stack spilling. "All-in. Seven hundred and twenty-five thousand." Turning to Don, he goaded, "Is this big enough?"

Don shrugged as he met the challenge. "Work with what you've got, brother."

Taking a secret breath, Fin added her chips. "Let's see the river."

The river card landed beside the others. "Ten of hearts."

An Italian oath rose from the table, presaging the disgusted turn of Massimo's hole cards. Indeed, an ace of diamonds stared up impotently beside a queen of clubs. He held a pair, ace high, a poor showing and certain defeat.

Don, on the other hand, eagerly tossed in his pair of nines. "Three German Virgins, Massimo." He chortled, his hands reaching. "Reminds me that it's time to visit Berlin."

"Tut, tut." Fin swatted his hand lightly where it hovered over the pot. "I believe it's my turn." With a practiced flick of her wrist, she revealed an eight of diamonds and a jack of clubs. "Inside straight, Don."

"Well, I'll be double damned." He stared at the woman who'd just won the lion's share of fifteen million. His short stack had maybe another hand to play, but not nearly the chips he'd need to catch her. "You are a cool one, Fin. I'd heard stories, but hell if they weren't all true. Hard as nails, they say. And she'll drive one of 'em through your wallet and another through your heart."

"I play to win," Fin demurred as she raked in her chips.

Don propped his elbows on the table. "Why don't you tell me where you learned to fleece old men like me?"

Shaking her head, Fin tutted, "Sorry, Don. A woman has to keep a few secrets."

Massimo snorted. "A few secrets? The elusive Fin is the Mona Lisa of Monte Carlo. A vision to behold and impossible to know. Not even a last name."

"Come on, Fin. Who are your people?" Don inquired. "I hear a touch of the South in your voice. Where do you call home?"

An interesting question, Fin thought as she raked in her winnings. She had a house in Los Angeles, another in Las Vegas, and a condo in Johannesburg. Permanent residency at the St. Regis in New York and a villa in Tuscany.

She lived everywhere, but there was only one place she considered home. And she'd never go back. Grinning at the older man, she summoned a glass of champagne from a hovering waiter. "Home is where the game is, Don. Shall I finish relieving you of your money?"

Before he could answer, a bell chimed throughout the suite. The butler opened the door, and in strode Jake Devon, Fin's business manager and the closest thing she had to a friend these days. He carried a cell phone and wore an expression of vague annoyance.

With an unconscious elegance, Fin rose and crossed the room to meet him. "What's going on?"

"You tell me." He thrust the phone at her. "It's someone named Kell. She says it's urgent."

Fin snatched the phone and raced over to stand near a bank of windows overlooking the Mediterranean. "Kell? What's wrong?"

"Fin, you've got to come home."

Horror grabbed her by the throat. "What? Did something happen to Mrs. F?"

"No, no. She's fine," Kell assured her. "But we need you here. Pack some clothes and grab the next flight to Atlanta. I'll be at the airport to pick you up tomorrow. I'll explain everything when you arrive."

A thousand questions crowded on her tongue, but Fin knew better than to ask. Especially with an audience. But a single query managed to slip through. "What about Julia?"

"She's coming too. Hurry home, Fin. It's time."

Caleb Matthews sat at the card table that masqueraded as a desk in his cramped office. The environs of the Hallden County district attorney offices lacked the niceties of space and ambience. Instead, the ten-person office settled for peeling beige paint, a defective coffeemaker, and a copy machine with a vendetta against him. None of which occupied his thoughts; at the moment, his entire attention was focused on the haranguing that speared across four states into his burning ears.

"Would you mind explaining to me one more time what the hell happened?" The request from the division chief for major crimes held more than a hint of annoyance. It bordered on exasperation, tinged with disgust. Shirley Benton did not suffer fools well, especially on her payroll. According to her tone, he now headed the list.

Caleb didn't blame her. "As I indicated in my report, Chief Graves manufactured evidence to implicate the defendant, Mrs. Eliza Faraday. He bribed our key witness into falsifying his statement about seeing her at the scene of the crime. Mrs. Faraday's attorney raised the issue during the probable cause hearing, and Judge Majors found it compelling. She dismissed charges."

"Did you object?"

"I did not. In my estimation at the time and given the events that followed, Mrs. Faraday is not a likely suspect in the Griffin murder."

Papers shuffled in Washington, D.C., their sound clear across the lines. "Ah yes, the events that followed. Namely the shoot-out at the O.K. Corral, where your only lead on Stark disappeared in a hail of gunfire. Is that correct?"

"Yes. However, the sheriff searched Graves's home and located the knife we think was used to kill Clay Griffin. It had been wiped clean, but the lab is testing the blood specks. Given that Mrs. Faraday's set is intact, I intend to seek an indictment for murder against Graves as soon as forensics confirms."

"Which tells me that you've lost the killer and your link to Stark."

He didn't bother to argue. They both realized that the Faraday case had spiraled away from him, and he saw no reason to pretend otherwise. But he'd gained valuable intel, a fresh lead to pursue. "If we can find Chief Graves, we can find Stark. With the city's permission,

Sheriff Calder has put his deputy in charge of the police department, and a number of Graves's officers are under investigation."

"Hmm, Sheriff Calder. Your report clears him as a suspect despite the death of his squad in Chicago under questionable circumstances. And in spite of his links to the defense attorney for your former murder suspect. Having reviewed your reports, I question his judgment—and yours."

Caleb cringed but answered firmly. "I have no reason to believe Sheriff Calder is involved in Stark. I've spoken with his superiors in Chicago, and I am confident that the deaths there were the result of a tragic accident, not malfeasance. As for his relationship with Ms. Jameson, I did not find it relevant to the prosecution of Mrs. Faraday."

"Because Graves and Stark killed Griffin."

"Graves lost control when Mrs. Faraday was released. His behavior in court tells me that he had no reason to lie. He asked me to have him arrested. Those are the actions of a man terrified for his life. Terrified of Stark."

"Or a clever ruse to help him elude responsibility." The bland tone should have warned him. Benton continued, "To summarize, your latest defendant in the Griffin murder is on the run from the elusive Stark, a criminal enterprise being operated out of Georgia's answer to Mayberry. Did I miss anything, Agent Matthews?"

Caleb resisted the urge to shift in his seat. "No, ma'am. You didn't miss anything."

"Then please explain to me why one of my formerly better field agents is playing Perry Mason, chasing a mysterious racket that may or may not exist."

"Because Stark has been the missing link in hundreds

of drug trafficking cases and illegal gun sales. Because they expect us to not look for them in a tiny Southern town, and they have been right for decades. We have at least two bodies to attribute to them, and I may have found a few more. Because, Chief Benton, they killed Agent Eric Baldwin, and for that alone, they should pay."

The mention of Eric Baldwin's name halted the sarcastic retort she'd planned. Instead, Benton replied, "Matthews, I am sympathetic to your motives, but you've been digging into this Stark case for nearly four years. I let you convince me to send you undercover to Savannah and then to Hallden to pretend to be a prosecutor. At the time, it struck me as a novel approach to learning more about this enterprise."

"During my time in Savannah and here, I've found proof that traffickers coming through Hallden have been unusually adept at avoiding detection," he reminded her sharply. "Information I was able to piece together and feed you because of my undercover posting as an assistant district attorney."

Grudgingly, she acknowledged, "Yes, we've been able to move on your intel, but in that time, you've offered little actual proof that these crimes were orchestrated by Stark." She paused, her voice firming. "We don't have unlimited resources, Caleb. I have a preliminary budget hearing in a month, and at that time, I'll have to justify every agent working in my division. That includes you."

"I understand."

"No, I don't think you do." Her tone grew ominous. "You've got three weeks to connect the dots to Stark and bring them in, or not only am I shutting down this case, you may be looking for permanent employment in Hallden. Do you understand?"

"Yes, ma'am. I understand." Accomplish in three weeks what he and Eric couldn't in years. Impossible. "I'll get you what you need."

"Good." Benton hesitated, then added, "I miss Eric too, Caleb. But I can't let you chase shadows forever."

The line disconnected with a click. Caleb stared at the receiver for a few seconds. Three weeks to reveal a conspiracy that he'd dogged since Eric's death. With his only contact in the wind and his lead suspect exonerated. All he had left to track was a violent outburst by Chief Graves, a signet ring, and a cryptic conversation with defense attorney Kell Jameson. She'd feigned ignorance about Stark, as had he. She knew more than she'd let on. More that he desperately needed to know. *Now.*

Making his decision, he depressed the line button and dialed a new number. The phone picked up on the second ring. "Sheriff's office, Luke Calder speaking."

"Luke, it's Caleb. I need to meet with you about the Griffin case."

Luke had known the call would come, but he'd hoped to buy a few more days. At least one more. No such luck. He reclined in his chair, staring at the stack of reports awaiting his review. With his chief deputy assigned to be the temporary police chief and most of his squad hunting for former police chief Graves, he could scarcely find time to sleep or take the biggest step in his life. He lifted the black velvet box and flipped it open. The luster beneath the fluorescents eased the knot in his neck but did nothing to relieve the one in his gut.

Today, he decided, *before anyone or anything else intrudes.* Including the ADA. "Sure, Caleb. I'm on my way to Atlanta in a couple of hours, and I've got to get a request for more help into the GBI. Can it wait until I get back?"

"No, it can't. It involves Kell and Mrs. Faraday. And Stark." Luke greeted Caleb's use of the name with silence. When the quiet lengthened, Caleb prodded, "Luke, I don't want to use the DA's office as leverage, but it is imperative that I speak with them immediately."

"What for?"

"Kell and Mrs. Faraday are material witnesses to what I believe is an ongoing criminal conspiracy."

More than witnesses, Luke thought. "I've questioned them already. You were there. Anything they can tell us, they already have." Luke was hanging his integrity on the word *can*. Kell had assured him that she couldn't say more until her guests arrived, and he trusted her.

"I've got new questions. What is this Stark that Graves mentioned? And who are the 'they' Kell said you were bringing to town? When are *they* arriving, and how soon can I speak with them?" Caleb responded.

Torn, Luke made an executive decision. "Do you know how to handle a gun?"

"I've got a registered weapon in my possession. Why?"

"I have to drive to Atlanta today. I'd planned to take one of my deputies, but I'm stretched pretty thin."

Picking up the suggestion, Caleb said, "I can ride along. I'm not due in court again until next week. When do we leave?"

"This afternoon."

"Who are we picking up?"

Going with his gut, Luke responded, "The 'they' Kell mentioned at the courthouse. Give me a chance to clear it with Kell. If she agrees, I'll swing by the DA's office on my way."

Caleb nodded in satisfaction. "I'll be waiting."

"Calder and Kell Jameson are going to Atlanta to pick up her friends."

James Worley felt his pulse speed. "Does anyone else know?"

In his dingy motel room off I-16, former Hallden police chief Michael Graves snorted derisively. "Of course not. I've got ears around his shop. Leftover trick from when Patmos's fat ass sat in my sheriff's seat. Still comes in handy."

"When do the girls arrive?"

"Said this afternoon." A talk show droned in the background, chairs flying across the thirteen-inch screen. He stubbed out a cigarette and lit a new stick of tobacco. He missed the Cuban cigars of his previous life, the thick smoke and mellow taste. Soon enough, though, he'd be inside again. If his partner did his job and they finally cut off the monster's head, killing Stark, it would leave the spoils for them. "We can solve all of our problems today, Jimmy."

"What should I do?"

"Call the crew. Tell them you want to order a number three."

"Number three?" Try as he might, James couldn't keep from feeling squeamish. His world was a tidy one, not the more violent one Graves preferred. He followed numbers, counted money. He didn't get his hands dirty, which kept his conscience mostly clean. Until gambling debts had piled up higher and faster. Until they'd decided to end things. "What if we're found out?"

Graves blustered, "We won't be. Do what I say, and we'll be in charge, won't we, Jimmy? You and me." He'd had a momentary attack of conscience in the courthouse. Telling Kell about Stark's plans for her and her friends had been a mistake, a second of weakness that he had to rectify. And nothing fixed problems better than a number three. "You do what I say, and we'll have tied up all the loose ends."

"Will that mean . . ." He stumbled on the question, preferring not to have an answer.

But Graves knew his old friend. "You pull this off and then you won't have to explain what happened to their millions."

"But killing all of them seems extreme," James reasoned, his breath wheezing in. "We could negotiate with Mrs. Faraday. She's always been a very nice customer at the bank. I can convince her not to put the girls in charge, if I could just talk to her about the land one more time."

"After you've been given explicit instructions not to? You got a death wish, Jimmy?"

"No. But they haven't done anything."

Graves chortled, struck by the stupidity of his partner. "No one is innocent, Jimmy. But just think of them as casualties of war."

"Isn't there another way?" he whined.

What a pansy-ass, Graves realized. More baggage to be cut loose after he took over Stark. But since he had to hide, he required Jimmy's sweaty hands on the controls. "We've got a plan, don't we? We knock off the women and take out that damned sheriff and the stupid ADA. Then all of our problems get solved. Unless you want to explain your error to Stark?"

Chills of trepidation made already cold skin clammier. James Worley knew he couldn't afford another mistake. And if Graves helped him, they'd both be sitting pretty soon. He summoned his courage, thinking of his tai chi DVD. *Breathe in, breathe out. Find your center.* "What's the phone number?"

CHAPTER 2

Standing in the library at the Faraday Center, Luke braced for the explosion.

"You invited Caleb Matthews to come to Atlanta with us?" Kell asked the question in slow, measured tones, certain she'd misunderstood. After all, forty-eight hours ago, the ADA had attempted to put her client—and surrogate mother—in prison for a murder she hadn't committed. Forty-eight hours ago, she'd broken her most inviolate promise and told the man she loved about a secret she'd kept buried for sixteen years. Forty-eight hours ago, she'd placed the lives dearest to her in his hands. And now, a betrayal? "Would you care to explain why?"

Bridging the distance between them, Luke closed his hands on rigid shoulders, thumbs soothing angry lines along her collarbone. He'd practiced his explanation on the drive over. Winning an argument with Kell Jameson required preparation, skill, and a healthy dose of charm. And prayer. "Listen, honey—"

"Don't call me 'honey' when you're trying to manipulate me, Luke Calder. It only makes me angry." Still, she relaxed slightly beneath his ministrations. The roughened touch shivered nerves that ought to have been as outraged as she, but this one man had the ability to thwart even her most righteous indignation. "Explain yourself. Quickly."

"Okay, Counselor." Luke knew better than to smile at his small victory. Instead, he offered, "Caleb called my office and asked for a meeting about Stark. With you and Mrs. Faraday."

"We'll see him tomorrow. Or Monday."

"He insisted, Kell. And how much longer did you expect me to put him off? You told him yourself that he was in danger and that he should trust me."

"You know what I meant."

"As the sheriff, I have an obligation to be straight with him. This is bigger than the four of you."

Kell lifted her hands to cover the strong ones on her shoulders, and her eyes were steady on his. "I know you respect him, but Caleb is the prosecutor, Luke. He has no reason to trust what I've told you. No reason not to indict all three of us for murder."

"I won't let that happen."

"You may not be able to stop it. The truth will come out, Luke. It's already started."

Luke seized on this admission. "Exactly. Which is why he needs to hear your story. Today." Luke had played the scenarios over and over. If they didn't take control and do this right, he'd be faced with an untenable situation—arresting the woman he loved or turning in his badge. "With Caleb along, we can control the information. And if he comes today, I can use the help.

We've got most of our people looking for Graves or covering for the officers Cheryl had to fire. And I lost a deputy too."

"He was leaking information, Luke. You had no choice."

"I know," he acknowledged, "but I don't like it." The itch at his neck refused to be soothed. "I'd feel better if Caleb rode along. And if he heard the full story from you directly." Luke could recount Kell's version on his own, or he could let Caleb hear it firsthand. His dealings with prosecutors over the years argued for the latter. Besides, no one sold a tale like Kell Jameson. "We are playing against borrowed time, love. With Graves in the wind, we have no idea what Stark is planning. The chief may have told him more than Caleb realizes. We need him on board."

"Or you can question him and find out that way," countered Kell. "I haven't told Fin or Julia about you, let alone Caleb. What if he doesn't believe us? I'm not sending my best friends to jail."

"Trust me. I won't let that happen." The fingers on her skin tightened. "Stark could have shot at you instead of Chief Graves." He could still hear the report of gunfire, his frantic search for Kell in the courthouse crowd. "I'm not willing to risk your life trying to do this alone. Matthews will have to be on board, and the sooner the better." He leaned his forehead against hers. "I love you. Let me help you."

"I love you too." She expelled a long breath. "Fine. He can come. But—"

"No, wait. Me first." Luke thought about restaurants and candlelight, park benches under the moonlight. Then he looked around the sitting room. His personal favorite and the perfect place. "This is where I met you the second time."

"Ah, yes. When you threatened to arrest me."

"Well, let's see if I can do better this time." He took her hand, drew her to the sofa with its faded rose silk. "Sit here and close your eyes for me."

"What are you doing, Luke?" Kell asked, her eyes closing, her mind spinning through reasons. Had he hit her car? Broken something? Raising her voice, she warned, "If Caleb is outside, you'd better be armed when you come in here again."

"Do these count?"

A soft weight landed in her lap, a fragrance wafting up. Kell peeked through veiled lashes. "Oh, Luke!"

Dozens of lilies rested in her arms, with more strewn across the cushions—white petals with delicate pink hearts, her favorite flower. Feeling tears rise, she choked out, "I said Caleb could come. You didn't have to rob a florist to bribe me." But her heart tripped and stuttered as Luke knelt, his hand going to his pocket.

Their eyes met, held.

"I do love you, Kell." He caught her chin in his palm. "No one has ever made me feel the way you do. No one will ever love you the way I will." With hands that shook slightly, he opened the box. A black pearl glowed inside, radiant and perfect. "I know this isn't traditional, but then, neither are you." He took her hand, brushed a kiss across knuckles that trembled beneath his lips. The subtle quiver strengthened his voice, firmed his declaration.

"Black pearls are prized for being rare. The stone is made by fighting against any who threaten." Luke shook his head. "I've never known a stronger, braver woman. You will always fight to protect those you love. You'll always stand up for what's good and right. And I want to spend the rest of my life standing with you." Taking her ring finger, he presented his promise. "Will you marry me?"

Kell felt her heart fill, overwhelming the love she'd already known for this man who'd changed her life. Stroking his cheek, she whispered, "Every day. I love you."

"I love you, Kell." The silver band slipped on and Luke stood, carrying her palm to his heart. "I wanted to do this before your friends arrived. Wanted you to know that no matter what else I learn, you're stuck with me. Forever."

With a sigh, she slipped her arms around his waist, lifted her mouth to brush his in a tender kiss. Their lips tasted, explored. For an instant, the world fell away, leaving her alone with a man that she loved more than she imagined possible. She'd placed her life in his hands, as well as the lives of those she loved, and she knew that he would do all in his power to help protect them.

But, she decided as the kiss spun to a close, she was still a damned good defense attorney. "Immunity," she murmured against his searching mouth.

"Hmm?" Luke sampled the elegant line of her throat, the hollow at its base. "What?"

"Immunity." Kell arched against his forays, feeling her skin heat and nerves dance delightfully. "I want full immunity for me and my clients, in writing. Then he can come with us."

As her words penetrated, Luke lifted his head. "You're negotiating with me? Now?"

Kell slipped her hands lower, then lower still. "I'm a defense attorney, sweetheart. I'll use all of the tools at my disposal." She stroked her palm once, nipped at his lower lip. "Full immunity."

Hard and faintly amused, Luke stifled a groan. "You play dirty, Counselor."

"I win." Kell kissed him again and stepped away, satisfied. "Give ADA Matthews a call. I'll review the terms of our agreement on our way to Atlanta."

The plane landed with the customary scrape of rubber against tarmac. Behind her first-class seat, Fin could hear the first stirrings of coach passengers reaching into purses and pockets, fishing for cell phones. She remained still, her eyes closed. She was in Atlanta, only three hours away from Hallden.

Kell's call had stirred up the restlessness she'd been fighting off for months. The games had gotten bigger, the purses fatter, and the hole inside her had gotten deeper. She'd never considered herself one for introspection, but after sixteen years of hustling and playing the odds, she longed for something more . . . permanent.

Her eyes flickered open, and she peered out the window, stifling a self-deprecating laugh. Fin, the one-named wonder of the poker tables and the woman with a heart of iron and nerves to match, was homesick.

She wanted her family. Kell and Julia and Mrs. F. She missed the smell of magnolias in the springtime, the humid heat of Georgia in the summer. She missed home.

Jake had balked at her decision to leave Cannes, pointing out how long they'd worked to get her into a tournament set to start tomorrow. But one look at her face, and Jake had backed off. Once his business in Cannes finished up, he would return to their base in Las Vegas and start planning her next rout.

For the first time in memory, Fin didn't care.

A chirpy flight attendant announced that the plane had taxied to its destination. After she exhorted passengers to be mindful of their fellow travelers, the seatbelt sign dinged off. Fin impatiently waited for her turn to deplane. Then she stood, retrieved her suitcase, and entered the terminal. The bag rolled silently behind, and she moved past the rows of chairs where passengers waited to embark. Fin ignored the faces, her mind skipping ahead.

"Hey, stranger!"

Fin stopped and turned around slowly, a frown furrowing her brow. She gave the speaker an inquiring look. "Couldn't swing that extra inch, could you? Still pocket-sized, I see."

The petite woman with sherry brown eyes and a pixie's face grinned, unperturbed. "Coming from the Jolly Green Giant, I'll take that as a compliment." She rushed forward, hands outstretched. "Oh, Fin."

"Julia." With a sob that reached no further than her heart, Fin folded Julia into a fierce hug.

The younger woman wrapped her arms around the slender waist she'd always envied. "I'd always hoped you'd shrink and put on an extra fifty pounds," Julia muttered as tears poured heedlessly, proudly. Her sister had finally returned. Leaning away, she presented a wobbly, watery smile. "Or gotten ugly. Couldn't you at least have gotten ugly?"

Fin smirked. "I tried hard, Jules. But we all have to

learn to live with our limitations." Squeezing Julia, she shut her eyes. "God, I've missed you."

"Me, too. A phone call just isn't the same."

"No, it's not," Fin agreed, wiping at a tear on Julia's cheek. "It's not the same at all."

"Come on." Julia brushed at her damp skin and grabbed the handle of her bright pink suitcase. With her free hand, she clasped Fin's. "Kell's waiting at baggage claim. She's called a dozen times asking if your flight had come in. In fact, she threatened to buy a ticket so she could meet us here."

Because she could feel tears threatening still, Fin mocked, "Kell couldn't finagle her way past security? What's this world coming to?"

"It's the apocalypse, I'm sure." Julia barreled through slow-moving passengers, Fin's hand still in hers. She wove between knots of people, shifting them aside so gracefully that few noticed they'd been displaced. Fin had always marveled at Julia's uncanny ability to order the world to her liking—and to convince the world it was happy with the outcome.

Sooner than Fin could have expected, they stood on the escalator, climbing out of the bowels of Atlanta's airport. Julia looked down the step at her. "By the way, Kell's not alone."

"Mrs. F came with her?" Fin couldn't mask her note of hope.

Gently, Julia shook her head. "No, not Mrs. F. She decided to wait for us at the center. But Kell did bring her sheriff."

"No kidding?" Fin raised a brow. "Kell and a cop. Will wonders never cease?" Then her eyes flattened. "Kell brought a police officer to meet us at the airport?"

Prepared for the reaction, Julia spoke quickly. "She assures me that everything is okay. Luke knows a little bit about what happened."

"She told him?"

"Broad outline," Julia rushed to assure her. "But she's refused to give him the details until we say it's okay."

The escalator steps disappeared into the metal landing. Julia alighted first, followed by Fin. They turned toward the baggage claim, Julia scanning the crowd. But Fin spotted Kell first.

Before Fin realized it, she'd launched herself forward, Julia on her heels. Arms flung wide, the trio collided in the middle of the path, embracing. A tumble of words, a tangle of scents, a lifetime apart.

"My God, you're here. You're really here." Kell felt her breath hitch. "I've missed you guys so much. Julia. Fin. God, you're here."

Eyes burning, Fin confessed, "I've wanted to see you a thousand times. I've even boarded the plane. But I couldn't come. Couldn't risk it."

Her head against Kell's shoulder, Julia confessed hoarsely, "When I visited Mrs. F, I'd drive to Atlanta to watch you in trial. You're splendid."

"I never knew. I never saw you."

Controlling her voice, Fin lifted her head and looked down at her sisters. Nearly two decades of distance because of her. The apologies she owed tumbled out. "I'm sorry, Kell. Julia. Sorry I did this to us."

Kell glared at her through glistening eyes, refusing to accept Fin's apology. This was her fault, her burden. "You didn't do it. I did. If I hadn't tried to outmaneuver you—"

Eyes flashing, Fin stepped back a pace. She'd done

this, and she'd damn well own up to it. "You tried to save me. You both did."

Kell planted her fists on her hips. "I planned it. Me. Not you. So this is my deal. My fault. My apology."

"Keep your voice down," warned Julia.

Fin harshed, "If Ms. Know-It-All would let me speak, I could finish this and be done with it." Moving, she brought herself nose to nose with Kell.

Not to be intimidated, Kell rolled her eyes. "And if the Rebel without a Clue would stop rewriting history, I'd shut up."

"Nothing ever changes. Always trying to be the one in charge. Just be quiet, both of you," Julia ordered, shoving herself between them. Fin and Kell looked down at her, bemused by her ferocity.

She glowered at the mutinous faces. "You both screwed up, but I'm trying to weep with joy right now, if you don't mind. We can save the blame assignments for later."

Fin caught Kell's eye and nodded. Bending at the waist, they swooped Julia up and over their heads.

"Evil! Put me down. Now!"

Giggling, they turned in a dizzy circle, laughing hysterically. Around them, passengers stopped to watch, entertained by the sight of three beautiful women making complete fools of themselves.

Finally, overcome with laughter, Fin and Kell relented and placed Julia on her feet. Julia lifted a hand to her head and swayed with vertigo. "I hate you both, you know that," she grated out. But the sloppy grin that slipped across her face ruined the effect. Grasping futilely at dignity, Julia instructed, "Kell, introduce us to your friend."

Kell beckoned and Luke approached, wary and amused. Fin glimpsed the engagement ring and sized up Luke Calder as she would any opponent at a table. The khaki shirt and gold badge told her less than the absolute devotion gleaming out of dark brown eyes. He watched Kell as though afraid she'd disappear if he blinked.

Joining them, he immediately slipped his hand around Kell's waist, less a mark of possession than a compulsion to touch. Then Kell smiled up at him.

"You plan to marry him." Fin spoke softly, a question buried in the statement. She had a low opinion of the institution, having never actually seen a successful attempt. "'Til death do you part and all that?"

"All of that." Kell beamed. "I love him."

Keeping her cynical thoughts to herself, Fin welcomed Luke with a cautious smile. "Congratulations. Nice choice on the stone." She held out her hand. "I'm Fin Borders, Kell's best friend and the person who'll put out a hit on you if you break her heart."

"Luke Calder and thanks for the warning."

Luke turned to meet the smaller woman, whose sleek cap of sable hair became her as much as the lurid pink suitcase. Extending his hand, he said, "You must be Dr. Julia."

"Julia Warner, Sheriff." She batted his hand away and slid in for a hug. "I can't shake the hand of my future brother-in-law."

"Apparently, some can," he commented as he accepted the friendly welcome.

"You'll have to forgive Fin. She was born without a romantic bone in her body."

Luke gave a good-natured shrug. "At least you know where you stand."

Handsome and a sense of humor, Julia thought approvingly. "Mrs. Faraday sings your praises, but our paths never managed to cross during my visits."

"We'll have plenty of time to get to know one another." He tilted his head at Fin. "Maybe cut down on the threats."

Mildly amused, Fin stared over his shoulder. A second man stood with his foot hooked through the metal gate separating terminal from baggage claim. He was watching the reunion closely. Copper skin stretched over a narrow, ascetic face. Black hair cropped close to the scalp emphasized the stark male beauty of angular bones and deep hollows. Fin had seen a similar face, carved into a statue in Tunisia. That man had been an ancient god, rather than this modern manifestation.

Brown eyes, a shade too dark for honey, too light for cognac, were framed by luxurious lashes. Below a prominent nose that had been broken before, his mouth promised sinful delights, worth a trip to hell. The firm, sculpted lips neither smiled nor frowned. Her gaze traveled lower, to the spare, runner's body dressed in a well-cut, but modest, gray suit with lighter gray pinstripes. Broad shoulders filled out the jacket, adding elegance to the pedestrian garment.

He stood still, watching the scene with an unnerving patience. The stance was deceptively relaxed, militarily precise. The hooded eyes met hers, held. A shiver of almost recognition and something more elemental chased through her.

When Luke waved him forward to join the tight clutch, the shiver of awareness became a shrill of warning. She'd made her living sizing up folks in a glance, noticing the minutiae and the incongruent.

The man walking toward them had the look of a bureaucrat and the bearing of a man more used to the field than a desk. And she'd be willing to bet there was a gun under that jacket. If she had to put money on his occupation, she'd double down on the call that he worked for the feds. FBI, CIA, or another initialed group that had no place in Hallden, Georgia.

Fin turned to Luke and asked laconically, "Who's your friend?"

CHAPTER 3

"Caleb Matthews. Assistant district attorney for Hall-den County," Caleb responded as he walked forward to stop within a breath of the woman who studied him with a mix of suspicion and knowledge. His eyes locked on hers, and the awareness was like a fist to his solar plexus.

"Findley Borders."

Up close, he noted the striking face composed of angles and planes, too sharp for beauty, too singular for any description less than stunning. A single dimple winked beside a ripe mouth that verged on a pout. Below, her chin jutted to a stubborn point. With mere inches separating them, Caleb confirmed with proximity what his instincts had warned at a distance.

Findley Borders was a dangerous woman. Smoke and heat given form.

A sundress of unrelieved white skimmed over curves and shadows that taunted a man's senses. Hanging from skinny straps that crossed in the back and teased with glimpses of smooth, bronze skin, the dress ended abruptly an inch after interesting. Skyscraper heels added unnecessary height, bringing her nearly to eye level. An intriguing sensation, to look into eyes the color of burnt cinnamon and see only contempt. Experimenting, he shifted to a distance best described as rude. "Ms. Borders."

Fin fought the urge to move. For one thing, she wasn't sure if she wanted to move in or step away. As she watched him, his expression remained blank, his eyes observant. Missing nothing.

Definitely a government agent. She wondered if Luke and Kell knew it. Fin glanced at them, saw nothing out of the ordinary. *Apparently not,* she surmised. In a voice still pitched low in case of listeners, she asked plainly, "Who did you say you work for, Mr. Matthews?"

"Caleb is the assistant district attorney," Kell volunteered. "And a friend." She walked past Luke to flank Fin. Laying a hand on her shoulder, she explained quietly, "Luke asked him to come along—to ride shotgun."

Fin held her examination of the lean, handsome face and the unsmiling expression. A man trained to share nothing, to hold onto secrets. A man trained to lie. Apparently, he was very good at it.

Without turning to Kell, she scoffed softly. "An attorney? Interesting." Angling her head, she perused him, from the buffed black oxfords, along the suit that hinted at Armani but lacked the thread count. "I wouldn't have guessed." To test, she prodded, "I'd have pegged you as having a more active job. Maybe law enforcement."

"Hallden County district attorney," Caleb insisted blandly, wondering how in the hell she knew. Because she did.

Somehow she'd made him, and her jibes demonstrating that knowledge weren't subtle. Fin Borders knew he wasn't simply a county attorney. But until they were alone, he couldn't learn how.

He'd been undercover for years, and no one had ever tagged him as FBI. Not even seasoned professionals like Luke Calder. Either a breach had developed in his division, or he needed to take a good look at her file as soon as possible. In any event, the middle of the Atlanta airport was scarcely the place for the discussion to come.

He turned slightly to meet Julia. "Dr. Warner."

Julia nodded warmly, reserving judgment. She didn't share Fin's preternatural instincts or Kell's professional ones, but she could read currents. The sparks arcing between Fin and the lawyer could ignite a room. "A pleasure to meet you, Mr. Matthews." Taking matters in hand, she slid her suitcase toward Caleb. "If you'd be so kind."

Caleb stared down at the neon pink fabric and felt his first smile of the day spread across his face. "I'd be honored."

With a laugh that glittered, she linked her arm in his and tugged at Fin's hand. Fin stowed her suspicions and allowed herself to be dragged along. Luke and Kell brought up the rear, with Julia leading the group through the sliding glass doors. On the curb, a massive black SUV emblazoned with HALLDEN COUNTY SHERIFF'S DEPARTMENT sat patiently.

"Our chariot, I presume?" Julia stopped at the side door while Luke unlocked the vehicle.

"Only the best." Kell climbed inside, and soon Fin and Julia joined her on the second bench.

Caleb shut the truck door and climbed in front, while Luke circled the bonnet to the driver's side. A police officer directed traffic from the central median.

"Thanks, Officer Morgan!" Luke called out to the cop. The man flashed him a thumbs-up.

Fin waited until the truck pulled away from the curb and merged onto the interstate. She leaned against the window, ignoring the safety belt. The time had come for answers. "So, Kell, why did we need an armed escort to pick us up from the airport?"

"Straight to the point, as always, Fin," Julia commented, but she too angled toward Kell. "What's going on?"

Choosing her words carefully, Kell began, "You know that Mrs. F was accused of killing Clay Griffin."

"Ah, yes. A brilliant bit of police work," Fin taunted. No way would anyone with half a brain suspect Eliza Faraday of murder. In her experience, though, half a brain in a cop would be an improvement. "I read online that you'd gotten the case dismissed."

Kell nodded. "I did, Fin, but the police had good reason to suspect her."

An unladylike snort clearly expressed Fin's opinion. "Why? Because she knew Clay? Will she be accused in the murder of every orphan who dies in Hallden?"

"Of course not," Kell answered before Luke could. "She became a suspect because she owned a version of the murder weapon, and she'd had a fight with Clay. Where she threatened to kill him in front of witnesses."

Kell pinned Fin with a warning stare begging her to throttle back the disdain. She couldn't explain everything yet, not until she and Caleb came to terms. Hoping Fin could still read her signals, Kell continued, "Neither

Luke nor Caleb were out to get Mrs. F. In fact, Luke worked hard to help me prove her innocence."

Receiving the message, Fin slanted a look toward the front of the truck. "I assume Mr. Matthews prosecuted."

"Based on what seemed like credible evidence," explained Kell, trying to soothe. If Fin ticked Caleb off, he might not agree to her request for immunity. The Fin she knew had both a remarkable ability to hold a grudge and a temper to match. Speaking quickly, Kell added, "Look, both Luke and Caleb were doing their jobs. And I did mine." Before Fin could respond, Kell ran through the case and the hearings. "In the end, Caleb concurred with my motion for dismissal, and the charges were dropped."

Charges that never should have been brought, groused Fin. However, she accepted Kell's lead and shifted gears. "What happened to Graves? Is he in custody?"

"Graves is in the wind," Caleb said as he twisted to face the women, Fin in particular. She made no secret of her disdain—a reaction that told him she'd spent some time in the company of law enforcement. "As soon as the judge dismissed the charges, Graves told me that a group named Stark was trying to kill him. Before I could get any more out of him, he took off."

"But before he got away, he accosted Kell in the courthouse lobby and told her that she was in danger." Luke checked the rearview mirror, his eyes catching the trio. "Kell believes you two are in jeopardy as well. Stark is coming after all three of you."

Caleb lasered in on Fin. "Do you know why?"

Hidden by the front seat, Julia clenched her hands in her lap, and Fin reached over to cover the tightened fist. Stark, a name she hadn't heard in years. Yet she'd thought of them often, wondered what they had become. In her time, Stark had been the code word to describe a network that had operated illegal bars and sold drugs and smuggled guns into town.

Fin met Caleb's questioning look coolly, then lied. "I have no idea." Unless they were still angry about a stolen $300,000, the burning of their casino, and the death of one of their chief lieutenants. "Do you?"

Caleb marveled how easily the lie came to her, without a slip or a pause. A useful skill to possess, one honed by training and practice. He wanted to know where she'd learned the trick. Was it training or a natural talent for deception? "What do you do for a living, Ms. Borders?"

"Call me Fin." She read the inquiry that lay behind the bland question and weighed the value of the truth. "I'm a professional gambler. I play poker for a living."

Made perfect sense, he decided. The keen observation, the brashness. All the hallmarks of someone bred to take risks. "Are you any good?"

"One of the best," she replied without a hint of arrogance. Fact was fact. "And you, Mr. Matthews? Are you any good at your . . . job?"

Caleb heard the deliberate pause. With a quick scan, he checked the others' faces, but no one else in the SUV appeared to notice her hesitation. But he was certain she was testing him.

Returning his gaze to Fin, he confirmed his suspicion. The woman was baiting him and, if he could tell by the unholy gleam in the unusual brown eyes, enjoying herself immensely. She watched him carefully, waiting to see if he'd confront her innuendo, knowing he couldn't.

Accepting the challenge and an unexpected spark of desire, he nodded once, in silent acknowledgment. "I am quite good at my job. I find the practice of law to be rewarding, especially when I can bring a criminal to justice. In my line of work, you do what you have to do to keep society safe."

"So noble." Fin leaned over to prop her elbow on the back of the seat, resting her chin in her hand. Impressed by his deftness, she goaded, "You ever think about a change of careers? Maybe a more exciting career than practicing law in middle Georgia?"

His gaze sharpened on hers, and he could hear the disbelief layered beneath the question. "No. What about you? Ever considered a grown-up occupation, or do you intend to play for a living for the rest of your life?"

The dart hit its target, but Fin batted the sting away. "I like playing for a living, although I have thought about becoming a spy. Or a secret government agent," she taunted slyly. When the cool brown eyes heated on hers in anger, she could feel her pulse begin to race. "What do you think?"

"I think you'd have to pass a background check first." Two could play at this, he decided. "What would a government agent find in your personal history, Fin? Any skeletons?"

"Children, to your corners." Kell scooted forward and cut her eyes toward Fin. She didn't understand the rising tension, but whatever was going on had to stop. "Caleb, you'll have to forgive Fin. She's always been the shy, retiring one."

"Caleb."

Luke caught his attention, and Caleb turned. "What?"

"Behind us, three car lengths. There's a black sedan."

Caleb looked out the rear window. The stream of cars had thinned as they'd left metropolitan Atlanta. The Thursday afternoon traffic was growing more and more sparse the farther they drove. By habit, Caleb had catalogued the automobiles on the road, and Luke's question jarred his memory. In a subdued tone, he asked Luke, "You expecting any company?"

Luke shook his head. "No."

"Well, we've got some. Black Ford Taurus. You're right. It's been with us since we left the airport."

"Hasn't gotten closer or further behind. A steady three lengths."

"So, the driver is either very careful or—"

"Very interested in the contents of this truck."

Caleb looked at the three women in the backseat. "Did anyone else know they were coming?" he asked Kell.

She shook her head. "Mrs. Faraday, Luke, and me."

"Luke? Anyone from your shop?"

"No," Luke answered, but he had experienced leaks in his office before. He'd thought he'd plugged them, but anyone who knew his itinerary had to have been at the sheriff's department. Or somehow listening in. Cursing himself for not thinking of it sooner, Luke made a mental note to have his office swept for bugs. "They know who's in this truck."

Caleb assumed as much. Quickly, he shrugged out of his jacket, revealing a shoulder holster and a .45 millimeter automatic. "If we've got a tail, we need to shake them loose."

The revelation of Caleb's gun had Fin scrambling over the seat. Her skirt hiked perilous inches before she scooted to the center of the bench and leaned between the two men. She swept both with a hard look. "How can I help?"

"It might be nothing," Luke hedged, reluctant to alarm his passengers. "Could be a careful driver."

"Or not," Fin countered dryly. She checked the distance of the trim black car in the mirror, then watched Luke thoughtfully. "I assume we're about to figure out which one."

"Buckle up." Luke scanned the road ahead and noted an RV dragging a classic Mustang on a towline. Ahead, on the right, a green sign announced a forgotten town and a truck stop. "Let's see if our friend is ready to go off road."

Accelerating steadily, Luke brought the SUV within a car length of the RV. Behind them, the black sedan kept pace but did not come abreast. Without warning, Luke zipped into the passing lane and overtook the RV. Then, with a jerk of the wheel, he shot off the interstate onto the exit ramp. The ramp curved steeply, but he drove into the embankment, effortlessly leveling off with a spin of the wheel. In seconds, the Taurus jogged off the highway to follow.

"Definitely company." From the second row, Kell examined the road and noted a sign up ahead. "Turn left, Luke. That looks like a logging road."

"Get down," he instructed tersely as he spun the wheel and aimed for the unpaved, rutted road. The four-wheel drive of the SUV would handle the ridges and dips without issue, unlike the exposed undercarriage of a car designed for city commutes.

Undaunted, the Taurus matched their course, closing

in with spurts of speed. Lighter than the SUV, it tightened the gap between the vehicles, and the sound of a straining engine pierced the roar of the truck's motor. Luke shot the SUV forward, tires gripping the clay and gravel until they'd sped a quarter of a mile.

In the rear, glass shattered, showering the interior. Julia yelped once, then lapsed into silence. Fin peeked up and shouted, "Move! They've got a rifle!"

"Hold on!" Luke bellowed, jamming hard on the gas.

Caleb flipped in his seat and released the pistol from its holster. "Stay down," he warned them.

In rapid fire, he shot through the broken rear window, peppering the pockmarked road with bullets. The passenger in the sedan returned fire as the driver swerved to escape the onslaught. As Caleb fired, the driver veered out of Caleb's line of sight.

"He's going to come up on your left, Luke," Caleb warned. "I'll try to pin them down as long as I can."

Adrenaline pumping, Fin poked her head between the seats. "I can take the left. What else do you have in here?"

Luke floored the gas, gaining precious seconds. Caleb continued to fire, but he'd predicted their next move accurately. Already, the Taurus edged along the rear bumper, gaining ground. Shells peppered the SUV, screaming into metal. Sparing Fin a rapid glance in the mirror, Luke jerked his head toward the glove compartment. "There's a Glock in there. Clip is inside." He didn't ask if she knew how to use it.

The Taurus vanished between one shot and the next. Caleb used the time to reload and to plan. He hadn't bargained on being trapped in a gunfight with civilians. As of now, his cover was truly blown, at least as far as Fin and Luke were concerned.

And, he wondered again, who in the hell was Fin Borders?

Slithering between the seats, she eased open the compartment and blindly fished inside for the weapon. Her hand brushed cold steel, gripped the familiar barrel. She removed the gun and snaked along the carpeted floor. With an economy of movement, she positioned herself behind Luke. She rolled down the window with a hiss of sound. "I'm ready."

As if on cue, the sedan gunned its engine and came alongside the SUV, looking to take Luke down. Instead, Fin aimed carefully and fired. One. Two. Three. The hiss and pop of a destroyed tire, then a jolt as the car banged into the SUV. The Taurus's driver lost control, sliding across the shoulder and tumbling over. Metal ripped against the exposed rocks, glass crunched beneath the car's weight. A hundred feet past the crash, Luke slammed on the brake and reached for his own holstered weapon.

"Stay inside until I give the all clear," he yelled as he and Caleb bolted from the truck. Moving in tandem, they approached the overturned car, guns leveled. From the wreckage, they could hear a man cursing, another moaning in agony.

"Cover me," Luke instructed. Caleb fell back, eyes scanning the road. Crouching low, Luke approached the smashed passenger door. A bloody arm lay across the crumpled metal and flattened grass, the body held motionless inside the Taurus. A Winchester rifle glinted dully in the grass. Luke retrieved the shotgun and adroitly removed the shells. Weapon secured, he motioned to Caleb, who approached the other side.

Beyond the smashed windshield, the driver's body lay in the gully carved into the shoulder. He groaned weakly and fell silent.

Caleb approached the driver cautiously, wary of a trap. Despite Luke's retrieval of the rifle, a second, hideaway weapon could appear at any moment. Still, Caleb crouched next to the twisted body ejected by the car's rollover. Showered as the man had been by broken glass, a dozen cuts oozed blood. Green glass bit into skin, lacerating cheeks, forehead, and scalp. The scars from the crash would join a cacophony of other, older marks. Chalky skin had been gouged and bruised by acne and fistfights.

Lower down, a shard the size of a man's forearm protruded from the driver's abdomen. Crimson pooled, poured out of the wound. The location of the glass told the story. He'd been thrown through the window when Fin's shot had taken out their tires. He'd begun to die the minute the glass had cut into his stomach, piercing vital organs. No ambulance would reach them soon enough to repair the internal destruction.

Caleb studied the face, paying scant heed to the groans for help coming from the other side of the car. As he looked into the man's half-closed eyes, blood slugged through veins drawn cold.

Was this one of the men, he thought grimly, who'd killed his partner? Did he know where Eric's body lay?

How badly did this man want to stay alive?

"Do you know him?"

Caleb spun on his heel to find Fin standing a few feet away. A grim rage flashed for an instant and disappeared. His voice was irritated but calm when he reminded her, "You're supposed to stay in the truck."

Fin rolled her eyes and took a tentative step closer. "I have a hard time following orders. Bad genes." She looked past him to the unconscious man, wondering at the flare of rage she'd seen before Caleb had banked it. "Do you know him?" she repeated.

"No, why?"

"Because you looked like you did." *And hated him.* The look Caleb had given the man had been anything but blank. Fury had leaped out, mingled with what had looked like sorrow and something else. The fury she understood, but the rest was mystery she wasn't certain she wished to solve. No one understood better than she that not every puzzle warranted an answer.

Waving at the ruined body, she warned, "If you want to find out what he knows, ask him now. He looks like he could go soon."

Caleb looked askance at her. "Are you a paramedic too? Among your other vocations." Perhaps during an EMT regimen, she'd taken some additional courses, including weapons training. That would explain her ease around the blood and gore, and her aplomb with the car chase.

"No. I told you, I'm a professional gambler," Fin corrected. "But I've seen my share of accidents."

Caleb lifted a brow at the word "accident." The attack on the truck had been anything but. And it all came back to Fin and her friends. "You've seen this before? When you learned how to handle a Glock like a pro?"

She sidestepped his question, aware of where any answer might lead. Instead, she pointed at the shard of glass protruding obscenely from the driver's belly.

"We've both seen gut wounds before. That much blood, he won't last long enough for the cavalry. You want answers, you'll have to ask your questions. Fast."

He turned back to the prostrate man. "I'd prefer to ask them alone."

The icy tone, as cold as the dismissal, shivered over her. It was then that Fin finally realized what she'd seen in his eyes.

Death.

CHAPTER 4

Before Fin could respond, Julia hurried across the rutted red clay to the scene, her pastels washed out in the plumes of smoke. Her voice reached them before she did. "Who's in the worst shape?"

Luke rose from the opposite side of the car, walking as he spoke. "Check the man with Caleb. This one is talking and cursing. He can wait."

Kell reached Luke's side quickly. "I've called 911, but the nearest ambulance is at least twenty minutes away. Luckily, Julia is one of the top ER doctors in the country."

"I'd feel better if the three of you would go back to the truck," Luke said as they stopped a few feet away from where Julia knelt with the man. "We don't know if this car is leaking gas or not. It's not safe."

With morbid logic, Fin interceded, "Neither is being shot at. We need to find out who these men are and how they knew we were coming. Julia can treat them while you and Caleb interrogate." Casting a shuttered look at the driver, she explained, "I think Julia would agree, he doesn't have much time."

Julia carried a clear plastic kit, which she dropped beside her. For emergency first aid, the gauze, bandages, tape, and disinfectant could do in a pinch, but their meager efforts wouldn't begin to repair the man dying at her feet.

Pushing aside the horror of the last few minutes, she examined her patient. From his side, she considered the insertion of glass and the position of the wound. Instantly, she knew what lay ahead for the man who'd tried to kill them. With efficient motions, she checked his pulse, listened to the labored sounds of breathing rattling through his lungs. The man's pasty skin color confirmed her diagnosis. "The fragment from the windshield likely pierced his kidney and is causing internal bleeding. Right now, the glass has staunched the flow of blood. I try to remove it, and he'll hemorrhage. I leave it inside, he's got ten minutes. Maybe fifteen." With real regret, she shook her head. "There's nothing I can do."

"Should we try to move him?" Fin asked.

"No."

From the man's heaving side, Caleb probed, "I need to ask him questions. How long do I have?"

After a career spent in one of Boston's busiest trauma centers, she was familiar with the impatience of law enforcement. Still, Julia compressed her lips. The driver of the car had tried to kill them, but now he was her patient and therefore deserved her protection. But so did her sisters. Splitting the difference, she temporized, "I can't advise you to question him, Caleb. He's bleeding to death and will soon be going into shock. He needs to conserve his strength, but he doesn't have much time."

Fin looked down at the man, her eyes steady. Her bullets had blown out the sedan's tires, which had caused the rollover. Later she would process her part in this man's death, but that time had not yet come. She'd returned to Hallden for answers, and this man might prove to be a key informant. Asking Julia what Caleb hadn't, she demanded, "Will talking kill him?"

"No. But anxiety might." Julia watched the man, then looked to Fin and Caleb. "Be very careful."

With that admonition, Julia crossed to the passenger side, where Luke and Kell had returned to wait with the trapped man. Kneeling, Julia peered inside the interior. A seat belt pinned a middle-aged man against the seat, holding him immobile. From what she could determine, the flip had collapsed the hood, pinning his legs inside. But his endless stream of pleas and curses signaled lucidity. "He's conscious and responsive to pain," she said as she leaned in, touching the man's bloodied arm. A gold ring with an emerald stone caught her eye, but she focused on her patient. "Sir, can you tell me your name?"

A hiss of agony peppered by reflections on her womanhood answered her query. "Get me out of here."

"I'm Dr. Warner. Do you know your name?"

"John-freakin'-Doe." He cursed loudly, trembling within the confines of the smashed vehicle. "I can't feel my legs."

"The front of the car is crumpled," Julia told him. "I think your leg may be broken, but I don't want to move you."

"Get me out of here!" he screamed, beating at the

window with his fist. The ring knocked against the remaining glass and caught Luke's attention. "Get me out!"

Julia waited until he paused for breath. "Sir, I can't move you. Screaming at me won't change that."

"Then give me a shot of something. Knock me out."

"Before you get started, Julia, I've got something to tell him," Luke interrupted. The heavy gold signet ring clanging against the glass matched the ones from Clay Griffin and Michael Graves. He'd bet his post the dying man had a matching ring.

When the shooter turned his head to focus on Luke, he began, "You have the right to remain silent. Anything you say . . ."

While Julia tended the shooter, Fin and Caleb waited for the driver to regain consciousness. Already, his ragged breathing had slowed considerably.

"He's not going to make it much longer," Fin prompted. "If you've got questions, ask them now."

Caleb agreed and tapped the side of the man's face. "Wake up." When the driver failed to respond, Caleb tapped both wan cheeks. Had he been alone, he would have struck harder or used a more direct method. But with a witness, he went by the book. "Sir, wake up."

A moan greeted the second attempt, but the half-closed eyes remained still. "Caleb, he's slipping away," Fin prompted. Sensing that Caleb's restraint was for her benefit, Fin placed a hand on his forearm, where he'd rolled up his sleeves. The white of the fabric was touched with blood. Muscles bunched beneath her fingers, and she felt the gallop of pulse that belied the tight control she read on his face. Caught by the division, Fin urged, "Do what you have to."

He paused a beat, wondering if she understood what he intended to do. Caleb looked at Fin and saw comprehension. Satisfied, Caleb reached for a slice of glass that had found a home in the man's upper arm. With a vicious yank, he pulled the fragment free. He could track the path as agony raced the man into consciousness. Dull ice-blue eyes fluttered open on a wave of distress. When his feeble scream died, Caleb asked, "What is your name?"

"Harold Jacoby," Fin replied instantly. Caleb turned his head to find her on the man's other side, his wallet in hand. "Aged forty-six, resident of Hallden, Georgia."

"Mr. Jacoby. Harold." His voice solid and patient, Caleb shifted to the man's first name. The voice of a friend. With the dying, kindness worked better than fear. "My name is Caleb Matthews. I work for the DA's office in Hallden." He touched the man's shoulder lightly. "Who hired you?"

"Need a doctor," came the wheezed response.

"An ambulance is on the way," Fin offered, her tone pitched to match Caleb's play. Concerned law enforcement, not outraged victim. Soothe the man into complacency, then slide information from him—a more subtle avenue than she would have expected from the man she'd seen standing over Jacoby's body. That man would have reached for the shard of glass embedded in Jacoby's guts and twisted it until Jacoby pleaded to share what he knew.

But, as was often the case with force, Caleb would never have been certain of the truth of Jacoby's confession. With coaxing, though, they might learn more, as she did every second she spent with Caleb Matthews.

Approving of the approach, she spoke gently to Jacoby,

her hands wrapping around his clammy one. "I'll sit with you until the paramedics arrive. Don't worry, we won't leave you."

The clouded eyes looked at her, noticed the comforting touch, and softened. "Thank you."

Spinning out her act, she stroked at his furrowed brow. She murmured regret at his pain. "Harold, we'd like to help you. Find out what happened. Can you tell Mr. Matthews who hired you?"

"Hired me?"

"To force us off the road, Harold. Remember?"

"I'm just muscle," he rasped. Pain skated along his skin, skewered his belly. He wanted to lift his head, to look down, but the anguish scared him into stillness. He'd done many horrible things in his life, but he'd never tried to kill anyone before. "Pete told me to just drive the car. That's all. What I always do. Didn't know about shooting at you."

"Who hired you to drive the car?" Fin asked tensely. "Who told you to shoot at us?"

"Don't know." Jacoby grimaced against another wave of agony. "Pete just told me we had"—a cough shook him, stealing his breath—"a job. I was supposed to drive. No mention of killing no one."

"A job?" Caleb pressed.

"Uh-huh." He clenched his jaw and tightened the fingers within Fin's grip. "Aahh! It hurts. Damn, but it hurts." Jacoby's hand jerked, and Caleb saw a flash of red on his pinky. A signet ring.

He had the right man. Adrenaline surged through him, but he forced himself to remain controlled. Impassive. "There's a fragment of glass in your kidney, Mr. Jacoby. You're bleeding inside," Caleb explained calmly. Then he forced the agonized eyes to meet his own. "Do you believe in God, Mr. Jacoby?"

Harold's eyes filled and his lips flattened as a wave of torture ripped through him. "What'd you say?"

"I asked if you believed in God."

"Yes. Sure." To prove it, he cried out on the next stab of anguish, "Oh, Lord. Help me."

"The Lord's not coming, Harold." Bending in until they were nose to nose, Caleb contemplated Jacoby. The pallor deepened, the breathing shortened. Death skated on the periphery of his consciousness; perhaps it would nudge his conscience.

Caleb pitched his tone between soothing and terrifying. Harold Jacoby had information that would help him locate Eric's killers. The ring on his finger tied him to Michael Graves and to Stark. Jacoby might not have been involved with Eric's death, but he knew something, some scrap of information. Desperation hoarsened Caleb's words. "Harold, that piece of glass is saving your life right now, but in a few minutes, it's going to kill you. Five minutes left in a life we both know hasn't been the holiest."

Torment flickered in response, but Harold said nothing.

"You're going to die on a dirt road, Harold. Today. Now, you can either die with your conscience clean, or you can go to meet your maker with a lie staining your soul." Caleb laid his hand over Jacoby's heart, felt the tepid pump beneath his palm. Felt the fear of mortality shiver over the damp skin. "Which do you want to do, Harold?"

Before Harold could respond, a shudder racked the trembling body. Beneath her fingertips, Fin felt his pulse slow as blood strived to reach a heart cut off by broken vessels. Over his body, she shook her head at Caleb.

Urgent now, Caleb pressed, "You're dying, Harold. Heaven or hell? Which one?"

Another spasm chased the first. Harsher, longer. Jacoby shifted his gaze to the bulge at his gut, feeling himself dying. He thought of his forty-odd years on earth, of the sins that had been etched across his records. Maybe, Harold considered hazily, a truth could erase a few of the blacker marks. He started haltingly, "Pete called . . . said we'd . . . get five thousand . . . for trailing the sheriff."

"Just trailing?" asked Caleb.

"We've done security before."

"Where?"

"At the gambling joint. And at the lab."

"What lab?"

"In the woods. For Chief Graves." Tremors began in his hands. *Not long. Not long enough.* "He paid good."

"Chief Graves, did he give you your ring, Harold?"

"Yes." Harold coughed, blood strangling in his throat. "Said the rings were special. Showed that we were a team."

Fin's eyes landed on the signet ring and its bloody red center. "A team? Who?"

"Me. Pete. Clay." Another cough. "Better than them."

"Better than who? Stark?"

At the mention of the name, Harold shook his head wildly. "Don't tell them I said nothing. I've got a wife. Kids. Please." Tears welled and ran down his face. "Please don't tell them I said nothing."

"I won't," Caleb promised. "But you have to tell me

who sent you to follow the sheriff and what they told you to do."

"I don't know."

"Sure you do, Harold," Fin prompted. "Someone told you to shoot at us."

"That was Pete. When you made us. Pete said—" He broke off again. Black spots flashed in his dimming eyes. "Pete said we'd make ten."

"Ten thousand dollars? For what?" Fin probed.

"Killing the folks inside."

Caleb froze. "All of them?"

"Yes. All of them."

"On whose orders?" dug Fin. The fingers in her hands felt like slivers of ice. They had seconds, a minute at most. "Did Chief Graves hire you to kill us, Harold?"

"Don't know. Pete wouldn't tell me. I didn't want to know." He shook spasmodically, his body temperature dropping.

Caleb could feel the man's life slipping free beneath his hand. "Harold?"

Reaching for his final breaths, he wheezed out, "Graves had a partner. Squirrelly guy. Named—"

Fin squeezed his hand as his words trailed into a whisper. "Harold?" she urged.

He blinked once as his heart ceased to fight. "God forgive me."

Not knowing if she agreed, Fin offered absolution anyway. "He probably does," she murmured as she reached out and closed the dead man's eyes.

"Come on, Fin." Caleb stood and drew her to her feet. He expected her to sway, but she stood firm. Which concerned him more. "You okay?"

She tugged her arm free. "Sure. Why wouldn't I be?"

Why would her stomach be flipping in tight somer-saults? Why did it feel like she couldn't catch her breath? "I'm okay."

"You've just watched a man die, Fin," Caleb reasoned. "It takes a toll on you. Want to take a walk?"

"No." Fin took a step, then swung toward him. "I've seen dead people before. Death doesn't scare me."

"It terrifies the hell out of me," he countered. Careful not to touch her, he eased closer. "Have you ever killed anyone, Fin?"

"I didn't kill him." The staccato response shot out of her. "I blew out their tires, but I didn't make the car turn over."

"You're right. You didn't kill him." His tone was neutral, offering neither comfort nor congratulations. Right now, a shock feeling surged through her, and soon, she'd shake with the aftermath unless she walked it off or sat down. "You saved our lives. Why don't you come with me, Fin?" He held out a hand, praying she would take it. Certain she would not.

Because she desperately needed to touch him, Fin shoved her hands behind her back. "I'll go check in with Julia and Kell. Let Luke know Jacoby is dead." Before she could give in or he could contradict her, Fin loped off to the other side of the car.

"How's it going?" she asked as she dropped down beside Kell. On the gravel, out of sight, her fingers trembled.

The paramedics loaded the body of Harold Jacoby into the waiting ambulance, white cotton shrouding his still expression. In a second vehicle, the man identified as Pete writhed on a stretcher. Curses flowed into the open air, punctuating the heavy, late-summer heat. Two paramedics hovered over him as they attempted treatment. An IV slid saline through his veins, and another needle punctuated skin to deliver a dose of numbing narcotics. The arm receiving the jolt of morphine wore black plastic manacles binding him to the railed stretcher.

At the wreckage, Luke briefed Caleb alone. "We should ride with Pete to the hospital. I Mirandized him, and shock of shocks, he clammed up. If he decides to become chatty, I'd feel better if you were along to let me know how far I can push."

Hoping it would be far enough for answers, Luke extended the black leather wallet with its white creases. "Wouldn't tell me his name, but we found his wallet once they pried him out of the car. Peter Franklin of Macon."

"Pete. That's what Jacoby called him." Caleb jerked a thumb at the closing ambulance. "Told us that Pete called him and asked him to drive. They used to do security work for Graves, including out at the lab you and Kell found."

"Graves hired them to kill us?"

"He didn't know. Said Graves had a partner, but he died before we could find out who."

Luke's ripe curse spoke for both of them. Caleb continued, "Whoever hired them offered ten thousand bucks to kill us."

Luke raised a brow. "Ten thousand dollars. Stark has gotten serious very fast. Ordering a hit on the sheriff and the ADA is major league."

"Do you really think we were the targets?" Caleb asked dryly. When Luke hesitated, he shook his head. "I know, I know. Later."

Grateful, Luke asked, "What else did he tell you? I asked Fin not to say anything within Pete's earshot."

"Good call. Because according to Jacoby, Pete was the contact. Jacoby was just the driver." Anticipating the next question, he added quickly, "Jacoby didn't know much else. But he had a ring, just like Graves."

"So did Pete." Luke had taken Franklin's ring, over his vociferous protests; he'd be sure to collect Jacoby's for evidence. "It can't be that easy—just look around town for tacky signet rings and we'll find Stark."

"Jacoby listed Pete, Clay Griffin, and himself. These men aren't that smart. From what I know of Stark, they've got to be henchmen, not masterminds." Caleb started to add more, but Fin approached at a fast clip. "We've got company," he warned Luke in an undertone.

In seconds, Fin appeared at Luke's elbow. As far as she was concerned, Caleb and Luke wouldn't be holding private conferences until she had better answers. Staying out of trouble had never been her strong suit, and she saw no reason for that to change.

As though she belonged, she inserted herself between the men. "The ambulances are almost ready to go."

"Good." Luke nodded at Kell and Julia. "I've asked a deputy to drive you all back to the Center. I've already sent a car to watch the house."

"Thanks," Fin said.

"How are you doing?" Caleb asked, touching her elbow.

A frisson of sensation coursed along her skin where callused pads caressed her flesh. Her voice, when she spoke, was huskier than she liked. "I'm fine. How are you?"

"Concerned. Jacoby and Franklin haven't given us

much to go on." Caleb left his hand on her arm, let his thumb drift across the skin to soothe. "I plan to keep trying, though. Maybe in the ambulance, he'll be more forthcoming."

Fin frowned. "Why would you be in the ambulance? It makes more sense for Julia to ride in with Franklin." Hopefully, Julia would hear useful information. "She's ready to go."

"No need," Caleb answered flatly. "Luke and I will ride with him."

"Julia's a doctor. I think that trumps lawyer."

Luke jumped in, hearing the start of an argument. "Man's got a broken leg, a vial of morphine, and a couple of paramedics to see to him. He won't need a doctor until we get to the hospital."

She angled her head at Caleb and curled her lip. "Do you expect him to have a legal emergency along the way?"

"You never know," Caleb deadpanned, his thumb tracing the angle of her elbow. "Tracheotomy, interrogatory. Happens all the time."

Fin refused to smile or to admit the ribbons of heat coursing along her captive flesh. "Who's coming with us?"

"A deputy will escort you three to the center and wait until we return from the hospital." Luke laid out the plan while he trailed a bemused look over Kell's best friend and fellow fugitive. Blood and clay spattered the alabaster dress with streaks of red and orange. Knowing Kell, Luke figured the dress had cost more than he made in a week, maybe two. Yet Fin didn't seem to care.

Caleb noted the same disregard. The cavalier attitude

toward ruining an expensive dress caught his attention, but her reaction to attempted murder, a fatal car crash, and a deathbed confession intrigued him more. Much more. Composed, unemotional, and, when the crisis passed, a self-mastery he respected.

She also possessed a heated temper and a sharp tongue. The contradiction opened a myriad of possibilities, none of which could be explored on the side of a highway. Fin and the others had to get to safety, and he needed to probe Luke for more information. Aiming for her jugular, Caleb added, "We assumed you'd want to stick together until we have a better handle on what we're dealing with."

Indicating the two women huddled near the open ambulance bay, Luke added, for good measure, "I'd consider it a favor, Fin. I don't trust her life with anyone else."

"Cheap shots," Fin murmured, but she fought down the urge to argue. She *would* feel better with the three of them in the same vehicle. Also, if Caleb and Luke went to the hospital first, she and the others could coordinate their stories. They still had to decide which stories to tell and how. With a slight bob of her head, she accepted the decision. "I'll let them know."

Relieved, Luke shook his head. "I'll do it. I want to remind the paramedics not to tell Franklin that Jacoby is dead." He jogged off toward the ambulance.

Caleb didn't buy Fin's easy capitulation. He slipped his hold from elbow to upper arm before she walked away. The play of firm yet feminine muscle beneath his touch distracted him for an instant. Holding her still, he poked, "Giving up so easily?"

"The plan made sense," Fin explained quietly, trying

to pay no heed to the frissons streaking along her flushed skin. She gave a pointed look to his hand, then lifted narrowed eyes to meet his. "Julia, Kell, and I will go to the center. We'll wait to hear from you."

Refusing the silent command, Caleb lazily stroked the contours of skin. "You don't strike me as the waiting type."

"I've learned patience," she returned flatly. "But I have my limits." Once more, she glared at his hand, willing herself not to break contact first. She wouldn't give him the satisfaction.

Devilry spurred him, made him want to see the flash of temper he'd started to prefer to her cooler demeanor. Fin didn't strike him as a woman who'd allow herself to be touched if she didn't like it. One way or another, he'd learn something about her. "Where did you learn to shoot like that?"

"A guy in Las Vegas. Ex-military." After a disastrous run at the tables that had left her with just five hundred dollars and her wits.

Plucking her free hand up, he turned the palm over and studied the fine-grained skin. He looked at her and inquired softly, "Did you pick up other useful skills from him?"

You'd be surprised. "I know how to spot a phony," she reminded Caleb. "Comes in handy."

Still refusing to concede, he lifted a brow. "For criminals, perhaps."

Fin grinned, unoffended. "We all have our secrets, don't we?"

"So it seems."

"I'm glad we agree on something." With a nimble twist, Fin turned aside. He released her hand and her arm, but not without sliding down to snag her wrist. She paused, looked up at him. "Yes?"

"I appreciate your help back there." Caleb felt the tapered bones move between his fingers. Where his thumb pressed at her wrist, her pulse skittered. The urge to pull her to him, to taste the source of the smoke and heat pummeled through him. Desire, usually a banked emotion, reared against reason and location demanded action.

But he ignored temptation, saying simply, "You're a complex woman, Fin Borders."

"I'll take that as a compliment."

"It might be. I'm not sure yet."

His look warned he intended to pursue, but she had no intention of being figured out by this federal agent who'd already lied to her friends.

Still, she couldn't dismiss the spark of attraction, the fluke of chemistry between them. She wanted to test the beautifully sculpted mouth with hers. To know how the firm, confident hands would caress more than her wrist.

Intense, gravely still brown eyes watched her with a predator's patience. Waiting. Expecting. Pulling her careening thoughts back, Fin focused on the present situation instead of the demands in the fathomless depths. "Are you going to tell me what you're doing here?"

"Not yet." Caleb inclined his head, bringing his mouth within a breath of hers. He whispered, though no one was around to hear them. "I've been here nearly two years without anyone questioning me."

"Your point?"

He shifted more, the space imperceptible. "My point

is, either you've had experience with my kind or you are my kind. Which one is it, Fin Borders?"

The query brought a smile to lips bare of gloss. Clay dust flecked her cheeks, caught in the black curls. She leaned away but didn't break eye contact. "You can bet I'm not on the side of angels, Mr. Matthews."

Compelled, he traced the curve of her ear with his free hand tucking an errant coil behind the delicate shell. "But you offered Jacoby pardon."

Her skin warmed, heated. With effort, she countered lightly, "I have it on good authority that God listens to sinners too." Because the craving to stay, to allow his touch to linger, rose faster than she expected, Fin tugged at her wrist.

Caleb released her with a reluctance he didn't attempt to hide. "Running away?"

"Not ever again," Fin declared firmly. With a dismissive nod, she pointed at the ambulance, where the paramedic motioned from the running board. "Mr. Matthews, your ride is waiting."

CHAPTER 5

Sirens blared as the caravan sped along I-75. One of Luke's deputies, introduced as Deputy Little, drove the SUV in silence. Every few minutes, he peered into the rearview mirror and braced for danger, but nothing followed the SUV or other vehicles except the light traffic of the interstate.

Julia sat on the middle bench, surrounded by antibacterial wipes stained red. Kell rode shotgun. Fin actually carried the borrowed Glock. Deputy Little had protested at first, until Luke had given his authorization. Little had subsided, and Fin had taken up post on the rear bench, watching the two ambulances through the shattered glass. Wind rushed past and rendered conversation almost impossible.

Which gave Fin ample time to run through the events of the morning. An interminable flight from Cannes to Atlanta. Reunion with her dearest friends. Introduction to the county sheriff and an ersatz attorney.

Then the extraction of a deathbed confession while working beside the most compelling man she'd encountered in a long time.

Ever, corrected her traitorous brain. Caleb Matthews of the cool, dispassionate eyes and the low, hard voice. A voice that slid from grilling to guileless in an instant. She appreciated the effect, was wary of the impact. Harold Jacoby had died imagining himself among friends, a useful skill for a consummate liar.

One to be on guard against, when lies were all the protection she had left. Caleb would probe their story with the same ruthless skill, but she'd be damned if he'd get the results he expected.

In her lap, the familiar weight of the handgun reminded her of other lives she'd slipped out of as the money had come more quickly. In the time before success, there had been other bodies lifted onto stretchers or worse.

"Penny for your thoughts?"

Fin blinked, turned to Julia. Shoving aside bleak memory, she replied flippantly, "I'm thinking about my dry-cleaning bill. White linen doesn't take too kindly to red clay and hemoglobin."

"Tell me about it. Try getting plasma out of raw silk." Julia shifted on the seat and propped her chin on her draped arms. "You handle that gun well."

"I'm a quick study." Fin scanned the road automatically. Other than rigs heading south and the occasional car, the caravan had much of the freeway to itself. Relaxing her guard slightly, she looked at Julia again. "Very impressive, Dr. Warner. Setting Franklin's leg without pulling it out and beating him with it."

"Recalcitrant patients are a specialty in the trauma center," she demurred. Too muted for Little to hear, she demanded, "Fin, what in the world is going on here?"

Fin glanced at Little in the rearview mirror. "Would you like to be more specific? We've had a bit of an afternoon so far."

"Don't play cute with me." Julia leaned in, her eyes searching. "Why did someone try to kill us?"

"I don't know." But by the end of the day, she intended to. "We'll talk about it later, Jules. In the meantime, why don't you catch me up on life in sunny Boston?"

Soon, the SUV parked in the cul-de-sac of the Faraday Center. Children, reveling in the last days of vacation, tore across freshly mown grass. Shouts melded with delirious laughter and the pleasant drone of late-summer afternoons.

Fin alighted from the truck, heels crunching on gravel. The familiar rise of the center, with its white columns and shady oaks, shook her more than she'd anticipated. A lump rose in a throat unexpectedly constricted. She blinked once, to clear vision that had gone suddenly hazy. Fatigue, she determined sternly, not remorse. She'd left the center because she'd been made for larger, grander dreams. The incident at the Warehouse had moved up her timetable, she reminded herself, but she'd have been leaving anyway.

But, a tinny thought chided, she'd always known before that she could come back.

"Fin, here's your bag," Kell announced from the rear of the truck, jarring her out of her reverie.

Julia joined Fin, with Deputy Little nipping at her heels. "Thanks so much, Morty." Julia smiled. "If you'll

just carry it up to the house?" The besotted Little gave
Julia a dopey grin and took her bag to the front porch.

"You always did manage to have boys carry your
stuff," Kell teased from the open truck doors.

"We all have our talents." Julia gave a honeyed smile
that dimmed as she watched Fin. "What's wrong?"

Kell came to where they stood and shoved the handle of Fin's bag into her suddenly nerveless fingers. She
noted the flicker of dread mixed with regret and cut her
gaze to encompass Julia. "Everything okay here?"

"Hey, Fin?" Julia nudged her friend gently. "You in
there?"

Giving herself a shake, Fin tried a smirk. "I'm fine.
Just jet-lagged."

"And scared," added Kell mildly.

"Not at all," Fin dismissed, ignoring the slamming of
her heart into her ribs. "Just absorbing everything. It's
been a long time. I'm not sure if—"

Putting her fingers on Fin's where they clutched the
handle, Kell supplied, "If she'll be happy to see you?"

Fin's shrug spoke volumes. "Why should she be?"

Always ready to defend, Julia countered, "Why
shouldn't she be?"

Fin laughed, the sound harsh even to her own ears.
"Because Kell here is a famous attorney who saved her
life last week. And you are Dr. Julia Warner, bleeding
heart and general do-gooder. I, on the other hand, refused to go to college, and I make my living as a gambler." She heard her voice quaver, and she hardened it.
"I don't imagine she'll be too pleased with two out of
three."

"Give Mrs. F some credit." Kell saw the edges of

nerves and taunted, "Maybe all these years of good living have made you soft. Scared of what an old woman thinks of you? You never gave a damn before."

"And I don't now," Fin protested, glaring at Kell. "The last time she saw me, I was a kid."

Julia stepped forward, adding her touch to Kell's. "And now you're all grown up. So go and take your punishment like a woman." With her free hand, she rubbed at her bloodstained belly. "I'm filthy and I'm starving. So move it."

With Kell in the lead, they traipsed up the broad steps to the front porch. Deputy Little stood with Julia's suitcase at his side. "Need me to carry it inside, Dr. Warner?"

"Call me Julia," she corrected winningly. "And no, I've got it from here. Thanks for the lift." Kell and Fin added their thanks.

Deputy Little tipped his olive green brim. "Sheriff said I'm to relieve Sergeant Marane out there." He indicated the end of the driveway, where a marked car stood sentinel. "You come running if there's a problem."

"Absolutely," Julia agreed.

He tipped his hat again and reluctantly headed out to the SUV.

Kell moved to the door, noting how Fin angled herself out of the way. She understood the distance, the stance of defense. But, unlike Fin, she understood better what waited behind the imposing mahogany. *Better to rip the Band-Aid off quickly,* she decided, and she knocked at the door.

The door flung open before she completed the first pass. A cherub in denim coveralls streaked past. Kell grinned as he deftly avoided a collision with Julia and bounded down the stairs. Kell entered the foyer as Eliza hurried across the polished floor, her scolding of Jorden breaking off at the sight of Kell.

"They're here," Kell announced unnecessarily.

Julia rushed inside and flung herself into Eliza's waiting hug. Leaning away, Julia cupped Eliza's face and grinned. "How come you don't get any older, Mrs. F?" she demanded, pressing a kiss to the barely lined cheek. "I want three of whatever you take."

"Silly girl." Pleasure welled up, brimmed. "I haven't seen you in months. Thought you had a vacation coming up?"

"For attendings, vacation is an urban myth. But I'm here now."

"Indeed you are," Eliza murmured, staring over her shoulder expectantly.

Because she could feel tension thread through the pleasantly rounded body, Julia shifted, but she kept an arm around Eliza's shoulder.

Fin moved into the open door and halted. In a rush, years evaporated, as if they'd never been. A lifetime of experiences shrank into a single afternoon, when her hand had reached for a shiny brass knocker. On that summer day, she'd worn frayed and faded jeans too high at the ankle for a girl who'd grown an inch since the end of school. Another band of children had ripped across the lawn, had whooped at the freedom of the summer.

She'd been ten then, had felt a decade older. Her mother had been buried, her father sentenced to prison for the crime. Determined, she'd prepared her speech in her mind, the one that would save her from foster care or a group home. Fin could feel her knuckles strike against the solid wood. Could hear the swift hiss of air as the door swung open on oiled hinges.

And then, as now, in the frame of the doorway, stood salvation.

Then, as now, she chose bravado over begging.

"Mrs. F." Fin slowly crossed the polished hardwood and stopped a polite distance away. A chasm of her own making, yet she couldn't move her feet closer, make her voice warmer. "Hello."

Eliza Faraday stood next to Kell and Julia. Embraces had been so easy with both; now, she waited for her last wayward child. Her gaze swept over Fin, taking in nothing of the grimy dress. She saw only a tall, confident woman with styled, tousled hair and edges honed by experience. Light from an antique chandelier gilded hollows and heightened angles of a face grown into its promise. But before the brown eyes had not been as hard, the jaw so rigid.

Guilt flooded Eliza in a terrible rush. She'd let her go, had let her chase danger. Unable to find the words for apology, she reached for courtesy. "Findley. Welcome home."

Fin took a mincing step, eyes determinedly flat as they watched the older woman, brown searching hazel for accusation and condemnation. Braced for disappointment, she stood straight and taut an arm's length away. At this distance, rejection would be swift, impersonal. She lifted a hand, allowed it to drop to her side. *Don't offer what she might not take,* came the internal warning. Instead, she managed a stiff, "You're looking well. How are you?"

"Well," Eliza answered politely, her heart rending even more. So cool, so unforgiving. "And you?"

"Hanging in there." Fin's throat constricted, cutting off the inclination to plead. To apologize. To weep. She lifted her chin, bit desperately at her bottom lip to still the sudden trembling.

Eliza caught the movement, and her heart gave a grateful sigh. Shunting remorse aside, she studied her prodigal daughter, saw her. "Findley?"

"Yes, ma'am?"

Eliza took a single step forward, then another. After all, she knew her children. The first step would never be Fin's. "I love you."

Fin flowed into her arms, into her heart, muffled exclamation caught between them. No hot tears, no noisy sobs. Eliza understood those would come later, when witnesses could not overhear. For now, though, the clench of fingers and the ragged inhalation told her of affection and forgiveness and homecoming. Told her all she needed to know for now of the intervening years.

They stood together for minutes, each absorbing scent and feel of family. For Eliza, Kell had been gone but always within reach. A newspaper article, a snippet on television. Although it had been from a distance, she'd been privileged to watch the brilliant girl grow into a famed attorney. Julia's path had taken her to Boston, but she'd had holidays and phone calls and letters to track the time.

Only Fin had disappeared. Vanished from sight, leaving only whispers of her life to be passed along by Julia. No postcards had announced her whereabouts, and Eliza had learned early not to expect letters filled with stories of her escapades. "I've missed you," she murmured softly.

Lifting her head, Fin tried a cocky grin. "Of course

you've missed me. I hear life's been really dull in my absence."

"She's held her own," Kell responded, eyes damp with emotion. The speech she'd prepared to ease the reunion slipped away, unneeded. Julia reached out and squeezed her hand, sharing the relief and celebration.

But more had to be said before all could be forgiven by Mrs. Faraday. Taking charge, Kell instructed, "Fin, you and Julia are taking the green guest room. Why don't we put your luggage away?"

Eliza nodded serenely. "Freshen up and decide who's going to tell me why you're all covered in blood. You have twenty minutes."

"What do we tell her?" Julia posed the question as she sprawled across an emerald green duvet in the guest bedroom they'd all envied as kids. Watercolors adorned silk-papered walls, and furniture they'd once waxed and dusted accepted Julia's folded clothes. "She should know what happened."

"Agreed," Kell replied as she ran a brush through her tangled locks. "She's already in this pretty deep. She deserves the whole truth."

"But not today." Fin's tone brooked no argument.

Kell stopped brushing. "Why not? Someone just tried to kill us. If they're that anxious, who knows what they'll do next?"

"Until we know more, I don't see the point in worrying her," Fin said in her own defense. Then, before Kell could rebut, she added, "Tomorrow we'll tell her all of it. I swear. Just give me today, alright?"

Kell thought about the immunity agreement she still needed to get finalized, and decided to relent—to a point. "We at least have to warn her about the gun-men."

"Agreed." Fin loathed confession, but for once, she saw no reason to argue. She'd been given a second chance—though, truth be told, she was probably on her fifth or sixth. Eliza Faraday had earned the right to absolute honesty from her, and if it resulted in being banished, she'd take it. Tomorrow. "Let's go then. The guillotine awaits."

In single file, they entered Eliza's study, with its paneled walls and eclectic art. More than any other room in the center, it reflected its owner. Equal parts grace and sturdiness, form and function seamlessly aligned.

Fin claimed one of two sapphire Queen Anne chairs flanking the antique desk that dominated the space. Julia perched quietly in its twin. Dragging an ottoman from the corner, Kell folded her legs beneath her as she arranged herself on the seat.

Eliza occupied the captain's chair, which fairly dwarfed her diminutive form. As though it had always been, a Meissen service waited with four dainty cups and a steaming pot of fragrant tea.

"No fatted calf?" Kell asked as Eliza poured a cup and passed it to Fin. "Mrs. F, I thought that was mandatory when prodigal children returned."

"Funny, Kell. Very funny." Fin reached for a cookie, not eager to begin part one of the inquisition. But the best defense, when a good lie wouldn't do, was selected parts of the truth. "Mrs. F, on the way back from the airport, two men tried to ambush us. They shot at the SUV Luke was driving."

Even as she reminded herself they'd survived, Eliza's hand traveled to her heart. "Luke? Is he okay?"

"Yes, ma'am," Kell rushed to assure her. "He and Caleb took the men to the hospital."

Eliza shot a concerned look at Julia. "Was anyone hurt?"

Julia nodded tightly. "One of the men in the car died. The other is in the hospital with a broken leg."

"Pete Franklin," Kell supplied quickly. "Do you know him?"

Eliza shook her head. "No, should I?"

"He had one of the signet rings like the one Graves gave me. Both men did."

"Then they work for Stark?"

"Possibly." Kell prompted, "What about Harold Jacoby? Any connection to him?"

This time, the shake was slower in coming. "I know the Jacoby family, but I'm not familiar with Harold. They're involved in this?"

"The real question," Fin offered as she stood, too restless to sit, "is what 'this' is. Framing Mrs. F for murder and trying to kill the three of us doesn't make sense after sixteen years."

"I wouldn't know, now, would I? Given that all I know of that time is that Clay saw you running from the fire at the Warehouse." Eliza drummed her fingers against the desk. "Exactly what happened that night, girls?"

Fin, Kell, and Julia exchanged looks, wondering how to proceed. "Listen, Mrs. F," Fin began, only to be cut off by the ringing of the phone on the desk.

Eliza lifted the receiver, allowing them time to marshal their thoughts. "The Faraday Center. Eliza Faraday speaking."

"Such a lovely family reunion," said a mechanical

voice. "Your beautiful girls all together again. Enjoy your time with them, Eliza. It won't be long."

The line went dead. Eliza stared at the phone, panic lancing through her. She wouldn't lose them again.

"Mrs. F?" Fin rushed to her side, taking the receiver. She lifted it to her ear and heard the insistent beep of a disconnected line. "Mrs. F? Who was on the phone?"

Eliza managed an answer past the constriction in her throat. "A voice. Computerized, I think. Said that we should enjoy our time together because we didn't have long."

"They're watching the house," Julia realized in horror. "The children."

Eliza came to her feet quickly. "We must bring them inside. And call Luke."

"I'll call him," Kell said, reaching in her pocket for her phone.

"Wait," Fin cautioned. "Remember, someone may be listening in on calls to Luke. We don't know if it's his cell phone or the sheriff's line. We can't take a chance." She headed for the door. "Bring the kids inside and I'll go to the hospital and get them myself."

"It's not safe, Fin," Julia protested, hurrying across the carpet. "You shouldn't go alone."

"Julia is right." Eliza came toward her, Kell a step behind. "Take Julia or Kell with you. Or Deputy Little."

Fin jerked open the door. "The deputy stays. Plus, Kell and Julia need to be here in case you have to move quickly. Herding twenty-five children won't be easy." She broke off, then jogged up to her room.

She returned with her bag. Reaching inside, she

removed the nine millimeter handgun. "I know how to use this, Mrs. F. I can take care of myself."

Without a word, Kell disappeared into her room and returned with a set of keys. "Take my car. Do you remember how to get to the hospital?"

Fin twisted open the front door, pausing to give them a reassuring smile. "Don't worry. I remember everything."

CHAPTER 6

The ambulances careened into the emergency bay at Hallden General Hospital and screeched to a halt. Proficient hands lifted Pete Franklin's stretcher to the apron and rolled him toward the sliding glass doors emblazoned with red letters of caution. Caleb leaped out, landing lightly beside the paramedics and their patient. Knowing Caleb would watch Franklin, Luke went over to the second ambulance.

"Keep the body inside until Franklin enters the hospital," Luke instructed the driver. "Then we'll get him over to the morgue."

Outside the blue-and-green vehicles, Franklin shouted, "Where the hell is Harold? Why can't I see him?"

Caleb strode in beside the stretcher. "As Sheriff Calder explained several times on the ride over, Mr. Franklin, Harold Jacoby is in custody. Like you. And the first person to give me the information I want will walk out of the hospital a free man."

"I ain't saying shit until I see Harold." Contorting

awkwardly in the stretcher, he hollered out the door, "Harold, you keep your goddamn mouth shut, you hear me? Don't say a word!"

Caleb pressed a hand against the agitated man's shoulder. "Mr. Franklin. You've sustained severe injuries. Although the paramedics didn't detect any internal bleeding, if you keep this up, you could cause yourself further harm."

"Where's Harold?" he growled, snagging Caleb's arm in a grip of surprising strength. "You were over there beside him with that lady. Tell me how he is."

"I am not permitted to share another patient's condition with you, Mr. Franklin. It's against the law," Caleb reminded him. The stretcher turned down a long mauve corridor. At Julia's direction, they were taking him directly to the OR. "Only next of kin can receive medical status."

Franklin grunted. "Tell me how he is or you'll pay."

"How?" Caleb asked, keeping pace with the spinning wheels.

Franklin boasted, "My employer is very powerful and dangerous. Very dangerous."

"I wouldn't threaten me, Mr. Franklin." Caleb gave a sliver of a smile. He motioned for the paramedics to stop, then waved them away from the gurney. Bending low, he murmured, "My employer is powerful and dangerous too. Eager to meet your bosses. Besides, what will Stark think when they realize you failed? And that you came to the hospital in the custody of the district attorney."

The ramifications slammed into Franklin, and his eyes widened. "I didn't tell you anything." Afraid, he shouted, "I'm not telling the cops anything!" He tried to twist to get the paramedics' attention. "Take me to the doctor, dammit! Get him away from me."

"They won't move you until I say so," Caleb warned politely.

"I need to see a doctor," he whined. "Please, man. My leg is killing me." Then, in a frantic whisper, he hissed, "You've got to protect me."

Hearing the desperation, Caleb pressed his advantage. "Your only choice is to help us and help yourself. Or maybe we turn you over to Stark with our thanks."

Franklin looked over Caleb's shoulder and appeared to gain his composure. "I don't know anything about Stark. I was bluffing. I don't know a damned thing."

Following Franklin's line of sight, Caleb saw a doctor approaching. Soon, they'd wheel Franklin away. "Okay, so you don't know Stark. What about Graves?"

"I don't know nothing about him either."

"So when we drag your phones, we won't find any calls from him to you?"

Ever mindful of his own well-being, Franklin hedged, "Not lately, no. Not since he went missing from the courthouse."

"And before?"

"Before, I did work for the police. Got paid legally. That's why you'll find his number. But not since he went on the run."

The doctor was only a few meters away. Caleb insisted, "Tell me who called you, Pete. Tell me right now, and I'll agree to a plea bargain. Otherwise, you're looking at twenty-five years for attempted murder. Five counts, plus additional charges for trying to kill a cop and an officer of the law. You won't see freedom until your grandchildren are dead."

Franklin believed him, but there were worse places to hide than prison. And worse threats than life in jail. "I want to know about Harold," he insisted stubbornly.

Frustrated, Caleb glanced up as a white-coated man with weathered, olive skin and a shaved head came abreast of them. The paramedics rejoined them at the gurney. Caleb acknowledged the newcomer with a slight nod. Turning back to Franklin, he said, "When and if Mr. Jacoby gives me permission, I will share his medical status with you. For now, however, you need to be treated before we can haul you off to your new cell."

"Who are you?" The doctor glanced from his patient to Caleb.

"Caleb Matthews. Assistant district attorney. I'm here because your patient is under arrest," he explained, extending his hand to the physician.

The doctor accepted his hand gingerly, pumped it once. "Dr. Silas Hestor. Do you plan to guard him the whole time, or can I treat his injuries?"

Caleb heard the censure. "This man was responsible for a fairly serious crime."

"Is that how you got blood all over you?" Dr. Hestor queried. "Did you get checked out?"

"Not my blood," Caleb replied tersely. He shifted to allow one of the paramedics to report out. "There was a Dr. Warner on scene to treat the patient. According to her diagnosis, his femur is broken, and, while he's been conscious and responsive since the accident, she recommended an ultrasound and a CT."

"And where is this Dr. Warner?"

"Otherwise disposed." Caleb gave the short answer, knowing he stopped on the precipice of rude. But, for some reason, he'd taken an immediate dislike to

Dr. Hestor. "Dr. Warner treated the wounds on scene, and we can make her available if necessary."

"I think I can muddle through." Hestor tapped the stretcher, giving the paramedics the signal to move. Turning away, he looked over his shoulder at Caleb. "What did our patient do?"

"Why?"

"Curiosity, Mr. Matthews. Occupational hazard."

Caleb had no reason to doubt the doctor except instinct. And his instinct blared at him to keep quiet. "I'm not at liberty to release that information at this time. But we appreciate you patching him up for us."

Clearly irritated, Dr. Hestor nodded and followed his patient behind the swinging metal doors.

Caleb turned and headed toward the waiting room, moving quickly along the hospital's corridors. During his tenure in Hallden, he'd become very familiar with the hospital's layout. More than once, he'd been summoned to its sterile confines to meet an officer or talk to a witness.

This was his first trip to deliver a man who'd tried to kill him.

He turned the corridor, absently noting the row of private rooms that stretched past a swinging chartreuse door. As he passed, a figure emerged. Caleb stopped, surprised. "Judge Majors."

The trim, white-haired woman halted, then nodded in weary greeting. "Mr. Matthews."

Caleb noted that the gray eyes were rimmed with red and the suit she wore was rumpled. "How are you, Judge?"

"Tired." She didn't bother to stifle a yawn. "The chairs in these rooms weren't designed for long-term use."

Reading the question in his concerned eyes, she sighed. "My husband, Roger, is in ICU. He's had a heart attack." She took a deep draught of air, despite the staleness of the hallway. "What brings you here, Mr. Matthews? You've got blood on your shirt."

"Not mine, Judge. A man tried to kill the sheriff, and I happened to be in the car."

She asked anxiously, "Is Sheriff Calder okay?"

"Yes. We brought the suspect in for medical treatment." Caleb recognized the shocky look and the slight sway of sheer exhaustion. He touched her shoulder, as much out of comfort as to steady her. "I'm so sorry about your husband, Judge Majors. Is there anything I can do? Anyone you need me to call?"

The exhausted mouth managed a tremulous smile. "We're waiting on a prognosis now. It's his second one. Twenty years apart, but just as shocking. Just as terrifying."

He reached out to her, laid a hand on her arm. "Can I get you anything?"

Judge Majors patted the comforting hand. "A miracle would be lovely." With another pat, she crossed past him and down to the nurse's station.

Caleb shook his head. Mary Majors sat as the chief judge for the Superior Court of Hallden County, one of two regular judges on the bench. In his time in town, he'd appeared before both and was always pleased when he drew Majors. She was smart, fair, and evenhanded. Prosecutors and defense attorneys respected her, and neither suspected the other of favorable treatment.

Such a shame, he thought as he rounded the corner and saw Luke.

"How's our friend?" Luke asked.

"Franklin's being treated by a Dr. Hestor. Friendly guy," Caleb said dryly.

Luke had met Hestor a few times and had had the same reaction. "He's arrogant and obnoxious," he corrected. "They've taken Jacoby's body to the morgue. Coroner will do an autopsy." He indicated a smaller waiting room. "Let's talk."

Caleb preceded him into the cramped quarters. He snagged a chair, flipped it around, and straddled the seat while Luke pushed the door firmly shut. "You want to compare notes."

"You seem to know more about Stark than you let on at the courthouse," Luke replied. He handed Caleb a bottle of water he'd begged from the duty nurse. He was nursing his second bottle, drinking slowly. His first one had been drained in an instant, sluicing through his outrage. He prided himself on an even temper and a cool head. But attempted murder tended to stoke both. "What's your angle?"

Twisting the cap off the ice-cold bottle, Caleb took a long draught. "Same as yours. A gang of thugs operating with impunity in Hallden."

"Tuesday was the first time I heard the name, but the m.o. sounds right," Luke said. "Criminals trot out some nasty underground gang like the bogeyman, usually when they want to make a deal. These people have been accused of everything from illegal gambling to drug running."

"Ever get anything more than stories?"

"Nope. Anytime I asked for proof or a name, they shut down." Luke scrubbed his hand over his face wearily.

"To be honest, I haven't had the resources to chase after shadows, and I didn't have a reason to take the myths seriously."

"Now you think they're real." It wasn't a question. Proof rested on a slab in the morgue and in the terror he'd read in Franklin's eyes. "What exactly do you know about them?"

Luke took another swig. "Slick operation. According to what I've heard, they've operated out of Georgia for the past twenty years unchecked. You?"

"Some credit Stark with introducing meth to the Southeast and supplying a hefty number of the unregistered firearms that get resold up north."

"Sounds like the Mob."

With a sigh, Caleb rubbed the bottle's condensation against his forehead. "Not exactly. What we've got is a group that facilitates. They don't personally traffic the drugs or sell the guns. They grease the way for others, sliding them right through Hallden and up I-75 or I-16."

Luke lifted a brow. "How did you hear about all of this in the DA's office? We haven't received this information in the sheriff's office or over at the police department. The GBI hasn't been too helpful either."

Tread carefully, Caleb thought. "After the scene with Graves at the courthouse, I called my buddies in the FBI. They sent me what they had."

"You planning to share?"

"Yes. That's one of the reasons I wanted to tag along today." He admired Luke Calder, and if anyone had earned the right to know about him, Luke had. Still, Luke's ties with Kell and the others were troubling. Especially the enigmatic Fin Borders. Until he understood what was going on with all of them, he'd hold off on his real identity. "That, and to find out what Kell knows."

Luke scratched at the back of his neck, which tightened abruptly. "Kell plans to tell you what she knows, but she's got conditions. She expects full immunity for her and the others." Before Caleb could protest, he lifted his hands. "You've faced her in court, Caleb. Before you fight her on this one, you'd better decide how badly we want to capture Stark."

Caleb satisfied himself with an angry grunt. "Fine. I assume I'll get to draw up the papers, or has she done that already?"

"I'm sure she'll be willing to use your documents to start." Luke made a mental note to have Kell concede on that point. "We should head over to the center. I like Little, but he's fairly new." Luke dropped his bottle into a green bin and caught the empty bottle Caleb tossed to him. He opened the door to find Fin standing a few feet away with the receptionist.

"Fin? What's going on?"

She raced over to Luke and pushed him inside the room, shutting the door. Caleb stood still, waiting. Fin looked at them both. "Mrs. F got a phone call. Disguised voice, but the words were clear. They told her we're all in danger. The kids are all inside the house, but I didn't want to risk using your line until you're sure it's clean."

"Good thinking." Luke lifted the radio at his hip. "Dispatch."

"This is Curly."

"Curly, send Marane back over to the center and raise Cheryl on the horn. Get me a couple of uniforms over there too."

"Something happen?" Curly demanded. "I can still fire pretty straight."

"This is just a precaution, but I don't want to take any chances."

"Roger that."

Luke replaced the radio and fished in his pocket for his keys. "Let's go."

Together, they rushed out of the hospital. Kell's silver Porsche had been illegally parked along the curb, behind a patrol car Luke had ordered. A young deputy sat behind the steering wheel in the cop car, lights flashing on silent.

Fin noted the driver and offered, "Caleb, why don't you ride back with me?"

Luke agreed to the plan absentmindedly, his mind on Kell and the center. "Good, good. I'm going to use the lights. I'll see you at the center."

Luke vanished inside the patrol car, leaving Caleb and Fin on the curb. "I figure you and I should get to know each other better," Fin supplied as she unlocked the door. "And you can tell me what an FBI agent is doing in Hallden, masquerading as an attorney."

Knowing he had few options, Caleb got inside the low-slung car. He'd received clearance to bring the sheriff into his confidence if the need arose, but they hadn't discussed potential criminals. However, if today hadn't proven his need to breach protocol, he didn't know what would.

He waited while Fin started the car and drove toward the street. Ahead, sirens whirred as Luke sped toward the center. Caleb faced Fin. "How did you know?"

"Instinct." She glanced at him. "What division?"

"I started out in Violent Crime. My partner was from

Macon, and he spent his free time hunting a theory he'd been playing with for years. Read arrest reports and sheets from the DEA, Justice Department, and the GBI. After a while, he built a pattern."

"Pattern?" She zipped around a slow-moving pickup truck.

"Drug shipments we'd collar in North Carolina or D.C. Guns sold at shows in New Jersey or New York or Florida had a common point of origin if you backtracked."

"Hallden?" Fin gunned the engine and slid beneath a changing traffic light, then wove through a string of cars moving too slowly on the main thoroughfare.

She drove with speed and precision. No wasted movements and no fear. Relaxing, he took his eyes off the road and focused on her questions. "Nothing so clean. But when we got confessions, more than a few mentioned being able to sneak past patrols around middle Georgia, especially around here."

"When did you catch this case?"

"When Stark killed my partner, Eric Baldwin." Sorrow had years ago morphed into a simmering anger. "Eric convinced our boss to let him track some leads. He didn't have support, and he wasn't exactly seasoned. But his gut told him he was onto something in Savannah. Something that led him to Hallden."

Traffic lights gave way to open road, and the Porsche purred as she punched the gas toward seventy-five. "Where were you?"

"Undercover for a federal gang task force. We'd set up our own protocol. Contact every thirty-six hours, no deviations." He'd been on the brink of a major bust, distracted by a kingpin threatening to slip below the radar again. Impotent guilt had hung with him since.

"Eric missed a check-in. I sent up a flare, but he didn't surface. Ever."

Fin gave a short nod, knowing words did little to assuage guilt. "How did he die?"

Caleb dropped his shoulders and rolled his neck before responding. "I don't know. We never recovered his body."

"But you're still looking." She kept her eyes on the road. "He's lucky to have you in his corner. Any leads?"

"Just his last message to me. He said he'd found a lead around here. Was coming to check it out."

"Then why were you assigned to Savannah?"

"I focused on Savannah first because that's where he'd made his base. Port city, plenty of crime. But I didn't get a nibble."

"What led you to Hallden?"

Caleb nodded. "Eric was a pack rat. Kept every scrap of paper, every note scribbled on a napkin." He thought about the day he'd inventoried Eric's apartment. "The case went cold and my chief planned to yank me back to D.C. I got permission to go through his stuff again." He remembered the first new break he'd found. "We'd gone under together once on a vehicle theft ring in Virginia. Worked out a code. I found a note stuck in one of the boxes from his apartment. When I deciphered the message, it told me he suspected the epicenter was in Hallden." Flimsy evidence on which to request a transfer, but by then straws had been all he had had to go on. "I got reassigned here and started watching."

"See anything?"

Caleb turned to face her fully, the center coming into sight. "You tell me."

"I'm not saying anything until Kell gives me the okay."

Her experiences with the FBI hadn't been ones that promoted trust. Trust was a commodity she kept in short supply, particularly given how forthcoming a trained liar had been with her. Wary, she demanded, "Why did you tell me the truth? I could use this against you."

"You won't."

"How do you know?"

Caleb had been thinking the same thing. Other than her name and her handiness in a gunfight, Fin remained a mystery—except that he knew to his bones she wouldn't reveal his secret. "You won't do anything to harm the people inside that house. Stark is real, and the danger to you and everyone you care about is real. You're a woman who understands the importance of a good pretense." He fixed her with a solemn look. "Like recognizes like, doesn't it?"

"We're not the same," Fin dismissed.

"Of course we are. We both pretend to be who we need to be to survive," he countered patiently. "We both rely on our wits to beat the enemy. And we both see more than anyone expects."

Fin ignored him as she rolled up to the center's gates. A deputy she didn't recognize approached the car. After checking their licenses against a list she carried, she motioned them past.

"Is everything okay?" Fin asked the woman, before driving inside. "Did Sheriff Calder make it back?"

"Fine, ma'am. The sheriff is inside, but no one else has been in or out."

Satisfied, Fin continued into the center. For now, her family was safe. All that remained was figuring out how to stall Caleb until they could finish their plans on how to explain their connection to Stark. "Caleb," she said, turning into the driveway, "I'll make you a deal."

"What kind of deal?"

"You don't ask any questions tonight, and I won't let them know who you are." She put the car in park and released her seat belt. Turning to him, she covered his hand, where it rested on the console. "One night, and then you'll get your answers."

Caleb recognized the move. Touch him to convince him of her sincerity. And distract his libido. The second was definitely working. "My silence for yours?" He flipped his hand, linking their fingers. "Your secret's bigger. What else do I get?"

Their fingers laced, and Fin felt the friction of palm to palm in her belly. How had she never realized how erogenous hands could be? Flicking her eyes to his, she boldly countered, "You'll get absolutely nothing if you push us too hard. Cut your losses tonight, and I promise you'll get what you want tomorrow."

His gut tightened at the sultry smile, and her scent fluttered between them. She smelled clean, provocative. Dangerous. "What I want." He repeated her words and brought his free hand to the slender nape. Tugged her closer. "Do you know what I want right now?"

"You're not exactly being subtle," she whispered, already feeling the heat. Adrenaline mixed with chemistry, tying her stomach in knots. His mouth came closer, slowly. His free hand covered hers on the steering wheel, brought it to join the other. She looked at their hands and daringly raised her eyes to meet his. He wanted to kiss her, and she didn't object. After all, it was just a kiss. Playing along, she teased, "What are you going to do about it?"

"This." His mouth closed over hers, stealing inside.

Caleb intended the kiss to be brief, exploratory. To size up the reality of his attraction. He hadn't expected the slash of fire, the temptation of warm, molten secrets that drew him inside. Held him there, dizzily drowning. Her flavors stormed his senses, driving him to plunder, but he kept their hands on the console, his fingers on the silken skin at her throat. Not yet, he warned himself, scarcely heeding his own admonition.

A contained explosion rocketed through Fin. A kiss shouldn't shake her and muddle her thoughts. She'd done too much, seen too much for the press of lips to matter. Yet, she couldn't remember another kiss, another taste like him. Like Caleb. Masculine and strong, cunning and deliberate. She opened her mouth to invite him inside, and her breath hitched as he explored. Every thought, every sensation, centered there, where his clever mouth feasted.

Reaching for sanity, she broke away first, her breathing not quite steady. "We should go inside," she strangled out. "Now."

Breathing hard, Caleb had to agree. A simple kiss had nearly turned into more than he'd planned. Had prepared for. "Good idea."

Reluctantly, he released her nape, let go of her hand. Later, he'd explore why letting go felt so difficult. Forcing himself to open his door, he resisted the urge to swoop back in, to take one more taste. It was neither the time nor the place. They'd go inside, make sure everything was fine, then he'd head home. Tomorrow would be soon enough, he thought. Soon enough to find out everything he had to know.

"Do we have a deal?" Fin asked when he came

around to open her door. "We don't talk tonight." *About what happened in the car or anything else,* she thought. Not until she'd figured it out.

Mirroring her thoughts, Caleb took her hand. "Deal."

In his hospital room, Pete Franklin drifted on a cloud of morphine delight. His tastes in drugs were simple. Liquor, maybe some weed if a friend decided to share. Meth ruined your teeth, and crack messed up the head and the body. At forty-six, he had a good racket going, one that he didn't plan to screw up by getting hooked on junk.

He was a ladies' man and a major player. Pete lifted his hand and scowled. The cops had taken his ring off. A wave of sickness rolled through him, but he wasn't sure if it was the meds or fear. He didn't like jail, but there were worse things in the world, he knew. Like Stark.

"How are you feeling, Mr. Franklin?"

Peeling his eyes open, Pete vainly tried to focus. A white coat. A doctor? "Feeling fine," he chirped, slurring his words. "Might need more of that stuff there." He tilted his head toward the morphine drip. "Sss good."

"Yes, Mr. Franklin. It is good." Hands removed a syringe, held it aloft. "I've got some questions for you, Mr. Franklin. This will make you more relaxed."

Pete considered the offer and decided that morphine wasn't the same as the bad stuff. It was medicine. "Whatcha wanna know?"

Efficient hands made the injection and waited for the drugs to stream through the plastic IV. "I hear you were arrested for shooting at Sheriff Calder. Is that true?"

Narcotics tickled at his senses, but he hesitated to answer, though he wasn't sure why. "What of it?"

"Because I'd like to know why."

"Maybe I got my reasons. Or ten thousand reasons to kill him, that DA and some girls too. Ten thousand reasons. All green." The joke amused him and he laughed, the laughter strangling in a cough. "None of your damned business."

Ten thousand dollars. To kill Sheriff Calder and three women riding in his vehicle. A hot spurt of anger tightened the fingers holding the syringe. More disobedience. More disorganization. "Did Michael ask you to help him?"

"Graves is hiding from them. Don't wanna die. We get our orders from Jimmy now," Pete corrected sloppily. "All of us down in Macon call him Jimmy. Stuck-up sumbitch, but he pays good."

"You've been very helpful, Mr. Franklin."

"Sss okay," he slurred. "Jimmy works for them too. They'll take care of me."

"Absolutely."

CHAPTER 7

Friday morning, Fin entered the study as Eliza served tea. Pausing, Fin contemplated the women in the room. After more than a decade and a half, she realized, they'd come full circle.

A circle she'd begun, and now would begin to close. Reverie gave way to determination; she sat in one of the wing chairs and propped her elbows on the desk's glossy surface. "It's zero hour, Mrs. F. What do you want to know?"

"Blunt, as always." Eliza brought a dainty painted cup to her mouth, lips thinned in mild censure. A warning to anyone paying attention. "I would like to believe that I did a fair to middling job of raising you." In a slow sweep, she scanned the very adult faces of her three most beloved. "And yet, when faced with a crisis, none of you turned to me. Kell and Fin slip off into the dead of night without a cent between you, leaving poor Julia here to lie to me."

"I never lied to you, Mrs. F," Julia protested, flushing

lightly. Spurred by jagged scruples, she amended, "Not much, anyway."

"Such as when I asked if you knew why Kell and Fin ran away?"

"I showed you their diaries," came her tepid defense. "I never said the words aloud."

When Julia squirmed, Kell gamely intervened. "Mrs. F, we didn't want you to be involved. To get in trouble for what we did."

"For what I did," Fin amended. All of it. She popped up from her seat. "For the record, Kell and Julia were just trying to save me." Fin faced Eliza, shoulders squared. "They came to the Warehouse that night because of me. I'm the reason Kell and I ran. I'm sorry." She scanned the women's faces. "To all of you. I screwed up."

"Yes, you did." Eliza sipped at her tea. "Apology accepted."

"Just like that?" Fin asked. She'd prepared herself for the worst. "You and the kids are in danger because of me. Aren't you angry?"

"Do you regret what happened?"

"Yes," Fin said, then amended, determined to be upfront, "well, most of it."

"Fin."

She dug balled fists into her pockets. "I don't want to lie to you, Mrs. F." She would admit to making dozens of mistakes leading up to the fire, but she couldn't regret how the night ended. "We did what we had to—and I did what I needed to. What I have to understand is what's going on now."

"That night set off a chain of events," Kell explained. "Apparently, Clay saw us the night of the Warehouse fire. He blackmailed Mrs. F for the next sixteen years, until she cut him off when he tried to attack one of the girls."

Julia inhaled sharply and rose to stand near Eliza. She tucked her chin on the woman's shoulder, arms encircling her shoulders. "You never told me."

Aware of the sting, Eliza patted her hand. "I couldn't. Not without knowing the truth."

"So our actions made you a target for blackmail." Fin felt the unfamiliar rush of shame. "That's why the police thought you killed him."

"With some aid from Stark." Kell picked up her tea and fiddled with the cup. "Clay dealt drugs for years, and abruptly closed up shop a few months ago and went to work for new employers."

"He went straight?" Fin jeered.

"No. He earned a ring just like the men who attacked us yesterday. Luke and I discovered an abandoned laboratory on County Road. And Clay had a form of resin on his shoes and hands when he died."

"Pine?" Julia frowned thoughtfully.

"Not according to the preliminary tests. They sent the sample to Georgia Tech for analysis. Luke should be getting the results in a few days."

"Where did the resin come from?"

"We found the lab hidden in the forest between Hallden and Taylor County. Five thousand virgin acres that have never been cut."

Fin let out a low whistle. After poker, real estate had to be the biggest gamble with the highest payoffs. That much land lying untouched would fetch a tidy sum in the right hands. For them to remain pristine meant one of two options. The most likely answer came quickly. "State land?"

"Nope. Private conservation. Belongs to the Metanoia Foundation." Kell looked pointedly at Eliza. "Whose sole beneficiary is one Mrs. Eliza Faraday."

"Holy crap!" Fin stared at Eliza in amazement. "You own all that land?"

"Plus the Grove and a few thousand acres on the coast," Kell added. She'd done more digging into Eliza's finances and had been stunned to discover the extent of the wealth held by their modest Mrs. F. But her discovery did explain the priceless art and the antique furniture replaced without complaint when destroyed by clumsy children. She almost winced when she thought of how much she alone had cost.

Shoving that aside, Kell focused on her most important reveal. "If she's incapacitated in any way, the Georgia Bank makes fiduciary decisions until she regains control."

"So, we've got a dead drug dealer, millions in unforested trees, and Mrs. F on trial for a drug dealer's murder." Fin played the angles in her mind, considering the possibilities. "Someone tried to frame you for murder in order to take control of the foundation."

"Bingo." Kell had run the same scenario past Luke, drawn the same conclusion. "The bank received several offers for the land holdings, but Mrs. F has consistently refused."

Eliza folded her hands atop the desk. "In the last year or so, there's been more pressure to sell, including from the bank. I've refused to do so, but the offers keep coming."

"All of a sudden?" Fin asked.

"I've held that land since my parents died. Before last year, I could count the number of offers on one hand."

"Mrs. F kept a list of company names, and I'm going to start researching them," finished Kell.

"If what they want is for you to sell the land, why not simply kill you instead of Clay? Why frame you for murder?" The cold, steely question shivered across the room's occupants, but they'd each had the thought. Fin continued, "Knocking off one woman is a lot easier than setting up a frame for murder. Conspiracies require more planning than a simple hit."

"Which is knowledge you possess?" Hearing the icy summation, Eliza worried about the experience that gave Fin's voice such authority. "Fin?"

"I'm not a hit woman, Mrs. F," Fin dismissed with an airy wave. "But my business isn't exactly populated with insurance salesmen. I run into all sorts. Including federal agents and men who'd slit your throat for a negotiated fee."

Eager to steer the conversation away from Fin's past, but caught by her analysis, Julia asked, "So why not simply hurt Mrs. F? Why did they kill Clay?"

"I have a theory, but no evidence," Kell said. "The terms of the foundation's trust are fairly straightforward. As long as Mrs. F lives, she makes decisions about the disposition of the holdings. But in the event she's incapacitated, the indenture gives the bank the authority to make decisions. Under state law, serving a life sentence for murder would probably count. If Mrs. F tried to sue, they could argue that she can't meet her fiduciary duties while incarcerated."

"And if she dies?" Julia asked uncertainly.

"In the event of her death, a new beneficiary is named," Kell explained.

"Who is that?" Fin asked. "You?"

"No, it's the Faraday Center." Kell glanced at Eliza, who gave a short nod. "But if she dies, the foundation has new trustees to replace the Georgia Bank."

"The ones who want her out of the way?" Julia surmised.

"No," Eliza corrected. "I've named the three of you to become its trustees."

Fin and Julia turned to Eliza. "What?" they asked in unison.

"However, I decided not to wait until my death. As of Wednesday, you three are now the trustees of the Metanoia Foundation. I've always intended to leave my most precious possessions to my most precious ones," Eliza explained simply. "Now part of trusteeship will be insuring the continuation of the center. However, there's sufficient funding to guarantee its survival."

"Why do this now?" Fin asked quietly.

"You three were not my first children. You certainly weren't the most obedient or docile. But you have always been mine." She'd made this decision so easily, knowing her daughters would not disappoint her. "If this past few weeks taught me nothing, it is that the center must be protected. By you three. Together."

"We will." The words a vow, Fin straightened, determined not to disappoint. "Which means we need to settle on the story for Luke and Caleb. What do you think, Counselor? What exactly do we tell them?"

Kell nearly strangled over the suggestion no defense attorney should make. "I say we tell them everything. Beginning to end."

Fin didn't try to hide her reaction. "Everything? That can't be necessary." She sliced a look at Mrs. F. Forgiveness or not, she intended to keep some things to herself. "Why not just start with the night before the fire?"

"Because they'll want context," Kell explained. "We can trust Luke. I promise, Fin."

Julia turned to Fin. "Are you okay with that?"

Fin gained her feet, unable to sit. "Someone wants us dead, and I'm not willing to be the reason they succeed. If Kell trusts Luke, then we've got no choice." She paced over to Kell. "But isn't there some legal maneuver you can work? Caleb has no reason to believe anything we tell him."

"I've got an immunity agreement for us ready over here." She lifted a slim file. "One for each of us. Full protection for any crimes committed. Caleb sent his version over last night."

"Full immunity." Fin rolled the idea around, measured it against what she'd learned about Caleb. A small-town attorney might be convinced, but what about an FBI agent? "Are you sure it will protect us?"

"What happened that night was self-defense. We'll tell our story, and they'll see."

"And if it wasn't self-defense?" Fin pressed, returning to her abandoned chair. "Are we risking too much? If they had proof, we'd all be in jail already. Maybe we hedge a bit," she suggested.

Eliza intervened. "Fin, it's time."

"You don't know what happened, Mrs. F," Fin protested.

"Yes, it would help to know what you're seeking absolution from," Eliza conceded. "However, assuming these were truly acts of self-defense, I see no reason to fall on your swords or to cover one lie with another. You will tell the truth." Her gaze measured each in turn, leaving no doubt. "I expect you to take responsibility for your actions. I didn't raise you to shirk your obligations, regardless of how difficult they are." She paused, hearing the front door chime. "But I also didn't raise you to be martyrs. Kell, make sure those agreements are ironclad." Eliza glided out of the study, and the women quickly huddled.

Kell spoke first. "It's a good agreement," she told them. "And we've got a solid justification. Pippin didn't leave us any alternative."

"Are we sure?" Julia clenched her fingers together.

"I'm sure that if Kell hadn't acted fast, we'd be having a very different conversation," Fin retorted. "So, we're going with the truth. Great."

The tableau of three beautiful women greeted Caleb's curious eyes. But only one held his attention. Fin lounged in a blue chair, legs bared by the smattering of material she wore. Once he could breathe, he thought, he'd lecture her on the dangers of catching cold from inadequate clothing.

"Ladies." Eliza and Luke walked in side by side. "Your visitors."

Fin took the lead. She straightened in the chair, acutely aware of Caleb's attention. "Before we say anything, I think Caleb has something he'd like to share."

"What's she talking about?" Luke moved to face Caleb.

"She's talking about what I am." He shot Fin a look of approval. "What Fin figured out yesterday."

Luke cocked a brow. "Which is what, exactly?"

"I've got a couple of roles," he began. Glances darted toward Fin but eventually returned to focus squarely on Caleb. The phalanx of stares warned him this room wouldn't accept his story with the aplomb Fin had yesterday. He tucked his hands in his pockets. "I am the assistant district attorney for Hallden County. I'm a member of the Georgia, Virginia, D.C., and New York bars. And I am a special agent for the Federal Bureau of Investigation, Criminal Investigative division."

"FBI?" Luke repeated in disbelief. "You're a field agent for the FBI?"

"Yes. I've been undercover. Sent here to investigate the potential for an ongoing criminal enterprise here in Hallden, Georgia." He faced Luke, regretting that he'd deceived a colleague and a new friend. "I didn't get clearance to tell you until yesterday, but we got distracted."

The specter of Chicago rose, and disappointment tightened Luke's jaw. "Were you sent to investigate my office? To look at me?"

Caleb quickly denied the possibility. "I have one target, Luke. Bringing down Stark."

"Fin figured this out?" Eliza asked, watching him warily. "Exactly what is a field agent, Mr. Matthews?"

Standing in the center of the room, Caleb understood the anxiety of rats in a lab. Human eyes searching for weakness, the rat trapped, unable to flee. "I've been trained in law enforcement and investigations. I'm basically a police officer, for the U.S. government."

"You're an FBI agent, who's still on the federal payroll." Kell picked up the questioning. "But you've been practicing law in Georgia?"

Caleb replied, "Nearly four years ago, my partner disappeared here in Georgia." Caleb paused, buffeted by a cascade of memories. "Eric requested permission to come and investigate. Several months in, he vanished. The last message I received from him warned that he was closing in on the source. Stark."

Luke interjected, "Did he tell you who Stark was?"

"He didn't have the chance. I believe Stark had him killed because he'd gotten too close."

"Do you have any proof?"

"Not yet, but I'll find it. Eric deserves justice." Outside the study window, he watched the children as they raced across the rolling lawn. Carefree, exuberant. "I thought I could find it here in Hallden. So I convinced our division chief to assign me to go undercover, using my legal training."

Julia asked quietly, reeling, "Did anyone else here know about your other identity?"

"Absolutely not." Caleb trusted no one. "Until Fin made me at the airport, I've been invisible. I got permission to tell you all this morning. They've given me three weeks to find out who Stark is before I'm recalled to D.C."

"Three weeks?" Three weeks to protect her children from an enemy she didn't understand. Eliza stood up, decision made. "How can we help?"

Grateful, Caleb responded, "Stark is the key. They scared Chief Graves into running, and we've got at least one murder to pin on them already. Maybe three, if both of the bodies from the Warehouse are their handiwork."

Kell and Fin exchanged looks, and Kell walked over to the desk. "Before we go any further, I'll need you to sign these." She motioned to the immunity agreements. "One for each of us."

Caleb left the window and accepted the pen Kell extended. She'd e-mailed the final version to him, and he'd had to admire her handiwork. "I don't normally agree to blanket immunity without having some inkling of what's to come." He bent over and scrawled his name across each sheet. "Let's be clear. This agreement covers state charges only. I have no authority to act for the federal government."

"Understood." Kell accepted the pen, gathered the pages, and tucked them in her file. "Only the state will likely have jurisdiction anyway. Immunity is the only way I can allow us to tell you what happened to Louis Pippin."

"Louis Pippin?" Caleb asked, a frown forming. "One of the bodies Luke found in the Warehouse?"

Fin stepped forward, shifting his attention to her. After all, the time had indeed come. "Louis Pippin died at the Warehouse in 1991, before a fire destroyed the building. We know for a fact that Stark didn't kill him."

Fearing the answer, Caleb nevertheless asked, "How? How do you know?"

Kell and Julia moved as one to stand beside Fin. As they closed ranks, Fin answered simply, "We know because we killed him."

CHAPTER 8

Eliza broke from the group and approached a china cabinet nestled between towering bookcases. Without a word, she removed two stout glasses. Without a word, she returned to the desk, reached into the bottom drawer, and removed a crystal decanter filled with amber liquid.

With practiced, brisk movements, she splashed brandy into the glasses and poured the liquor into the four cups of rapidly cooling tea. She set the decanter down and passed the cups and glasses to the waiting hands. Catching the looks that ranged from gratitude to amazement, she permitted a brief, knowing smile. "Two dozen children underfoot each day. Please."

Fin gave a startled laugh, joined quickly by the others. She lifted her cup to sip, then gulped the spiked tea. A trail of fire slipped along her throat. She welcomed the heat as she continued, "Louis Pippin ran a juke joint out of the Grove Warehouse," she began. "Alcohol. Dancing. Gambling. All available at the Warehouse."

For Caleb and Luke's benefit, she explained, "Hallden was a dry county back then. Completely."

She'd set the chain of events in motion long before she'd understood the consequences. Abruptly, it was vital that Mrs. F and the others comprehend what had driven her then. Drove her still. "My pop taught me to play cards young. By the time I was nine, I could play anything. Poker, blackjack, spades." Fin gained her feet again, too edgy to remain still. "By high school, I was very good. Louis had a younger brother named Victor, who was still in high school. One night, Victor brought me to the Warehouse."

She could recall her first moments inside the seedy bar and casino. Flimsy tables strewn across a cement block floor, sticky with spilled beers and less appetizing substances. Raucous music had poured from speakers mounted on the walls, and dim lamps had flickered thin streams of light across the crowded dance floor. For most, the best action had occurred on the main level, where cheap liquor and cheaper pleasures had been had for the asking.

However, Fin had come for the delights to be found belowground. A narrow staircase hidden near the bar had descended into a gaming hall complete with pool, card tables, and the click of craps' dice. Her first visit had been a revelation. She'd bet her life savings at the time, a grand total of $162. She'd left minutes before her eleven o'clock curfew with fifteen dollars left.

She'd returned the following night and lost all but three bucks. By the third night, she'd been up $578 and steadily climbing. The clientele, almost exclusively men, had paid good money to watch her work. Later, appreciation had shifted into admiration as the more hard-core players had learned to stop leering at the scenery while their dollars had vanished into her pockets.

"I picked up games wherever I could, and I was there almost every night after curfew by my senior year. I got really, really good."

Pride flashed in Fin's eyes, and Caleb saw its predatory gleam. As Fin described her escapades, he listened but allowed his mind to sift below the story. To the woman with a keen intelligence who'd become a formidable gambler as a teenager. What, he wondered, had brought her to the Faraday Center? What had she carried inside her that had made her sneak out to flirt with disaster?

He watched her as she spoke. Long, endless legs stood slightly braced, as though preparing for a blow. Like a prizefighter, she leaned in almost intangibly, inviting the attempt with a tilt of that willful chin. Read together, she stood like a woman who expected the worst and welcomed all comers.

"Louis noticed how guys would sit at my table to flirt and leave several hours later with an empty wallet. He offered me a regular cut if I'd keep playing with his out-of-town clients."

"You were a ringer," Caleb summarized.

Fin raised a brow. "And I made good money at it. Until—" She stopped, realizing she hadn't spoken the words aloud in years. Not to Jake or anyone else. A secret held for sixteen years.

"Go on," Kell prompted softly. "Fin, tell them what happened."

Fin remembered the night with perfect clarity. "Louis got used to having me around. After a while, he started getting careless. He'd brag to me about his connections and how no cops would ever shut him down. Even showed me where he stashed the night's take. Told anyone who'd listen that the police worked for him."

"Graves."

She nodded at Luke. "Graves came in a couple of times a week. He'd disappear with Louis and leave with a brown paper bag. I realize now, he was collecting for Stark. That summer, he'd been coming around more often, and the bags had gotten bigger." Draining her cup, she crossed to the desk and added more brandy. "One night, Louis and Graves got into a fight. Most of the people upstairs had gone, but a few of us were still playing in the basement. Graves threatened to arrest Louis unless he got an increase in the payments." She hesitated, the words burning in her throat.

Kell urged, "Finish it, or I will."

Fin gripped the cup so tightly that she feared it would snap. Carefully, she set the china on its saucer, the sound loud in the quiet of the study. "Louis told Graves he couldn't have more money. Graves said that Stark wouldn't be happy with him, given all the money it had poured into the club. Said Stark had a way of dealing with their folks who got out of line or refused to do as they were told. Graves demanded that Louis give him something to keep his mouth shut.

"Louis stormed over to me and jerked me out of my seat and pushed me toward Graves. Told him more money was out of the question, but I was available. Said my mother used to screw for a living, and my dad sold her. He laughed. Told Graves it was a family business."

Wandering over to the corner, she let her voice carry across the room. "I shoved at Graves, but he was too big and too drunk. The pig tried to kiss me, put his hands on me. All the men in the place started laughing. Egging him on. I took a swing at him and broke his nose." She remembered that blood had poured from his face and he'd dropped like a stone. "One of the players grabbed me and pinned my arms."

"Fin, no," Caleb murmured the words, too easily imagining the scene. A teenaged Fin trapped in a basement with angry, drunken, lecherous men. "How—did you get away?"

"Graves threatened to arrest me, but Louis told him no. Said he had other plans for me. He had two of his goons lock me in his office." She'd been trapped inside with only a single bulb dangling overhead. No windows, no air ducts. Only a phone. "I decided to do what Graves suggested. I called the cops."

The sound of sirens had sent the patrons scurrying like cockroaches. Louis had snatched her from the office. Had warned her that he and Graves worked for people who would kill her if she ever tried to rat them out. "He said I just needed to remember one word. Stark."

Kell picked up the thread. "Fin climbed in through the bedroom window, and I could see she'd been attacked. Her shirt was ripped, her skin bruised. I made her tell me what happened." She'd gotten Fin into bed, her mind whirling with outrage. "The next day, I went to the Warehouse. I don't know what I expected to accomplish, but I knew I wasn't going to let them get away with hurting Fin."

"I was coming from the Grove, around the building, when I heard Louis. He was talking to someone about a buy. Said he had the cash inside. They agreed to meet later to make an exchange." Taking a breath, she told them, "Then Louis said he'd be out at a meeting until midnight. The police coming had angered Stark, and he had to close the club for a while and make nice. Said it was 'all that little bitch's fault' and that he had a surprise for Fin. She'd be working off her debt for him on her back for a long time."

Fin crossed to where Kell stood near the chairs. "Kell told me what she'd heard, and I realized I had to get out of Hallden before Louis found me. I'd saved up some money, but not nearly as much as I'd planned."

"So I suggested we steal Louis's money." Kell turned to face Eliza, her eyes defiant. "I know we should have come to you, but we didn't want to drag you into this. You or Julia." Kell took a deep breath. "Fin refused to take the money, thought it was too dangerous. But I didn't believe her. I went to the Warehouse that night on my own."

"Kell, what in the hell were you thinking?" Luke demanded. "You went by yourself?"

"No." Julia finally spoke. "When Kell snuck out that night, I went to find Fin. I'd heard them arguing, and I figured out what Kell had done. Fin and I went to the Warehouse. Kell was already inside."

"Julia and I followed her inside," Fin continued. "I had them stand as lookouts while I broke into the safe. I grabbed his stash and came out of the office. Only Louis had Julia by the throat and a gun on Kell. He kept saying what he planned to do to Julia, then Kell, while I watched. Then, he said, it would be my turn." The rest had happened in a blur of memory. "I remember swinging the satchel, and Julia bit him. We all ran up the stairs, and he caught me by the leg."

"Then Kell came out of nowhere with a piece of

pipe," Fin recalled darkly. "She hit him in the head and he went down."

"I could feel it strike him," Kell said dully. "Feel it break against his skull. Then he fell. He fell and didn't move." She lifted eyes glazed with memory to meet Luke's. "I killed Louis Pippin that night, Luke. To save my friends."

In his mind's eye, Caleb could see the three of them, trapped and fighting for their lives. Even without the immunity agreement, he doubted any DA would get a conviction. But he had to hear the rest. "What about the fire? Did you all set it on purpose?"

Fin dropped into the chair, leaned her head back on the fabric. "The fire was an accident. As we were running out, I knocked over a canister of something. Gas, kerosene, I don't know. Apparently, Louis had left a cigarette butt burning. It caught fire, and the grass and shrubs ignited. We just ran." She finally summoned the courage to look at Eliza. "I'm so sorry, Mrs. F."

Moving around the desk, Eliza came to Fin's side. She extended her hands, beckoning Julia and Kell. They clustered together, a circle that permitted few outsiders. "You saved yourselves and you protected one another. I couldn't ask for more."

Luke spoke, his voice strained. He couldn't erase the image of Kell in the basement with a madman, but one part of their story confused him. "The updated forensic report I just received showed that Pippin burned years after he died."

"What?" Fin squinted, sure she misunderstood. "Pippin's body burned that night."

"According to the report and the evidence, it couldn't have." The reports had puzzled him, and there still wasn't a clear explanation. "The fire set that night didn't reach the basement. His body was burned later. In fact, the coroner suspects it happened in the last few years. The meth lab that we found during excavation looked nothing like the place Fin described." He proffered, "I think someone burned the second body in the basement and tried to make it look like they died together."

"No one else was there that night." Kell broke from the circle and went to Luke. "Only Pippin. I swear it."

Luke cupped her cheek. "I believe you."

Kell kept her eyes on Luke. She looked up at the uncompromising man who had promised her devotion. Regardless of its cost to him. "I'm not sorry for what I did, my love. He was willing to rape Julia, would have hurt Fin if he'd had the chance. I didn't mean to kill him, but I'm not sorry he's dead."

"I understand," Luke whispered in hoarse response as he gathered her against him. Images of Kell trapped in the concrete tomb he'd visited only last week flashed in terrifying clarity. He took her chin, lifted her eyes to his. "He left you no choice."

"Mr. Matthews?" Turning, Eliza searched Caleb's shuttered look. Before his revelation, she'd liked the ADA, with his patient demeanor and innate civility. He'd been kind to her children and polite to her, despite his attempt to convict her of murder. But as she studied him, his eyes remained flat. And focused on Fin.

She couldn't read the expression buried beneath years of training and subterfuge. But, as Fin had described their frantic race from the burning building, she'd detected a tightening that could have been fear. More, she could see a concern for Fin that went well beyond casual interest. "Caleb, do you believe them?"

"Yes, what do you think, Matthews?" Fin, like Eliza, kept her attention on the ADA, but she couldn't penetrate the impassive look that focused solely on her. "Do you think we're killers?"

Caleb measured the taunt and heard the muted plea that he doubted even Fin was aware of. He'd taken a life before, as had she. No amount of penance or rationalization erased the stain, lessened the remorse. He moved soundlessly to the desk. Lifting the immunity agreements he'd brought, he methodically ripped the pages in half.

"Caleb." Luke said his name, shocked. Before he could argue, he caught a look in the man's eyes and went silent.

Caleb returned to the decimated agreement, turning the ripped pages and tearing them into quarters and eighths.

Other than the hiss of tearing paper, the room was silent. Fin tucked her tongue in her cheek and waited, a fiery ball in her throat. After all, she'd never expected to escape responsibility forever. She'd accepted the possibility of prison when she'd boarded the plane in Nice.

But she'd be damned if Kell was going to lose a shot at happiness because of her. Marching to Caleb, she snatched up the shredded pages and threw the pieces at him, like bitter confetti. "You're breaking your word."

"Fin—," he began, but she cut him off.

"I should have known." She didn't curse, knowing the vicious anger streaking through her wouldn't rewind the clock, undo their confession. But the snarl was harder to control. "But since you plan to try someone for Louis's murder, pick me. Leave Kell and Julia out of this."

Caleb folded his arms and turned to fully face her. As she had in the truck, her first instinct was to defend her friends. He realized he could fall in love with her for that alone. To be sure, he probed, "You'll take the fall for them both?"

"In a heartbeat," Fin assured him nastily, certain he wouldn't comprehend such loyalty. "Julia happened to be in the wrong place at the wrong time. More importantly, she matters. She saves lives. Every day. And Kell is a hotshot attorney who still remembers the little people. If either of them goes down for this, the world loses out. Big."

To hear her dismiss herself as irrelevant stoked an anger hotter than the one burning in him at Graves. "And you, Fin? What if you go to prison?"

Fin lifted a shoulder in a gesture of dismissal. "Then my business manager has to get an honest job, and I take up smoking and fleecing my cell mates." She released a grim chuckle that held little humor. "Let's face it. I'm not exactly a grand contributor to society. I gamble for a living, and I've never saved anyone's life. From prison or otherwise."

"That's not quite true," Caleb retorted. Did she really not understand who she was? What she'd done? Yesterday, she'd been a hero. "You saved our lives, Fin. If you hadn't taken out the tires on that sedan, we might all be dead."

Like Harold Jacoby. Another stupid bastard who'd played the wrong odds. Like they did, trusting Caleb. "I had a lucky shot."

"Damned lucky." He confronted her, letting the outrage fuel him, struggling not to resent how quickly she'd forced him to care. But he did. He cared about a woman who would hide for sixteen years, cutting herself off from everyone she loved, then fly halfway around the world the instant one of them called. A woman too oblivious to know what that meant. "You're an idiot, Fin."

Righteous indignation kept her pinned to the floor. "Excuse me?"

"I said you're an idiot." He returned the blistering look, ignoring the jolt of heat. Sitting on the ledge of the desk, he rested his fist on his knee, his free hand braced on the surface of the desk, scraps of paper beneath his palm. "For such a sharp lady, you've got some huge blind spots."

"I know what I see," she replied, crumpling a handful of white from the desk. Disappointment swirled inside, ruthlessly doused. She barely knew the man, and she'd been a fool to imagine he'd give up the chance to notch another win—even at the expense of their lives. "You've got at least one case you can close."

"We thought we could trust you," Julia protested from her post near Eliza.

At that, Fin sneered, looking over her shoulder at Julia. For that naïveté alone, she'd go to prison proudly. "Jules here never learned to distrust the system. Fortunately for me, I gave up believing in fairy tales and honor a long time ago." With a mocking smile, she extended her wrists. "Have Luke arrest me and leave them out of it, and I swear I'll go quietly, G-Man."

"No, she won't," Kell countered, breaking free of Luke's hold. When he tried to stop her, she shook off his hand. "For God's sake, Caleb, we had a deal. I expect you to abide by it. Either that, or we all go in."

"Stay out of this, Kell," Fin said. The tinny note of

alarm in Kell's demand made Fin clutch at Caleb's wrist. No way Kell was going to throw away her hard-won bliss because of their mistake. And Julia had always been innocent. Despite their loyal defense, the Warehouse debacle was hers alone.

As was the error in judgment today. Kell clearly loved Luke, had faith in his word. But Fin had no such excuse when it came to Caleb. And no reason to expect mercy from him. They'd just met, and she barely knew anything about him. Except that he had a handsome face and that he'd protected her friends from harm. That her pulse jittered when he brushed against her or merely sent a mocking look in her direction. That he'd kissed her as though there could have been more.

Being fooled by the chemical cocktail of passion, taken in by a façade of solid reliability, was a rookie mistake. So she'd pay for their folly and hope Kell was as good a lawyer as she seemed. Fin aimed a level look at Caleb. "We both know how the game is played. Only one person needs to be held accountable. Even if you're willing to ignore your agreement, there's nothing to be gained by destroying their lives."

"What about your life?" He grabbed at her hand, unconcerned about their audience. "Do you really think so little of your value? Damn it, Fin, what do you deserve?"

"Get your hands off me," Fin demanded, jerking at his hold, using her free hand to push him away. "Don't touch me."

Launching up, he opened his mouth to yell at her, but the chill of her fingers on his wrist penetrated his anger. She was terrified, he realized, but the panic had been contained, banked. Only the bloodless fingers on his skin had communicated her distress.

What kind of life demanded that level of control?

Shaken, Caleb placed a hand on Fin's shoulders, his other sliding unbidden beneath her chin to lift her damning eyes to meet his own. "Fin, I'm not planning to arrest you or Kell or Julia." With a hard swipe of one hand, he scattered the pieces onto the carpet. "I signed the agreement in good faith."

"And ripped it up the minute you had the whole story," she reminded him, unwilling to believe.

"I was being dramatic," Caleb admitted gruffly. "Too dramatic. I have no interest in revealing what you've told me today." He softened his hold on her, lightly chafing the cold from her skin. "Any immunity agreement is a public record. What I heard in here today doesn't warrant public embarrassment or an investigation. Assuming the sheriff's forensic reports bear out your story, I don't intend to press charges." Looking down at Fin, he murmured, "No charges, no agreement necessary. And no need for the grand sacrifice."

Embarrassed, Fin shot back, "What was I supposed to think?" She angled her chin at him, hair falling in ebony profusion between her shoulders. "I'm not a psychic."

"I'd have appreciated the benefit of the doubt and a couple of seconds to explain. Which now I understand I'll need to earn."

Fin braced herself against relief and desire. Remorse led her to cover his hand on her arm, and a fear she hadn't acknowledged seeped away in a rush that left her shaky. Knowing she should, she let her touch linger in mute apology. "So, maybe I misunderstood."

Caleb arched a brow in disbelief. "Maybe?"

Fin gave an unladylike snort, aimed at herself as much as him. " 'Maybe' is the best you're going to get. Don't push it."

Where he held her, the skin warmed, smoothed. Forgetting their audience, he leaned closer, drawn. "I wouldn't deceive you, Fin." And so much more, he accepted.

"Don't make promises you can't keep," counseled Fin in a tone only he could hear. Promises she might be tempted to believe. She stepped away, and his hand fell to his side. "Now that we've got that cleared up, what's next?"

As if on cue, a phone shrilled in the study. Luke snatched out his cell and flipped open the receiver. "Sheriff Calder." He listened, scowling. "How the hell did he manage that?"

Another pause, then Luke muttered an oath. "Call Acting Chief Richardson and tell her to meet me at the hospital. I'm on my way." He shut the phone and skimmed the room with a look. "Pete Franklin tried to sneak out of the hospital. Convinced a nurse to get him a wheelchair and take him outside. Then he knocked her over with his cast and tried to hobble away."

"How far did he get?" Caleb asked, already moving to the door.

Luke matched his stride. "To the elevators. One of my deputies caught him, and he swore to them he was a target for murder. They took him seriously and called me."

"Did he say who was after him?"

"Nurse says he's too terrified to be questioned."

"If Franklin's terrified, we've got to push him now, find out who hired him."

Luke agreed. They stopped at the door, deep in strategy mode. The potential for a chink in Stark's armor spurred adrenaline. "Maybe it's time to tell him Jacoby is dead. Remind him that we can protect him. How are you at good cop/bad cop?"

"Which one do I get?" Caleb asked.

Luke's feral grin answered him silently.

"Gentlemen."

Both men turned to Fin. Caleb masked his impatience. Franklin was primed and ready. Terror swayed more confessions than conscience did. With him working with Luke, they could stoke the panic, build it to a crescendo that revealed evidence. "We've got to get to the hospital, Fin."

"We're not finished here." She advanced, jaw set. They had their goal, and she had hers. "Since you're in a hurry, we'll go with you."

"Out of the question." Caleb rejected the idea immediately. No way would he sanction bringing them to the hospital, especially if Stark had eyes and ears on the scene. Their best protection rested within the confines of the center's walls with Luke's team on twenty-four-hour watch. "As of this minute, you four are out of the detective business. Leave this to the sheriff and me. We'll take care of it."

CHAPTER 9

"You'll take care of it?" Fin repeated the dismissal silkily. "So we shouldn't worry our pretty little heads about Stark?"

Seeing the trap, Caleb marched into it boldly. The ready escape of the door receded, and he came nose to nose with her. "That's correct."

"I'm not staying here while you go off and play hero."

He searched her face for a hint of amusement. Surely, she couldn't be serious. Within an hour of her arrival in town, she'd been shot at and nearly killed. He had no illusions about what more Stark might do to accomplish their ends.

Already, the idea of calling in professional reinforcements had crossed his mind. There was no way he'd put Fin or her friends in harm's way. "We appreciate your information, but we see no need to bring you in any deeper. Right, Luke?" Caleb looked to the sheriff for support.

"Oh, no," Luke demurred, hands shoved into his pockets. But, in a show of unity, he meandered back to the center of the room. "I didn't say a word."

"Which you might want to consider," Fin cautioned grimly, sure he wouldn't. Being relegated to the sidelines chafed, but she resisted the instinct to pounce again so soon. Before she exploded, she decided, she'd try reason. "Listen, Matthews. We've got as much at stake here as you do. Stark killed your partner. They tried to kill us. So we don't intend to sit idly by when we can be of help."

"Help? How?" He folded his arms. Fin had no sense of her limits, but he did. "While I admit you handled yourselves well yesterday, you're not cops. You have no business being involved at all." Anticipating her protest, he added, "I accept that you have provided valuable information, but I've got to draw the line."

"Really?"

"Absolutely." He felt the shaky ground beneath him shift, decided to brazen out the quake. "As of this moment, the Stark matter and all surrounding issues are under federal jurisdiction. I'm authorizing local law enforcement to assist, but under no circumstances will civilians be involved." Which, he decided, she'd eventually accept and understand. But determination gilded with haughtiness stared at him evenly. She gave no sign of concern, no indication of uncertainty. Caleb shook his head once. "I mean it, Fin. There isn't room for civilians in a case like this."

"We're not your average civilians," she countered. "Especially me. Check with your superiors. I've done it before." She swept past him, allowing her revelation to sink in.

Stark had upped the ante, and she had no intention of

sitting on the sidelines. Caleb and Luke were facing an enemy with years of practice keeping their secrets. And Stark was getting overeager, which meant something big was on the horizon. She'd returned to protect her own, and protection meant helping the sheriff and the FBI keep her family safe.

Caleb refused to let the revelation go. "You've never faced an opponent who tried to kill you with the sheriff in the car."

Direct hit. Wanting to regroup, she waved her hand in dismissal. "I understand that you and Luke need to get to the hospital. We can discuss how we'll be involved later."

"There's nothing to discuss," he replied flatly. "And let me stand corrected. *I* don't use civilians. Ever." Not when he couldn't even manage to keep his own partner safe. The familiar twist of guilt and vengeance slid sickly in his gut, making his voice harsher than intended. He added politely, "I do appreciate the information you've given. All of you. But this is a matter for Luke and me."

"This matter," Fin retorted dryly, "almost killed us yesterday."

"And I'm not sitting on the sidelines," Kell advised the men mutinously. She advanced on Luke, jabbed his chest in emphasis. "I've got dibs on revenge, Luke. They tried to frame Mrs. F for murder. Tried to shoot us off the highway."

"Which is why Caleb and I will bring them to justice." The black pearl gleamed on the hand boring a hole into his chest. In defense, Luke tucked a lock of hair behind her ear and tried not to wince as Kell glared up at him. He drew his hand back, vaguely surprised it was intact. "Though I might have phrased it better," he said with a veiled look at Caleb, "he's right. We're dealing with a criminal enterprise that's been operational for at least two decades. I won't have you four or the center in the middle of this."

"With all due respect," Eliza said, her lady-of-the-manor voice threaded with ripe impatience, "we seem to be dead center of this mess already. Not only have these thugs tried to put me in prison, they hurt my children. Or, Luke, don't you remember coming to the center the morning one of them attacked Jorden? Should I ignore the threat to my family and wait for the very police that helped orchestrate my arrest to save me?"

Luke flinched. "Mrs. F, please. I'm not Chief Graves."

"I understand, and so should you," she reproved sternly. "I don't relish the thought of any one of us participating in your investigation, but we will not be relegated to the role of spectators." Drawing herself to her full five foot two, she sailed over to Fin, Julia on her heels. She faced both men down, the hazel eyes a mirror image of the other looks aimed their way. "We know more about this town than either of you. Without our help, you won't stand an ice cube's chance in Hades of identifying who is involved, let alone protecting us."

"I've been here for a fair number of years," Luke protested as exasperation bumped against the instinct to mollify. "Hopefully, I'm adequate to the rigors of my job without putting the lives of women and children at risk."

Kell patted his cheek fondly. "Honey, we're not damsels in distress. In fact, I think only yesterday, we stopped a gunman from killing you and we set a patient's leg, and today we solved a homicide." She saw no benefit in pointing out their role in the latter. "We're not asking to be deputized, but we're all in this together."

"And if I refuse?"

She smiled easily. "Then we'll figure something out."

His lips thinned at the threat, and wisely, Kell plowed on. "I'm a defense attorney, my darling. Which means I can—and will—use every means at my disposal."

"As we all will," Eliza added calmly.

"So, you see," Julia interjected, "you're outnumbered."

Luke and Caleb exchanged looks, and Fin took the opening. "We won't interfere in any official actions, guys. But we won't be kept in the dark. How about a compromise? You keep us up to speed and give us safe tasks, and we won't go mucking around in your investigations. Deal?"

Luke relented first. "Fine. We'll keep you in the loop. But no one is to take any actions without clearing it through us first. Agreed?"

"Agreed," came the chorus of responses.

"Now see, that wasn't so bad." Fin twisted the knob, pleased with her victory. Maybe after a few days of spinning their wheels, Caleb and Luke would realize they needed the women of the Faraday Center. "Shouldn't you men be on your mighty way?"

Fin held open the door as Luke and Kell, then Julia and Mrs. F filed past. The foyer remained clear of children, who played outside under armed guard, determined to wring out their last moments of freedom. Kell walked Luke to his car, and Julia followed Eliza around the grand staircase to the guest room. Fin leaned against the jamb. "You going with Luke?" she asked Caleb, who still stood inside the study.

"I'll meet him there." Caleb stepped forward and stopped in the frame of the doorway. Today, she wore slim khaki shorts and a black top made of a slinky material that shimmered in the light and fell from two slender straps. Newly formed habit compelled him to slide the tip of his finger along the blunt edge of her collarbone, stopping at the hollow of the graceful, bare throat. "What plot are you hatching in that fascinating mind?"

Startled that he suspected, she covered by mocking, "You're too suspicious, Matthews."

No denial, he noted. No false protests. Nicely done. Sketching the delicate indentation where her blood beat in rapid tattoo, he instructed, "Occupational hazard."

"Every job's got them." Shivers ranged where he stroked. Aroused, exasperated, Fin lifted her hand to capture his. "You should learn to ask permission before you touch."

He allowed her to move his hand, enjoying the taut hold of her fingers on his. Smoothly, seamlessly, he shifted to stroke his thumb against her palm. "I prefer asking forgiveness instead. Less threat of being told no."

"Better chance of losing your fingers," she parried, but the single dimple winked in good humor and reluctant admiration. "I could like you."

"I could like you too." Caleb smiled at the grudging admission tempered by amusement. He appreciated both, in equal, disconcerting measure. Wanted both. But now was neither the time nor the place. Fin Borders deserved his undivided attention, and he deserved more privacy than an open doorway for the exploration. "However, I meant what I said, Fin. This is a federal matter now. Behave yourself."

She grinned wickedly. "I told you I would."

"I'm not reassured."

"I'm hurt." The longer they lingered in the doorway, the harder it was to remember why she didn't like law enforcement. "You should go."

"And you should worry."

Hackles rising, her nostrils flared. "Worry? About you?"

"You've caught my attention. I have a hard time letting go of mysteries." Caleb released her and made it to the end of the balustrade before looking over his shoulder. "I plan to figure you out."

Leaving her with his parting shot, he strolled out to the car he'd parked at the center mere hours before. Quickly, he slipped behind the wheel of the sedate Accord, his thoughts still on Fin. More than beauty, more than brains, he couldn't help but admire slyness. A cunning mind that could leverage assets and liabilities and convince the victim that neither label mattered. A trait Fin appeared to own in spades.

Finding all three—beauty, brains, and slyness—in one woman? Caleb felt his entire system churn, the notion making him jumpy. At best, Fin served as a link to a criminal enterprise. More likely, given her disdain for rules, she had darker ties.

And either way, he couldn't wait to see her again.

By dusk, Fin had nearly shaken off the disturbing encounter with Caleb. It was difficult, she discovered, to concentrate on a man's erotic upper lip while playing hopscotch in ninety-degree weather. Mercifully, Eliza appeared on the porch to summon them all inside.

"It's time for evening chores and supper."

Grousing, the children straggled into the house, with the three adults stumbling in behind. Eliza stopped them on the porch. "Julia, please help the older kids tidy up. Kell, you should get the little ones cleaned up and ready for dinner. Fin, you come and help me in the kitchen."

"Why does Fin get to cook?" Julia asked plaintively.

"Because I don't burn water," came Fin's teasing response as she trailed Eliza into the house. Before they reached the kitchen, a trill of notes rang out from the guest bedroom she was using. "Let me grab that, Mrs. F. I'll be right with you."

She jogged into the room and scooped up the telephone, not bothering to check the number. "Hello?"

"Fin, it's Jake."

Flopping onto the mattress, she toed off the sandals that had never been intended for actual use. "Back in Vegas yet?"

"Not quite yet."

"Cocktail waitress or heiress?"

"Heiress."

"Figures." Fin shimmied out of her shorts, phone tucked to her ear. "What's up?"

"Thought you'd want a heads-up. Someone has been putting out feelers on you. Asking about outstanding markers."

With a jerk, she sat up, blood sloshing noisily in her brain. "Who?"

"Don't know. But I've got alarms on your accounts, so I get notices whenever folks start to pry too much."

Her thoughts zipped to Caleb. "Could it be the FBI, maybe?" It would make sense to investigate her, to check out her past. Despite his magnanimity with the immunity agreement, he had no reason to trust her. Her thudding pulse slowed modestly. "Yes, it's probably them. I've recently come to know an agent with a very suspicious mind."

"Fin, this wasn't a government search. They'd have no trouble accessing your records." He hated to worry her, but he had no choice. "Whoever it is asked about buying up your debt. At a premium. Why would anyone want to do that?"

Blackmail, she thought forbiddingly. *Extortion.* "What did they find out?"

Jake shook his head before he remembered she couldn't see him. "You don't have any markers, Fin. Nothing that I know of, anyway. That's part of the reason I called." Cautiously, he prodded, "Do I need to be worried?"

"No," she placated quickly. The only outstanding marker on her head had been revealed to the FBI and the DA's office that morning. Three hundred grand stolen from Stark. "Keep your ear to the ground, will you, Jake? Let me know if anything else pops."

"Will do. And Fin?"

"Yes?"

"Be careful. Call me if you need something. Anything."

"I will." Fin rang off and drew her legs up. Before she could talk herself out of it, she punched in a number she'd memorized.

"Caleb Matthews."

"Matthews, it's Fin. Can you stop by the center tomorrow?"

Sitting on his sofa, Caleb let his book fall shut. "I've got a seminar in the morning in Atlanta. Is this an emergency?"

The urge to say yes, to convince him to come over, disturbed her. "No. It's not an emergency, but it is important." She wouldn't allow herself to become dependent on him. On anyone. "Actually, on second thought—" she started.

"No second thought, Fin. I'll see you at three tomorrow." Pleased with himself, he added, "Good night, Fin. Dream of me."

CHAPTER 10

"Heads up!"

In response to the shouted alert, Fin lifted her head in time to snag a Frisbee sailing in on a collision course. Expertly, she spun the disc of plastic on a coral-tipped nail, waiting for the owner to reclaim his toy. She didn't move, content to remain where she was. All in all, she admitted, a perfect day. A lazy Saturday afternoon spent lolling beneath a towering oak, complete with a tall glass of lemonade and a rattan lounger rescued from the garage.

A perfect afternoon, if she ignored the numbing circuit of the deputy's cruiser and the dead weight of worry from her conversation with Jake. Worry that had her bending her pride and asking Caleb to meet her at the center. She glanced at the slim gold watch on her wrist. He'd agreed to stop by around three, which gave her fifteen minutes. She moved to sit up, rescued Frisbee in hand.

"Nice catch," the lanky teenager commended breathlessly, braking beside her seat. Blond hair darkened with sweat fell over a tanned brow and lake blue eyes. A ratty T-shirt cautioned he didn't play well with others. Raking his hand through the damp strands, he apologized, "Sorry about that."

"No worry," Fin said as she relinquished the orange plastic, tipping oversized shades down her nose. "Thanks for the warning."

With the insouciance of youth, he complimented, "Wish we had more women in town who looked like you." Giving her the teenage version of a come-hither look, he asked in a practiced drawl, "You dating anyone?"

"Patrick." The quelling voice came from behind her. Over her shoulder, Caleb cocked a disapproving eyebrow at the teenager but silently admitted he wondered the same. "Stop hitting on Mrs. Faraday's guests."

"Come on, man. Do you see her?" But Patrick took a respectful step back. "Mrs. F says we should learn to appreciate beauty. That's all I'm doing."

Caleb muffled a laugh at the impertinence. Giving the boy a level look, he replied, "I expect to see you Saturday. Nine o'clock sharp."

The cocky shoulders slumped in disappointment. "Ah, Mr. Matthews. It's the last Saturday before school starts. Can't we do it the next week?"

Caleb's ebony brow lifted again. "What do you think?"

Scuffing a worn sneaker on the grass, he mumbled, "See you next Saturday. Bye, Fin." He turned and jogged to the group of boys he'd been playing with. Additional comments on adults and their ability to kill fun floated across the lawn.

"I see you know how to win friends and influence people," Fin commented dryly as she slanted her head to look at Caleb. His proximity rattled nerves that were usually rock steady. And the intense scrutiny of his shaded eyes left her feeling more exposed in the denim shorts and tank top than she did in a bikini. She swung her legs over and pushed up from the lounger. "Will he be scrubbing toilets with his toothbrush?"

"Worse. Repainting the benches in the city's park." Caleb shifted forward and took her elbow, ostensibly to help her stand. Even beneath the tree's shadow, her skin glowed with the luminosity certain women possessed. He allowed his fingers to dance along the satiny skin. The dizzying scent of her drifted up, filled his head. "Patrick's got a creative vocabulary and a penchant for graffiti."

"And you've got a soft spot for strays." Cornered against the lounger and the oak tree, Fin rested against the rough bark. Beneath the branchy overhang, her sunglasses shaded his expression, so she slipped the frames into her hair. Uncovered, her eyes narrowed on his. "Is that tendency limited to wayward children?"

"I don't know," he answered honestly. "I've never tested it. What about you, Ms. Borders? Do you have a soft spot for strays?"

Her eyes twinkled briefly, humor mixed with self-deprecation. "I am a stray, Mr. Matthews. But no, I don't have any soft spots."

The lounger and tree blocked escape, and he another—an experience he was certain she rarely faced. Fin struck him as a woman who would always find an out. But he believed in taking advantage when-ever it appeared. Curious fingertips brushed the inside of her upper arm, a gentle caress that blazed through his senses. "No soft spots? Now, that's not true."

Bones melting, Fin gave his chest a shove. "Back off, Matthews."

He obligingly moved away a couple of steps. "You called me, remember?"

Fin nodded, hoping to shake some sense back into her head. "Let's walk." Without waiting for his agreement, she sidled between him and the lounger, her stride long and quick.

He fell into step with her easily, matching her swift gait. Like the woman, her movements were smooth and sure, no wasted motion, no quarter given in case others couldn't keep up. Together, they rounded the house to the backyard, where games of tag and jump rope were in full swing.

Fin saw Julia playing dolls with a trio of little girls. "We're taking a walk," she called out. A wave of Julia's hand indicated she'd received the message.

"Do you have a destination in mind?" Caleb inquired politely when they'd strayed deep into the wooded copse that spread behind the house. He'd already tucked his sunglasses away, the gloom of the trees unbroken by the afternoon sun. Below his feet, he could discern no actual path, though Fin seemed to be following one. "Or should I be scattering bread crumbs?"

With a rueful chuckle, Fin stopped and angled her head to look up. Leafy branches met overhead, providing a dense green canopy. The loamy smell of earth and nature reached out, and she inhaled slowly, savoring. "I've been to almost every continent, and I've never found a place quite like this. Pine trees and honeysuckle, wild blackberries. Elephant ears."

"Elephant ears?"

Fin laughed again, meeting Caleb's quizzical look. "Big green leaves that grow in the summertime. Kell always tried to teach us the correct botanical name, but Jules and I called them elephant ears."

"You missed them."

The statement was simple, filled with understanding. Fin wrapped her arms around her waist, let out a pent-up breath. So much time lost. "I panicked that night. Instead of saying we should run, I should have told Mrs. F what happened."

"Why didn't you?"

"Because I'd been looking for a reason to leave. Some dramatic moment that would give me the courage to go." The truth of it hit her with stunning force. She never realized she'd been afraid to leave. "I wanted to go, but I was too much of a coward to escape on my own. Not until the night at the Warehouse. After the fire, if I left, my reasons were noble. I was saving them, not abandoning them. Turned out to be the same thing."

Caleb snorted derisively. "Give yourself a break, Fin. You were just a kid. You didn't abandon anyone." Except whatever remnants of childhood she'd had left.

She sneered at herself, at her excuses. "I was selfish and wild, and I dragged my best friends into my mess of a life."

"And they obviously hate you for it."

Her eyes snapped to his. Sarcasm gleamed out at her, mocking her. She heard herself, gave a rueful chuckle. "Look, I'm trying to own up to my failings."

"No, you're whining. Owning up sounds different."

"What would you know about it, Captain America?

When have you ever done something so out of bounds
you had to own up?"

"Right now." He yanked her into his arms, brought
his mouth down to cover hers. The first taste of her
sizzled through him. Heat. Smoke. He fisted one hand
in the mass of curls, clamped the other on the firm indentation of her waist. Sunglasses fell to the loamy
ground. The kiss burned through him. Smoke clouded
his brain, the heat blazed his control.

Breath seared out as his mouth explored hers. Fin
struggled for sanity, for air. But she found only the
male taste of him streaming through her as before. She
clutched at his shoulders, anchoring herself as she spun
dizzily beneath his kiss.

This time, he drew back, wanting only to go under.
Caleb lifted his head, pleased when Fin wasn't quite
steady on her feet. His felt none too solid either. "Forgive me."

The insincere request was coupled with a slow feath-
ering of her lips by his thumb.

Insides liquified, temper flaring, Fin willed herself to
settle. Her voice strained, she managed, "You're pretty
good at that."

Pleased, Caleb slowly released her hair, letting his
fingers stroke through. "I've always been a good student.
A plus."

A laugh gurgled in her throat, wholly contrary to the
tumbling of nerves in her stomach. She didn't want to
like Caleb Matthews. Only to use him to save her
friends. "I had a reason for bringing you out here," she
reminded them both, slapping a hand to his chest when
he took a step closer. Her mouth tingled in anticipation,

but she found she needed time to process. To plan. "No more of that."

Caleb stooped and retrieved her glasses, then tucked his hands into his pockets. "I'm listening."

"My business manager called me last night. Someone has been trying to buy up gambling debts for me."

"How much do you owe?"

Gone was the flirtation man, replaced by the cool agent in a heartbeat. Fin angled her chin proudly. "I don't owe. I'm good at winning, and Jake is even better about watching my money."

"Jake?" How did a woman who kissed him like that have a man named Jake in her life? "I assume Jake is a short, fat balding accountant of advanced years."

An impish grin spread across her mouth. "Jake is six feet tall, has a full head of hair, and turned thirty-five in June."

A single brow lifted. "Does he only watch your money?"

"Jake is very capable. A multitasker."

"How convenient," Caleb nearly snarled, but he kept his temper penned. "I'll keep that in mind."

"Do." She returned to the hidden trail, and Caleb stomped beside her. Relenting, she pointed out, "I've known Jake for ten years. He's my business manager, and we have a hands-off policy that has worked well for us both."

Disbelief had him stopping, turning. "Is he gay? A eunuch?"

"No, he's very rich because he does an excellent job of managing me and my investments."

"A leech."

"On the contrary." Fin tried not to rock on her heels

in delight. "Jake doesn't need my money. Devon Industries is his family company."

Caleb snapped his mouth shut. Devon Industries? An international conglomerate with money to burn. "Interesting choice for a business manager." And he'd be running a make on Jake Devon tonight, just in case. Find out why a scion of one of America's richest families was playing accountant to a lady gambler.

Scooping her elbow, he propelled them both forward. "So Jake called to warn you that someone's checking your finances. Looking for something to hold over your head."

"Stark knows I'm back, and they'll figure I'm the weakest link. Kell has Luke, and Julia probably hasn't even gotten a parking ticket."

Which left Fin as their prey. Ice formed in his gut, and he asked, "What else can they hold over you?"

Fin lowered her lashes. "I've had a busy sixteen years, Caleb," she demurred. "Other than the money we stole, they've got nothing on me that would work. But I thought you should know." Concentrating on the ground, she missed his speculative look.

"Are you sure that's everything, Fin?" He stopped again, and held her shoulders steady. "If they can hurt you, I need to know. Right now."

Shaking off the hold and the concern, she led them back toward the house. "I won't let them use me to hurt my family. Ever again."

Pete Franklin lay against stingy hospital pillows, his mouth moving in uninterrupted prayer. Beyond his closed hospital door, a sheriff's deputy stood guard. Still, he started at every squeak of a stretcher, at every clash of bedpans on a cart. He might have survived the car rolling over, but he knew his continued existence would be short-lived. With the new drugs seeping out of his system, he had remembered his visitor dimly. But he could definitely recall all of Graves's warnings to them about the consequences of failure. How his bosses dealt with failed soldiers. After all, even the big man himself had run when the Griffin deal had gone south.

His heart raced, and the monitor attached to his arm echoed the gruesome imaginings. Tonight, he figured, they'd sneak into his room. Probably shoot him in the face. Stark could do that, he knew. Sweat beaded on a flushed brow bandaged with tape. Flecks of glass had etched scars into the puffy skin. Permanent scars, according to the doctor.

He wondered how Harold was doing. They hadn't let him see him at all. With a sickening lurch, he remembered the instant Harold had lost control of the car. The way the Taurus had skidded off the highway and somersaulted through the air. He'd seen cars do that on television, hadn't expected it to ever happen to him.

Vaguely, he recalled the scream of glass. Or had they been Harold's screams as he'd flown through the broken windshield? Images jumbled in the haze of morphine and terror. He thought he saw glass sticking out of Harold's belly, but the picture slipped away when he tried to hold it.

Wherever Harold was, hopefully he had a guard too. Someone to stop visitors from sneaking to his bedside and finishing what the car crash had started.

What Graves had started. Too many years of mopping cleanup had readied Franklin to take on the police chief's more important assignments. Help build a shed in the woods and watch over a drug dealer with a flair for chemistry. The skinny punk Clay Griffin had worked on the equipment, and all he and Harold had had to do was ferry him around and keep Graves up to date. In exchange, he'd given up blue coveralls for suits and ties and fancy rings. More money than he'd ever made doing the mail scams for Jimmy.

Being muscle for Graves's crew had become a regular gig with a bunch of perks. Paid for alimony and the ladies at the Pink Pony. Pete Franklin didn't deal drugs, and he refused to mess with kids, but otherwise, he had no problem with his employer.

Until recently, when the requests had gotten stranger and riskier. When he'd started to see his coworkers die and his boss go into hiding.

"Mr. Franklin, how are you feeling?"

Pete blinked once at the white-coated man standing by his bed. Dr. Hestor. He hadn't liked the guy out in the woods. Foreigners made him antsy. "My leg hurts like hell, Doc."

"Remember, you shattered your femur, Mr. Franklin." Dr. Hestor lifted his IV and adjusted the drip of morphine. "If you'd stayed in bed and hadn't tried to wheel your way to freedom, you'd have allowed the cast time to set."

Fighting through suddenly fuzzy thoughts, Pete struggled to cling to awareness. "What'd you do, Doc?"

"My job." Hestor circled the bed and checked the monitor. "You know, my other job."

Stark. The terrible truth wound through Franklin's brain. They'd come for him. "I didn't tell the cops anything," Pete babbled. "Honest. And Harold wouldn't either."

"What about Chief Graves?" Red numbers cycled downward in a steady decline. "Your pulse is slowing down, Mr. Franklin."

"Feel. Sick."

"Too much morphine, Mr. Franklin." Hestor reached into his pocket for a syringe. "We have some questions for you, Pete. About where Graves is. What Jimmy told you."

Panic surged but could find no answering speed in Franklin's heart. "Didn't tell me. Nothing."

"You're lying, Mr. Franklin." Again, the syringe pierced the clear tube, added a second liquid into the constricting veins. "Jimmy asked you to help him, and you failed. First, you manage to get caught, and then you tried to run from us."

Brown eyes widened as he felt the beginnings of his heart attack. "I didn't tell."

"I can't believe you, Mr. Franklin. But not to worry. You'll soon be at the morgue with Harold." He saw the eyes widen, then fill with sorrow. Tears trickled along now sallow cheeks. "He died on the scene. We're not sure what he told Sheriff Calder, but we can't take a risk. You understand."

"No." The moan warbled out on a cry. Neither carried further than the bedside. Pete died trying to scream for help.

Hot spray stung legs lathered with ginger-scented soap. Fin circled lissomely beneath the shower's fall, head tipped away from the cascading drops. Behind tightly closed eyes, she forced her teeming mind to empty. She wouldn't think about her plans for Caleb Matthews or the way her skin seemed to vibrate when he touched her. She certainly wouldn't dwell on the blistering kiss beneath the trees.

"Are you gonna stay in there all night?" Julia demanded. "Where are you going, anyway?"

A draft swept behind the partially lifted curtain, and Fin jerked it closed. "Some privacy, please."

"What's with the dress on the bed, Fin?" Kell entered the bathroom, having helped Eliza finish serving dinner. Fin had whipped up a meat loaf, and Julia had drawn kitchen detail. "Going out?"

"I need to make a visit."

"To Caleb?" Kell guessed easily. With a smirk to

Julia, she added, "I haven't seen her this stirred up by a guy since Kevin Ladaris."

"Kevin had a fantastic butt," Fin reminded them, ignoring the jibe about Caleb. Though she couldn't see them, she knew that Julia had taken up vigil on the toilet seat and Kell held post by the sink. If old habit held, she had about forty-five seconds before Kell reached over and flushed the toilet.

"So does Caleb Matthews," Kell added helpfully. "Thirty seconds, Fin."

"Flip that handle and I'll kill you," she muttered. But she twisted beneath the jets of water and quickly rinsed clean. Fin shoved out a hand, and a fluffy yellow towel materialized in her grip. She dutifully wrapped herself and emerged from the shower. "You could show some sympathy. My clock is still off from my flight. Plus, I had to fly in coach from Cannes to New York." Fin saw no reason to explain that she could have secured a first-class seat from France if she'd been willing to wait another twelve hours. But half-a-day delay had been too high a price. "I haven't done that in years."

"Poor baby," mocked Kell. She sneered as Fin strolled to the sink and nudged her aside with a terry-cloth-covered hip.

"When stuck between Bert and Ernestine on a second honeymoon, absolutely." An array of products marched across the surface of the double sink. Starting with her face, Fin flipped on the taps and squeezed a cream-filled bottle. A stream of soap poured into her hands, and she returned the bottle to its place in line.

Julia reached for the tube. Her eyes widened as she

read the label. "This stuff costs as much as my car note," she gasped.

"I've moved up," Fin confirmed as she massaged the frothy concoction onto her skin. Like her entire toilette, the contents were worth their weight in gold or thereabouts. An extravagance, she knew, but she'd promised herself luxury years ago, and she'd kept her word.

When they were younger, she'd envied the wealthier girls in school who had been able to afford the creams and perfumes and lotions from the local department store, while she'd made due with Ivory soap and homemade steam baths. Now, she received shipments from Swiss spas and Italian perfumeries. A far cry from Je Naté and Vaseline. Decadent cream glided on like a cloud. She ducked her face to rinse and lifted her head with a haughty grin. "Worth every penny."

Kell reached over and squeezed a dollop into her palm. Lifting her hand, she sniffed at the light blue blob. "I've tried it. Overpriced."

A hand towel patted delicately at the freshly washed skin. Fin glared playfully at Kell in the mirror. "Philistine."

"Princess." Kell flipped the bottle to her, and Fin snatched it easily from the air. "You never change."

Julia beamed, eyes misting. "God, I've missed you two."

"Oh, Lord, she's about to start blubbering again," Fin grumbled, speaking over the lump that filled her own throat. The steam-fogged mirror reflected the dream she'd been haunted by for too many years. Kell, willowy and confident, the gorgeous face made for magazine covers and shrewd eyes that swayed jurors to her cause. And Julia, quietly lovely with sherry brown eyes too soft to see beyond her belief in you. "Cry and I'll throw you into the tub."

"Try it." With a swift dash at the tears clinging to her lashes, Julia flexed an arm to display a diminutive bicep. She was as proud of the tiny lump as she was of the many successful operations she'd performed. "I've been working out."

"In Lilliputian-ville," Fin ribbed her as she dutifully pushed at the muscle. "Hmm, not bad for a girl who thought rolling her hair had cardio value."

Julia grinned. "Amazing what they teach you in med school." She reached out, brushed at Kell's knee. "I saw you on *Entertainment Tonight*. You've taken Senator Marley's case?"

Relaxed by the pleasant mix of feminine scents, Kell nodded. "We've got a suppression hearing next week, so I'll be back and forth to Atlanta. I'm trying to get the gun kicked."

"The one she was holding when she called the police?" Fin queried. "The one engraved with her initials?"

"The very same." Kell lifted a shoulder and watched Fin sweep the contents of another expensive jar across the strong, distinctive bone structure Kell had longed for as a teenager. Widely spaced eyes received a brush of shadow, with the color repeated along high planes, accenting the hollows beneath. The yellow towel swathed a lushly curved body that wore cotton as stylishly as silk.

Kell wondered if her best friend realized how beautiful she'd become. If she finally understood how deep that beauty was rooted. But the time for heavy conver-

sations would come later. "In all the excitement of arresting the good senator, the police neglected to log the
evidence for a full thirty-six hours."

"Break in the chain of evidence." Fin curved her lips,
as much to slick on lipstick as to show approval. "Who
arrested her, the Keystone Cops?"

"A rookie and a drunk took the call. Dispatch assumed it was a prank call. Not every day a politician
calls in a double homicide."

"God bless the American justice system."

"And its federal agents," Julia added coyly, switching
the conversation to her preferred topic. "Speaking of
federal agents, Caleb watches you like he'd like to—"

"Frisk her," supplied Kell. "Full body."

"Drop it. Both of you." Outnumbered, Fin relented.
"I do plan to meet Caleb for dinner to convince him to
expand our role."

"What's going on, Fin?" Shooting her a concerned
look, Kell went on, "He's over this afternoon and now
you're meeting him. Talk."

Because Fin hadn't mentioned Jake's call, she replied
evasively, "There's nothing to tell. He stopped by because I wanted to know more about his plans."

"What did you find out?"

Meeting Kell's eyes in the mirror, she admitted, "Not
much, which is why I plan to beard him in his den."

"That's all?" Julia teased, enjoying the light flush
that swept over Fin. "That's all you want tonight?"

"I'm going for more info," Fin retorted. "Not to make
out with a cop."

"Cops have terrific hands," Kell offered with a knowing smile. "And amazing mouths."

"And a penchant for disliking the criminal element,"

Fin finished cynically. "Right now, Mr. FBI is on the phone with some guy in a rumpled suit and striped tie, pulling up all known records on Findley Ann Borders."

"What will he find?" Kell asked. "Do we need to be prepared? I can have you on the next flight out of here. Just say the word."

Fin turned and rested against the sink. "I've got flags but no outstanding warrants."

"Outstanding warrants?" Frowning, Kell demanded, "Exactly how many times have you been arrested?"

"That's not import," Fin dodged. "Suffice it to say, after I left here, I bumped around for a couple of years until I hooked up with a guy named Sebastian." Which is where she learned to shoot and a variety of other useful skills.

" 'Hooked up'?" Kell asked.

Fin's smile this time was sly with memory. "A very creative man," she murmured. "And now, very married."

"What, exactly, did Sebastian do?" The question came from Julia, who watched Fin with widened eyes.

"He was a recovery specialist."

"Recovering what?"

"Anything for a price." She'd been twenty-three and stuck in a hovel in Amsterdam. She'd provided a diversion to help Sebastian sneak into a casino, and he'd staked her in a tournament the following night. Both had reaped rewards, separately and together. Until they'd reached the mutual conclusion of friendship.

"His wife?"

"An ethnobotanist who thwarted a pharmaceutical giant's conspiracy. Last I heard, they were living between Bahia and New York."

"Nice, but will either of them have reason to turn on you?"

Fin smoothed body cream over her skin and shook her head. "I've only met Katelyn once, and she's as straight as they come. Except for the Girl Scout over there."

"I resent that," sniffed Julia.

"You resemble that," Fin corrected. "Anyway, after I worked with Sebastian, I learned to fly pretty low. Then I had a hiccup in L.A. I worked out a deal with the agent in charge. Three weeks of wearing a wire and I got off the hook." The story of the Bejkos was left best untold.

Kell picked through the tubes and pots. "Not so fast. Who were you eavesdropping on?"

"Midlevel crime lords who hadn't earned their stripes. A few guys who ran a ground game in Beverly Hills, snookering diplomats and dignitaries."

"What was your role?"

"Snookering diplomats and dignitaries." Propping her leg on the tub, Fin creamed lotion into each limb. Only she knew that her fingers trembled with memory. "The head of the family offered me a cut of each take. The FBI collared me and used me to get invited to the game. I worked off my debt and promised to keep my nose clean."

Warily, Kell asked, "And did you?"

"There's no proof otherwise." Fin scooped up the cream and tossed the canister to Kell. "Take it, it smells better on you."

The casual generosity didn't draw a remark from Kell or Julia, both familiar with Fin's unsolicited acts of kindness. Both knew that if they made a comment, she'd probably snatch the lotion back.

So they held their peace as she passed from the bathroom into the adjoining bedroom. Lifting the slender column of black she'd laid out for dinner, Fin caught Kell's look of concern. "I won't be needing a lawyer today, Counselor. By the time I hit twenty-five, I'd learned my lesson. Got myself a business manager to locate legitimate games for me." She turned back to the bed and the silky scraps of black lace she'd laid out beside the dress.

"Jake Devon scouts the tournaments, finds a stake for me when I need one, and makes sure my taxes are paid on time." Unconcerned about her audience, she shimmied into the fragile triangles and snapped the low-cut bra into place. "He's been a godsend."

Julia gawked from her bed. On what she earned in a public hospital, she couldn't afford the set hugging Fin's curves. Using her hefty trust fund never occurred to her. Mildly envious, she teased, "He must love your underwear."

Fin gave a husky laugh. "Jake only cares about my underwear if he thinks it could be a write-off."

"Sounds like a fun guy."

"He's great, actually. More importantly, Jake knows me too well to be at all interested." Loneliness stirred briefly, unexpectedly. She hadn't spent her years in exile alone, but she hadn't formed close ties to anyone besides Jake. No one who expected her home at night. No one to miss her. She'd been alone, but content—never thinking about what wasn't in her life.

Which is why her reaction to Caleb rocked her. In a matter of days, he'd snuck under skin she thought too thick to be pierced, and he'd drawn out emotions she'd barely acknowledged.

His defense of her yesterday, then their conversation by the tree, showed more insight than she'd expected. The first had made her uneasy, and the second had made her wonder if there might be more.

And his kisses melted through the steel of her resistance with barely a touch.

It was all too quick. Too easy.

Too right.

Bothered by her train of thought, Fin hurriedly stepped into the dress, knowing how the cuts of fabric transformed on the wearer. She'd give Caleb a taste of his own medicine and prove to herself she didn't need any. Right after she'd convinced him to go along with her plan. She gave herself a brisk nod and asked, "Can someone zip me up?"

Kell came forward to perform the task, while Fin released the clip holding her hair in place. Curls tumbled free, skating lightly across shoulders left bare by the generous descent of the dress's neckline. Straps supported gossamer weight, which danced at midthigh. Sleek, glowing legs ended in strappy heels she'd coveted a week ago. "How'd you get those? They're back ordered," Kell gawked.

Fin stood in front of the full-length mirror inset in the bathroom door. Glancing down at the shoes, she replied, "A gift from an admirer."

"Who?" Kell asked, brow arched, prepared for the answer.

"Franco himself."

Shaking her head, Kell stepped back to study this gorgeous creature she'd once padded into a brasserie.

"Caleb is going to swallow his tongue," she praised, then frowned. "I'm damned glad Luke met me before he ever got a look at you."

"Luke's only got eyes for you. He'd do anything for you." Fin smiled and reached for Kell. "He makes you happy?"

"Every day. Especially today." Kell linked her fingers with flesh as different and as familiar as life itself. "He helped me bring you home."

"Thank God."

Julia rose to join them, completing the circle. "Amen."

In a lushly appointed study, three members of Stark met in emergency conference. The leader reclined in a favored chair, listening to the report.

"Franklin and Jacoby are dead," Silas Hestor reported. He reclined in the capacious leather chair, puffing on the thick Cuban he'd selected from the carved wooden box reportedly owned by Napoleon. Smoke wafted into the cloistered space, and he enjoyed the rich decadence of scent.

"Any word on Graves?"

"Nothing yet. Jimmy, you know something?"

The question was more of a dare. James Worley brandished his cigarette, well aware Hestor despised the things. Red glowed at the tip, and the pungent aroma blended with the heavier cigar smoke. "I swear I don't have any idea where he is." The lie had been practiced a thousand times. Puffing on the cigarette, he added, "I know I made a mistake with the sheriff, but I did it on my own."

"Just have never known you to be much of an independent thinker, Jimmy. Except when it comes to money."

James nearly coughed on the smoke. Money was his forte. After all, that's how they'd found him. An abandoned embezzlement scheme that hung over his head, even as he controlled the coffers of Hallden. President of its premier bank and launderer of Stark's funds. Funds they wanted and couldn't have. Terror streamed through him. They had to get the land, he thought frantically, before they asked for the cash. "I saw the papers naming the three girls as trustees. With them in charge, the bank will have no say in the land transaction. I wanted to be proactive."

"Instead, you handed witnesses to our enemies," the room's third occupant rebuked. "If I hadn't been there, hadn't been able to rely on Silas, we might all be sitting in Calder's jail."

"You said you wanted the land," wheedled Worley. "I was trying to help. Time's running out."

"We're all quite aware of the deadline. And the land, while crucial, is not your concern, James. Continue to make arrangements for our withdrawals, and you'll be doing your part."

"I can do more." He had to. Soon. "We should focus on getting the deed, but with the other ones returning, it gets harder. Kell Jameson is practically living there, and Sheriff Calder has authorized an around-the-clock guard."

"Brute force won't cut it." The third voice paused, considered. "We tried to purchase the land and to seize it. And then there was your asinine idea of trying to kill Borders, Jameson, and Warner. Exactly what would you have done if Franklin had succeeded? Let's assume the three women and the men died. What would your plan have been then, James?"

Worley flinched, but he couldn't tell them it was Graves's idea. Instead, he blustered, "Um, Eliza Faraday would have been crushed. Losing all of them at the same time. While she was in mourning, I'd sell the land. Claim that she was too distraught to act in the best interest of the foundation. Once the sale's made, she can't undo it."

"Clever." The third voice grew hard. "But James, you do not commission hits on your own. That is way above your pay grade."

"I was trying to help. To fix—"

"You're a banker, James. A bean counter. Your only function is to protect our funds, and to have them ready for us by the month's end. This is my warning to you."

Worley's teeth snapped shut. A warning occurred only once. The second warning came just before death. Too late to run and hide, too late to make it right. Burned houses with families trapped inside. Unsolved car accidents and faked suicides. All the handiwork of their founder. He sputtered, "I understand. I thought—"

"Don't think, James." Standing, the hard look given encompassed both Worley and Hestor. "Findley Borders has an interesting background, one that you, James, are well aware of. While she's proven to be smart about her gaming debts, there's still the matter of the money she stole from us."

Hestor inquired, "Do you think she'll play ball?"

"According to her record, she's either turned over a new leaf or learned to hide her basic nature better. My instinct is the latter. But she may require a push to assist us. Let's start with the three hundred thousand she stole from us."

"What do we want from her?" James ventured.

"Exactly what you so ineptly attempted to secure. Fin Borders will simply have to convince Eliza and the others to sell us the land. Or suffer the consequences."

"Should I call her?"

"Not you, James." The regal head inclined toward Hestor. "Silas, contact her. Convince her to work with us. Remind her of what we do to thieves in our organization."

Hestor nodded. "And if she won't?"

"Then we'll return to James's ill-conceived plan to deal with all of the center's occupants. At once."

"Yes, Judge Majors."

Mary nodded. "Keep me informed."

CHAPTER 12

Fin parked in an open slot and bent to gather her supplies. She slipped a light red Beaujolais, the only vintage on hand at market, into the canvas bag containing two uncooked steaks and a plastic bag filled with crisp greens. She opened the door of Kell's car, careful not to scrape the black sedan in the next slot. Not that she cared about the other car. Wheedling the borrowed wheels a second time had required an oath nearly signed in blood and a threat of death followed by imprisonment.

She stepped out of the car and paused to study Caleb's building. Covington Arms occupied a squat corner of the center city block. Main Street wound past on the west, with the county road jutting across to the south. But the primary entrance faced a quiet, tree-lined street with charming cottages and sturdy bungalows. Red brick trimmed with freshly painted white awnings rose multiple stories, flattening at the top into kempt rooftop gardens scattered with a clutch of wrought-iron tables and chairs one could glimpse from below. Oak trees spread green fronds across a cobbled walk in faded red stone, accented by white pebbles in channels along either side.

At the entrance, she scanned the metal panel for Caleb's name. Apartment 611. Taking a breath, she pressed the buzzer once, then again.

"Yes?"

"Fin Borders. I come bearing gifts."

A moment of silence, then, "Come on up."

The buzzer sounded, releasing the lock. Fin shifted her parcels and made her way inside. Mailboxes lined the wall to the left, a console table with fresh daffodils greeted visitors on the right. Straight ahead, an elevator with an old-fashioned gate stood at the ready. She entered, pulled the gate shut, and jabbed the button for the sixth floor.

The elevator opened onto a wide hallway with five apartments along either side of the corridor. The eleventh had been carved into the end of the hallway and spanned the width. Paintings of flora and fauna in black matte frames decorated the space, melding nicely with the blue-gray carpet that gave slightly beneath her feet.

A nice, featureless apartment building, she mused. Tasteful, edging toward shabby chic. Comfortable and quickly forgotten once you pulled into traffic. Handy.

Fin lifted her hand to knock, only to find the door opened before her fist struck. He wore blue jeans and a black T-shirt. Both molded a body that carried not a spare ounce of flesh. The simple uniform of men everywhere, made marvelous on this man. She spoke through the sudden knot in her throat. "Hi, Caleb."

"Hi, yourself." Caleb opened the door wider and

reached out for the bag she carried. "This is unexpected."

"Spur of the moment."

"Nice surprise." He closed his fist over the bag's strap, then froze as she stepped into the doorway. Into the light. Black had been poured over her into a semblance of a dress. Skimming over high breasts and a taut waist. Stopping inches above legs that could drive a man to oblivion, where he'd still dream of her.

Dark imaginings forced him to take the sack before he reached for more than either of them was ready for. He knew better. He didn't know her. Volatile reactions belonged to rookies who'd never seen women like Fin. He had. And he remembered the consequences. He cleared his suddenly dry throat. "Come on in."

Fin noted the reaction, and the brief flash of annoyance. She relinquished her bag and strolled inside. As she passed him, she glanced over her shoulder and asked, "Did I interrupt?"

What? he thought dimly, trying not to stare at the sleek expanse of skin left bare except for a light ribbing of string and the generous curves below the helpful V. *Oh, yeah.* "Just working on a case for next week."

"Do you have time for a break?"

"Sure." Caleb led her further into the apartment, grateful he was the type of man who put his toys away. Except for a stray glass on the coffee table, the place was immaculate. "To what do I owe the pleasure?"

"I was hungry. Thought you might be too." She stopped in the living room, examining the interior for clues about one Caleb Matthews. A simple floor plan led from the entryway to a spacious living room furnished with a sofa in rich chocolate leather and a fireplace in the red brick that decorated the building. Prints depicting dramatic landscapes graced walls painted golden amber. In the morning, the western exposure would make the color glow. Evenings like tonight would burnish the subtle hues.

In a silver frame on the mantel, a boy and girl knelt beside a sleepy basset hound. A handsome couple posed behind them, with a gangly teenager standing beside the older man. The quirk of a smile immediately identified Caleb. Getting closer, Fin peered at the younger children. The resemblance was uncanny. "Twins?"

"Jonas and Mariah. My parents. And the master of the house, Casey. Although Mariah always insisted on calling him Fred." He spoke from the bar of the kitchen, where he'd set the canvas sack. Though he didn't mind speaking of his family, he fell silent. Watching her examine his living area intrigued him. What did she see in the rooms? In him?

She traced the picture, herself framed by the mantel. A new thought crept in to disturb him. Why did she seem to fit?

Unaware of his scrutiny, Fin wandered around the room. Drawn by the bay windows spearing the last rays of sunlight, she pushed aside gauzy sheers. Banks of flowers, dutifully tended, spread in a profusion of colors. The garden lacked a formal plan. Instead, pale white asters sidled up to vivid crimson zinnias, necked with lovely daylilies.

Mrs. F had once sentenced her to tending the center's garden for a summer, she recalled wistfully. Every Saturday, she'd scrabbled in moist soil beside her mentor, nursing begonias and geraniums through a summer drought. How long had it been since she'd dug into the dirt, touched something more vibrant than a poker chip or the slick of a card?

Shaking off the disquietude, she crossed to the middle of the living room. Books were piled high on the low-slung coffee table, teetered on the matching side table. Tattered paperbacks squeezed into one long column of built-in bookshelves, which flanked the fireplace. Fin drifted to the shelves. Doyle. Fleming. Christie. It was fitting, she thought, that Caleb preferred mysteries. From floor to ceiling, all read several times, if the creased bindings were any indication. On the other shelves, law books jostled for space with art texts and biographies. A middle shelf had been reserved for a television, which slid out on a concealed track.

"Clever," she said, pushing the shelf into place. He'd taken a sterile apartment and made it home. Not a talent everyone possessed. Certainly not her. "Nice digs."

"Thank you." Caleb set the wine in the refrigerator and checked the label with a smile. "I see you found our only wine seller in town."

Sharing his amusement, she shrugged. "When I left Hallden, we were technically dry. I guess we've moved to damp. Maybe in another decade or so, we can aim for wet."

"You were eighteen when you left town, right?" He removed a bottle of white from his personal stash, lifted the label for her inspection. "Better?"

"Much better," she approved, unoffended that he'd set hers aside. Sliding onto the stool at the breakfast bar, she accepted the glass and took a sip. Closing her eyes to savor the wine, she allowed her mind to drift. "Yes, I was eighteen. I'd been planning my escape for months."

"Escape." The word choice caught him, bothered him. Just as it had that afternoon. "Watching the four of you, I'd have thought you'd never have separated if it hadn't been for the fire. Why were you so desperate to get away?"

"Restlessness. My great curse." She shook her head. "I'd gotten a scholarship to college, to run track. But academia wasn't my bag of tricks."

"You were a runner?"

Wine, chilly and smooth, glided over her tongue. "I was all-state three years in a row. One hundred, two hundred, and relay. Hurdles if Coach bribed me."

Caleb gave a satisfied nod. "Well, that explains it." As though a mystery had been solved, he brought his glass to his lips.

Fin frowned. "Explains what?"

"Why you have the legs of a goddess. Endless, with lean muscles, taut skin, and the perfect shape." Caleb caught her look, a mix of flattered and embarrassed. "But I'm sure you're used to compliments about them. And that face of yours. Bold. Stunning. Beautiful."

Moved, she found herself holding her breath. She released it on a throaty laugh. "A woman rarely hears enough of her beauty."

"But you'd prefer compliments about your brains, I'd imagine," Caleb deduced, elbows resting on the bar. When he leaned in, he could catch stray thoughts in the shimmery eyes before she marshaled them into obedient blankness. He answered the hidden question anyway. "Beauty is a handy distraction, but when you outwit an opponent, you want him to know you were smarter, quicker."

The accuracy caught her, made her wonder. Those

shrewd eyes saw more than she'd expected from a man in uniform. His type tended to surrender insight in exchange for a badge and a gun. Once again, she reordered her concept of him. "I rely on whatever works at the moment," she refuted lightly.

"And what are you counting on tonight?" He pushed away from the bar, came around to the stool. To her. "You don't strike me as the domestic type, Fin. Plus, I'm fairly certain you don't really trust me. So, what gives?"

Though he stood a polite distance away, she couldn't shake the sensation of being cornered. Trapped. She stood, putting the stool between them, a poor but essential barrier. "I wanted to talk to you about Stark and how we can help. How I can help."

"And the steak?"

"I'm an excellent cook, and I'm hungry." The last word hung between them, a declaration with a myriad of solutions. "For steak," she rushed to add.

"And salad," he offered blandly.

Fin ignored the taunt. She circled the opposite end of the bar and entered the kitchen. Like the living room, it was pristine. Pots dangled from a rack above head. A quick search of cabinets revealed pans in near-perfect condition. She chose her weapons, then raided the refrigerator. Armed and ready, she asked, "Got an apron?"

"Sure." Caleb tugged open a drawer and removed a length of green that demanded a kiss for the cook. He grinned. "Too easy."

She draped the opening over her head, reached behind her to tie it. After a brief fumble for the ties, masculine hands brushed hers aside. Deft fingers grazed bare skin as he knotted the strings. Warm air drifted along her temple, echoed by the furnace of male body heat. As soon as the apron was secured, she shifted to the stove, pressed her hands to the cold metal. Which did little good. The simple proximity of the man sent her system into turmoil.

A third kiss would be devastating.

Fin dipped her head to light the stove and melt butter in a skillet that had never touched heat. "Thanks," she murmured.

"My pleasure." Caleb eagerly reached for his wine. Seconds in her presence had him as hard as iron. But until he learned her angle, he wouldn't act. Shouldn't.

She'd better talk fast, he thought, measuring the limits of his patience.

Wax paper peeled open as she uncovered the steaks. "How do you like your meat?"

"Medium well." To occupy his hands as much as anything, he busied himself with preparing the salad. "Where did you learn to cook?"

"The center." In a bowl, she blended a concoction of spices he didn't realize he owned. With skillful motions, she dredged the fillets in the rub and settled them in butter to cook. "Mrs. F didn't believe in corporal punishment. She preferred to find your least favorite activity and make it the whole of your existence."

"Didn't care for cooking?"

"Or gardening or any of the domestic arts. Which guaranteed that I learned to sauté a mean salmon, and I can grow a garden in the desert."

"I take it you stayed in trouble?"

"It would be easier to count the days I wasn't on punishment." Her mouth softened in memory. "Usually, if

Julia got involved, we avoided actual mayhem. She had this effortless way of steering me onto a path of righteousness, despite my determination to sin."

Caleb fished two potatoes from the pantry and set them in the microwave. "Where was Kell?"

"Oh, she was usually egging me on and preparing our defense."

The easy affection belied the tough exterior she preferred. "You love them."

She lifted her shoulders in a gesture that spoke eloquently of loss and rediscovery. "They are my sisters."

"Then how did you stay away so long?" He'd been wondering since he'd first seen them together, more since their confession. "You're resourceful, Fin. Why didn't you try to come back before?"

"Because of Stark."

"I don't believe you."

Fin tossed her head back. "You have a theory?"

"I think just like you were afraid to go, you were afraid of what you'd find when you came back."

"Afraid of what?" she challenged, sneering as she transferred the steaks to a ceramic platter. "The men who'd threatened to hurt me before I stole their money? Absolutely."

"Nope." Caleb raised his wineglass, considered her over the rim. "You were afraid of coming home to where people knew you. Expected more of you than a glib answer and hard shell."

"Dime-store psychology," she sniffed, annoyed. She'd had excellent reasons for steering clear. Maybe if she'd tried harder, she could have returned earlier, but she'd been busy. "I'm not afraid of who I am, Caleb. I'm proud of the woman I've become."

"Good. You should be." He reached for the platter of steaks. "I'm just surprised you know it." Exiting the kitchen, he left her standing, hands reaching absently for the side dishes, filing away the tangle of emotions in her eyes.

Soon they were seated at his dining room table. He brought a bite to his mouth and nearly moaned. "I didn't know I could adore a piece of meat."

Pleased, Fin speared a piece and sampled. "Hmm. I did good."

"An understatement." Focused on his meal, he nudged Fin into regaling him with tales of her travels, wincing in some places, cheering silently in others. In exchange, he talked about his parents and siblings, about his first few years in the FBI.

Dinner soon disappeared, and Caleb stared forlornly at the empty plates. "All of these ingredients are in my kitchen?" he asked in disbelief.

Fin laughed and reached out to pat his hand. "One day, I'll give you a cooking lesson."

"In exchange for what?" he asked, savoring the last morsel. "A kidney? A lung?"

She saw the opening and seized it. "Your help." Knowing the value of timing, she paused a beat. "I want to go undercover to catch Stark."

CHAPTER 13

To his credit, Caleb didn't drop his fork. Instead, he set the utensil by his plate and reached for his wine. Glass drained, he looked at the woman who watched him expectantly while he considered her request. "Absolutely not."

The rejection was swift, firm. Final. Just as she'd expected. Ignoring his reaction, she splayed her hands on the table and leveled her eyes toward his. "Stark has an agenda that includes Mrs. F and, therefore, the rest of us. They're probably the ones nosing around my finances. Why not let them use me and allow me to find out what they want?"

"Because they'll kill you." He shoved away from the table and paced into the living room. "Luke wanted to tell you all in person tomorrow." Spinning around, he pinned her with a hard look. "Pete Franklin is dead."

Fin blanched. "What? How?"

"Murdered. Luke called me just before you arrived.

One of the nurses came to check on him and he was dead."

"Are you sure it wasn't an accident?" Even as she posed the question, she knew the truth. "How did he die?"

"The killer made it look like a heart attack." Caleb raked his hand through his hair. "Could be a dozen drugs, some detectable, others not. My guess is we won't find a cause of death besides heart failure."

"They got to him in the hospital." Fin absorbed the news, a shudder coursing through her. She was no stranger to death, but two men in as many days . . . "What do they want?"

Caleb shook his head. "I don't know. But I do know I'm not risking you or anyone else to find out."

"What are your leads?"

"We don't have any. The car was registered to Franklin, and the guns had their serial numbers filed off. We've got nothing."

Fin squared her shoulders. "Wrong. You have me. Like I said, send me in undercover, Caleb. I've done it before."

Without a word, Caleb left the room. Fin chased after him, forgotten wine in hand. He flung open a door that revealed a small office. On the desk, a manila folder lay open. Fin didn't have to read it to know the contents. "You pulled my record."

"Yes. And Kell and Julia. Both of them are clean."

"But not me."

"No, not you." He snatched up a sheet. "You've been arrested three times. Each time, though, you've avoided prosecution. How?" He'd made calls, but no one had given him a satisfactory answer.

She colored but didn't flinch. "According to your tone, I assume you think I slept my way to freedom."

He didn't dignify the accusation. "I don't assume anything. That's why I'm asking."

Fin picked up the folder, scanned the contents. Seeing her life in black and white, realizing he'd read a litany of her mistakes, smarted. With a negligent motion, she released the file to fall on the desk. "The first time, I was underage at a club in Vegas. I did too well and the owners had me pinched. Charges were dropped because one of the waiters came to my arraignment and helped me out with the judge."

"You were twenty-one the second time." He didn't glance at the report, having committed the contents to memory. "Grand larceny. Possession of an unregistered firearm."

Heat flooded her cheeks. "A misunderstanding. One I was able to clear up."

"What about the third one, Fin?"

Her eyes closed briefly, shuttering embarrassment. "The RICO charge."

"Racketeering is a serious crime. Those cases take years to build." Caleb watched her, waiting. No glib answer explained a hefty accusation like that. "The Bejko crime family, Fin. You were accused of a federal crime, but you've got a clean record unless a person goes hunting."

Her throat like sand, she spoke in flat, even tones. But nothing could erase the distress threaded beneath. "Because one of your brethren decided I could work off my misdeeds by wearing a wire. I'd already become acquainted with Aleksander Bejko, the oldest son. His father was working to establish another branch of the

Albanian crime family in L.A. Aleksander grew up in the city and developed a penchant for exotic women."

She'd glossed over her escapade earlier, but Caleb had to understand. She understood the risks, had an intimate knowledge of the stakes involved. "The agent had gotten too cozy with his marks. I'd been working for Bejko, fleecing high-flying diplomats who couldn't tell a straight from a flush. Your man lost his shirt and collared me that night. Told me if I'd wear a wire, he'd drop the charges."

"My God." Sickness formed in his gut, oily and slick. Despite crime drama depictions, an agent wearing a wire risked his life each time. The Bureau taught courses on avoiding detection and blustering through revelation, because discovery could get you killed. No one went in miked without backup and training. Yet, according to her sheet, she'd have been barely twenty-five. Brash, fearless, and terribly vulnerable. And alone in a pit of vipers. "He made you spy on the Bejkos?"

Fin forced her voice to hold steady. "For almost a month." Time, she imagined, had numbed the memory to a haze she didn't dare to penetrate. If she focused, the past would whip out like a lash, shredding the fragile illusion. So she crested on the surface, giving Caleb sufficient information to convince him. "I had to play with these men, trying not to short out the mike or give myself away. Twenty-three days of hell."

Rage fired, grinding against control. Twenty-three days. Twenty-three nights. Lying to men who valued women only slightly more than dogs. Men who did not accept no from a woman's lips. "You weren't . . . discovered?"

The glass of wine in her hand bobbed and steadied.

"No. No thanks to Agent Palento." Bitterness coated her words. "After the first couple of weeks, he decided he deserved part of my take. Then he upped the ante."

"Fin."

He'd cornered her that night, in an alley behind the club. Caleb didn't need to know that. No one did. In response, she said, "I refused, threatened to go to his superiors."

He heard the evasion and saw the pallor creep under her skin, but he held his tongue. Later, he decided, he would hear the entire story. "The Bejkos?"

"Palento appeared to have sufficient evidence to make the RICO case stick. Turns out he didn't need my information."

Relief coursed through Caleb, settled the tumult that brewed inside. "They didn't find out?"

"I'm still alive." She made the quip, but both of them realized how accurate her assessment was. And how capricious.

"The Bejkos preferred gambling and human trafficking," he offered.

"By and large. From what I heard, they didn't seem to have much of a problem with the occasional murder for hire, either." Fin set the wineglass on the desktop with a sharp sound. "Pull the Bejko file, Caleb. I wore a wire to stay out of prison. I'm willing to do much more to save my family."

Caleb met her eyes. Their determined look was empty of the anger that shimmered in his own. He'd not only pull the Bejko file but by tomorrow he'd also have Agent Palento's jacket. "I'm still not convinced, Fin. Stark isn't a newbie trying to make its mark. They've been operating under the radar for years."

The waver was slight, but she pounced on the opening. "I know. I know because the drug shipment, the money we stole—all of it was connected to Stark. I know that some of the men who used to come to the Warehouse weren't there for the card games or the booze. Men like James Worley and Ernest King."

Caleb frowned, running through the names. "Worley is the president of the Georgia Bank."

"Correct. And when I left, Ernest King was the head of the county commission," Fin provided.

"King? He retired last month." Ernest King, a gruff, bantam rooster of a man who had treated him to dinner his first week in town. "You're sure both men were involved?"

Fin heard the skepticism, accepted it. She'd wondered at her own memories. Youth often stitched together memory made of dubious recollection. She knew how it would sound, the reminiscences of an eighteen-year-old gambler. Though she desperately needed to convince him, she wouldn't lie. "I'm saying both men spent hours in the Warehouse losing money and never seemed to be very upset."

"Wealthy men don't always play for money," Caleb argued. "Perhaps they simply came to watch the show. Or you."

"I've watched men play games, watched how they counted their winnings. These men spent hours discussing cruises and vacations and women. What I wrote down, what I heard, was code, I'm sure of it. For drug shipments and guns and prostitution, whatever else they were into. The Warehouse was a front for them, and a lucrative sideline. And if they are willing to surface long enough to try and snuff out Mrs. F and

Luke, then what's on Stark's radar now is worth millions."

Despite his reservations, Caleb could feel adrenaline course through veins tight with anticipation. A solid lead on Stark. Two live bodies with links to his nemesis. "So what do you suggest?"

Carefully, she laid out her plan while he listened, asking no questions. Sensing victory, Fin finished, "Once I'm in, I feed you and Luke what I learn. Either they'll reveal something to me or they won't. Given their urgency, I think whatever they're after has a short time line. You have three weeks. It strikes me that they have even less."

"Why would they let you inside, allow you back into their organization? You stole from them. Disappeared." He pressed hard, looking for a hole. Because, he thought with cautious excitement, her idea could work. "How do you convince them that you're worth the risk?"

Fin kept her gaze level on his. She'd never wanted to be on the side of right or wrong, never considered herself a friend of angels or the demons. But, it appeared, Stark had left her little choice. "They'll take me because I can give them Mrs. F."

Caleb circled the desk, reached out, traced his thumb over one of the wrinkles that appeared between the almond-shaped eyes. Beneath his touch, the wrinkle deepened, as did his worry. "I don't know that I can risk you, Fin."

He skimmed the curve of her jaw, and she could feel her breath hitch. She told herself to move away, but her body remained stubbornly still. Only her mouth moved. "I'm at risk either way."

"Perhaps." The unasked question that vibrated between them was, *From what?* Caleb allowed his thumb to graze the mouth painted in a color to loosen a man's will. He thought of kissing her, as he had this afternoon. Of steeping himself in her. But what she'd told him of Agent Palento wedged between thought and action. Murmuring, he said, "I have no right to mix business and pleasure. If I kiss you, I'll be no better than Palento."

"You're right," Fin murmured in agreement. Decided, she stretched up, framed his face with her hands. "So I guess I'll have to do the honors."

Her lips met his, a torrent of heat that jolted both. Fin trembled, pulled away. "Too much."

"Not enough," retorted Caleb as he dragged her against him, fingers releasing her bound hair to have the skeins cascade over his sensitized flesh. His arms slipped low around her, lifting her higher. She fit him perfectly, every curve, every plane. Greedy, he sampled the courtesan mouth that teased with a smirk. Arousal, already riding hard, shot past caution and restraint. He dived into the kiss, already gorging on flavors.

Spice where her lips parted at their moist seam. Sweet, achingly sweet, when her tongue smoothed over his demanding forays. Tart now, as they tangled in a duel to give more, to find more.

Fin had kissed men, had reveled in the dance. But no man had quaked through her system like Caleb, fire singeing control, burning judgment to ash. Suddenly, wonderfully, all that mattered was the hold of his gloriously agile hands at her waist. Then, in an instant, the stroke of wildness as his tongue sampled the lobe of her ear, the hollow of her throat.

She tested the resilient flesh at his neck with delicate nips. A groan rumbled through him, shivering her with delight. Emboldened, she gave herself rein to explore the hot, sleek skin beneath the black T-shirt. With a sigh of triumph, she found the solid heat of his chest, felt it heave beneath her questing hands.

Knowing he moved too fast, Caleb whirled them to the edge of his desk. Fin stepped into the cradle of his legs, her skirt ruched higher by the rough denim. When she shifted, the caress hardened steel and he gasped into her mouth. The kiss this time held a keenness, a fevered mating demanding release.

Because she wanted nothing more, nothing less, Fin fought to surface. As glazed eyes snapped open, she saw herself nearly astride a flexed, muscled thigh. One thin black strap dangled off her shoulder, where his lips wreaked havoc perilous inches above her breasts.

"Caleb."

He heard his name on her lips, a sound it seemed he'd craved forever. But he also heard the tone beneath, felt her retreat. Need thrummed beneath his mouth, yes. And a measure of trepidation that stopped him. Curses rang in his head. "Fin."

"We can't. Not now."

He didn't reply. Instead, he eased her away and drew the fallen strap into place. Black coils tumbled in erotic disarray. Unable to resist, he dove in for another kiss.

Fin resisted until his mouth softened in tender salute. She released a sigh, and the kiss spun slowly, gently out.

Before they drowned, he raised his head. "Soon, Fin. Very soon."

Unable to argue, she dragged her thumb across his mouth, erasing evidence. "Good night, Caleb."

They walked together to the door, gathering Fin's purse from the sofa. Hand on the knob, she reminded him, "You didn't give me your answer."

Knowing he should refuse, he nodded his head. "If you do anything other than what I tell you, the deal's off. I'll snatch you out and put you so deep in protective custody, you'll wish you'd never met me."

"Thank you, Caleb."

"Don't," he muttered, jerking the door open. "I'm not doing you any favors."

With an inscrutable smile, she kissed his cheek. "If only you knew."

CHAPTER 14

By Sunday morning, when she was surrounded by a gaggle of children hungry for promised waffles, Fin had convinced herself the interlude with Caleb should be forgotten, except for his agreement to her plan. An affair with him made no sense, had folly written all over it. She stirred batter expertly at the kitchen island, determined to focus on the task at hand. But scorching images of the night before flashed uninvited and threatened to undermine her resolve.

His mouth on hers, diving deep, demanding a response. His hand streaking fire across her naked skin. The rub of denim against silk, hard against soft.

"Hey, Fin, the waffles are burning!"

Jolted, Fin blinked, then smothered a curse. On the blue tiled counter, the waffle iron seeped gray, blueberry-scented smoke. She dropped the whisk and reached for the smoldering appliance. Gingerly, she pried open the top and glared at the blackened breakfast. "Thanks, Nina."

The younger woman grinned. "Kell does that all the time. But even your burnt food smells better than hers."

"I heard that," Kell chided, entering the kitchen. Kids tittered when she poked her tongue at the smirking teenager. "You have no respect for your elders."

"I do when they can cook," Nina muttered.

Guilelessly, Faith added, "Good thing you're dating Sheriff Luke. Otherwise, you'd probably have to go to a restaurant every day."

Nina took juice glasses from the cabinet and passed them to a lean, quiet young man named Brandon. Sotto voce, she told him, "Or she'd just starve to death."

Unable to argue, Kell settled for a faux glare. "Go set the table, brat. You go with her, you traitors." She pointed at the door, but no one believed she was really mad. After three weeks of living with Kell, they'd grown to understand that the lawyer was a sucker for kids.

A chorus of "yes, ma'am's" followed the children from the kitchen into the dining room. Nina, Faith, Brandon, and the older kids gathered up glasses, dishes, and cutlery already stacked for use. Pushing through the swinging door, Nina caught Fin's eye and begged, "Don't let her help cook. Please. We're famished."

"Out!" Kell threw a kitchen towel at the disappearing, chuckling form. Laughing herself, she joined Fin at the waffle iron and poked at the burnt husks with a fork. "I recognize this stage of cooking. I'm an expert at removal, let me handle it."

"Deal." Fin relinquished the hot pad and returned to the workstation, where a stack of blueberry waffles, a tray of scrambled eggs, and strips of crisp bacon had mysteriously vanished as well. "Eat slowly!" she called into the dining room, knowing she had mere minutes before the demand for more food would come. "They're like locusts," she commented in amazement. "Where does it all go?"

"You've seen them play," Kell reminded her. "Harness a few eight-year-olds, and we could solve the energy crisis."

"Couldn't grow enough food." Fin lifted a jug of milk, already depleted. While Kell wiped down the eight plates, she redoubled the batter. And firmly dismissed Caleb Matthews and his agile mouth from her thoughts.

Kell had other ideas, Fin soon discovered.

"You were out late," Kell remarked as she sprayed the newly cleaned waffle iron with a generous hand. "Way past curfew. Like always."

Fin ignored the provocative comment, saying only, "That's too much oil. We're not going for a deep fry. Just a light coat."

Adjusting her volume and filing the tip away, Kell continued, undaunted. "You didn't even stop by to give me an update."

"I thought you'd be asleep."

"I was. Why weren't you?" Kell set the canister down, leaned back against the counter, and propped her elbows on the tiled surface. "Did you and Caleb do more than eat steak?"

"We talked." Fin stirred the whisk faster and added a dash of milk.

The terse response raised Kell's brow—and her antennae. *If she stares any harder at the mixing bowl,* Kell thought, *she'll bore a hole in the bottom.* "You left for dinner at seven o'clock. Heard you come in around eleven. Car break down?"

"Your precious car is safely in the driveway," Fin replied evenly as she added a generous handful of berries. "Not a scratch on her."

Kell watched her carefully, noting the light flush of color. "Then it must have been out of gas."

"Full tank. Is the waffle iron hot?"

Intrigued by the dogged avoidance, Kell shoved away from the counter and came to the island, where Fin was scooping a heaping cup of flour from an open jar. Even to Kell's untrained eye, it seemed overly full. "Watch out," she warned.

Fin glanced down at her absent movements and bit off a fresh curse. Jerkily, she speared the measuring spoon into the flour bin. She picked up the mixing bowl and circled around Kell. "Dinner was fine. Uneventful."

"Liar. Something happened." Kell was certain of it now. Not once in all their years had she ever been able to outbluff Fin Borders. But guilt and an emotion harder to name skated over the blank expression. "Tell me."

Filling the ladle, Fin poured batter into the eight round slots. *Uneventful* was less a lie than strategic denial. She didn't see any reason to admit how accurate Kell was—or might have been. "We had steak, talked, and I left Caleb's at nine."

Anticipating the next question, she added, "Then I went for a drive." That much, at least, was completely true. After she'd left Caleb's, nostalgia had driven her to a nighttime tour of the city she'd tried so hard to forget. Magnolias lined quiet streets, their glossy green leaves black in the moonlight. Neighborhoods settled in for the evening, lamplight dancing behind drawn shades. She'd even driven close to the Red District, where she'd spent her first ten years. Kell had lived there too, on the better side of the wrong side of the tracks.

"I drove by Brockett Street."

Kell stiffened. Fin had grown up on Brockett, a slum by only the most forgiving of descriptions. *Shantytown* was a more accurate assessment. Single-frame wood houses with peeling, cheap, florid paint. Porches sagged, eaten away by rot and neglect. "You hate going over there."

Fin flipped the lid on the waffle maker and set the dial. "House is still there. Vacant." The dilapidated house where she'd awakened to the screams of obscenities night after night. Where her mother had shoved her into a closet to wait when customers had visited.

"Did you go inside?"

"No." Fin picked at a nail. "There were kids on the street, running and shouting. Ten o'clock at night and no one gave a damn."

"I know."

"Do you ever think about who we'd be if Mrs. F hadn't taken us in?" The question rose unbidden. Fin lifted her eyes to meet and hold Kell's sober gaze. "If your parents hadn't skipped town, do you think you'd have been a lawyer?"

Despite the fact that she'd asked herself the same thing almost every day, Kell stumbled over her answer. "Don't know." She folded her arms, feeling cold in the sunny room. "I'd have the same mind. The same drive. But without her, or y'all, I don't know what I would have used them for." Giving her skin a brisk rub, she asked, "Why?"

"I'm no better than they were." Fin had idled in a car that cost more than the entire block, one she could have bought with her last big win. But a car, a house, or a yacht changed nothing. She could win millions, but she'd still be the same—the child of a pimp and a prostitute. "My folks sold themselves. How is what I do any different? Better class of people where I work, but same difference."

"Fin."

"Save it, Kell." The realization had tangled her up last night as much as memories of kissing Caleb had. Both carried the same warning. "He had my rap sheet. He'd run a background on you and Julia, but of course you both came up clean. Me, on the other hand, I had a lot of tap dancing to do."

"You made some stupid choices. That's tough, but fixable." Kell stepped closer but knew better than to touch. Tension wired through Fin's slender form, blazed in the eyes that held a self-contempt Kell recognized. "Fin, don't start this again. You're not your parents."

"Why not? Because I make hundreds of thousands of dollars doing what I do? Hell, I remember what my mom looked like. Put her in Versace, and she'd have made millions as a high-class hooker."

The caustic tone did nothing to disguise the raw stripe of pain. Kell had seen this woman before, when doubt had churned and yielded destruction. "Okay, so you're not a schoolteacher or the executive of some company. Big deal. Maybe you don't save the world, but what you do takes more skill than lying on your back, Fin. I've gambled a time or two in Vegas, and I'll tell you, I've got nothing but awe for you. We both know winning isn't luck. It's skill and smarts and savvy. Three traits you have in shameless abundance." Revving up, she flung out her hands in frustration.

"They even carry the World Series of Poker on ESPN. So, basically, you're like a world-class athlete. All we've got to do is get you endorsements and a nickname. Maybe Firestarter?"

Mood broken, Fin chuckled. "Nasty. Very nasty."

Patting her cheek, Kell grinned. "Whatever works." Then her smile faded. "We survived the worst kind of parents, Fin. Mrs. F helped, but something inside us did it too. For the first part of her life, Julia had two parents who loved her, but she had her own battles to fight. I love you because I know who you are. I admire you because I know who you could have been."

"That's not fair," Fin managed softly. "Not fair at all."

"And it will be worse if you burn another batch of waffles. Believe me, I know." Kell glanced toward the dining room. "It's too quiet in there. I'll be right back."

Grateful for the reprieve, Fin salvaged waffles on the brink of overheating. She filled a tray, added more batter, and joined Kell in the dining room.

And froze in the doorway. The unnatural calm from the children had an easy explanation. Krispy Kreme donuts were being munched in reverent silence. Caleb stood by one greedy child's chair, filching a ring of glazed, fried dough for himself.

He wore jeans, a faded blue strained white at the knees. The black T-shirt had been replaced by a gray one emblazoned with Georgetown's logo. The frayed cuffs swept over ridges of firm muscle she'd clung to yesterday. Burnished skin stretched over the flex of arms trained by weights as well as physical activity. Arms that could bind a woman against a chest hewn from granite.

Tearing her eyes away, she lifted them to meet his

amused brown ones. "Good morning." He picked up a box, extended it to her. "Hungry?"

Fin heard the double entendre, appreciated the jibe. "I'm trying to watch my diet," she returned casually. "Not everything you enjoy is good for you."

"Hmm," Caleb offered in low agreement. He traced her mouth with a look that flushed heat across her skin. Then he smiled, the edges tinged with regret. "But what a way to go."

The dining room door swung wide, admitting Julia. "I thought I smelled death in a box," Julia chided. "Thank God." She pinched a chocolate donut from the box Caleb held, then hunted around the table for a seat. Squeezing in beside Brandon and Jorden, she announced, "Mrs. F wants everyone ready for church in twenty minutes."

Halfhearted groans met the announcement, and the plate of waffles diminished as children attempted to gorge before beginning morning ablutions. Kell had already secured a plate and a place near Nina, who protested when she tried to steal a strip of bacon.

Fin saw Caleb's look of amazement as food evaporated in seconds. Taking pity, she tucked her hand in his arm. "Come in the kitchen," she instructed in an undertone. "I've got a few more waffles they haven't devoured."

Caleb let himself be led away, still astonished. "Do they do that every day?"

"Three times a day," she cautioned. "If you'd been any earlier with the donuts, you might have lost a hand."

He laughed and settled on a stool at the island. "I appreciate the warning."

"My pleasure." Fin reached into the cabinet for plates and glasses. "Juice is in the refrigerator."

He rose to retrieve the carton and swished it unhappily. "You've got maybe a swallow left."

"Guests first," she offered graciously. "I'm having coffee."

"Do you brew as well as you cook?"

Smiling smugly, she piled waffles onto each plate and replied, "Better. I can do things with an Arabica bean that would blow your mind."

"Nothing about you surprises me, Fin." Caleb walked to the coffeepot and found cups overhead. "Cream? Sugar?"

"Black."

Nodding, he filled the cups and replaced the pot. "You're a remarkable woman."

The unexpected compliment stilled her hand. "Remarkable? You barely know me."

With a lifted brow, he crossed to her, coffee in hand. The heady aroma rose between them. "In our lines of work, we learn to read people in an instant. That's how we win. How we survive."

"And we've both been wrong, I bet."

Nodding, he gave her the sturdy ceramic mug. "Occasionally. But not this time." Caleb set his mug on the counter and did as he'd wanted to the instant he'd woken up. He hooked his arm around her and brought her flush against him. With his eyes open on hers, he kissed her, lips soft and searching. In the sun-drenched kitchen, he steeped himself in the lush give of the mouth that haunted his dreams. When her lips parted, he slipped inside. Slowly, he explored the mystery of her, content to simply taste what he'd plundered last night. The sweetness she strived to hide, the bite that was essentially Fin.

She emitted a low moan, an erotic sound threatening to claw at the simplicity of pleasure. Caleb lifted his head, dazed. Kissing her wasn't, as he'd intended, a sate to the endless craving. He had the stark suspicion nothing short of all would do. Panic set in, gilded by a desire stronger than any he'd known.

Fighting the first as viciously as the second, he forced himself to step clear. Before he dove again, fell deeper. All the way.

"Good morning," he repeated, his hand fingering the hem of her top.

"For some of us, at least." The dry response came from the kitchen doorway.

CHAPTER 15

Fin whipped her head around to meet Kell's speculative look and Julia's moue of amused shock. She wriggled out of Caleb's loose hold and took a swig of coffee to calm the gallop of her pulse. She muttered, "Did you need something?"

"Luke's here," Kell volunteered with banked laughter. She'd rarely seen Fin embarrassed, and the look Kell sent Fin warned of a follow-up conversation. "He wants to brief us on something."

"We'll be right there." The kitchen door swung on its hinges, closing them inside again. Fin used the brief seconds of respite to collect her scattered thoughts. Now was neither the time nor place for the conversation they had to have about what was blooming between them. Turning to face him, she found him grinning at her, eyes dark with intent. Determinedly, she stepped away. "You should know, I haven't told them about me and Stark yet."

"Why the devil not?" A scowl instantly replaced the

indulgent grin. He'd assumed she'd already introduced the idea, hashed out the pros and cons and beaten them into submission. After his last encounter with the Faraday brigade, he was in no hurry to repeat the experience. He'd no doubt they'd be as opposed to Fin's scheme as he'd been at first. Now, he thought dismally, they'd blame him for this too. His mood spiraled down as he pictured the coming scene. "They'll think I put you up to this."

"I'll take the blame." But she was perversely glad Caleb was there. She intentionally hadn't broached the subject with anyone—and she easily acknowledged cowardice as the chief cause. Already, she could predict their reactions. Mrs. F would forbid her from endangering her life. Julia's bent would tend toward fretting. From Kell, she'd get sharp disapproval guised as logic and reason. "I'll tell them it was my idea."

"It is your idea," he reminded her sardonically. An idea he'd already received a caustic reprimand for even suggesting. He'd called his division chief at eight, violating the well-known sanctity of her Sunday morning ritual. Tea, the *Washington Post* and the *Times* crossword puzzle. The scathing denunciation of his plan still burned in his ears. "I've already taken my beating for the day. This one is on you."

"Coward."

"Sticks and stones, Fin. Sticks and stones." In support, he draped an arm around her shoulders. She grumbled but walked with him to the study door. Caleb paused outside and recalled the dressing down he'd gotten for suggesting they steer clear of his investigation. In commiseration, he squeezed her shoulders, bussed a kiss along the clenched jaw. At her ear, he admonished, "If you want to take on Stark, you'll have to start with Eliza Faraday. After that, organized crime should be a breeze."

Before she could snip at him, he gave her an ungentle prod toward what had become Command Central. Eliza, already dressed for service in a simple coral suit and a discreet strand of pearls, peered out onto the verdant expanse of the backyard. Julia wore a cornflower blue sheath that accented the delicacy of her features. Luke stood by the arm of the divan, a gentle hand on Kell's silk-covered shoulder. She nestled against him, a relaxed pose that Fin realized was unconscious.

Startled by the prick of envy, she cleared her throat. *Showtime.* "Hey, Luke."

"Not going to church today?"

"I prefer holidays and weddings." They'd already had the discussion, a pitched battle settled in a draw. "Mrs. F has agreed to let me ease into regular attendance. Don't want to attract bolts of lightning my first week back."

"Findley." Eliza refrained from igniting the argument anew, but she couldn't resist a small dig. "Reverend Abrams will be invited to visit later this week. We can discuss your lapsed soul then."

"I look forward to it," Fin muttered.

"Luke, didn't you have something to tell us?" Kell elbowed him gently. "Now?"

Luke took a half step away, his hand still on her shoulder. "I would have called last night, but Farmer Henry's goat got loose again."

Remembering the last time, Kell laughed. "Nadine? Did you have to catch her?"

"Me, Curly, and Deputy Little. Evil beast." He rubbed

at the spot on his thigh where she'd tried to bite him. "I intended to come here and talk to you all, but after Nadine, we had a flurry of calls."

"What happened?" Julia asked. "Did you learn something new about Stark?"

He gave a disgusted nod. "Two things. One, my phone was bugged. We've cleared the microphones, but there's no way to tell how long they've been in place. The tech who removed it thought it pretty old."

"Any clue who put it there?" Fin asked.

"My guess is Graves, but I haven't got any proof." Haunted, he blew out a sigh. "Stark may have someone in the hospital. Pete Franklin died last night."

"How?" Kell demanded.

"We'll have to wait on the autopsy, but for now, it's been ruled a simple heart attack. The only people to enter his room yesterday were my deputies, the duty nurses, and his doctor. Caleb already had the FBI run the names," he added before Kell could ask.

"Any suspects yet?"

"I did a run through GCIC, and no one came up." Luke clenched his jaw. "My team has been accounted for, and I've got no clear suspect on the hospital staff. Dr. Hestor said his heart simply gave out from the trauma and stress. Unless the autopsy reveals otherwise, that's what it will be."

"Dr. Hestor called it a heart attack?" Julia quizzed. "What were his symptoms?"

"According to the nurses, he complained nonstop about his leg and demanded more morphine."

Julia frowned. "Did he complain of chest pains? Shortness of breath?"

"Don't know," Luke admitted. "Why do you ask?"

"I'm not a cardiologist, but Mr. Franklin had strong vitals after the accident. That level of trauma, even if it only resulted in a broken leg, should have given a man with a history of heart disease some symptoms." She paced forward, hands fisted on her hips. "If he didn't have a weakened heart, a cardiac incident the next day is unusual."

Caleb spoke quietly. "Impossible?"

"You told us he tried to escape. That he was terrified Stark would find him in the hospital." Julia considered the circumstances and the man she'd treated. "Perhaps, if he became sufficiently agitated when he couldn't leave. But I'm stunned he didn't tell them about other symptoms. He had no such qualms with me."

"I don't think he died of natural causes," concurred Luke, his voice low and angry. "I think he was murdered, but until the autopsy comes back, I have no proof." Frustrated, he balled his fist tight. "It's like tracking shadows. Every time we get near an actual person, they slip free. Or die."

On the desk, the telephone jangled for attention. Eliza hurried to the desk to answer. "The Faraday Center."

"Findley Borders," a gruff voice requested.

Eliza tensed. "May I ask who's calling?"

"An old friend."

Eyes troubled, she said politely, "Please hold on while I find her." She pressed the appropriate button on the handset, then turned to the room's curious occupants. "It's a call for Fin. He wouldn't say who."

Before Luke could, Caleb reached for the phone and checked the caller ID. "Unknown number." Though the caller could be harmless, Caleb refused to take any chances. Apprehension bloomed, his mind returning to the image of Fin crouched in the truck, aiming a handgun. Going with his gut, he asked, "Mrs. Faraday, is there another receiver?"

"Next door, in the sitting room." She sped out of the study, returning hastily. Giving the second handset to Caleb, she waited for instructions. Fin had moved to the desk, hand outstretched.

Caleb instructed, "Give Fin the phone."

"Fin Borders," Fin greeted pleasantly, working hard to keep anxiety low. She felt foolish that a phone call worried her, but nothing about this situation was normal. "Can I help you?"

"I've been asked to extend an invitation."

"To what?"

"One of your favorite pastimes. Some old friends would like to reestablish their acquaintance. Tonight, at the Warehouse. If you're willing."

She masked her fright at his choice of locations with effort. "Depends on the activity and the friends. Is this business or pleasure?"

"Why draw distinctions? You never used to." The man's voice grew brisk. "This is a one-person invitation. Leave the sheriff at home."

"And if I decline?"

"Saying no wouldn't be healthy. Just ask your friend the doctor. Or the lady lawyer." He chuckled once, a nasty sound. "Or the mama hen and all those lost little chicks."

Fin became rigid, incensed. "Are you threatening me?"

"I'm telling you that my friends would like to see you. This isn't a request. Ten o'clock. Tomorrow night."

Abruptly, the call clicked off. Caleb plucked the

receiver from her, cut off both phones. "Did you recognize the voice?"

"Not at all," she responded. Facing the others, she recounted the conversation. "I should add that my business manager contacted me yesterday. Someone is trying to find out my financial shape, see if there's any leverage to be had."

"Leverage?" Julia asked the question, afraid of the answer. "They want to blackmail you?"

"So it seems." First the inquiries and then a cryptic demand for her attendance. "Stark must know about us, about the Warehouse." She willed away nerves and continued. "Last night, I brought an idea to Caleb. He didn't like it, but he understood why it made sense. Makes even more sense now."

Dread filled Eliza, and she closed the distance between her and Fin. She reached up, cupped the stubborn chin, read the daredevil eyes. "What are you planning to do?"

"What I have to, Mrs. F."

Last night, after leaving Caleb's apartment, she'd driven to Brockett Street to find the truth of her. The man and woman who'd given her life. The hovel that had sheltered and shaped her soul. A soul steeped in avarice, a greed for more that she'd never thought to question. Until now. She squared her shoulders, summoned her will. "I'm going inside Stark."

"Out of the question." Kell jumped to her feet, arms akimbo. She surged past Fin to confront Caleb. "It's dangerous, ill-advised, and will do absolutely nothing to stop Stark except give them another body to add to their count."

Caleb bristled at the accusation. "I don't care for the idea any more than you do, but she's got a plan. A solid plan that can help us. Especially now that they've made first contact."

"How?" Kell taunted. "By tagging her dead body so it's easier to identify when they're through?"

A swift murmur of distress from Eliza had Fin ordering, "Cut it out, Kell!" Focusing on Eliza, she clutched at her wrist in appeal. "Please, just hear me out before you react. Or overreact."

She tossed the last statement over her shoulder, shooting a look of disgust at Kell. "Stark has its power base here in Hallden. Stands to reason its biggest players occupy the upper echelon of key institutions. We know for a fact they had access to Chief Graves at the police department. And, as I told Caleb, I'm fairly certain the president of the bank and one of the county commissioners used to gamble in the Warehouse."

"Then powerful men know you can identify them," Luke countered sharply. He'd seen the real Mafia in Chicago. Bloated corpses fished from Lake Michigan or unearthed during a construction project. Men riddled with bullet holes for simply talking to cops. "That means you should get out of Hallden, not join them."

"I'm not leaving." Fin moved away to meet four pairs of eyes that were watching her with varying degrees of doubt. She intentionally avoided the fifth pair. Stark had to end now, before Mrs. Faraday or the children who depended on her got hurt. Before Stark shifted its attentions to Kell or Julia. "They know who I am, and I might know them. James Worley, a bank teller who becomes bank president. Or Ernest

King, an assistant in a politician's office. What if Worley laundered their money? Or King eased some permits and suddenly, he's got financial backing for his own bid for office?"

"You can prove this?" Kell asked, considering the angles.

Fin shook her head. "I've remembered bits and pieces. Conversations they thought I wasn't listening to."

Intervening, Caleb said, "Which means we've got a place to start looking. Civic leaders with unexplained wealth or interesting paths to power." He focused on Luke. "It's a solid lead. More than we have right now."

"They've invited me to come in, and they haven't left me much choice." Her eyes hardened to flint. "I can use this. Use them."

"How?" Julia spoke now, her belly a knot of fear. She too had seen the viscera left by the Mob. Had stitched together limbs mangled by the worst of human imagination. "Why would they let you inside, and, my God, how would you get out? This must be a trap."

Fin jammed her hands into her pockets, pulling the shorts low on her waist. "They're desperate, Julia. And I'm easy pickings. I've got a record. A criminal record. Plus, I've got money I might not want Uncle Sam to know about." She'd played out the scenarios, read the patterns in how they operated. "They're willing to risk a lot to get the land Mrs. F owns on County Road. They've tried to buy it from her, then tried to frame her to get it. A frontal assault didn't work, and neither did an ambush. Best play for them now is to rig the game from the inside. Me."

Luke gave her a dubious look. "Why would they believe you'd betray her?"

It was Kell who answered desolately. "Because they think Fin already did."

Bingo, Fin thought. "I skipped town with one hundred thousand dollars of their money. And unlike my pals here, I didn't do good with my life. I joined up with the scum of the earth and worked my way up. You don't do that without some of their habits rubbing off on you." Bemoaning poor choices wouldn't do any good now. But using her unique talent for screwing up would. "I can speak their language, and, because Mrs. F is seen as a pushover, they won't question that she let her prodigal daughter come home."

"I won't allow it," Eliza declared. "I will not let you set yourself as bait."

Fin drew herself stiff, prepared. "I'm not asking permission. I can help you, Mrs. F. Whether you like it or not."

"If you choose to do this, to risk your life, then you are no longer welcome here."

"Mrs. F," the whisper ripped from a throat gone arid. Terror more feral than any found at the barrel of a gun swarmed Fin. "You promised. If I wanted to come home. You promised."

"Not if you came home to die." Eliza didn't turn to her, didn't look at her. "I will not have you risk your life and ours."

Grasping, Fin reminded her, "We're already at risk, Mrs. F. I'm trying to help." Silently, she begged Mrs. F to look at her. Surely, she couldn't be serious. "Mrs. F, I know what I'm doing."

Eliza heard herself, but the pain in Fin's voice bore no comparison to what rended through her. *Not again,* screamed the heart that had lost Fin once. Stiffly, angrily, she shook her head. "This isn't one of your games. You've escaped these people twice, but I won't let you stay here and put yourself in harm's way again."

"This can save all of you. I want to do this."

"By putting a target on your back? I'm not impressed."

"Fine. Then I'll go. Because I'm not walking away from our best chance to bring Stark down."

The straight back grew impossibly stiff. Then Eliza turned, speaking before she could stop herself. "Your choice. You do this, and I won't have you here."

Caleb saw Fin's eyes go dark and glassy, felt as much as heard the hiss of pain. She swayed for a moment, as though reeling from a blow. In the next instant, she stood immobile, the anguish dismissed, relegated to a place he imagined filled with grief and agony and a misery he could only glimpse if she didn't see anyone looking. He couldn't go to her, he knew, without her spitting at him. But, he thought, he could give her this chance that seemed to mean so much to her.

"Mrs. Faraday, I've agreed to let Fin go undercover. Stark has operated with impunity for nearly twenty years. Children have died from drugs they helped move, from guns sold when they let them through. Your own kids have been their victims." Impatience coiled inside him, and he allowed its teeth to show. "If you kick Fin out, it simply gives her a different story line. We can convince them she knows whatever they'll need her to know. We'll make it work. With or without your help."

Even as he spoke the words, he understood he'd lost any hope of friendship with Eliza Faraday, an instinct confirmed when the hazel eyes flickered in sour distaste.

"I see." She sized him up, a cutting examination that stripped him raw. "I misjudged you, Mr. Matthews. I assumed your zeal to prosecute me was based on your commitment to justice. Not on your desire to win at any cost."

Turning to Fin, she continued. "Fin, if you decide to proceed, I'll expect you to clear your things out. I'm sure Kell will drive you into town." Without a look to the woman she'd once sworn to always welcome home, she glared at Caleb. "If she comes to any harm, you will pay."

In grave silence, she swept from the room, the door closing quietly behind her.

CHAPTER 16

When Fin finally moved, she drifted to the unshaded window. Sunlight streamed through, creating a pool of warmth. She wondered if she'd ever forget the cold of losing Mrs. F.

"She didn't mean it, Fin." Kell spoke from behind her, close enough to support, careful not to touch. "She's afraid and angry."

"Whether she meant it or not, it's done." In her own ears, her voice seemed brittle. With effort, she forced a bleak laugh. "I did it. Didn't think it could be done, but I managed it."

"Did what?" Kell lifted a hand, let it fall to her side.

"Got Mrs. F so pissed off she finally gave up on me."

Julia walked over to Fin. Since her arrival at the center, Julia had accepted the bond between Kell and Fin and the boundaries neither crossed. She respected one out of understanding, the other out of habit. Both at that moment made her mad. Despite Kell's unspoken caution, she stroked a firm hand along Fin's stiffened spine. Fin permitted the touch but gave no sign it mattered. "For pity's sake, Fin. She didn't give up on you. She's mad and so are you. You'll both get over it." She angled around to face her staunchest champion, to tease out a smile. And froze.

There was nothing in the stark, fixed expression. Not sorrow, not anger. Empty eyes stared out onto the jumble of flowers and gentle roll of the lawn. Skin the color of bronze dulled, the creamy hue tarnished.

"Fin?"

"I'm fine, Julia." She almost meant it. Like a child, she'd held on to a bedside promise as a talisman against her own selfish impulses and their results. A pledge made by a woman whose bond she'd thought unbreakable.

Get out, came the wild, frantic thought. Before she shattered and lost sight of the pieces. She heard her breath saw into her lungs, could see her paling face in the glass. This wouldn't do, she decided dimly. To collapse here, in *her* house. To fold because she'd been discarded once again.

No, a gambler had the tightest dominion over herself. You couldn't pick the cards, but you decided how to lay them down. When to bluff a mismatched hand into a rout. When to drop a made set to lure an opponent into a hotheaded play. When to chuck the whole damned game and leave the table.

Her knees trembled, once, and she understood how close she stood to the edge. But leaving was impossible. She was trapped—no wheels, no one to call for escape. Kell would take her somewhere, but Fin didn't want to hear reasonable. Julia might help, but Fin couldn't stand pity.

Tremors moved, slowly, imperceptibly. She was running out of time. To run.

From his place near the desk, Caleb observed the three women. Comfort offered and stoically rejected by one too proud to admit she could be hurt. The rigid back annoyed him. The grieving silence angered him. And the care her best friends took to protect her from her own emotional stupidity fired a rage that spit for release.

Then the slim, solid body quivered for an instant before she ruthlessly controlled the motion. Fin Borders wasn't a fragile woman, but she wasn't indestructible. And if she didn't find an outlet soon, she'd explode.

"Screw it." He marched to the window, grabbed Fin's elbow, and hauled her from between the startled women. "Fin is coming with me. I'll have her back here after church." He nearly snarled when Kell moved to intercept. "What?"

Kell lifted both hands in the universal sign of surrender. "She's surly when she's hurt. And nasty when she wants to cry and doesn't," she advised remorsefully. "Take care of her."

"I will," he swore as he propelled the unresisting form through the foyer and out to his car. She said nothing as he stuffed her into the black leather seat and slammed the door. He climbed into the driver's side and keyed the ignition. A glance at Fin showed she'd yet to buckle her seat belt. In her lap, her fingers were linked together, immobile. No trembling, no shaking. Simply limp and unmoving.

"For Christ's sake," he muttered, leaning over to snap the restraint in place. His arm brushed against her breasts, but she gave scant sign of noticing. Her breath rose and fell evenly, placidly.

Shaken, Caleb released the cold metal buckle and stroked at the sculpted lines of her profile. "Where'd you go, honey?"

He didn't expect an answer.

Caleb shoved the car into drive and steered onto the road, tires shooting gravel. For the first ten minutes, he drove in silence, listening to the rush of wind as it whipped past the car. On the barren highway, he indulged himself by punching off the air conditioner. A flick of buttons slid the windows down and retracted the sunroof. Warm summer air whipped inside the car, chased by humidity eager to crowd inside the speeding vehicle.

Hallden fell behind them and he headed south, away from Hallden and Stark.

Fin blinked, turned her head to gaze out the window. Thinking she should, she asked dully, "Where are we going?"

Hearing the lack of interest, Caleb challenged, "Do you care?"

Fin considered the question and lapsed into silence. Miles sped past, changing the scenery from stretches of red clay to towering pines and sturdy oaks. Four lanes narrowed to two, warranted by the sparse traffic. She'd driven this way before, she thought. With Mrs. F.

"We drove down to this way once," she murmured absently.

"Where were you going?"

"To Autry County." Fin settled against the leather, lifted her face to the air zipping past.

Autry County. The site of one of the state's few maximum-security prisons. "How old were you?"

"Thirteen." She'd been getting into trouble more and

more. Fights at school, fights at the center. "At school, there was this kid Alan. He was the only boy in middle school taller than me and he was a year older. So, of course, I had a tremendous crush on him."

"Of course."

"Kell dared me to talk to him." She smiled wistfully. "I wasn't like her. She could talk to anyone. About anything."

"You weren't shy."

"No, I wasn't shy. I just didn't like most people." She braced an elbow on the lowered window dropped her head onto her folded arm. Her voice rose louder to compete with the muted roar from the outside. "But Kell dared me. So I walked over to him at recess and said hello."

"Very brave."

"Alan was sitting on a bench, reading a book. He wore wire-rimmed glasses that made his eyes shine like diamonds. Made him look smart."

"Hmm."

"I asked what he was reading." She'd been nervous, almost giggly, like the insipid girls who'd painted their nails and fluttered their lashes. It had been a couple of years before she learned the wisdom of those uniquely feminine rituals. At thirteen, she'd preferred the charm of her fists to the guile of a well-timed pout. "My voice nearly squeaked, but I did it. He looked smug, though I didn't understand why. After a second, he handed me the book. Said it was about my family."

"What was it?" He checked the rearview mirror, caught the passage of memory. Unhappy, he thought. Like too much of what he'd learned of her life. "What was he reading?"

"In Cold Blood."

"Little punk." Effortlessly, Caleb recalled the page in her file about Daniel Borders, a part-time pimp who used as much of his drug product as he sold. Her father's sentence to a maximum-security prison had warranted a flag in her FBI file. Murder of her mother in a drunken rage had netted him a life sentence without possibility of parole. "What did he say?"

"He was smart." Alan had had a look of glee as she'd flipped over the book and read the synopsis. Nerves had congealed into humiliation as her feet had frozen to the concrete. "By then, one of his friends had come over. Alan pointed to the book, and then he laughed at me. Asked me if they were planning to do one on my dad. It took three teachers to pull me off of him, and he needed six stitches." She examined knuckles long since healed with remembered satisfaction. "That was the last time anyone mentioned my father."

"I've never wanted to kick an eighth grader's ass before," he admitted. But he could too easily picture her then, a gangly young girl, fueled by the compulsive ardor of outrage and disgrace. "What did you say his last name was?"

Oddly pleased, Fin gave an ironic smile. "Alan Wentworth. But there's no need to avenge my honor. I also knocked out his front tooth. His parents threatened to sue Mrs. F."

"What stopped them?"

"Don't know." She'd asked, but Mrs. F had refused to divulge the secrets of grown-up meetings. "All I know is that Mrs. F met with them in her office, and when they left, his mom gave me a hug. Mr. Wentworth said something about Alan and military school." Resting her head on the seat, she shut burning eyes, soothed by the muted rumble of tread on asphalt. "That next week, she told me I'd be missing school on Friday."

"Court hearing?" he teased, but he thought he knew what had followed. What a woman like Eliza Faraday would have deemed necessary. "Is that the only time you saw your father?"

Fin didn't question how he knew. "Yes. Mrs. F drove all the way down to Autry in this green convertible she used to have. We wore chiffon scarves on our hair that blew in the wind. Halfway there, we stopped for Mississippi mud pie and orange floats at a café." They'd talked, Fin remembered wistfully. About how women made themselves from steel and silk and smarts. About how Fin had mastered the steel and appreciated why intelligence mattered, but appeared to have no appetite for the niceties.

"Then she took me to see my father."

Her voice trailed off; her eyes were glued to the road. "What happened?"

"Nothing." Even twenty years hadn't cured the slash of rejection. "He refused to see me. Told the guard to say he wasn't in the mood to see the bitch's bastard."

"Fin."

"Doesn't matter. Whether he's my real father or not, he shaped who I was. Who I am. Like she did."

The grim curve of her mouth broke his heart. "Eliza too."

"Yet another parent who's decided to cut me loose."

"She loves you." Pity would be met with the icy stare she favored. But, if he understood her at all, she'd accept facts. Caleb needed to give her enough to salve the wounds that gaped still. "Think what you will of how she acted today, but you can't doubt how she feels."

"Then why throw me out?"

"Your fault." The bald pronouncement whipped her head to him. Caleb kept his eyes on the road. "Springing the idea of you going under wasn't the brightest approach, especially right after they summoned you to their lair. Stark terrifies her. As it should."

"I'm doing this for her." *Surely, he understands that,* she thought bleakly. "Kell grew up like I did, but she made good. For pity's sake, she's a famous lawyer, sought after by celebrities and politicians."

"She's good at saving the guilty." Caleb permitted himself the petty dig. "Yes, I get it. Kell became an attorney and Julia is a doctor. You think you have to measure up. Prove you can do a good deed."

"No," Fin corrected, speaking to herself more than to him. An image formed, memory or dream, she'd yet to decipher. "I owe it to her to prove that she was right." She broke off, unable to finish.

"Right to what?"

She sat silent for so long that Caleb assumed she had no intention of answering. But then she spoke on a thin whisper of sound. "That she was right to save me."

The stricken confession sliced at him, and he veered off the deserted highway. Dust plumed, and he slammed the gear into park. Whipping toward her, he caressed her cheek, bringing her eyes to his. "Of course she was, darling. How can you doubt it?"

"How can I not?" She wrenched free of his hold, wanting only to sink into the comfort offered. To share the knot of guilt, the urgency of penance. To be intimate, she realized with a sprint of panic, emotionally naked without the shields and guards and walls.

Fin snatched at the door handle and scrambled from the car. Heat punched her like a fist. Sweat, kept at bay by the car's motion, beaded on her forehead. Recklessly, she dashed into the trees, to get away from him and his comfort. Away from her yearning to stay.

Damn him, he had no right to pry. To sneak into her thoughts, to make her want. *Need.* He'd earned the right to her silence, not her secrets. After all, what did she know about him? Other than the fact that he'd lied to her best friend about who he was and what he wanted? *Needed.*

Racing her demons, she charged into the woods lining the highway, unmindful of the scrape of branches against her bare legs. Caleb Matthews had one agenda— find Stark and make his case. Mrs. F had surely read him right. And here she was, on the verge of confessing to a virtual stranger what she'd barely admit to herself.

Consumed with building her outrage, she failed to notice the tracking sounds behind her. The acid, steady stream of curses that dogged her. When he spun her around, her eyes flew up to meet his.

Caleb read the chaos in frenzied brown, confusion masquerading as anger. Besieged by the turbulence raging within her, he drew Fin to him.

She decided later that she had intended to protest. To thrust him away and refuse anything from him.

Except the crush of his mouth against hers.

CHAPTER 17

But before she could adjust, the kiss evolved beyond her ability to prepare. To guard against. He explored her mouth with an affection that stammered her breath. A benediction where she expected fireworks. Instead of the heat she comprehended, she found compassion cloaked in passionate restraint. His lips danced across hers, sampling and praising. She pressed into him, to insist on the bite and the fire, to sweep away thought and feeling.

Because, sweet heavens, she could feel. Emotions crested, compelling reaction. Desire raced through her, chased by a yearning to know the man whose hands traced her skin. Arousal jangled in her veins, stoked by a kinship that whispered this man could see past the shields and into her soul.

"Kiss me harder," she begged, afraid of the leisurely stroke of his tongue against hers, the unraveling of barriers. "Damn it, Caleb. Please."

"No." Caleb settled into the mating of mouths, gave

himself over to the wave of tenderness carrying his hands along the long drape of her spine. Tension vibrated beneath his hands, and he murmured reassurance. "So beautiful. This lovely face, a goddess ready for war. With the heart of a lioness." His hand drifted over, captured her breast. Expertly, he called forth a rigid peak. "You're so lean, and yet voluptuous. A woman of contradiction."

She bowed up, into him, wresting at his control. He clawed to maintain it, refusing to rush. Instead, he trailed his teeth along the sensitive nerves where her shoulder curved. "Here, you taste like sunlight and storms." Craving softer, smoother flesh, he slid beneath her thin cotton shirt to free the taut globes that filled his palms. Lace gave way under his touch, and he released the clasp with a deft twist. He satisfied his hands with the warm satin mass, drew away to see her. "Undress for me, Fin," he whispered, nibbling at her jaw.

She yanked the top over her head, felt her bra fall to the leaves beneath their feet. When she would have spoken, his tongue slicked over one crest, and she whimpered. The sound stunned her. Liquid pulls arrowed through her belly. Longing merged with greed as she clutched at his shoulders, stripped off the offensive cotton barring her from him.

Reveling in her senses, she found the flat male disks, so different from her, so wickedly similar. She mimicked the slow mouth that had tormented with tantalizing licks and gentle bites. Tracked the faint line of hair, sampled the rock of his bicep.

They lowered to the spread of leaves. Caleb turned to range her over him. To flow over his hard, ready body, her thigh nestled against him. Claiming her mouth anew, he searched for the heat that flooded through her, into him. He was sinking, he thought dimly, drowning in the taste of her, the scent of woman. Of Fin.

This scared, audacious woman who deserved more from him than a roll in the leaves and muck. He stroked her naked back, fingertips memorizing the perfect length. Her gentle murmur of pleasure soothed him, and he wound out the kiss. Now, it spun for them both, floated with them. Without words, he told her of burgeoning care, softer emotions ensnaring his better intentions.

The compulsion to cherish rocked through him, trailed by a whip of fear. End this, he told his mouth, his hands. Palms curled at the narrow indention of her waist. He sipped at the corner of her mouth and traced the richness of her bottom lip. "Fin."

"Hmm?" She sensed the hesitation, the withdrawal. Hazily, she thought briefly of embarrassment but couldn't summon the feeling. Not with his arms around her. Not with proof of his desire pressed against her. Care and desire were a dangerous combination, and neither of them could afford its aftermath. She released a long breath. "You cheat."

He laughed hoarsely. "When I have to." Both heard the dark promise.

She nipped at his chest and muttered, "Did you lose my shirt?"

Caleb laughed at the slightly grumpy response and reached out blindly. His fingers closed over lace and, with another quick sweep, cotton. He dropped both onto her back, vainly trying to not cup the warm weights that pressed into his chest. Nearly desperate, he asked harshly, "Need some help?"

Giving a short, disbelieving laugh, Fin rolled over and jackknifed up. With swift movements, she shook out both garments and pulled them into place. Decently clothed, she glanced over her shoulder. The broad chest she'd admired before looked even better in daylight. Dappled rays gleamed on polished muscle and highlighted the tapered hips and powerful flex of muscle. Her mouth watered and sanity wavered. "Cover up, will you?"

"Find me irresistible?" he teased lightly. But it had been he who'd forgotten to dress while he'd watched her. His blood quickened at the sight of the athletic, rangy form toned with supple skin and deep curves to capture a man's fantasies. Coupled with a face to churn longings best denied.

On that disturbing thought, he rose to his feet and took her hand. Both brushed away errant leaves, and she reached up to remove more from his hair. Her breath stirred his mouth, and she gave herself a brief, smoldering taste. When his arms banded against her hips, she waltzed away. "You said no." With a mocking look below his waist, she taunted, "Suffer the consequences."

"Truce." Caleb captured her hand again and led her toward their abandoned car in a companionable silence. After he'd tucked her inside and rounded the hood to enter, he held the key without inserting it in the ignition. "You okay?"

"I am." And she meant it, oddly. The fight with Mrs. F wounded her, but it wouldn't deter her from her goal. No running off this time. It hadn't worked before, it wouldn't now. "You might want to patent your version of shock therapy."

Caleb gave her a long, solemn look. "I'm only interested in one patient, Fin."

Her eyes flickered away. "You barely know me. I know even less about you."

"Then ask," he instructed warningly. He'd found that time had little meaning with her, a thought as disturbing as it was alluring. He started the car and turned on to the highway, heading toward Hallden.

"I've told you about my family. Younger brother and sister. Twins, age twenty-six. Jonas is a musician. A cellist with the Baltimore Symphony who longs to be in a rock band. Mariah is a schoolteacher. Dreams of being a novelist."

"Parents?"

"Mom is a high school principal, and Dad is an accountant. They live in Severn, Maryland, right outside Baltimore."

"Where you grew up?"

"Yep. Went to public school, learned to play the bass guitar and shortstop for the baseball team." He drove fast but with confidence. Absently, he reached out to link their fingers.

Fin froze at the intimacy but forced herself to relax. A truce, she reminded herself. Simply a careless touch between new friends. "Did you want to go pro?"

"Of course." He rubbed his thumb along the velvety sweep of her knuckles. "Always thought I'd be drafted out of high school to start with the Mets."

"Lofty goals." Her heartbeat, rarely steady around Caleb, jittered with the caress. *Focus,* she commanded silently. "I assume there's a tragic end to the tale?"

In his hand, he felt her tension, the instinct to pull free. The desire to stay. The same tension ground through him, but he'd accepted in the last hour the futility of his cause. He wanted Fin Borders, in and out of his bed. And waiting was already near impossible.

"Caleb?"

"Yes?" He cast his mind back for their topic. *Baseball. Shortstop. Right.* "An absolutely devastating story. Senior year, I'm covering third. A power hitter is up. He cracks the ball and I stretch for the out. Then, wham! Here comes the runner from second. A klutzy kid who played for a school with a 'no-cut' rule. Guy barrels into me and steps on my wrist."

"Did he break it?"

"Nope, a severe sprain, but it put me out for the season." He surrendered and raised her hands to his mouth, skimming heat across the pulse point. "To this day, it aches when rain's coming."

Fin laughed, despite the surge of fire where his tongue traced the rush of blood beneath her skin. Good sense cautioned her to pull back from his errant touch and the want to know more about this man, but she consoled herself that she'd been leaping before she'd looked for years. "Why did you join the FBI?"

Caleb paused before answering. "In college, I studied political science. Knew I wanted to become a lawyer."

"Visions of Perry Mason?"

"And Columbo," he added wryly. "I appreciated the lawyer's job of defending justice, but I found Columbo's role in discerning the truth equally compelling."

"A one-man version of *Law & Order*?"

Caleb slanted her a startled look. "You watch entirely too much television."

"They love American syndication in Europe." Warming to her inquisition, she swiveled in the seat as far as the belt would allow and drew her knee up. She propped up her chin, but didn't reclaim her hand. "So, you're torn between being a broken-down detective or a preternaturally successful attorney. How'd you wind up doing both?"

"During my third year of law school, I applied to an internship at the Justice Department. Happened to be assigned to an attorney who'd once worked for the FBI. He sent over my resumé and got me an interview."

"Georgetown?"

He glanced down at his T-shirt. "Clever deduction. College and law school. Didn't discover my yen for adventure until later. After I went into the program."

For a second, a shutter fell over his eyes. Fin saw and wondered. "Who else was there? Your friend Eric?"

He nodded once and dropped her hand. Instead, he clutched the steering wheel, accelerated slightly. "I met Eric in the training program. He was taking courses in the policy school. Thought he'd serve a tour in the Bureau then apply for an administrative job."

"He didn't want to be a field agent?"

"Not at all." Caleb thought of the early morning jogs, the hours in the gym. "Eric hated the life of a field agent. Didn't like to run, shoot a gun, or interrogate a suspect. But he loved criminal justice. For his thesis, he developed computer models for predicting crime. Algorithms for the most likely hot spots in a city."

"Impressive."

"He was. He was brilliant. And his greatest ambition was to become the next J. Edgar Hoover and run the Bureau."

"So why take the long way around?"

"Because Eric was a policy wonk who understood

that only those who'd climbed the ranks had a shot at the top job."

Fin frowned. "Then ask for an assignment to art theft or cyber crime. Why request the assignment to here? Why follow Stark?"

Caleb had asked Eric the same question, had hated the answer and the consequences. "Ambition." He derided the response, the single word dripping with loathing. "Eric decided Stark would make him the way Capone did Eliot Ness. One of his infernal models pinpointed a site for drug and gun distribution in Georgia. While I was out on assignment, he asked our division chief to send him down to take a look. She agreed."

"She believed him?"

"Not at all." Bitterness twisted with disgust. "Eric was a terrible field agent, but he was too smart to lose. She thought letting him ply his theories in a safe place like Savannah would get him out of her hair."

Fin touched Caleb's shoulder lightly. "But he found something. Something real."

"And they killed him for it." The message on his answering machine had been frenzied. A plea for his partner and best friend to come and help him. To protect him. A call Caleb had missed because he'd been undercover. A call that had come a day too early. "I was undercover on a drug bust. But we had a system, checked in every thirty-six hours. But Eric called a day early, and I was out of range."

"You couldn't have known."

Caleb spun the wheel and shot up the gravel driveway to the center, slowing only when he remembered children might be playing. But the front yard was deserted, the van and other cars missing. He cut the engine and sat motionless, fingers clenched. That she was right could never erase the ache. "When Kell called, you came running."

"Caleb," she protested. "That's not the same."

"Why?"

"Because I could and you couldn't." She knew what he wanted to hear, but she understood the grip of remorse, the relentless tearing of culpability. "Caleb, don't do this. Don't take on guilt for the sake of it. It's not fair to you or Eric."

"My best friend calls, and I'm not there." He dropped his head, stared at the steering wheel. Other than the FBI-required shrink, he hadn't spoken of Eric or his guilt. Until now. "Eric would have liked you."

"Why? He had a penchant for lost causes?"

"No, because he hated wasted emotion."

Rubbing at knuckles that bore a faint tracery of scars, she asked, "What did his message say?"

"He told me he had more evidence, but that he needed me to see it. He'd found some connection, and he was afraid."

She let her touch linger. "What happened?"

"We don't know."

"After all these years." Fin whispered it as a statement, not as a question.

"The department shrink advised me that closure would come when I accepted Eric's flawed decision to violate protocol."

"And you say?"

"Eric didn't violate protocol. He worshipped the rules. If they got to him, it wasn't his fault."

"Then what's your plan, Caleb? How will you forgive yourself?"

"By finding Eric's body and bringing his killer to justice." He turned to her then, his eyes burning. "I don't want to risk you, Fin. But, by God, you're my last hope. And if I send you in, I'm damned."

"You're not sending me, G-Man. I volunteered." She stroked the tight line of his mouth, brushed a kiss across his scowl. Then she stared at the white columns of the center. "After all, what else have either of us got to lose?"

The green Spitfire parked on the cobbled driveway, the top closed. Rosebushes had been planted in the center of the front lawn, then surrounded by stone and water. Red brick and fluted columns decorated the Greek Revival mansion, its low-pitched roof shading a white portico. Regularly trimmed hedges guarded the perimeter, stretching into a backyard profuse with flowers and a small greenhouse. Eliza loved the Majors home, the stately grounds and modest charm.

Inside, one of her oldest and dearest friends grappled with the illness of her husband of more than thirty years. Eliza had come to offer comfort, but she could only feel her own biting grief. And, if she was honest, her shame.

In all her time at the Faraday Center, she'd turned away only one of her wards—Clay Griffin, who'd made it impossible to keep him. Today, she'd discarded another, but for vastly inferior reasons.

"Are you going to skulk in that car all afternoon?" Mary Majors rapped lightly on the window, then placed her hands on her hips. "Come on out and say hello."

Opening the door, Eliza apologized as she exited the car. Despite the humidity, the judge's chignon knew better than to relinquish its austere shape. Mary was a formidable woman, and even the elements knew better than to mess with her. Pasting on a smile, and giving her friend a hug, Eliza admitted, "I'm trying to get a bit of self-flagellation in before I come inside. But I came to check on you and ask about Roger. How is he?"

"Stabilized. Doctors found another blockage, just like before."

"Will they operate?"

"Tomorrow." Mary linked her arm with Eliza's, drawing her up to the porch. "Why don't we sit outside, sip mint juleps, and you tell me all about your sins?"

Chagrined, Eliza paused on the lower step. "I'm not here to burden you with my problems, Mary. That was a petty whine that I should have kept to myself."

"Nonsense." With a tug, they reached the porch, where a fan circled lazily. "I don't have mint juleps, but I've got a pitcher of lemonade. And"—she raised her hand, palm out—"before you start, I'd like nothing better than to focus on another person's worries. I can't do any more for Roger right now, so let me wallow with you. As a favor?"

Eliza gave a weary sigh. "Where should I begin?"

"How about after I got to dismiss those nasty charges against you?" Mary pressed Eliza into a rocking chair painted the dusky pink of her favorite roses. "Let me go grab the pitcher and glasses."

Escaping inside the house, Mary commended the luck that seemed perennially on her side. After accepting the doctor's demand that she go home for a break, she'd been holed up in her office. Her investigation into Fin Borders had not turned up any new tidbits for Hestor to use, but a financial report had given her forbidding news. James Worley, so long a trusted ally, seemed to have a gambling habit that was eating into Stark's funds. Her funds.

Oh, he'd hidden his perfidy well, reporting higher numbers in their web of corporations, but she hadn't spent years managing their enterprise without being able to spot phony records. If he didn't provide an adequate explanation, she'd be forced to dispose of him.

Gladys would have to go as well, she decided. Men like Worley shared too much with their wives, whether the women knew it or not. Stark's disappearance would have to be as flawless as its inception.

Lifting the pitcher from the refrigerator, she retrieved two glasses and decorated a china dish with cookies baked by her housekeeper. Careful hands arranged the treats, and Mary recalled that Eliza had always liked pecan sandies.

Mary started for the front porch, tray in hand and plan set. A timely gab session with the upstanding Eliza and she'd have a better handle on what to do with Fin. A few probing questions, a willing ear, and she'd be able to update her instructions to Hestor for tomorrow's inquisition.

Mary settled the tray on the table between the rocking chairs and filled their glasses to brimming. Sprigs of mint floated in the pitcher, adding a brightness to the flavor. Mary took a sip, turned to Eliza. "Might I assume that your favorite urchin has been at it again? The return of Findley Borders."

Eliza bristled at the description, but she recognized that Mary intended no harm. "Fin and I did have words today. Harsh ones."

"What about?"

"The context isn't important," Elisa said, dismissing the matter. "But I said things to her I deeply regret."

"Such as?"

"I told her to leave the center." Eliza downed the lemonade in a rush, her throat arid with guilt. "I didn't mean it, but I was angry." *Terrified.*

Giving Eliza a gentle pat on the hand allowed Mary a moment to marshal her glee. A rift so soon? Providential. "Surely you can take it back."

"Probably, but I hurt her, Mary. Deeply." Eliza's head hung and her shoulders slumped. "I'm supposed to be the adult."

"For goodness' sake, Eliza, the girl is in her thirties. You've earned the right to expect some adult behavior from her."

"And she should expect honesty from me." But she'd lied. Either then, in that bedroom, or today, in the study, she'd lied. "I owe her an apology, but she's known such betrayal. I don't know that she'll accept it."

Hoping she wouldn't, Mary counseled, "The most you can do is ask for what you want, Eliza. Nothing is given freely."

Wise, sad eyes met Mary's. "Friendship is, Mary. And love. The question is whether it's too late to offer them back."

CHAPTER 18

"Just go and talk to her. Stop being so stubborn."

Fin continued to arrange clothes in the suitcase splayed open on the unmade bed. The multihued quilt jumbled against the headboard. Articles dumped from the armoire lay strewn across the rumpled sheets.

With a cursory fold, she packed a designer dress, unmindful of the creased fabric. "Kell, she told me to go, and I'm going. I would have left last night, but the Magnolia was full." She plucked her makeup case from Julia's resisting hold. "If she had changed her mind, she had all night to tell me."

"When, exactly?" Kell scoffed from the edge of Julia's bed. Her duvet had been pulled over perfect hospital corners, and the fluffy pillows were propped at the headboard. "Before or after you slunk into your room and decided to hide out all night? Julia had to tell the kids you were sick."

Fin lifted her head, taken aback. "The kids asked about me? Why should they care?"

Rearranging the untidy mess forming in Fin's suitcase, Julia reminded her sternly, "Because you told them you'd make spaghetti for dinner, remember?"

Fin winced. She'd completely forgotten. "I'm sorry," she began, then caught herself. Stuffing another tank top into her case, she reasoned, "But they're used to disappointment."

"That's not an excuse." Kell shoved off the bed and stopped nose to nose with Fin. The couple of inches Fin had on her in height didn't matter. She still managed to look down on her. "You know better."

The arrow hit its mark, but Fin refused to yield. "I know better than what? To give my word and break it?" She turned away and rolled up a pair of brief ivory shorts. With jerky motions, she jammed them into a crevice between a curling iron and a pair of strappy black sandals. "I said I'm sorry. What more do you want?"

"For you to stop acting like a brat and to go and talk to Mrs. F," insisted Julia. "She was devastated at church. I know she regrets what she said."

"Mrs. F meant every word." Fin had accepted as much last night, barricaded in the guest room, eager to be gone. "I'm threatening her precious center, and I've got to go. I'm just amazed it took so long for her to say it out loud."

"She's worried for you too," Kell added, her voice filled with sympathy. She dropped onto the bed close to where Julia stood. "Did you hear that part?"

"Must have gotten lost in translation." Seeing nothing more to repack, Fin bent over and shut the hardtop firmly. Five days before being exiled, she thought, was better than she'd had any right to expect. More than she'd earned. She looked down at the carpet, scuffed her tennis shoe against the soft nap. "I appreciate the attempts at fence-mending, ladies, but we all know this has been years in coming. Should have happened before, but I was a minor then." Head lifted, she added, "I'm a grown woman this time. I've made my choices, so I'm on my own."

"You don't have to be," Kell said gently. "We're not kids anymore. You leave this time, it's really on you."

Fin swung the case from the bed. "Then good riddance."

"Don't say that. Mrs. F is hurting too." Julia placed a restraining hand on her arm, where strain made Fin's arm as tense as a wire. "Kell's right, she was torn up yesterday. Barely spoke to anyone. Disappeared after church." Heart aching for both obstinate women, Julia pleaded, "Take the first step, Fin. Tell her you want to stay."

"And what, all will be forgiven?" Rolling her eyes, Fin scorned, "God, sometimes your Pollyanna crap gives me a headache. She said what she meant. I'm a danger to the ones that matter to her now. So, I'm out." Brittle fingers gripped the handle of the suitcase, and she glared at Julia. "Leave it alone."

"Bull." Julia blocked her path, teeth bared. "Better Pollyanna than a lonely curmudgeon who can't see past the chip on her shoulder." In full swing, she accused, "She loved you then, and she loves you now. But, as usual, you refuse to make it easy."

"Easy?" Fin's voice hardened, sharpened. "Is it hard being perfect, Jules? Never a misstep, never a fumble."

"Back off, Fin." Kell shouldered between the women, grabbed Fin's shoulder. "This isn't about Julia."

Fin knocked Kell's hand aside. Even as she lashed out, she knew she'd regret it. But the words spewed out, fueled by a churn of emotion she couldn't still. Sneering, she jibed, "That's right. St. Kell to the rescue. Always the peacemaker and champion advocate. World must look great from your pedestal."

"Saved your ass more than once."

"Of course you did." She shouldered past them, suitcase forgotten. On the other side, she whirled to face her closest friends. If she'd really looked, she might have seen the look of comprehension arc between them. "Without me, though, you'd have been the most boring kids on the planet. I taught you how to take risks."

"Which is why it shocks the hell out of us that you won't take one now," Kell retorted calmly. "How come, when it matters, you won't ever take a chance for yourself?"

"What?" The question stumbled out. "I take chances all the time. I gamble for a living."

"Money." Julia shot Kell a placid smile. "She thinks because she wagers money that she's really putting herself on the line."

Confused by the shift from rage to what seemed like amusement—at her expense—Fin narrowed her eyes. "I bet millions of dollars at a time."

Kell pursed her lips in consideration. "Your money?"

"Some of it." Feeling on the defensive, she charged, "I pick my games, but I'm not afraid to risk everything."

"Except what really matters." Julia came to her, anger forgotten. "Yesterday, you announced to Mrs. F that you intended to risk your life to catch the criminals who harmed her. That you would put yourself in jeopardy to protect her. And you think she's going to be happy about it? Don't be stupid, Fin."

"I'm not—"

Kell cut her off and moved to flank her. "You'd brave a bullet for us, but you won't ask if you can stay?"

Fin shut her eyes tight and bowed her head. She could tell them, if no one else. "What if she says no?"

Kell brushed the cascade of ebony curls. "She won't say no, Fin. Because she loves you and she regrets hurting you."

"Go talk to her," Julia added.

Fin took a deep breath. They were right, as usual. She could outwait a table full of rounders, but the possibility of one pint-sized woman's rejection immobilized her. "I hate you two."

Julia rose up and pecked a kiss on her cheek. "I forgive you for calling me Pollyanna."

Fin had the grace to blush. "Um, sorry about that."

"And the pedestal crack?" Kell nudged.

"Come down and we'll talk," Fin smirked at her, prepared to duck as a shirt flew past her head. She twisted the knob, took another breath. "Here goes."

In the foyer, kids scrambled around, preparing to enjoy the last week before school started. A grandfather clock chimed out the quarter hour. Fin slowly climbed the stairs to the second floor, where Mrs. F maintained a suite of rooms—a bedroom with an attached sitting room and a full bath. Fin summoned her courage and raised her hand to knock.

The door opened before her fist struck the wood. One of the kids, a girl Fin recognized as Faith, came out. "Thanks, Mrs. F," she called out before she hurried down the stairs. "Hey, Fin."

"Findley?"

Caught, Fin poked her head in the door. "Can we talk?"

"Please," Eliza said from where she sat in a brocaded chair near the windows, threading a needle. She nodded and offered in polite tones, "Come in."

Despite the invitation, Fin hovered in the doorway, prepared to bolt. "I won't take much of your time."

"Sit down, Fin." Eliza waved Fin toward a settee covered in a delicate floral pattern of spring flowers.

The sofa faced double doors that led to the master bedroom. Inside sat a wide, ornate bed Fin had been taught to recognize as Hepplewhite. A hand-stitched quilt had been draped across the footboard. Like every room in the house, windows stretched from floor to ceiling, admitting natural light. The same light poured into the sitting room and gilded the walls. "You've changed some things."

"Refreshed," Eliza corrected, pleased she'd noticed. "New drapes for the windows. And I painted the walls last year."

Fin studied the warm apricot shade. "It suits you."

"Thank you." A shirt she'd been mending rested in her lap. Her fingers worried the worn fabric. Common sense told her to toss the shirt away, but it was the favorite of a little boy who'd brought precious else with him. She'd repair it, stitching together seams frayed from use. "You have a question for me?"

Eliza immediately regretted the stiffness in her voice, but fear that she'd broken more than her word kept it rigid.

"Yes." Fin heard the distance and almost came to her feet. Why ask for what would clearly be denied? She scooted forward to stand, but then she saw the way Mrs. F clutched the fabric. Hope rose cautiously, and she cleared her throat. In for a penny, she recited, in for a pound. "I don't want to go," she blurted out.

Eliza nearly wept, but she allowed herself only a silent prayer of thanks. It appeared, she realized, that Fin could take a first step. "That's not a question, Findley."

Stung, Fin came to her feet and paced over to the glossy Chippendale bureau. Pots of fragrant creams and exotic bottles of scents clustered together. She remembered sneaking in with Kell, Julia keeping watch at the door. Carefully handling a rose-colored crystal bottle, she demanded, "Then here's one. Why did you break your promise?"

"I don't want you working with Mr. Matthews. It's too dangerous."

"That's not an answer." Fin faced Eliza, accusation mixed with disappointment. "You've never lied to me before, Mrs. F. Why?"

Eliza accepted both the accusation and the disappointment and sighed. "Because I got scared." Dipping her head, she studied the hands she'd folded into her lap. "Raising you was a terrifying experience," she explained slowly. "All of my other children needed me. To get them dressed for school. To help with their homework. To kiss a skinned knee. But you, you were different."

"How?"

"You didn't need me." At Fin's frown, she continued. "By the time you arrived here, you had nothing but contempt for adults. We rarely discussed it, but you'd been on your own a lot longer than a few days by the time you came to me."

"I came to you because I didn't have anyone for those things," Fin protested.

"I know. So, with you, I had to be careful. You'd watch me with those shrewd eyes, waiting for a misstep. For betrayal."

"I was waiting for you to kick me out," Fin confessed. "I figured you'd realize I didn't belong." She thought of the notes from teachers and the fights on the playground. "I wasn't a good kid."

"No," Eliza concurred. She permitted herself a wisp of a smile. "Thank God."

"I want to stay, Mrs. F." Fin knelt beside the woman who'd been more than her mother. "And I need to do this. To help."

"You are quite dear to me," Eliza replied. She brushed a curl back from the high, intelligent forehead. Her Fin would try to be careful. She'd fail. But habit required the request. "I don't want you risking your life. Promise me."

"I'll do my best," Fin temporized, unwilling to lie.

The measured response didn't ease the worry, but nothing Fin could offer as a guarantee would. So Eliza did as she always had. She accepted. Cupping her chin, she met Fin's eyes with a steady look. "I am so very sorry for making you doubt my word to you. I overreacted."

"Maybe I could have taken a different approach," Fin conceded dryly, lifting her shoulders. Eyes twinkling, she asked, "Does this mean I can unpack?"

Eliza bussed Fin's forehead tenderly and whispered, "Always."

"The judge is really angry, Mike." James chewed anxiously on the pen in his mouth, his cigarettes having been tossed out by his wife. She'd caught the smell of smoke on him and had chucked every last pack. "Told me that I'd received my one warning."

"Calm down, Jimmy. So it didn't go the way we planned." Tucked away in his motel room, Graves wiped at his brow. He could feel Jimmy's flop sweat, and it seemed to be contagious. Mary Majors ruled her court and Stark with an iron fist. Graves knew, from personal experience in both domains, that she had no qualms about using that iron fist to twist a man's head off. Either one. "Did you mention my name?"

"Of course not!" But, James had decided, the time might come. "They tried to trip me up, but I stood firm. Like we discussed."

"So what's their next play?"

"A meeting with Fin Borders tonight. They want to find out if she's willing to help us get the land. I've explained that she's only one of the new trustees—it will take all three to sell the trees to the company I've set up."

"One of Stark's fronts, right?" An idea sparked, grew. "Jimmy, you're a freaking genius."

"What?"

"That's what we'll do." Graves smacked his hands together, relishing the possibilities. "We don't need Stark, Jimmy. We don't need Judge Nut-cracker."

"You want to buy the land ourselves." Worry, his constant companion, reared up. "I'd have to transfer a lot out of Stark's accounts to cover the purchase."

Graves nearly cursed at Jimmy, but he held himself quiet. A whiskey bottle sat on the scarred table, its contents almost gone. Graves swigged the rest, savored the fire. There was a reason he and Jimmy had partnered up. The clod had delusions of criminal mastery, but he was a penny-ante player in a high-stakes world. "We won't need Stark's money. Not if we convince Fin Borders to transfer the land to us. And she keeps a cut."

"Will she do it?"

"For a price," Graves decided. "We just have to figure out her going rate."

CHAPTER 19

"Give me the keys and stop complaining." Fin stood with her palm out, waiting. "We don't have any other options."

"Why does it have to be my car?" As she clutched the keys, Kell cast about for an alternative. "Why not take the van?"

"I'm not taking the Faraday Center van to an illicit rendezvous in the middle of the district." The argument had been going on for more than ten minutes. "Mrs. Faraday has gone to the hospital to visit with Judge Majors. Julia doesn't have a car, and I'm not driving a police vehicle to the site of their attempt to blackmail me."

Logic rammed brutally into desperation. Kell's baby had already been smacked by a baseball and scraped when she'd been forced to park in a public lot for court. A rental car was the obvious answer, but at a quarter past nine on a Monday night, the only vendor had long since cut out his lights. Then, inspiration struck. "What about Caleb?"

She turned to the man who'd been listening to the fight. "Can't she take your car?"

Sitting on the lowest stair, his legs stretched out before him, he considered the question. "Nope."

"Why not?" Fin, whose fingers itched to get behind the wheel of the Porsche again, took mild offense. She didn't want to drive his car, but his quick denial compelled her to respond. "I'm a superb driver."

"I don't doubt that you are. Which is why Kell should have no qualms about loaning you hers."

"You drive an Accord," Kell pointed out. "I drive a 911 Carrera."

"You're her best friend. I'm not." His PDA blinked with another message. "Insulting my car won't help your cause, either."

Stymied, Kell searched for another tack. "Mine's a two-seater But in your car, you could hide in the back. Go with Fin to protect her."

Caleb had to admire the underhanded approach, the simplicity of her attack. "You are good. But it won't work. She can't arrive at a clandestine meeting driving the DA's car. Just isn't done in the criminal world."

Brilliant, applauded Fin. Smiling, she strode over to her traitor of a friend and took the keys. "It's for my safety." Besides, she didn't require a babysitter. Especially not one who could raise her blood pressure lounging on a staircase. With him in close proximity, she wouldn't be able to concentrate. To focus. "They said to come alone, and that's what I plan to do."

"You're not going alone," Caleb admonished her

lightly. "I didn't want to loan you my car because I intended to use it to follow you."

Fin whipped around, ready to spring. At the last moment, she throttled back her temper, opting for reason. "These aren't first timers, Caleb. They'll be looking for tails. Plus, it's out in the woods. Exactly where were you planning to hide?"

"They've done a bunch of construction over there, Fin. Cut new roads into the area. Everything came to a halt when they found the bodies, but equipment is being allowed back on site. Can't spook a developer for long." Caleb explained, "I'm parking my car in the woods and monitoring the scene from the comfort of one of the bulldozers. I scoped it out this afternoon. I'll be able to climb into the cab and keep an eye on you."

"Which means you can make sure she doesn't do anything to damage my car." Unhappy with the plan, but outgunned, Kell stormed out of the foyer.

Caleb turned to Fin. "After your meeting with Stark, you and I will come back to my apartment." Agreeing to let Fin meet with Stark didn't include sending her out unprotected. Luke had concurred, had gotten him the keys for a bulldozer. If Stark had someone check, they'd find all the construction vehicles locked. "Does that meet with your approval?"

Fin acknowledged that relief lurked behind her annoyance. "Sure." She scoped out the black jeans, black T-shirt, and requisite black boots. "That outfit come with a grappling hook or a utility belt?"

Lazily gaining his feet, he glanced down at his clothes. "I thought I looked rather dashing."

The colors highlighted the solid build, the lean sexy lines of the man. "You'll do."

"Thank you." Caleb stopped within touching distance, but he slipped his hands into his pockets. "I hear you asked Mrs. Faraday if you could stay."

Embarrassed, she looked away. "Kell talks too much."

"Actually, it was Julia. She's very proud of you." He tipped her eyes up to his. Held them. "So am I."

"I aim to please," she bantered, fighting off embarrassment. The steady, unwavering eyes left her nowhere to hide. A flurry of butterflies erupted in her stomach at the notion that she didn't want to. "Thanks for helping me."

Conscious she wasn't referring to tonight, he grazed her mouth with a friendly kiss. "You're welcome." Then he released her as his lips threatened to cling. "We need to leave for the meeting soon."

"I'll be right back."

He watched her disappear around the banister, then lowered his head into his hands. Sunday, he'd dropped her off at the center and had spent the rest of the night hunting and mulling. Looking for a way to eliminate the need for her as his entry to Stark. A smoking gun, even a smoldering ember to light the way to the center of the organization and its destruction.

Anything that would unravel the tangle of guilt and desire warring within him.

He could slake lust with a willing partner who understood the rules—work first, second, and last. No messy emotional ties, no expectations. But Fin enchanted him. For every minute with her, he wanted a hundred more.

But while the decision he'd come to that day wrenched at him, it was the right one. The proper way to handle his ungovernable attraction. The only way to assure her safety and his judgment. And one of the hardest things he'd ever have to do.

Cinder blocks lay scattered across the site, steel girders gleamed in the moonlight. Fin parked in front of what had been the back entrance to the Grove Warehouse and braced for the onslaught of memory.

Hours spent honing what was to become her craft. The frenzied escape from the death scene, surrounded by the blaze of accidental fire. But, according to Luke, the fire hadn't penetrated the casino. A second fire had been set to burn a second man. The identity of the second man remained a mystery. Somewhere, a family grieved for a missing person. As Louis Pippin's family had.

Faced with her life to live over, she'd have chosen better, absolutely. But try as she might, however, she couldn't summon remorse that she'd survived instead of Pippin. It was that coldness that shook her, that ability to not feel.

Then, as now, she thanked whichever parent had granted her the gift of compartmentalization. The ability to cordon off remorse and guilt and pay attention to the task at hand.

Finding out what Stark wanted from her.

Caleb had parked in the Grove, his vehicle hidden in the dense thicket of trees. By now, he'd be climbing one of the massive machines yards from her location, stealing into the cab. Knowing he could see her, she picked her way across construction debris and entered the hull of a building. Sheetrock had been hung on a portion of the frame, creating an enclosure. A tarp hung overhead, protecting equipment, she assumed. Instantly, she wished for a flashlight.

"Welcome, Ms. Borders. Punctual, I see."

Fin peered into the darkened space but was unable to make out more than a shape in the shadows. Out here, no streetlights illumined the pitch-black interior. Her only orientation came from the lightly accented voice inside. "A little help, please."

Hands closed over her outstretched ones, guided her over more steel and plaster. Dressed in a chicer version of Caleb's outfit, her black clothes blended into the night. Ahead of them, moonlight penetrated the exposed space, but the hands stopped her before they reached the shadowy light.

"Far enough, Ms. Borders."

"Do I get a name to call you?"

A cultured laugh met her query. "I think you already know who I represent."

"Stark."

"Yes. I am of Stark. The organization to whom you owe one and a half million. Payable immediately. Or we'll take aggressive action to collect."

Though she'd expected a demand for their funds, her stomach clutched at the number. She hid the reaction, her face placid, considering. "One and a half million dollars? A hefty interest rate."

"Prime plus two on a sixteen-year loan of three hundred thousand. Technically, it's $1.47 million, but given that you didn't actually ask us for our money, we decided to round up."

Three hundred thousand. Fin clung to the number, which meant they didn't know Kell and Julia had taken any of it. "I'm happy to get on a payment plan. However, I am assuming you have another alternative in mind."

Hestor approved of the woman's quick wit and her bravery in the face of danger. Though his sexual preferences lay elsewhere, he appreciated why men might want to bed her. He prided himself on his ability to instill fear, yet she showed only bravado. Admirable. "A favor may be required of you, Ms. Borders. A substantial request that we expect you to fulfill. Without question."

"I'd rather pay you your money." Shifting, she folded her arms across her chest. She couldn't give in too easily. Brazenly, she told him, "I've been rather successful in the intervening years. I can have your money for you tomorrow."

"You have access to sufficient cash?"

"I can get it." Jake would kill her, but hers was largely a cash business. One and a half million wasn't an easy hit, but she could take it. "I prefer not to be in anyone's debt. Or have their threats hanging over my head."

"Perhaps a compromise, Ms. Borders."

"I'm listening."

"We have need of information from two of the center's frequent visitors. Sheriff Calder and ADA Matthews. Like them, we are in search of our former colleague, Chief Graves. Provide us with your assistance, and we may be able to come to an agreement on your debt."

"Why not simply take my money?"

"Money is a fungible good for us. Your cooperation, at the moment, is imminently more valuable."

"And if I refuse?"

"Children are fragile creatures," he murmured. "Their bodies break with great ease. Their skin tears like tissue paper. Blood pours out of them in crimson rivers. The River Brandon. The River Nina. The River Faith. Ah, the River Jorden."

She nearly broke, but she held the shriek of disgust inside. "You've done your homework."

"Then there are the littlest ones. Less to play with, but worthy experiments. I'd think about that before you object to our terms." Without waiting for her reply, he clasped her elbow and led her to the rear of the building. "I'll be in touch. Good night, Ms. Borders."

Fin strode to the silver car, praying her knees would support her until she got inside. Her hand fumbled on the handle before she pried the door open. Nausea surged sickly. As he'd intended, she could picture the mangled, destroyed bodies of the center's children. The man inside would relish the experience, take his time with the desecration of innocence. She shoved the key into the ignition and forced herself to leave the site slowly. He had to believe she was unmoved, unaffected.

As Caleb had instructed her, she drove to his apartment, where she jammed the car into park and waited for him to arrive. Like a wraith, he appeared by the windows. "Fin."

She just shook her head and released the locks.

He got inside, flicked on the overhead light. Her face startled him. "What did he do to you?"

Fin shook her head, as much in denial as to dispel the images. "He threatened to kill the children if I don't cooperate."

Reaching out, he rubbed at her arms, trying to generate heat in skin cool beneath his touch. "And do what?"

"For now, they want information on the hunt for Graves." Fin tipped her head back, took a deep breath.

Nothing had happened to the kids and nothing would. Not if she did her job. "He was right to run. I wouldn't want that man to find me."

As she settled, Caleb slipped his hand up to knead at the tension in her neck. Her head dipped down, the ropes of black silk caressing his skin. "Can you describe him?"

"Tall, I think. Not American." She arched under the welcome massage, turned to give him better access. Her words trailed into staccato. Threats and murder dissolved beneath his touch.

Intent on his task, Caleb used his thumbs to press, his palms to soothe. Soon, she issued a rumble of pleasure that shot through him. Had him spinning her around. Before he could dive in, she plundered his mouth and forced Caleb's breath to saw out on a gasp of brutal arousal.

His hands, hers, claimed and tormented, voracious and shocking in their commands. Fin nipped at the hard line of his throat, laving the pulse that galloped beneath her tongue. When he groaned, she covered his mouth, whispering into the hot, lush cavern. "Shh."

Unable to resist, Caleb sank eager fingers into the silken curls at her nape. He feasted on the long, slender lines of her collar, delighting at the tension that arched her into him. Driven to seduce, he stroked the rise of her breast and claimed the tightly drawn peak.

Too soon, she eased away, gulped in reams of air. "Man, you can kiss."

Retreating to his side of the car, Caleb returned the compliment. "You're no slouch yourself." His heartbeat steadied, and his head began to clear. "Fin, we need to discuss this."

"Discuss what? Stark?" Fin pushed through the hazy web of arousal and focused. "Worley is one name I'm sure of. I'll go to the bank tomorrow and damage my credibility in front of him. Is there a problem?"

"No, not with that. I agree you should visit the bank."

The grim tone scared her, and she scooted closer. "Caleb? What's going on?"

"Us. This . . . this chemistry."

"We are rather combustible together."

She grinned, a sultry smile that nearly had him diving in again. "FBI protocol forbids sexual relationships between a civilian and a handler. You and me."

"We haven't gotten that far yet," she countered reasonably. "Though I like your ambition."

Laughter strangled his intent. "Come on, Fin. Whatever this is between us, it's heading in one direction. Which puts you and me off limits." Gritting his teeth, he admitted, "I realize I've shown a marked inability to keep my hands to myself. You're a gorgeous, desirable woman, but we've got a job to do. I have a responsibility to keep you safe. All we can have between us is dismantling Stark."

Hurt snaked in to wrap around her heart. Gorgeous. Desirable. Off-limits. She'd spent her entire adulthood trading on those three attributes, and when she'd finally found the man who'd broken through her guards, his life wouldn't allow it. Alone, she would laugh at the irony. "I see." She turned in her seat with as much dignity as she could muster. "I need to get back to the center now."

"Not until we talk about this," Caleb shot back.

"I don't know what we have to discuss. I work for you and you can't touch me." She flicked him a carefully blank look. "Did I miss something?"

"No, but why are you looking at me like that?"

"Like what?"

Despite the fact that he'd set the rules, her nonchalant response raised his ire. "I don't know. You tell me."

"I'm accepting your decision with grace, Caleb. Would you prefer a tantrum?"

"I'd prefer honesty." The thud of fury rising in his gut shocked him, puzzled him. After all, she'd simply agreed to his decision. And he wanted to throttle her. "Tell me what you're thinking."

"I'm thinking it's late, and I'm tired. I'm going home."

CHAPTER 20

The main thoroughfare shot straight through the center of town and did not end until Pike, the next town over. Like much of this part of Georgia, the main street was named for the state's most famed crop—the peach. This Peachtree Street, unlike its big-city counterpart in Atlanta, didn't flaunt high-rises and venerable hotels. On Hallden's Peachtree, a tourist would browse quaint shops with hand-painted signs selling homemade jam or hand-stitched sweaters.

Fin peered out from the passenger window as Kell wound her way through unexpectedly heavy morning traffic. Though she'd toured the Red District on Saturday, Fin hadn't ventured into Hallden's downtown.

The area hadn't changed much, from what she saw. Two stops down from the Bells Gas and Grocery sat a restaurant owned by one of the only wealthy black families in town. Foster's Foods offered everything from fried chicken and okra to linguine with clam sauce. The current owner, Elvin Foster, had lived in

Boston while in college, but he'd decided to come home after his father's second stroke. He'd agreed to take over the restaurant on the condition that he could update the menu and leave as soon as his father got better. Fifteen years later, Elvin was still running Foster's, waiting for one of his children to take it from him and let him return to Boston.

Slowing down beyond Foster's, Fin scanned the widened road for the venerable General Store. What greeted her startled. Where a single-door storefront had stood sixteen years ago, a strip mall now stretched the entire length of two blocks. According to the modern signage, Hallden's General Store now boasted a bookstore and a small café.

Shoppers toting bags laden with clothes crowded the sidewalks at 11:00 a.m. A petite, wand-slim woman touched the arm of her more ample companion and pulled out a dress Fin recognized as the latest finery from the Express or Banana Republic. Either way, the old-fashioned general store of her youth seemed to be the current home of a miniature strip mall.

"Now, when did that happen?" Fin muttered aloud as Kell zipped underneath one of the many new traffic lights in town. "When did Hallden become a real city?"

Kell gave an easy laugh. "This isn't Brigadoon, Fin."

"I hadn't expected so much to be different." She'd imagined her return to Hallden, but her renderings hadn't included an Arby's franchise across the street from the courthouse.

Kell found a parking space in the communal lot that served the town square. She released the windows and cut the engine. "I hadn't expected it either," she admitted. "You wouldn't believe it, but there's a French restaurant that rivals any four-star in New York. Luke took me there for dinner that first night. The chef is this gallant French Canadian named Hervé."

"Romantic place?"

"Hmm." Kell gave Fin a sidelong look. Between the shock of Fin's plan to go undercover and the crisis over Mrs. F's denouncement, she hadn't been able to prod Fin for details. Years might have separated them, but she knew her friend. Fingers tapping the steering wheel, she suggested, "Perhaps you and Caleb should meet there. To discuss the case, of course."

Fin refused to take the bait, though she'd known the interrogation about Caleb was coming. "What time is Luke supposed to arrive?"

"Eleven thirty and don't change the subject." Intrigued by the avoidance, Kell tried a more direct approach. "Come on, spill it. What's going on between you two?"

Her voice flat, Fin replied, "Caleb and I are colleagues."

"He didn't seem terribly platonic when he swept you from the study Sunday. Or kissed you senseless for breakfast. Julia found the gestures quite romantic." As had she. And, unless her friendship skills had gone terribly rusty, so had Fin. "Explain that."

"Caleb's a nice guy," Fin replied hollowly. "He saw that I was upset and wanted to give me space."

"With him. Alone."

"We went for a drive. Not to a motel," she retorted shortly, as the taste of his kiss shivered through her. For herself as much as Kell, she said firmly, "As of now, he's my handler. We're colleagues." And nothing more.

"I don't buy it, Fin."

"There's nothing to buy. Last night, after my meeting

with Stark, he made his feelings very clear. He's attracted to me, but Stark comes first."

"And?"

"And that's it."

"It's been a while since we could hash out men trouble face-to-face," Kell said. "I'd hate to see an opportunity go to waste."

Fin's mouth tightened. "He wants my body and my skills."

"A healthy start."

"Start and stop." Fin bit at her lip, preferring the small pain to the bruise to her ego. "How many times have you been in love, Kell?"

Thoughtful, she responded, "I imagined myself in love three times. That time in high school. With a professor in college." At the quick look, she waved a hand. "Don't ask. And then a lawyer I dated for a while when I first started out. But I've only really been in love once. With Luke."

"I've never been in love. Imaginary or real." The confession slipped out easily, feeling right. "Not once. I date men who expect nothing more than pleasure and mutual satisfaction. No nasty emotional ties or prolonged breakups."

"Sounds efficient."

"It is." Fin tilted her head into the headrest. "Has been. Because no one has ever wanted more. Asked for anything else."

"Did you give them room to ask?"

"I don't know." She let her head fall toward Kell, mystified. "But I would for Caleb. If he wanted me." The last emerged on a tight whisper.

"What about what you want?" Incensed at the idiot

who'd put that look in Fin's eyes, Kell railed, "What gives him the right to decide for both of you?"

"FBI protocol, for a start."

"He certainly wasn't concerned with protocol before."

"Well, he is now. *C'est la vie.*" Suddenly restless, she pushed open the car door. "Let's walk."

Kell obliged, and they crossed to the cobblestone walk surrounding the historical town square. First Missionary Baptist Church occupied the west corner, with the courthouse to its right. The Georgia Bank anchored the east corner, the eighteenth-century brick façade untouched by progress.

They made a slow circuit of the square and Fin pretended to window-shop, avoiding conversation. But her mind strayed to Kell's question. What did she want from Caleb?

The question had spun in her head since he'd dropped her off yesterday. Caleb represented the exact opposite of her requirements in a lover. She preferred the casual, itinerant type. A relationship with him would require depth and complexity, a commitment of her mind and heart, as well as her body. More than she intended to give to any man, she reminded herself dully.

"Sit down." Kell pulled her onto a bench in front of the parking lot. "You're scaring the tourists."

"Sorry."

"Don't apologize. And don't give in to Caleb."

"There's nothing to give. You've met him. He's not exactly the type to flout the rules."

"Every man will break the rules for the right woman. If you're that woman, do what you're best at."

A dark brow lifted in warning. "Which you think is what, exactly?"

"Taking a risk. Bluff him into it or some other gambling metaphor I don't know. But don't accept the hand you've been dealt."

"Nice one."

Kell preened. "Caleb obviously wants you, and he cares for you. That's a better start than most relationships have."

"You and Luke?"

"The first time Luke met me, he threatened to arrest me. There was nowhere to go but up." She glanced at her watch. "Speaking of which, we should be heading inside."

Fin stood and swept a hand over the trim carmine suit she'd borrowed from Kell. In her line of work, she preferred a less corporate image. However, she found herself enjoying the thrill of power exuded by the outfit. Kell wore a similar uniform, hers a cobalt blue trimmed in white piping. "Where will Luke meet us?"

"In the bank. Worley takes his lunch at precisely eleven forty-five, according to Mrs. F."

Oblivious to the attention they attracted, the women made their way to the bank's curved marble steps. Fin balanced lightly in the skyscraper heels, also courtesy of Kell. "Are you sure?" she asked quietly, her hand at Kell's elbow. Speaking urgently, she gave her best friend a final caution. "Once we start this, we can't change our minds. We go in, we're committed."

Kell closed her hand over Fin's. "We've lost sixteen years, Fin. They can't have any more."

No, Fin agreed silently with a glance at her watch, *they can't have any more.* Briskly, she hurried up the steps, Kell beside her. She tugged at the glass door and sailed inside. Chilled air fought off the early day heat and whispered through the broad expanse of the lobby. Teller bays in polished oak spread against the opposite wall. On the right, narrow cubbies had been carved into offices.

To her left, a lovely young woman with auburn hair bound in a chignon greeted new customers from behind a sleek ebony desk. The nameplate announced her as Katie Meredith. A gilt-edged clock hung on the side wall, ticking off banker's minutes. Eleven fifteen.

"Showtime," Fin murmured to Kell.

They approached the desk and were immediately greeted by a megawatt smile. "Welcome to the Georgia Bank."

"Thank you." Fin replied, then noted a moment of recognition.

"Ms. Jameson," Katie gushed, her perfectly straight teeth flashing at Kell. Her voice had been barely saved from perky by half an octave. "So happy to see you. You did a fabulous job with Mrs. Faraday."

"You saw the hearing?"

"Mr. Worley let me slip across the square to watch," she confessed. "I got hooked watching the Brodie trial on *CourtWatch*. Then, imagine, you here in our very own town." She glanced around sharply. "Would you mind if I asked for your autograph? It's not for me," she added quickly. "My mom loves Paul Brodie. She was so excited when you helped him get acquitted."

"Happy to." Kell accepted the proffered legal pad. "What's your mom's name?"

"Louisa," she answered breathlessly. "It's her birthday on Friday."

Kell jotted a note across the sheet, then scrawled her signature below. Passing the pad to Katie, she reached for a card. "How old will she be?"

"Fifty-three, though she still claims to be forty-five."

"Why don't I ask Paul to send me a collection of *American Dad* memorabilia for your mom?"

Bright blue eyes widened in astonished delight. "Oh, my goodness! She would just die."

"Well, we don't want to kill her," Kell teased. "I'll have the package sent here."

"Thank you, Ms. Jameson. Thank you so much." Katie gripped her hand, pumping it hard. "She'll be so excited. Thank you." Then, remembering Fin's presence, she released Kell's hand, eyes still beaming. "How can I help you today?"

"My friend, Ms. Borders, would like to open an account," Kell explained. "She will need to make a fairly sizeable deposit today and several more in the next few weeks. I assume you can also provide a brokerage account and a safety deposit box."

The blue eyes focused more tightly on Fin. Katie recognized the quality of the suit, the supple leather of the handbag. She considered her desire to move from the front desk into one of the side offices, then quickly made her decision. "If you'll have a seat," she said, indicating two club chairs at the side of her desk. "I'll only be a moment."

Katie gracefully stood and moved past the teller bays to the one large office on the ground floor. She nodded to the secretary. "Is Mr. Worley available?"

His secretary, a harridan of a woman named Tami Stephens, who disliked other humans but could organize an invasion force on a second's notice, gave an annoyed grunt. "He leaves for lunch in a few minutes, Ms. Meredith. Kindly hold your concerns until he returns."

"We have a potential customer I think he'd like to meet," she informed her smugly. "Unless you'd like to tell him we don't need the business." Katie's boyfriend worked for an upstart bank three blocks away. The Georgia Bank was a city institution, but the other bank had lower fees and free checking. If not for her job, she'd have moved her own accounts. "One of the customers is Kell Jameson."

Giving the young woman a speculative look, Tami lifted the black receiver. "Mr. Worley. Ms. Meredith is here to see you about a new customer."

She listened for a moment. "Go on," Tami instructed. "He's leaving soon."

Katie entered the bank president's sanctum and barely resisted the urge to curtsy. Plaques and photos covered every free inch of wall space, with Worley's wide, ruddy face beaming from each frame. "Mr. Worley?"

"What is it, Ms. Meredith?" He pointed to his gold watch with impatience. "I have a lunch appointment shortly."

"Yes, sir," she acknowledged hastily, "but I thought you might like to speak with a potential customer yourself."

"I would not," Worley dismissed. "Send him over to Mr. Lucas or Ms. Hugley."

"It's a woman, Mr. Worley. Her name is Findley Borders, and she's a friend of that attorney, Kell Jameson."

Worley froze. They were here? "Is it two women only?"

Katie nodded, puzzled. "Yes, sir. Ms. Jameson and Ms. Borders." She repeated the banking requests. "I didn't ask about the size of the deposit because it seemed inappropriate, but I thought you might want to handle this customer yourself."

Absently, his mind racing, he bobbed his head in agreement. "You did well, Ms. Meredith. Very good." He'd been given strict instructions to monitor these women, and here they were, standing in his bank. Graves would be pleased. At the thought of his partner, his happiness dimmed. Graves had brought Hestor into the fold a couple of years ago when one of their experimental sidelines had gone awry. Dr. Hestor had disposed of pesky details like autopsies by determining quick causes of death. Judge Majors was looking to Hestor to manage Stark's relationship with Fin Borders.

But if he could leverage today's coincidence, he'd be able to reassert his position. At fifty-two, he'd built a comfortable nest egg with his profits, but his penchant for gambling had gotten the better of him. Mrs. Worley expected to continue to live well above the means of a small-town bank president, and this latest opportunity would keep his bride in minks and Bentleys for the rest of her life.

Excitedly, Worley stood. "I'd like to enlist your aid, Ms. Meredith," he told her as he guided her to the door. "Ms. Borders and Ms. Jameson appear to be excellent potential customers for us. I intend to assign you to handle their accounts personally."

"I'd welcome the opportunity, Mr. Worley." She kept her voice level, masking her excitement. "Whatever you need."

He didn't miss the gleam that slid into the ambitious woman's eyes. Perhaps, he thought idly, she'd show her gratitude more personally later. Just as quickly, he dismissed the idea. Stark did not permit scandals that attracted attention to their members. And he had the strong suspicion that Ms. Meredith wouldn't take too kindly to his advances. He dropped back to follow her across the lobby, sighing ruefully as she preceded him.

Lust expanded when Kell and Fin came to their feet, especially when he saw what age had ripened in Fin Borders. She'd been the star of more than one of his prurient fantasies when she'd been a nubile sixteen-year-old with a penchant for miniskirts. The stunning woman possessed the same mile-long legs and sexy curves he'd imagined. It would be a pity to kill either of them without a sample first, he mused.

"Ms. Borders. Ms. Jameson." He extended his hand, held each one a touch too long. "I'm James Worley, the bank president."

Fin waited for the kick of recognition and was not disappointed when his eyes glinted into hers. She nodded, "Mr. Worley."

Would he admit knowing her, she wondered? Such an admission necessitated explanations a man like Worley couldn't slough off. So she followed his lead and pretended to not recognize him. "We appreciate you coming to talk with us," she said politely.

"My pleasure," he replied, motioning them to an empty conference room. "We have a board meeting this afternoon, but we can sit in here."

Before Katie could join them, a teller beckoned for her attention. Worley gave a genial smile. "Go ahead, Ms. Meredith. I'll speak with Ms. Borders and then let you get them squared away."

Katie nodded tightly, disappointed. "Alright. Yes, sir."

Grateful she'd been drawn away, Fin breathed a sigh

of relief. They followed him into the office. When everyone was seated, he steepled his fingers and reclined in the rolling chair. "Ms. Meredith indicated that you require special banking services."

"Yes." Fin slashed a look at Kell, then continued. "Ms. Jameson is not only my friend but my attorney as well." Remembering his penchant, she angled her chair and crossed her legs slowly, carelessly. "I'm not sure if you remember me, Mr. Worley, but in my formative years, I spent a bit of time at the old Grove Warehouse."

To his credit, Worley gave hardly any sign except for a short intake of breath. "The building that burnt down?" he challenged.

"That's the one." She reached for the pitcher of water, which was beading condensation. As she filled three glasses, she continued. "In my time since leaving Hallden, I've been fortunate to make my living on the international circuit."

"Circuit?" Worley frowned lightly while he accepted his glass, though he'd reviewed her dossier a dozen times last night. "What type of circuit?"

"Gambling." Sliding a glass to Kell, she poured one for herself. "I'm a professional poker player, Mr. Worley. A perfectly legal occupation, but entirely cash-based." She took a drink and watched him over the rim. "My earnings tend to come in lump sums, and occasionally, I require some creative handling of funds to meet all of my obligations."

Warily, he took a quick look at Kell. "How is Sheriff Calder doing these days, Ms. Jameson? I understand you two are quite an item." Worley caught Fin's grimace, which she masked instantly. He wondered aloud, "How does he feel about your clients?"

"The sheriff and I are very happy," Kell replied, meeting his speculative look with an even gaze. "We also understand one another. My clients enjoy my strictest confidence." Kell folded her hands on the slick tabletop. "Fin will be in town for a number of weeks, and she has specific needs that must be handled discreetly. While I can certainly find assistance for her in Atlanta, I tend to prefer the convivial atmosphere of local banks."

"We have the same reporting requirements," Worley pressed. "And the Georgia Bank is a thriving concern."

Fin interjected, "Let's be frank, Mr. Worley." She stood and moved to his end of the table. Resting a hand on his shoulder, she leaned in. "My last tournament netted me seven hundred and fifty-two thousand dollars. And during my travels, I've developed other— expensive—habits. Habits that are difficult to finance when Uncle Sam picks my pocket for almost half."

Her breasts grazed his arm as she bent to his ear. "I remember you, Mr. Worley. You had guts then. Brass—" She sat up. "Well, you know."

Throat as tight as his pants, Worley coughed once. "I'll need to consider your request, Ms. Borders. Check a few things."

"Thank you, Mr. Worley." With nimble fingers, she stroked the boring blue tie at his neck. "But please don't take too long."

"Give me a few hours," he managed. "I'll work fast."

Kell stood. "We appreciate your help, Mr. Worley." Nudging Fin, she flashed her watch. "Fin, we need to be on our way. I'm meeting Luke for lunch."

"So I'll make myself scarce," Fin retorted, edging her words with sarcasm.

"Fin." Kell lowered her voice but allowed it to carry to Worley. "He's concerned. You're not exactly his speed."

"Slow and laborious?" She mumbled the insult as Worley came abreast of them. "I'm joking," she explained, clearly not. "Sheriff Calder and I don't share common interests."

Worley opened the door and held it for them to pass through. Luke Calder stood waiting on the steps. He wore his sheriff's uniform and a Stetson that shaded his face from the sun. Tipping its brim, he said, "Good morning, James."

"Luke." Worley nodded in response. "I've just had the pleasure of talking with two of the most beautiful women in town about my favorite subject."

Luke's gaze narrowed. "Then you and Fin have a lot in common." He gained a step and gently pulled Kell to his side, creating a chasm between her and Fin. "We've got reservations for noon."

"Can Fin join us?" she asked lightly, her eyes pleading.

"I'd hoped for some alone time," he replied flatly. "I've barely seen you since they arrived."

Worley stood with Fin, fascinated. Kell had grown rigid, and he could fairly feel her anger. An interesting triangle, he decided. Obviously, the sheriff didn't trust the return of the playgirl and her possible effects on Kell. "I'd invite you to join me," he murmured to Fin, "but I'm afraid we'd bore a young woman like yourself silly."

Fin smiled at him wanly. "I appreciate the offer." She glared at Luke, who continued to argue with Kell. "I wonder how he manages to sit down," she said as an aside to Worley.

"What?"

"With the stick up his ass," she explained dryly. "He's afraid I'll get Kell in trouble."

Worley glanced at her, testing. "Will you?"

"Not if we don't get caught."

CHAPTER 21

Caleb didn't have to scan the study for Fin. Instinctively, his sights focused on her as he entered the room. She was lounging the window seat, munching the remnants of a sandwich.

Which gave him a moment to take in the transformation. Gone were the back-baring sundresses and the pulse-raising shorts. Today, she wore a tailored suit, but he silently blessed the tailor who'd designed the sleek lines that accented curves and framed the graceful body beneath.

Each time he saw her, he was certain the impact would dull. He'd known women more beautiful. Yet not one had required a constant regulation of his breathing in her vicinity. Not like Fin.

His fingers itched to stroke away the crumbs clinging to her overripe lips, to wrap one of the dark silken curls around his skin. Instead, he balled his fists. He'd decided touching Fin was now off limits. Damned if he could remember why as her tongue captured an errant crumb.

Responsibility, his conscience goaded. As long as he was responsible for her life, he would have to steer clear. Handler rule number one forbade relationships between the agent and his informant. Adrenaline masqueraded as affection. Sex got tangled up and called love. He'd already crossed a dozen lines, and with each one, the reasons he shouldn't have done so had blurred. Soon, he'd forget himself completely.

But she didn't know the rules. She was driven to prove herself, and helping her fulfill that agenda meant more than whatever was growing inside him. She meant more. So he'd protect her, from him and from herself.

"Did Worley take the bait?" Caleb directed the query to Kell, announcing his arrival. He wandered over to her, bussed her cheek with a kiss. Shook Luke's hand.

"Caleb." Fin greeted him, despite a full mouth. She waited for his response. He simply jutted his chin toward her as the only sign he knew she was in the room. *Okay,* she thought, *game on.* "Hello to you too."

He moved as far away as he could without being obvious. Eager to be gone, he demanded of Kell and Luke, "Was he at the bank? Were you able to make contact?"

"I'm the mole, remember?" Fin chided. "Give me a second to finish lunch. Then I will tell you."

Unable to forget that she was the mole, he folded his arms and let his impatience with rules and protocol transmit itself as exasperation. "Fine. Hurry up."

At the tone, Kell exchanged a veiled look with Fin.

For her part, Fin deliberately ate the last remnants of grilled bread with relish and no haste. She wiped her lap clean with a napkin, then swigged at a Diet Coke balanced on the sill. Swallowing, she slanted a look at Luke. "Unlike some, I didn't have lunch this afternoon. I had to forage for myself after baking in the car for ninety minutes."

Luke had the grace to wince. "We had to make it look good." Shielding himself from the angry glare, he told Caleb, "Like we suspected, Worley seemed suspicious about Fin and Kell, given our relationship."

"So Luke let it be known that I was persona non grata. And to put a fine point on the matter, he treated Kell to a leisurely lunch and left me to consider the error of my ways while they dined."

"I did bring you a panini," Kell managed lamely. "Besides, it worked. Luke gave a good performance, and Worley bought it."

"Appeared to," Fin corrected. Luke and Kell had taken the matching chairs, which created a natural circle. She shifted slightly on the cushions and patted the seat beside her.

Caleb waved the silent offer away, indicating his intention to stand.

Hurt pricked for a moment, then she thrust it aside. If he wanted to stand rather than sit next to her, so be it. Nursing her soda, she ran through the events of the morning. "We told Worley that I had money to move, and I hinted that laundering might be in order. He didn't accept right away, but he looked intrigued."

Caleb gave a satisfied nod. "Three quarters of a million dollars is a hefty sum for TGB. I got a friend at the Federal Reserve to pull their financial statements over the past decade. For a local bank, they've posted impressive balances and holdings."

"How impressive?" Kell asked. "Good for a community bank or the coffers of a budding third world dictator?"

"They've met their reserve requirements easily. In fact, they had been overdoing it," he responded. "A one-hundred and fifty percent ratio."

Kell gave a low whistle. "Nice."

"Nice?" Fin repeated, confused. Hers was a cash business, and Jake handled the formalities. Not that she couldn't recall her balance down to the penny, but she'd taken careful pains to avoid learning too much of the mechanics. "Why would a ratio of one and a half be noteworthy?"

"Because most banks must have on reserve a certain amount in case of a run on assets. Like the Great Depression," Caleb explained. "But TGB had more in reserve than they do on deposit. Much more."

Fin still didn't see the problem. "So they're careful savers. I'd expect that of a good bank."

Shaking his head, Caleb laid his files on the desk and joined her on the window seat. "TGB serves Hallden County and probably has some deposits from Pike. Even if you pool all the businesses in town, together they don't generate sufficient revenue to warrant even basic deposits at that level. And here, we're talking money actually in the bank's holdings. Extra cash."

"Money coming in that hasn't been earned." Comprehension settled and Fin deduced, "They're running a shell game. Bringing in money and hiding it with the bank's real assets."

"Exactly." Caleb had reached the same conclusion, and he'd spent the morning on the phone with an investigator at the Fed. "But I said 'had.' In the last year, the ratios have dropped. Not below what's permitted, but the drain has raised alarms."

"Is there an open file on them?" Kell had pled out a client who, among his other endeavors, had been involved in a mortgage fraud scheme. She'd wrangled a plea, but it had been difficult. "Is TGB under investigation?"

"Yes, and the focus is on the bank's president. Our friend Worley."

"Either the money is going to him or to Stark." Fin angled toward Caleb, aware of the gap he'd left between them. Stretching, she grazed his hand with her leg, murmured an apology. And noted the tightening at his knuckles. Amusement glittered through her, but she merely said, "I'm not an expert in money laundering, but if I were going to hide money in a small-town bank, I'd use dummy companies. Do we know where their extra deposits come from?"

"Most of the TGB depositors who haven't touched their cash are Georgia companies. I found a couple in the Carolinas and in Florida, but Georgia is their preferred base." With undo haste, Caleb left the window seat to remove one of his files. He spread several pages on the desk and motioned the others over to examine his findings. Strategically placing himself on the opposite side from Fin, he indicated a legal-sized sheet. "I tracked companies making deposits to TGB steadily over the last ten to fifteen years."

Fin skimmed the names and lifted her head, eyes widened by the multiple listings. "There are hundreds of companies here."

"Most of them don't provide any actual service that I

could discover. Under Georgia law, all you need to open a company is a registered agent and a physical address." He jabbed a finger at a column highlighted in yellow. "What do you see?"

Kell caught it first. "The same registered agent from Macon." She shrugged. "That's not remarkable, Caleb. This Karen Tompkins is probably a professional registered agent. A nice, cushy job, accepting service on lawsuits on behalf of companies with no liability."

He'd had the same thought last night when he'd downloaded the records and dismissed the coincidence. But this morning, he'd followed a hunch. "Karen Tompkins is ninety-eight years old and legally blind. She's also housebound and lives on Social Security and Medicare. There's no way she's actually registering companies like AccuComp Technologies and Watkins Products, Inc." He circled the common address with a pen he filched from a holder on the desk. "Luke, see anything else familiar?"

Luke bent over Kell's shoulder to read the company's information, as vouched for by Karen Tompkins of 1934 Benedict Lane, Macon, Georgia. "Benedict Lane. That's the same street Pete Franklin lived on. Son of a bitch."

Pleased, Caleb drew another circle around the address. "My guess is that Franklin probably collected Mrs. Tompkins's mail for her over the years. Friendly neighbor using her as a front."

"It's brilliant." Fin straightened and gestured to the pages. "Stark sets up phony companies and launders profits through TGB. They keep their circle small, placing key folks where they are most valuable."

"Exactly. Worley at the bank. Graves at the police

department." Luke had one more name to add to the list. "Hestor at the hospital. I wanted to wait for Julia and Mrs. F, but I've got the coroner's report on Franklin." He retrieved the case and splayed the manila file next to the corporate records. "Autopsy reveals that Franklin did die of heart failure. Caused by potassium chloride."

Chilled, Fin fished the death certificate from the stack of papers chronicling a man's demise. How long, she wondered, had Franklin worked for Stark? A loyalty rewarded by an injection of poison into a system weakened by doing their bidding. She had no sympathy for the attempted murderer, but she did believe in honor among thieves. Stark didn't. Shunting aside her darkening thoughts, she asked, "Do we know anything else about Dr. Hestor?"

"Not much," Caleb said. "I did a national search on him, since he was Franklin's doctor. The only blip is an assault conviction that got sealed in Michigan." He plucked out the folder labeled *Hestor*. "What at first looked like a homicide, pled down to a misdemeanor count of assault. The DA decided his actions were improper, but not the proximate cause of his patient's death."

"Neat trick," Fin complimented and earned herself twin looks of disapproval. Only Kell smirked in agreement. "I'm just saying—"

Not giving her a chance to finish, Caleb continued. "During his residency, Hestor had a reputation for medical zeal. Would aggressively treat patients and relied heavily on the full array of Schedule II drugs at his disposal."

"He overdosed a patient," Fin guessed.

"Exactly. An elderly woman complained of multiple issues. Hestor pumped her full of a drug cocktail. She went into shock, then a coma.'"

Luke snapped, "If they knew he overprescribed, how did he get off?"

"His attorney argued that he didn't violate any of the medical protocols. Simply showed poor judgment. DA agreed that she didn't have a case, but she slapped him with the misdemeanor assault charge. Because the record was sealed, no one else would know."

"Any clue how he made it from Michigan to Hallden?" Fin asked.

Caleb shook his head at her question. He'd been hunting for more on the good doctor, but nothing had popped up yet. Intensive research demanded hours of tedium at the computer and on the phone. Far away from Fin.

Counting on it, he told them, "I'm tracking him through the medical boards, but getting information is taking a while. I should have more soon."

"Until then," Fin responded, "Kell and I can try to gather more information on the dummy companies. See if any other names or similarities emerge."

Luke gave a short laugh. "Is there anything the actual sheriff should be doing?"

"Sorry, Luke," Caleb apologized. "Old habits and all." He'd spent almost two years behind a desk prosecuting cases, and it felt damned good to be on the other side of an investigation. "Have you gotten an ID back on the second body in the Warehouse? I'm hoping we might be able to connect it to one of them personally. The setting of a fire to hide the identity of the second man was either very smart or very serious."

"I've gotten word from Atlanta that they've reached

out to your shop. The decay and the burns stumped Atlanta's lab. No place to start to hunt for dental records. But the FBI agreed to help. If you can call in a favor, we'll get the results sooner."

"Consider it done." Caleb began to gather his papers. "I'm heading to the office for the rest of the afternoon. Try me there if you need me."

Fin laid a restraining hand on his arm. "Before you leave, I'd like a word."

Caleb saw the flare of temper, understood its source. "Sure, Fin. What's up?"

His glib response echoed in his eyes, which met hers easily. Blankly.

Except when she curled her fingers around his wrist and stroked lightly. Desire flared faster than he could disguise it. It radiated in his clenched jaw, his skipping pulse. "Oh, never mind," she said, stepping away. "I've figured it out."

Before he could retaliate, a scuffle sounded next door. Caleb could clearly hear Eliza, and her tone made him feel sorry for the recipient. "You know better. All of you. I didn't raise you to be so disrespectful." A pause. "Don't say a word. Come with me."

CHAPTER 22

Behind them, the study door opened.

"In here. Now."

Dragging his attention away from Fin, Caleb saw Eliza standing in the doorway. Julia walked in, her expression grim. Close on their heels trailed Brandon, Faith, and Nina. The kids wore identical expressions of fear. One of them carried a stethoscope. Eliza pointed to the leather sofa. "Sit down right now."

Feet scraping along the carpet, they crowded onto one end of the couch. Kell sat down in her abandoned chair, and Fin claimed the second. Julia joined the kids on the sofa, leaving Caleb and Luke to stand.

"I found these three in the library," Eliza announced, walking over to Nina. "They were using Julia's equipment to listen to your conversation." She removed the scope and handed it to Julia. "I will give you exactly one minute to explain why you shouldn't all be on punishment for the next six months."

In her visibly nervous hands, Nina carried a ream of

paper, and she leaned over to whisper to her companions. Nods followed, and she answered meekly, "We were trying to help."

"Trying to help?" Eliza moved behind her desk, pride battling worry, a familiar tumult these days. "By eavesdropping?"

"We knew it was the only way you could find out what was going on." Ducking her head, Nina stared intently at her sandals.

"What do you mean?" Julia prompted.

"We've got cops outside all the time. The sheriff and Mr. Matthews come almost every day, and you go in here and close the doors," Nina explained. "We're not regular children, Mrs. F. Something big is going on. Something scary."

Eliza studied her children, then glanced at the women in the room. Hadn't she learned that lesson once? "There are dangerous men who have tried to hurt us, but I promise you, you're safe."

"We don't want to be safe," Faith interjected, fear forgotten. "We want to help."

"How would you do that?" inquired Fin, torn between pride and concern. How much did they know?

Brandon responded, "You're trying to figure out why they want to take Mrs. F's land. So, we went on the internet. Nina, tell them what you found."

"First off, we're not sorry we listened in." Nina cast a look at her compatriots, who vigorously bobbled their heads in agreement. None of them looked at Mrs. F. "Like we told Kell before, we're not regular kids. We know what it means when the cops hang around outside the center, Sheriff Luke. And"—she pinned Caleb with a long examination mature for a teenage girl—"we understand that when adults go off for discussions with law people, someone is in trouble."

Brandon spoke, his voice soft but serious. "We had to do something. We couldn't let anything happen to Mrs. F again." He gestured in a wide circle. "The three of us are the oldest, and we have a responsibility."

"Like Kell and Fin and Julia." Faith picked up. "This is our home, and we won't let them hurt Mrs. F or any one of us ever again."

"Listening to you guys was wrong, but we're not sorry for it," Nina repeated. "Anyway, after we heard about the land over near the county road, I remembered Tony telling me about that trip he made with Clay out to the forest."

"Tony?" Fin prompted.

Faith snorted. "Her boyfriend. Tony Delgado."

"He's not my boyfriend," Nina snapped, embarrassed. She glared at Faith. "We're just friends."

"Who kiss," Faith mumbled in mock disgust.

"The point is," Brandon interceded, obviously used to the dispute, "Tony told Nina about the lab he'd seen out there. After we, um, overheard you all, I asked him to describe the place and what he saw." He held out his hand to Nina, who gave him a sheet of paper. Brandon rose and walked to the desk, laying the colored sheet on top. "This is a satellite image of the area."

Fin scooted closer to the image, eyes widened in amazement. "Where'd you get this?"

"Google Maps," Brandon replied diffidently. "It's not that hard. I could show you."

"Later," Faith instructed unceremoniously. She strode

to the table, Nina in tow. "See there? That's the Metanoia Nature Preserve. Mrs. Naughton took us there on a field trip in the sixth grade."

"Yeah, and Faith was telling us how the Metanoia had some types of plants that only grew in special areas."

Faith pulled out a new picture of a tall plant bearing bright green nuts. "The tree is called jatropha. Actually, it's really a shrub. And it's poisonous. It's from Central America, but it can grow anywhere."

"Tell her why it's important," Brandon said.

"Okay, well, when jatropha seeds are crushed, scientists have discovered that the oil can be processed to produce a"—she bent over her notes—"'a high-quality biodiesel that can be used in a standard diesel car.' And the residue can be processed into biomass to power electricity plants."

Brandon pulled a pencil from behind his ear and traced a ring around the preserve. "We found an article that says if just three percent of Africa had jatropha plants, the revenue would be in the tens of billions of dollars."

While the other adults goggled, Julia beamed. "Nina, tell them what you found."

"On NPR, I heard a story about Congress. There's a big law they passed that will pay for land currently producing biofuels. Basically, the government pays the owners to try to make alternative energy." She wrinkled her nose in disbelief. "The reporter was saying that a lot of environmentalists were mad because not only will the landowners get millions of dollars for the land, they get to keep all the money from generating the biofuels."

"The Metanoia is more than five thousand acres."

Kell inclined her head toward the map, and a crease appeared between her brows. "If I'm not mistaken, a consortium of environmental groups did sue to stop the program. They've asked for an injunction. Any harvesting that hadn't begun would have to halt immediately. But the case is still pending."

"I found an article," Nina said excitedly. "The appeals court for Florida already heard the case. I forget which court number it is."

"Eleventh Circuit," Caleb supplied uneasily. "Which includes Georgia."

"That's it. The Eleventh Circuit is planning to rule on the injunction, and if it goes through, no one who isn't in the program already will be able to get any money." Triumphantly, Nina laid another sheet on top of the growing pile. "Brandon and Faith did some math. If Mrs. F let her land become part of the program, she'd make about one hundred million dollars because of how many acres are in the Metanoia. Plus, if she could actually produce fuel, she'd make even more. Like billions."

"But Mrs. F won't let them have it," Faith explained, in case the adults hadn't made the connection. "And she shouldn't."

But the adults did understand. "Billions of dollars in trees growing in their own backyard," Fin murmured. "If the injunction takes effect, it will be years before the preserve could participate, right?"

Caleb felt his blood chill. "So they've got to get the land now."

"You did a fantastic job," Fin praised the trio. "This is a tremendous help."

"What else can we do?" The question came from Faith, but the other two waited for an answer.

Eliza provided it. "You won't be doing much immediately. Brandon, you will have kitchen duty for the next week. Faith and Nina, I expect to see every window in the center sparkling by Friday." Grumbles of protest began, only to be quelled by a single look. "I'd advise you to accept your punishment gracefully, or I will be forced to consider additional measures."

"Yes, ma'am," echoed three subdued voices at the desk.

Faith lifted mischievous eyes to meet Fin's. "She make you guys do stuff like that when you got into trouble?"

"I strongly recommend you start on the second floor. Less dust," she replied conspiratorially. "And the small one in the boys' bathroom has a stain that won't come out."

Faith giggled, despite the repressive stare from Mrs. F. "Go on. Chores begin at five." At Eliza's insistence, the children trooped out of the study, leaving their research behind. As she ushered them out, she murmured to them, "Very smart work."

The others waited until the door closed, then Fin spun around to Kell. "Even if their numbers are off, Mrs. F's land is worth hundreds of millions. Is there any chance Stark already knows when the injunction will be issued?"

"They shouldn't," Kell answered, frowning. "Lower courts have guidelines for hearing cases, but they can hold a decision until they're ready."

Caleb agreed but challenged, "Stark has managed to infiltrate a bank, a police station, and possibly a hospital. Getting to an administrative clerk on the court might not be that much of a stretch." Anticipating her, he said, "I'll get a list of the court staff this afternoon."

Julia swiveled around to face him. "Can the FBI ask for a speedy injunction? Take the preserve off the table?"

"The FBI can't interfere. They've already heard oral arguments."

"But we have proof," Julia pressed. "Stark has already tried to buy the land and steal it. Clearly, they have one option left."

"Unless I convince them I can deliver the deed to them," Fin stated.

All eyes turned to Fin. "What do you mean?" Kell asked.

"I go back to Worley. Tell him I know about their plot to take the land. Promise them that if they give me a cut, I'll get the deed turned over to them."

"It's not that simple," Kell argued. "The three of us would have to give our permission. How did you convince us?"

"Yesterday's conversation with Hestor is a pretty good motivator." His sinister demands continued to ring in her ears. "I'll convince them that Mrs. F has agreed to sell it and you two signed off."

Eliza had sat quietly through the discussion, listening. Though she'd agreed to Fin's involvement, misgivings continued to wreathe her thoughts. But Fin's suggestion drove her to chime in, "Why would Stark believe I agreed to sell? I've refused for several years."

Fin exhaled, the idea forming. "Because I'm in trouble." Warming to the plan, she continued. "I told Worley I had money to transfer. I'll tell him you think I've got more debts than my money can cover."

"Debts to whom?" Eliza asked. "Is there something I should know?"

"I'm not in debt, Mrs. F, but I can make Stark think there is an angry and motivated debt collector out for my blood." She curled her lip. "I'm supposed to be a step above a con artist. For a shot at billions, I'm the kind of woman who'd sell out her own grandmother. If I had one."

Still, Caleb frowned. His stomach, typically cast iron, churned. Sending Fin inside had scraped his conscience before, but with this new information, he was raw. Stark had its sights set on a potentially billion-dollar enterprise. He'd seen bodies mutilated for less. Much less.

But if she could deceive Stark and gain proof of their members and their corruption, lives would be saved.

"Fin." He spoke quietly, his voice taut. "I realize we've had this discussion before, but I need you to listen to me. Stark is ruthless, and they're getting careless. If they make you, you're dead. I won't hold you to your agreement. Say the word and I'll call D.C. Get another agent down here."

"To do what?" Fin heard his concern for her, heard it reverberate against the panic blooming inside. But she also heard reality, and she fought off the churn of dread in her belly. "Stark won't be fooled into accepting an outsider on such a short runway. I've already made contact."

"You can change your mind," he argued, the words harsher than he intended. "Luke and I can arrange protection for everyone, put you all in hiding until the decision from the court. If there's an injunction, game's over."

"And if there isn't?" She'd run the scenarios as well.

"If the courts don't stop Stark, then what? These children, who've already lost more than you can imagine, lose their home. The only parent they've got. There won't be a new center, and everyone in this room knows there won't ever be another Eliza Faraday for them."

"But there's only one Fin," Julia murmured, too softly to be heard.

Fin swallowed the fiery ball of terror lodged in her throat, forced her voice to be even. Calm. Resolute. "Worley is going to help us break Stark, Caleb. We can't afford to waste time arguing about it anymore." She headed for the door, hoping to escape before her shields faltered.

She made it as far as the hallway.

"Fin."

She heard Caleb behind her and veered off toward the sitting room, knowing he'd follow. She held her tongue until the door shut.

The lock clicked. At the sound, she turned slowly, deliberately. Sufficient time to mask the terror grinding away at her determination. "I'm not arguing the point with you, Caleb. When Worley calls . . ." she paused, repeated, "*when* Worley calls, I'm proceeding. With or without your sanction."

"You're scared." He heard the echo in his own voice but didn't try to disguise it. His hand reached for her, but she shifted away, leaving him gripping empty air. Bringing his hand to his side, he pleaded, "Let me pull you out of this. You can tell the others I forbid it."

The suggestion startled a laugh. "Forbid? Oh, please. If I wouldn't obey Mrs. F, you haven't got a chance in hell."

"I don't want to be responsible for you getting hurt."

Her laugh this time was humorless. "Don't worry, G-Man. I'm a big girl. I had a shaky moment, but I've recovered. So no reason for worry or for rescue."

"I didn't come to rescue you, Fin." The russet eyes that had watched her with disinterest blazed with passion.

"Then what?" She took a half step back, coming to the door. "What do you want, Caleb? You set the rules."

"I want to protect you." Her vulnerability tugged at him, a stark contrast to the woman he'd first met. Both women intrigued him, and he wished he could have both. But protocol was protocol. And, for now, Fin was his responsibility. He continued, his voice brisk, "In situations like this, people get confused. Mistake chemistry for true emotions."

"Again, I'm a big girl. I know what's real and what isn't." She'd planned to tease him, to make him beg. But now, all she felt was weariness. Flattening against the silk wallpaper, she gave up. "You changed your mind about whatever was happening between us, and that's your prerogative. But I can't have you chasing me every time I have a problem. That's a job for someone who cares about more than my great legs."

"I do care about more than your legs." Caleb didn't shout. He ground out the words, advancing on her. "But I called them endless, not great."

Fin held steady, her back flat against the door. "Whatever. I don't like being used to satisfy your more basic needs, Caleb. I've discovered I deserve a bit more than that."

"I haven't used you." The mere accusation tightened his mouth with rage. "You've been with me every time. So don't feed me any crap about being used."

Caleb had had every right to take what she'd offered, because he'd promised nothing more. Had nothing to apologize for. "You're right, of course." She met his livid gaze. "You set the rules, Caleb. I'm just trying to keep up."

Dissatisfied, he laid his forehead against hers. "I do care about you. More than I should."

"Should I say I'm sorry?" Her voice was firm, her eyes dry. "It's been a long day, a long week. The FBI has its rules for a reason. I'll follow them."

Perversely, he grew angrier. "There's more going on here, Fin. Talk to me." He kept his eyes on hers, searched for answers. Another facet of her to confuse and beguile. Conviction that he should leave her alone wavered. Here she was, the woman who could hold his heart and make it race.

If she survived the dangerous course he'd charted for her. "Fin," he whispered her name as he pressed a kiss to her forehead.

"We should get back to the others." She fumbled behind her for the knob, gave him a gentle push. "I want to know everything I can before they call."

Caleb gave way, but he closed his hand on her forearm to stop her. "Last chance."

Saying nothing, she slipped out of the room.

James Worley stood stiffly by the entryway as hands twice as wide as his own stripped away his dignity, as they had his outer layer of clothing. Each time he ventured to seek an audience, the humiliating ritual repeated itself. Lifting his arms, he felt the probe of cruel fingers into his armpits; he wanted to point out that he sweat too much to wear a wire there.

The investigation continued, and he focused his eyes on the samurai swords crossed on the mantel on the other side of the office. He'd always admired the artistry of the Japanese. In every craft, from forging metal to making money, they attacked their chosen profession with a keen attention to detail and a flair for beauty.

One day soon, when he cashed out, he planned to take his wife to Japan. They'd start in Tokyo, hire a guide and spend six months touring the islands. The trip he'd priced cost nearly twenty-seven million yen— about two hundred and fifty thousand dollars, give or take a yen or two. In his office at home, a box half the size of this one, he'd crammed bookcases with Japanese phrase books, erotic anime, and histories of the shogun. As a member of Stark, he fancied himself one of the American Yakuza.

Like the Japanese crime lords, Stark had a strict code of honor and behavior. Funds were to be spent carefully, not lavishly. Purchase a new house, but not more than one every five years, and with a limited increase in square footage. Vacations were permitted; however, locales should not invite inquiry. The contract he'd signed clearly delineated the roles of a Stark member and the consequences for failure.

Which is why he had to convince them to accept his plan.

The physical assault ceased and his clothing was returned. James shivered in the cold gusts of air blowing, and he eagerly shoved his feet into his shoes. "Ready," he announced unnecessarily. The goon, who also worked as baliff in the superior court, watched him re-dress as closely as he had when James had stripped down to his boxers.

He scurried behind the hulking man, skipping occasionally to keep pace. James had often wondered why Judge Majors was permitted to live in such lavish style. No requirements for muted wealth were observed here. He'd worked in a museum during college, and he recognized the value of the objets d'art. Jade shone from recessed nooks. Vases and paintings with soaring insurance values were scattered throughout the estate.

He'd heard rumors of old money, more often of the hoarded shares of Stark members expelled by her for some infraction. All six current members enjoyed a steady income, inviolate security against harm, and a generous retirement at the age of sixty. However, with James's help, they expected to cash out early, per Her Majesty's command.

But the money wasn't there.

The giant halted in front of the black-glass-paneled door. He didn't knock, and James knew to stand silently and wait for admittance. Soon enough, the panels whisked wide on hidden gliders. He stepped inside, and the bailiff disappeared.

Around the long sweep of table, four chairs were occupied. The fifth was his. The sixth belonged to Michael Graves, a deserter who'd forfeited his profits. Years before, there had been eleven chairs filled. None of the missing had died of natural causes.

James did not intend to lose his seat.

He sat at the table, next to Silas Hestor. "Good evening, ladies and gentlemen."

Murmurs greeted him in muted fashion. From the center of the table, Judge Majors spoke. "I received your request for a gathering, Worley. I trust you bring us good news."

"I believe so," he began. "Today I received a visit from Fin Borders and Kell Jameson."

Though no one made an audible sound, James sensed the mixed reactions and continued. "Ms. Borders requested my assistance with the transfer of sensitive assets. She'd prefer to not have too much attention drawn to them."

"Why did she come to you?" Hestor inquired in a pleasant tone that did not reach his flat black eyes. "During my conversation with her last night, your name didn't come up."

"According to her, she had to depart from her last location quickly and did not have time to make the necessary arrangements." He focused his attention on Ernest King, who sat in the third chair. "She remembers us from the Warehouse."

Ernest sucked at his teeth. "Blackmail?"

"Nothing of the kind." James recounted the conversation and the scene with the sheriff. "They left her on the steps of the bank. She was very unhappy."

"Do you think she can be trusted?" asked the other woman in the room. Ingrid Canton, associate editor of the *Hallden Telegraph,* had the striking looks of a woman who'd turned heads in her prime. Wheat blond hair had begun to gray, the journey halted by a standing appointment in Macon. Green eyes, as clear and cutting as Depression glass, watched him coolly. "If she can assist with our land acquisition, that would dispense with the need for more violence."

Hestor leaned forward. "And if she can't?"

"Then we'll likely act." She smiled at him, the curve of lips as insincere as her eyes. "Can we trust her, James?"

He shook his head. "I don't know yet, but I believe she can be manipulated. She was always the wildest of the three, the one with the most flexible character."

"And she does make her living as a gambler," Ingrid reminded the table. "Which likely means she has other, more prurient habits we can exploit if necessary."

Mary nodded. "I visited with Eliza the other day. Fin has already shown herself to be a nuisance. We can definitely use her. I'm assigning James and Silas to work on her separately. A little competition. I want the deed to the preserve by next Friday."

"Next Friday?" James swallowed. "Why the hurry?"

"Good question." Mary steepled her fingers, nails clicking in a faint dirge. "As you are well aware, our future has been jeopardized by your careless enthusiasm. Sheriff Calder and ADA Matthews have been making inquiries. Not just into Franklin's death, but into our companies. We haven't much time. You should be certain we are prepared to move according to our schedule."

"I understand." And he did. A failure with Fin would mean a solitary voyage to Japan for Gladys Worley. "I won't let you down."

CHAPTER 23

"Fin, your phone is ringing," Julia called through the closed bathroom door. Inside, the shower jets pounded, blocking the jazzy tone. Julia lifted the slim black case and flipped the receiver open. "Fin Borders's phone."

"Ms. Borders, please."

Julia hadn't glanced at the number, so she inquired, "May I ask who's calling?"

"James Worley. The Georgia Bank."

Though she itched to snap the phone shut, Julia forced herself to remain cordial. "If you'll hold on a moment, Mr. Worley, I'll see if I can locate her."

"Thank you. I'd appreciate that."

The rich Southern accent sounded genteel, nearly masking the man's impatience. Julia lay the phone on the bed and hurried to the bathroom. She twisted the knob, poked her head inside. "Fin!" she hissed to the drawn shower curtain. "Fin!"

A scowling face covered in a light blue goop appeared.

"What? I've only been in here five minutes. I swear I won't use all the hot water."

"No, no. It's Worley. On the phone for you. Should I take a message?"

Anticipation settled with a solid thud in Fin's chest, and alarm squeezed her throat like a fist. Bank presidents didn't call at 7:00 a.m. to decline business. She was in. Phase two had begun. Keeping her voice level, anxiety banked, she instructed, "Tell him I'll be right with him."

Julia gave a tentative nod, knowing it was too late to caution, to alter course. "Sure."

Inside the shower, Fin held her face up to the warm spray, scrubbing away cleanser and doubts. They'd stayed up well into the night, rehearsing answers and scouring Caleb's files for ammunition. At this point, she knew nearly as much about TGB as Worley did. About the dozen or so companies that made regular and steady deposits, never withdrawing their funds. Abandoned accounts dating back to the late 1980s, cash lying unclaimed in the bank's coffers. And modest, discreet withdrawals, irregular sums with regular timing, from other depositors handled by the duped Karen Tompkins.

Sluicing water over the rest of her, she emerged from the shower in a rush and grabbed a towel. Swathed in its folds, she flew into the bedroom and accepted the cell phone from Julia. "Mr. Worley." Her tone held no hint of breathlessness, no indication other than polite greeting. "Good morning."

"Morning to you, Ms. Borders. I hope I didn't pull you away from breakfast or anything."

"No, nothing so pleasant." She eased down onto the bed, hand folded over the edge of the towel beneath her arm. "What has you up so early? I thought banker's hours began at nine."

"Modern era, I'm afraid. I'm up by dawn to watch the Nikkei on cable. Fascinating stuff, the making of money."

"I agree. Though I much prefer the spending of it myself."

Worley chortled in appreciation. "My wife would agree with you. She takes spending my money as a personal mission. One I'm happy to finance."

Taking the initiative, Fin prompted, "I hope you're calling with good news, Mr. Worley."

"James." He settled deep into the leather chair behind his desk. One hand rested on the dossier compiled on Findley Borders, a read more intriguing than he'd first realized. "Please call me James, as we'll be working together to resolve your financial . . . um, shall we say . . . needs."

Relief coursed through Fin, and she replied dulcetly, "Then you should call me Fin." She glanced at the clock, noting the hour. "My business manager is in Europe, but I've alerted him that I might be transferring funds soon. Shall I meet you at the bank this morning?"

"I've got a few clients coming in at nine, then a weekly staff meeting. I was hoping I could invite you to lunch and we could review your portfolio. The Georgia Bank prides itself on its array of products. I'd like to walk through several of your options with you."

Lunch would give her an opportunity to probe for more details on the bank's structure and tease out de-

tails on Worley. "I'd be delighted. Shall I meet you at
the bank?"

"Perfect." He scribbled her name onto his blotter.
"How about eleven forty-five? I have a standing reser-
vation at the Magnolia on Tuesdays. Delicious fried
chicken."

"Sounds great. Thank you, Mr. Worley. I mean James."

"Have a good morning, Fin."

Fin shut the phone and turned to Julia, who watched
her with anxious eyes. Knowing she couldn't show the
same, Fin intentionally brightened her tone. "He took
the bait."

"So I gathered." Julia extended a cup of coffee to Fin.
Steam rose from its surface. Julia recognized the hard
gleam in Fin's eyes. Doctors' eyes sometimes carried
the same excitement, the thrust of adrenaline and the
challenge of the moment. When it dissipated, when the
patient had been saved or lost, the crash was brutal.
"How will you get to the bank?"

They hadn't discussed the car situation last night, but
Fin had been thinking about it. Kell had an appearance
in Atlanta, and Mrs. F planned to take the children to
the amusement park for the day. Julia had drawn chap-
erone duty, leaving Fin to her own devices until her
lunch with Worley. "Mrs. F has her Spitfire. I thought
I'd coax her into letting me borrow it."

"Last time you 'borrowed' her car, the police had to
tow it from the field near Planters Lake," Julia reminded
her with a grin. "If she lets you use it this time, remember to buy gas, and don't accept any dares."

"Misti Atwood shouldn't have spouted off at the
mouth about her father's Thunderbird. Especially when
she didn't know how to drive a stick."

"And you shouldn't have been caught with her boyfriend behind the school." Julia, who'd been up and dressed for hours, stood. "Finish your shower, and I'll go prime Mrs. F."

Julia sailed from the room, and Fin felt her grin fade. She trudged into the bathroom and finished preparing for the day. As she brushed on mascara, she noted the shadows forming beneath her eyes. Shadows that owed nothing to Worley and Stark and everything to a restless night thinking about Caleb.

Their fight in the sitting room had left her wrung out, but she'd managed to work shoulder to shoulder with him for hours. Trying not to recall how his mouth had moved against hers, how his hands maddened with their hunger.

How he could see into her faster, more astutely than anyone before. She prided herself on her sangfroid, her ability to skate above the tumult untouched. An ability that vanished when she was with him.

Accepting the inevitable, she reached for the phone, tapped in numbers she'd committed to memory.

"Matthews here."

The husky rasp of sleep skidded her imagination into overdrive. "Worley called. He wants to meet."

Caleb shot up in bed, wide awake. "When? Where?"

"We're having lunch at Magnolia, eleven forty-five."

"You ready?"

"Aye, aye, Captain. Today is just a friendly conversation. A salad, a wire transfer, and a casual mention of banking laws."

"I'm not happy about using your own money, Fin. If you'll give me a couple of days, I'll secure funds from the Bureau."

"We both know they won't agree to park that much money into one of my accounts, Caleb. You might trust me, but they won't."

"I do trust you, Fin. You know that, right?"

Warmth—a gooey, sappy warmth that had her sitting on the edge of the tub—spread through her. "Same here."

"Is that an admission, Ms. Borders?"

Though he couldn't see it, she grinned. "I find you worth believing, sure."

"Try not to gush. My head could swell."

Laughing, Fin conceded, "I do admire your style. In a purely platonic way." With that taunt, she disconnected the phone, eyes dancing. She finished her makeup and returned to the bedroom to dress.

From the shared closet, she chose slim pants in black paired with a pinstriped vest that cinched her waist with a wide black belt. After arranging her hair into a semblance of order, she left the bedroom to convince Mrs. F to relinquish the Spitfire's keys.

Chatter led her into the dining room, where pent-up excitement fairly bounced around the oversized space. Bowls of cereal and plates of eggs and breakfast meat disappeared along with carafes of orange juice. Dodging a mad scramble for the last link of sausage, Fin circled the table to reach Eliza. She waited patiently while a fluffy napkin, no longer white, gently swabbed at chocolate milk stains above a toddler's mouth.

"Can you handle all of them by yourself?" Fin asked with a worried frown. Since she'd left, the center had expanded to almost twenty children, ranging in age from four to sixteen. "Don't you need reinforcements?"

With a chuckle, Eliza tucked the child into a booster

seat and skimmed the length of the table for more mishaps. "We'll be fine. Faith, Brandon, and Julia are on call, and Luke has assigned Cheryl Richardson to accompany us. She's bringing along her husband and their two boys. Plenty of support."

Still dubious, Fin arched out of the way as a boy, then a girl, streaked past. As they made a second pass, Fin snagged the little boy by the scruff of his collar.

The girl, whom Fin identified as Lara O'Connor, had him by an inch. Lara lifted her fork, tines down. "Take it back!" she barked. "Take it back right now."

"Will not!" Jorden snapped, yanking against Fin's hold. "You stole it!"

"Did not!"

"Lara, don't stab Jorden with your fork," Eliza ordered mildly. "Jorden, what are you accusing Lara of this time?"

"She stole my marbles. I left them on the back porch and they're gone. She took 'em."

Lara whipped around to Mrs. F. "I didn't touch his stupid marbles. He's lying."

"Did so!"

"Did not!"

Fin grimaced. She'd gone out to the backyard to reflect and had stumbled on the cloth sack, spilling multicolored marbles onto the deck. "Actually, I'm the culprit, Jorden. I picked up a sack of marbles last night. Found them outside and thought someone had forgotten to bring them in. They're in the playroom, on the shelf."

Robbed of his anger, Jorden dropped his shoulders. "Oh. Thanks, Miss Fin."

"And what do you have to say to Lara?"

"That she probably would've taken 'em if she could," he sneered unrepentantly.

Eliza caught the girl's raised hand before she completed her arc. "Try again, Jorden."

"Sorry for saying you stole my marbles," he grumbled, eyes downcast.

Placated, Lara relinquished her fork into Eliza's waiting palm. "Okay." She waited a beat before asking Jorden, "Wanna shoot a game before we go?" She smiled winningly at Eliza. "We're done eating and our beds are made," she implored.

"Be ready to go when I call." Before they could go, she added sternly, "No more threatening people with forks, Lara."

"Yes, ma'am."

Released, the duo sprinted out of the dining room. Eliza laid Lara's makeshift weapon on the planked wood. "Did you need something, Fin?"

Feeling as old as Jorden, Fin shifted on her five-hundred-dollar heels. "Can I borrow your car, Mrs. F? I haven't gotten around to renting one, and I've got an appointment in town at noon."

Worry about Fin's meeting filtered into the corner of Eliza's heart where she kept all her fears for Fin. However, she'd decided to keep them unspoken, to lessen the burden Fin carried. Instead, she stood and began to stack dishes. "The last time you borrowed my car, I distinctly recall forbidding you to ever sit inside it again," Eliza reminded her plainly. "Particularly as I hadn't given permission the first time."

Fin gathered discarded cups, turning an empty platter into a carrying tray. "Come on, Mrs. F. I'm a much better driver now."

"Driving wasn't the issue before, as I recall. I believe it was stopping."

"I promise to be careful." She'd admired the Spitfire for years and still remembered her one turn behind the wheel. "Please?" Fin wheedled.

Pushing through the swinging door into the kitchen, Eliza relented. "My keys are in the study, top drawer."

"Thanks, Mrs. F." Fin smacked a kiss against Eliza's cheek. "I appreciate it."

"Be careful, Findley." Eliza permitted herself the dual warning, her eyes catching, holding Fin's. "Make it back safely."

"I will."

Near their appointed time, Fin slipped the two-seater into to a reserved space in front of the bank. The cerulean blue sky showed no hint of rain, tempting her to leave the top down. The Magnolia B&B was a couple of blocks away, and she assumed they'd walk from his office. She was early, a trait that belonged to Kell more than Fin. But with the center empty, she'd been too fidgety to stay inside.

Today would only be lunch, but the entire venture hinged on her. Worley had to trust her, to buy her desperation and her avarice—a bluff she'd managed before, but the stakes had risen dramatically.

Eyes shut behind tinted glasses, she searched for the cold center, where she stored pointless sensations like panic and dread. Where she'd tucked away the mystery of Caleb Matthews and her growing attachment.

"Penny for your thoughts."

Fin should have been surprised, but she wasn't. She drew down her oversized shades to rest on the tip of her nose. "Shouldn't you be prosecuting jaywalkers, Caleb?"

He curved his hand around the windowsill, rested his arm on the warm metal frame. He'd been crossing the square on his way to the courthouse when she'd tooled around in the snazzy green convertible. When she hadn't gotten out, he'd detoured.

"Is this the one?" he asked, admiring the sleek contours of the British import.

"The one?"

"That Mrs. F took you to Autry in."

Pleasantly moved that he remembered, she nodded. "She was less than thrilled when I drove it myself for the first time, so getting to take it out today is a huge concession on her part."

"I'm fairly certain you could convince Satan to loan you the keys to hell, Fin."

"I'm not sure if I should be insulted."

He smiled. "You're flattered."

"Maybe. But you should work on your lines."

Taking the shades from her nose, he murmured, "I like you, Findley Borders."

"Why?"

The bald, honest question gripped him, stirred him. "Because you are brave, beautiful, and devious. Because that heart of yours has more capacity than you'll ever acknowledge." He straightened before he gave in to the urge to kiss the stunned, parted lips. "Go inside before I do something I won't regret."

"Caleb." She said his name, unsure of what would follow.

"Go inside, Fin. Do good."

CHAPTER 24

"Ms. Borders, right on time." James Worley clasped her hands in his.

The gesture should have been gallant, but it seemed officious instead. Fin remained captive despite the tendril of unease. "I appreciate you fitting me into your schedule."

"My pleasure." Tucking her purloined fingers into his arm, he told the receptionist, "Ms. Meredith, please begin paperwork for Ms. Borders for her new accounts."

Katie gave a polite nod, but Fin saw the gleam of gratification. She considered the younger woman's role briefly, then dismissed her as a suspect. Given the pattern they'd established for Stark, recruiting another person inside the bank would be unnecessary.

Worley led her across the polished floor. "Was that ADA Matthews with you outside?"

"It was." Explaining Caleb had been part of her plan. "He's spending a great deal of time at the center. The Graves matter. He's shown an *interest* in me."

"That you share?"

"That I find useful." Her point made, she asked, "Where to for lunch?"

Accepting the information, Worley responded, "Magnolia's. Every day for lunch. I'm a creature of remarkable habit."

"While I enjoy caprice."

Steering her, he inquired, "I understand you've been away from home for a long time."

Fin exited ahead through the glass door, waiting to answer until he joined her on the stone steps. "Hallden is a quaint place, but I've become partial to the pace of the city."

"Where do you call home?"

"Home is where the action is," she rejoined. "Wouldn't you agree?"

"Well, now, Hallden isn't New York, but we're moving forward," he bragged, mimicking the Chamber of Commerce's current theme. They strolled along the sidewalk, Worley extolling the town's virtues, nodding to passersby, who greeted him with varying degrees of friendliness.

Her memories of him had faded with time; his amiability, however, was familiar. She recalled Worley as a ruddy-faced, middle-aged man with a receding hairline and a habit of underplaying strong hands. A rock who'd folded when anyone's ace had been showing. Night after night, he'd let himself be bullied out of a pot, even by a teenage novice.

Ernest King, on the other hand, had fancied himself a shark. He'd preyed on Worley's rickety confidence to take his chips. Later, Fin learned that men like King were actually referred to in the trade as lotto players—guys who'd chase a card down a black hole, playing anything they were dealt. Among amateurs like Worley and the Warehouse's regular guests, he'd run the table. Against her today, he'd be sucking wind by the third turn of the river.

Soon, they reached the Magnolia. Before Worley touched the front door, it was whisked open. A plump matron with vivid auburn hair and lake blue eyes welcomed them inside. "Mr. Worley," she cooed, "your table is ready."

The blue eyes lasered in on Fin, then the brows lifted in comic shock. "Well, as I live and breathe, Fin Borders really is back."

Fin blinked once, then dismal recognition set in. "Anamaria Akins?"

Over her head, Ingrid Canton beckoned to James. He gave a short nod and turned to Fin. "Will you excuse me for a moment?"

"Of course," Fin replied, trapped. Resigned, she pasted on a smile. "So, Anamaria Akins. How are you?"

"Just Ana these days. Anamaria is a mouthful for my customers. Actually, my last name is Philpot." A modest diamond fluttered on round, white fingers. Acquisitive blue eyes checked for a matching jewel on Fin's naked fingers. "Haven't caught yourself a man yet?"

"I prefer to catch and release."

Ana twittered, mildly irritated. Fin Borders had been the Jezebel of high school, entrapping boys with a sinful ease. "I couldn't wait. Graduated in May, married in September. You do remember Jason Philpot, the high school quarterback?" Who'd once drunkenly called out Fin's name while they'd groped in his backseat.

Because "no" seemed rude, Fin smiled noncommit-

tally. Jason Philpot, like most of his ilk, had left her
cold. She'd run track, which had put her in the vicinity
of the high school cheerleaders and jocks. By mutual
agreement, vicinity had rarely strayed into company.
Ana, head cheerleader, however, had been a thorn in
Kell's side. Lucky for the silly redhead, she'd been terrified of Fin.

Fright forgotten, Ana fairly twinkled, a feat that
amazed Fin, who preferred the terror. In high-pitched
tones that could scare dogs, Ana gushed, "I heard you
were in Hallden. With Kell home too, she must be so
excited to see you. And that other girl who used to follow you two around."

"Julia. Her name is Julia."

"Oh, yes. Julia." A rich, snobby child who'd garnered
everyone's sympathies with her big brown eyes. Ana
despised her. "When did you arrive?"

"Flew in last week from France. Cannes."

Jason had taken Ana to Miami once on vacation. Ten
years ago. "Are you going to be working at the bank?"
Ana asked, glancing around for Worley, who was approaching the maitre d's stand. "Is that what you do
now? Banking?"

Fin let her mouth curve. "No, I'm a professional gambler. Mainly poker."

Scandalized, Ana gaped. "Really?"

"Really." She touched Worley's arm. "Ready?"

Worley, who found Ana a bit cloying, appreciated the
effect. "All taken care of." They walked to their table,
and he clenched his teeth as they passed the booth
where Ingrid dined with Hestor. Though they claimed
to have already had the meal on the calendar, he couldn't
help but resent the supervision. His stupid mistake with

Franklin would haunt him until he salvaged the preserve project with Fin, either through Stark or Graves. He hadn't decided which, but the thought of making Hestor rich turned his ample stomach.

"James." Hestor called to him, forcing him to stop. "Who's your beautiful companion?"

Fin recognized the trill of syllables, as he'd intended. "I'm Fin Borders. And you?"

"Dr. Silas Hestor. A pleasure to meet you."

The hand extended to her was olive-toned, with a narrow palm and long fingers. Perfect for playing the piano or wielding a scalpel. She accepted the handshake, fighting off repulsion. "Nice to meet you."

"I'm Ingrid Canton."

A stone twice the size of Ana's flashed in white brilliance. On her right hand. "Lovely diamond."

"Only the best." Ingrid went with impulse. "What do you do, Fin?"

"I play poker. Professionally."

"Don't suppose you'd have any interest in joining our little neighborhood game one night?"

"As long as the table stakes are within my means, I'd be delighted. Need to keep my skills sharp."

Hestor asked, "Are you in town for a vacation or an extended stay?"

"Depends on the opportunities. If Mr. Worley is as helpful as I imagine, I might be changing occupations."

"I'm the assistant editor for the local paper. We'd love to run a story on you. We don't get many returnees to Hallden."

"Give me a call. I'm staying at the center." Fin turned to James. "I think our table is waiting. A pleasure to meet you both."

Relieved, James led her to his usual table. Menus appeared in their hands, and Ana ran through the daily specials. Worley admired Fin's swift perusal and firm orders. A woman who knew what she wanted. His libido stirred, incited equally by the tailored shirt that left her arms bare. Gladys hadn't been able to sport a top like that even when he'd married her. The shimmery material emphasized a waist he could span with his hands.

"James?"

Realizing his name had been repeated, he jolted. "Oh, yes. My order. The daily special, thank you."

"And your usual to drink?"

"Of course. Thank you, Ana."

They were alone in a corner booth, and Fin waited for him to speak. Although she required his assistance, she couldn't afford to appear completely vulnerable. Controlling the conversation lay in not rushing to fill the silence. She would let him come to her before she permitted him to save her.

"I did my homework on you, Fin." Worley shifted on the padded bench, his hands folded on the table. "You've had quite a career."

She inclined her head. "Excitement is addictive. Sometimes I lost my head."

"Like in Las Vegas?" The arrest had confirmed his recollection of her wilder bent. She'd been arrested twice more, none of the arrests with conviction. Proof of better skills rather than a change of heart. "Or Los Angeles?"

Fin pouted slightly, dimple appearing. "We all have our heads turned, don't we, James? Minor errors in judgment." She met his gaze steadily. "I'm a very careful woman these days, but there is some urgency to my request. If TGB is not the appropriate place for me, I can make other arrangements."

James savored the edge of panic, smoothly controlled. "According to banking regulations, I'll be required to report your financial transactions. You've been flagged."

Showing her first visible hint of concern, she let her fingers move restively. "I assumed as a community bank, you might have been less . . . visible . . . to the feds."

Satisfied by the flicker of distress, he smiled genially. "I have a measure of discretion," he conceded. "While I don't condone any illicit behavior, I do understand that our banking regulations in America have become a wee bit tedious."

"What avenues are available to a valuable customer?"

Satisfied, he laid out terms. "For a premium, we can assist with the relocation of assets. This will require specific investments for you, as a matter of protocol. I will advise on the purchases and will monitor your accounts personally."

"Timing?"

"We could accomplish most of the transactions by Friday." Suddenly, he covered her hand with his own, squeezing lightly. "The board of my bank dislikes attention, Fin. Will anyone be looking for your assets?"

Fin translated the question easily. Had she stolen the money? With a genuine grin, she shook her head. "I excel in my profession. Every dollar, yen, and euro are mine. I may have some exotic interests, but the revenue is my own."

Before he could push for details, their meal arrived. James waited impatiently for the server to leave. "Exotic interests?"

Fin lifted a bite of salad to her lips and smiled allur-
ingly. "One step at a time, James."

Caleb stood in the shadows of the courthouse, staring
into the Magnolia B&B. In a cozy booth in the back,
Fin tipped her head in a laugh. Her face, angled in the
light, bolted lust through him. He could hear the sultry
notes, as though he'd been inside with her. Which he
should be. Though, apparently, she and the crooked
James Worley were fast friends.

"Look any harder and I'll have to assume you're casing the joint." Luke stood on the sidewalk, leaning on a
parking meter. "See anything interesting?"

"Everything seems to be just fine. Hunky-freaking-
dory."

The muttered complaint amused Luke, but he knew
better than to smile. "Why don't you let me buy you a
root beer?"

Caleb met Luke's eyes, saw the laughter. "Am I that
pathetic?"

Shrugging, Luke responded, "Pretty close, but it's
not your fault." He started down the sidewalk toward
the general store. "The women at the Faraday Center
are lethal, man."

"Is it in the water?"

Luke chuckled. "If it is, Mrs. F should bottle it." He
thought of Kell, and his grin widened. "On second
thought, it should probably be regulated. Too much
could ruin an entire generation of men."

"But what a way to go." Caleb matched the sheriff's
long strides with his own. At six foot two, he rarely met
men taller than he. Or women who could look him in
the eye. His mind flashed to Fin and the scene in the

sitting room. She'd met him head-on. Then he recalled the flash of humiliation when she'd accused him of using her.

Blindly, he followed Luke into the store and took a seat at the old-fashioned counter. The white-capped teenager filled their orders and left them at their isolated end.

Luke lifted his mug. After a second, Caleb joined the toast. "To Kell and Fin. Riddles wrapped in mysteries wrapped in the sexiest damned enigmas to ever grace the earth."

"Cheers." Caleb gulped down the cold drink, wishing it had been stronger. "I don't understand why this is so damned hard. I just met her last week."

"That's how they get you." Luke heard the twist of longing and the deeper cadence he'd heard in his own voice. "They make it impossible not to fall in love. Time is irrelevant."

Caleb jerked his head up. "Am I that transparent?"

"Only once you've been there." Luke clapped his shoulder in commiseration. "Without becoming too personal, man, I'd like to offer some advice."

"Go for it."

"When I met Kell, it felt like I'd been kicked in the gut. Then I realized the ache kept spreading. She was on my mind all the time, even when she was pissing me off."

"Hmm."

"I couldn't figure out what I saw in this woman who flouted every rule I believed in." Then, being honest with himself, he tacked on, "She stayed a step ahead of me, and when I caught up, she moved with me. I didn't think she needed my help—a hard place for men like us."

"How did you handle it?"

"By accepting that they've lived lives more devastating than words could ever tell us. Kell took her wretched childhood and became a champion for the weak. Julia channeled her trauma into becoming a healer." He took a drink, letting Caleb finish it.

Caleb frowned. "And Fin is a fighter. So damned contrary. She doesn't wait for a blow. She sticks out her chin and dares you."

"Because she's had to. No one had taken care of her before Eliza." Luke didn't expound. What Kell had told him about Fin's past was hers to share.

Caleb admired the discretion, but it frustrated him. "I can't take advantage of that courage and look myself in the eye." Raggedly, he poured the contents of the glass down his throat. He'd wrestled with the question, tying himself up in the facts. This case had him trading Fin's well-being for the benefit of others. "We've got regulations about getting involved. How am I any different than the others who've put her last if I can't at least protect her from me?"

Understanding had Luke gripping Caleb's shoulder. "The best way to protect Fin, I think, is to stand with her but let her do what she has to."

"Are you sure?"

"Worked with Kell, but that's no guarantee." Luke drained his glass and stood, his grin sympathetic. "Last piece of ten-cent advice. When you're taking on a gambler, you've got to come in on her blind side."

Caleb sighed. "And since it's Fin, I'd better duck."

CHAPTER 25

By the following Monday afternoon, Fin's hand ached from scribbling her signature across dozens of forms in triplicate. Her rainy-day fund, as her business manager forlornly termed it, had been vigorously diversified into a handful of corporations scattered from Atlanta to Charlotte to Miami. Corporations she and Caleb had tracked through layers of misdirection to the home of Karen Tompkins.

While the research had been mind-numbing, spending time with Caleb had had its own compensations. She'd discovered a laconic wit that could skewer and a capacity for whimsy that enchanted. Over late-night hot dogs, she'd learned about his sick fascination for medical shows and their gory details. Julia had been delighted to find a kindred spirit, and Fin had vowed to hide the remote control.

He'd regaled her with stories of his childhood, coaxed out tales of her adventures. They'd laughed, shared meals, and swapped secret dreams. And yet, during the stretches of hours spent together, he hadn't touched her. Not once, even in the most innocent manner. At first, she'd thought it was her imagination, until Kell had made a comment last night.

Kell had sprawled across Julia's bed, legs kicked up while red paint had been drying on her toenails. Julia had been curled against the headboard, mending a tattered doll for Casey, one of the younger children. No one had commented on the incongruity of a skilled surgeon's hands darning a cheap rag doll. Fin had occupied the rocking chair, a thick file open on her lap, given to her by Caleb on his evening visit.

"It was nice of Caleb to bring over dinner," Julia had said. "I'd forgotten there was food you couldn't spell your name in."

"He's doing an excellent job of keeping his hands to himself," Kell had noted. "Like at dinner tonight. He nearly knocked the wine into my lap to avoid handing it to you."

Empathetic, Julia had given Kell a warning jab with her heel and had asked kindly, "Do you want to talk about it?"

Frustration had propelled Fin out of the chair, which she'd chosen because her own bed had been a tangled disaster. She hadn't wanted to be in it, and, it seemed, neither had Caleb. "Platonic colleagues. That's our agreement."

"How's that working out?"

"Miserably."

"Which one of you is the most miserable?" Julia had set aside her needle and thread. "I've seen the way he looks at you, Fin. All smoldering eyes and longing." She'd given a dramatic sigh, hand over her heart. "If a man who looked like him looked at me that way, I'd have *him* for dinner."

"Jules!" Kell had whipped her head around in mock appall. "I didn't think you had such prurient fantasies."

"And a vivid imagination," Julia had laughed with a caricature-like waggling of her brows.

"I'd hoped proximity would convince him that we weren't being fooled by our hormones," Fin had grumped, dropping down onto the clean bed. "We've spent every waking moment together, except when I've been trapped at the bank with Worley. Caleb tells terrible jokes, but I laugh. Lord, I even think some of them are funny."

Kell and Julia had exchanged smug looks over Fin's downcast head. "Fin, honey?"

Fin had looked warily at Kell. "What?"

"Have you fallen in love with him?"

Her recoil had been instant and comic. "Absolutely not!"

"Are you sure?" Julia had pressed gently. "Because when he's not devouring you with his eyes, you're usually doing the same."

"I've spent two weeks with the man. I like him and I want him, but most of the time, we've been face deep in files."

"And the rest of the time?"

Fin had said nothing, knowing they'd draw their own conclusions.

She'd studiously avoided coming to any of her own.

Mercifully, school had begun, leaving the center deserted. Julia coaxed Eliza into a spa day, an excuse for

Julia to bum a ride with Kell into Atlanta to shop. Hearing that Fin would be alone most of the day, Caleb and Luke decided that Caleb would babysit.

After a token protest, Fin yielded. She'd been stuck inside Worley's office that morning, evading questions and accidental touches. The man had eight hands, and all of them had found a way to graze her ass.

She'd escaped by noon with a calendar that required nothing more taxing than reviewing bank statements linked to the corporate accounts. Working with Caleb had stripped bare any romanticism in the world of detective work. This was a mind-numbing chore of paper pushing.

Eyes crossing from boredom, aching muscles tensed from hours of bending over endless reports, she shoved away from the desk that had become Command Central. Knuckling the cramped knots, she gave her head a slow roll.

"Let me do that." Caleb moved behind her, kneading along her spine.

She jumped as though stabbed.

"Did I hurt you?" he inquired, concerned.

"No," Fin managed. "You just surprised me." Especially since it was the first time he'd touched her in an interminable, frustrating week. "Thanks."

"My pleasure." With his thumbs, Caleb sought out the ridges of muscle and coaxed them into softening. For a solid week, he'd kept his hands to himself, giving them both physical space. Taking Luke's advice to heart, he'd tried to guess what Fin wouldn't expect. So, rather than making love to her in the million ways he'd imagined, he'd kept their interactions platonic or populated.

The longest week of his life.

But, given the low purring beneath his massage, worth every cold shower and torrid dream.

When her head fell forward, the scent of her rose between them. He'd begun to wake dreaming of the heady blend of sultry and sweet, uniquely Fin. Unable to resist, he lowered his mouth to the exposed line of her nape.

"Oh," she sighed as he nuzzled one bundle of nerves, unraveled another. In a hushed silence, she gave herself to his ministrations, twin assaults on her senses that asked only that she enjoy. Slowly, inexorably, he eased her between the taut cradle of his thighs, her hip teasing him to hardened arousal.

He traced the planes of her shoulders, creeping around to the inviting fullness of her breasts beneath a fabric so thin as to be indecent. It shifted easily as he caressed shadows below the enticing curves.

Like flame, she twisted in his hands, trying to capture the feather-light touch. Ready to be caught, Caleb tautened his hold.

The doorbell pealed.

His breathing unsteady, Caleb lowered his chin to her shoulder. "If we stand very still, they'll go away."

Tempted, Fin tipped her head to allow his teeth to nibble at her ear.

The bell rang a second time, followed by a determined knock.

"Damn." Reluctantly, Caleb stood, waiting for the piercingly sweet ache to subside, but he doubted it ever would as long as he was around Fin. Instead, he took her hand and they went to answer the door.

"Luke?" Fin saw his grim expression and imagined the worst. "Did something happen to Kell? Mrs. F?"

"No, nothing like that," he replied hurriedly, taking his hat off. In his other hand, he carried an oversized blue envelope. "Can I come in?"

"Of course." Fin shifted to admit him, her fingers still linked with Caleb's. "Do you need a drink or something? You look terrible."

Luke hesitated. "Let's go into Mrs. F's study. Maybe you can get three glasses."

"What's going on, Luke?" Caleb felt Fin's fingers tremble. "If something has happened, spill it."

Years of delivering the most horrible news had never eased the burden of the job. Experience had taught Luke that it was best to come out with the facts straight off, to soothe and comfort later. Standing in the foyer, he noted the tangle of their hands and released a sigh. "Caleb, we got the forensic analysis back from Virginia." He extended the envelope. "There's no easy way to tell you this. They identified the body as Special Agent Eric Baldwin."

The world fell away. He'd known for five years that Eric was dead. Had grieved for his lost partner and pledged to avenge his murder. In the seconds that followed Luke's announcement, Eric died again. Caleb felt his emotions rocket through the five stages of grief. No denial, no bargaining. Just a straight shot to anger. "How?"

"Single bullet wound to the back of the head. Execution style. They set the fire in the warehouse to eliminate any chance of identifying him. I'm so sorry, Caleb."

Unlike before, when they'd told him Eric was gone, he had images to fill the void. Eric, ambushed, bound by ropes or wire or steel. A barrel pressed to his skull, his mouth gagged to muffle screams. His corpse set aflame to disguise their crime, left in a burned-out shell of a building to rot in anonymity.

From a distance, he heard Fin ask him a question.

"Luke, the brandy is in the bottom drawer." She tugged at Caleb's hand, led him to the staircase. "Sit down, love."

Because his knees bent, he sat. "They mutilated him. Burned his body."

"Yes." She didn't offer pity or platitudes. Grief, true, savage grief, rejected trite attempts to diminish the horror.

He shot up abruptly. "I'll have to notify his parents. Tell his sister." Part of his brain knew that if Luke had gotten word, so had the chief. She'd call Eric's family. Send a car with the news. "They'll want to see him. God, can they see him?"

"We'll call your office, Caleb." Fin drew him onto the step a second time. The strength of the clever fingers dissolved into a fine tremor. Holding tight, she promised, "I'll find out if his family's been told."

Carrying a glass filled with amber liquid, Luke returned to the foyer and caught the tail end of Fin's reassurance. "Your division chief said she'd notify next of kin."

Grateful, Fin accepted the snifter of brandy, pushed it into Caleb's clenched fist. "Drink this."

He had seen the corpses exhumed from the Warehouse. Had stood over Eric's body and asked the dry questions of law, never knowing he'd quizzed over the remains of his best friend. In a single draught, he gulped down the liquid, oblivious to its fire. But it steadied him. "What kind of gun?"

Expecting the query, hearing the jagged edges of

pain, Luke replied in brisk cop tones. "Small caliber. A .22 millimeter. Techs peg it as a Saturday Night Special. Old-school professional. But the bullet didn't exit the skull, Caleb."

At that, Caleb's glazed eyes sharpened. "They have the bullet?"

"Intact. The FBI thinks they can lift a partial print. They promised the print package would come ASAP."

"Good."

Luke's beeper chimed. He lifted the screen and muttered a curse. "I've got a situation in the Red District. Cheryl's pulling double duty until they decide on a permanent police chief, so I'm pitching in."

Caleb released Fin's hand, set the empty glass on the carpeted step, picked up the blue envelope. Standing, he reached for the training that would keep him solid until he was alone. With a tone to match Luke's, he spoke officer to officer. "Thanks for coming by. For following up."

"I'm sorry, Caleb. Truly." The handshake between the men held firm for a moment. "I'll touch base once I'm off duty."

Fin remained on the staircase as Caleb walked Luke to the door. She scrambled to her feet as he prepared to leave with him. "Caleb?" He glanced over his shoulder, as though he'd forgotten her presence.

Caleb focused, impatient to be away. Worried brown eyes filled with compassion watched him.

Another person to be sacrificed. Yet Fin didn't have the training to defend herself against the menace of Stark. A menace he'd sent her to confront alone. Like Eric. Disgust swirled inside him, washing away Luke's admonitions about Fin's nature. Who gave a damn about her feelings if her life ended on a dingy warehouse floor?

"I need to go home," he said, his tone harsh and forbidding. *Get away from her before you crumble. Before you take the comfort, the solace, only she can offer.* "Is there something you need?"

She saw the sizzle of anger, thought she understood its source. What she needed, what he needed, was her. Her purse was in the study, along with the keys to the center. Fin turned, explaining, "Give me a second to grab my bag and lock up."

"Why?"

Fin halted near the doorway. Surely he grasped her reasons for wanting to be with him. To offer comfort if he'd accept it or companionship if that's all he could stand. "I'll come with you."

His eyes, watching her, went blank. "No. That's not necessary."

A tremor quaked in her belly at the absolute lack of emotion. She couldn't hear any resonance in his voice, and his eyes chilled her with their flat affect. But she owed him. "You shouldn't be alone right now."

"I appreciate the offer, but no, thanks."

Echoing him, she asked, "Why?"

A clean break, he told himself. One to slash at her pride and force her away. "Because I'm about to get roaringly drunk, Fin. And then I'll pass out."

"I can hold my liquor."

The sneer should have warned her. "If you come home with me, Fin, I won't need to drink. So stay here and mind your own damned business."

Caleb strode out of the center, leaving Fin to stand in the foyer. She didn't chase after him. He wouldn't welcome a witness to his grief. The man she knew, the man she might love—his grief would be private. Fin didn't begrudge him the desire to retreat and nurse his sorrow. Confirmation of Eric's death had sealed the guilt and erased the flicker of hope she knew he'd kindled.

He was a man who'd learned to rely on himself, to hold himself strong when those around him fell. Protecting others was his first instinct, his only recourse. Like her, he'd lived a life in shadows, and their dimness held no room for company.

No room for another to share his sorrow.

CHAPTER 26

Caleb whipped the Accord around a moving van, dodged a sputtering jalopy. On the seat beside him, the envelope containing the details of Eric's murder mocked his speed. No matter how fast he drove, the .22 had exploded through his partner's skull and lodged in bone. Behind him, he'd also left the woman he might have loved and who probably would never speak to him again.

The engine revved, shooting him forward past drivers who glared at his erratic passage. He couldn't outrace what was done, he conceded, but he could damn well beat them to their next victim.

He snatched up his cell phone and called D.C.

Chief Benton answered on the second ring. "Caleb. You've gotten the news about Eric. I'm so sorry."

"Thank you, ma'am." His voice was gruff, and he forced the grief to settle. "Sheriff Calder gave me the news. I hear the techs think they can lift a partial from the bullet."

"If there's a squiggle or a whorl, we'll find it and we'll match it." Neither mentioned the fact that the small caliber might not carry more than a three-point match. Insufficient for most convictions, but the death of a federal agent had swayed more than one jury.

Three points or six, he'd make sure it was enough. Before she could offer more condolences, he swung into his report. "Ms. Borders has set up her accounts at TGB. At this point, we've tracked more than seventy separate companies without assets and with fake boards. Mostly comprised of elderly men and women scattered from Hallden to Macon. I've sent the data to Agent Garland for analysis."

Benton had already told the forensic accountant to place the data on high priority. "What's the bottom line?"

"According to what we've been able to pull and what I've gotten from Garland so far, Stark has been pretty smart. From what we've pieced together from records and Fin's interactions this week, targeted clients of the bank are encouraged to make capital contributions to various shell companies. They're told the funds are investments to diversify their portfolios. A client pumps clean money in, and TGB accepts deposits from the companies that front for what has to be their drugs and arms trafficking operations. Mingle the funds and then flush them through the reserves of the bank."

"It's a win for everyone," Benton said, mildly impressed. "Bank has an impressive bottom line to report to the Fed, and clients get dividends to keep them quiet." She hadn't expected such sophistication. Baldwin had, and she'd fobbed him off. Another notch on a conscience that had made tough choices for decades.

She'd do it again and move on. "Do we have sufficient evidence to justify arrests?"

"Not yet. Fin—I mean Ms. Borders—has only had her money inside for a week. I've coordinated with Agents Senterfitt and Gay on the joint DEA-FBI task force. Based on what I'd been able to target, they've closed in on shipments into Savannah and Miami. Someone in the police department is tipping off traffickers to planned raids and watched routes. Sheriff Calder has his suspects, but proving their role is difficult. Still, he's making progress."

"I've seen the reports. The intel you were able to feed them from the sheriff's analysis helped. Chicago lost a good officer when he moved south."

Caleb agreed. Already, with his help, and the assistance of Fin, Kell, Julia, and Mrs. Faraday, he'd gathered evidence of money laundering, tax evasion, and bank fraud.

Caleb wanted them for murder.

Despite the lessons of Eliot Ness, Eric's death wouldn't be dealt with through a bloodless conviction on tax evasion. Which is why Caleb had decided on their final move.

"Stark is feeling the pinch," he began. "This land deal is their final project. By getting into the federal program, they'll net a windfall and be able to live off the biofuels proceeds."

"They're counting on a lot of ducks lining up," Benton scoffed. "A federal boondoggle as a retirement plan?"

"Look at the millions being raked in on ethanol today. Or farm subsidies. Call them what you will, farmers who own the crop du jour are raking in taxpayer dollars. Fin calculated their potential profit for one year's production."

The figure he gave her had Benton's eyes widening. "My family owns some land in Mississippi. Maybe I'm in the wrong business."

Caleb gave a short laugh, surprised he could. "Has to be the right kind of plants, Chief. But you might want to check it out."

"Not planning on muddying the waters, Matthews. I'll earn my ducats the old-fashioned way. Being underpaid as a public servant." She sank into her chair in D.C., her high, narrow window letting in scant light.

As he continued to report, she marveled at the mind and the cunning. Sticking one of her agents undercover as a lawyer hadn't been well received by her bosses. At first. But, in his methodical way, he'd chipped away, revealing what Baldwin had guessed at.

More, he'd done it like a lawyer. Fastidious attention to detail to combat waves of motions that would come from scrambling defense attorneys.

By the details he offered now, Matthews clearly had a plan. One that she wouldn't like. One that involved the Borders woman.

Sanctioning civilians wasn't new for the Bureau, but Matthews always resisted having outside help on his assignments. Until this one. Until this woman. The one he called Fin rather than using surnames, as was his custom.

But nothing on this case fit Bureau custom or Matthew's careful habits. And, Shirley Benton imagined, neither would his next step. She shifted, sighed. "Out with it, Matthews. What do you want to do?"

Caleb hesitated. "Ma'am?"

On the other side, she reached for a form. "Don't play dumb. You've got a trick up your sleeve and you want my go-ahead." When he didn't speak, she summarized. "The ATF and the DEA are putting pressure on their operations, their banker is gambling away their holdings. They've got to get the Faraday woman's land. So what's your play?"

"I want to force their hand. Shut off the tap at the bank."

"How?"

"By letting Fin tip them off to a potential raid." Placing her in greater jeopardy and carving out an opening for his move. "I'll need a fax from your office. A confidential memo to me about a planned raid on TGB."

"Why, exactly, would Ms. Borders have access to your personal fax machine?" Benton asked. "For the sake of argument."

Caleb refused the bait. "Stark is aware I've been spending time at the center. We've covered by using the false arrest of Eliza Faraday and our continuing investigation."

Thumbing the file of his reports, she said, "Then there's the link between the sheriff and the defense attorney. A cozy town you've picked, Matthews."

"I haven't crossed any lines, Chief." Toed them, yes. Peered over the side, absolutely. But, despite temptation, he'd stayed on his side. "I want to end this, for everyone's sake."

"You've got four more weeks on the clock. Use them if you need to."

"One will suffice." He was tough, he reminded himself. Surely, he'd survive another week of being near Fin and without her. "When can I expect the fax?"

"Give me an hour. I'll send it to your home machine," she confirmed. For a moment, she said nothing. Then she spoke. "Caleb, you've been under for nearly two years. You asked for this assignment, and I gave it to you because you're one of the best agents I've supervised."

"Thank you."

"Don't." Sentiment had scarce room in their business. She'd say it now and let it be done. "I liked Eric Baldwin. He had a first-rate mind. But he wasn't cut out to be a field agent."

Caleb bristled. "Eric uncovered Stark."

"Yes. From behind a desk." She let her tone soften. "I made a mistake sending him to Georgia alone. Let him chase one of his theories so I could avoid denying him a real assignment. I'll have to live with that."

"You didn't get him killed, Chief."

"And neither did you."

"I know that."

"Do you? You've got a bigger brain than most of your colleagues, Matthews. One that isn't afraid to leverage all the resources at your disposal. When you're on, you'll follow the rules, but you'll damned sure bend them."

"Is that an official complaint?"

"Don't get your back up. It's an observation. Like this one. I rely on your ability to sift through the data and find the information that truly matters. That's why I partnered you with Baldwin. Most of us glazed over with him, but you heard him. Saw what he saw."

Loss gnawed, its bite fresh. "I didn't see enough."

"But that's the other part of you. You don't blindly follow instinct. You're meticulous and thoughtful. And, Caleb, that's your chief failing."

"Ma'am?"

"Sometimes you think too damned much. Because when thinking slides into agonizing, it can paralyze you. Make you second-guess decisions, doubt your gut. You've got fine instincts. When you listen to them."

An image of Fin, hurt and humiliation blazing in her eyes, seared into his brain. Logic demanded he stay away. Far away from the woman he'd led into danger. And instinct? Instinct tightened his fingers on the steering wheel, urging him to turn the car around. To go back and apologize and tell her what whispered in his heart.

Almost angry, he retorted, "And if instinct can harm the innocent?"

"First off, if they've learned to talk, they aren't innocent." Still, Benton heard the confusion below the question. Affection overrode her usual distance. She glanced down at the gold band she'd worn for nearly thirty years. "We've sworn to protect and serve, and the best of us know it's more than a motto. But we aren't personal sentries. If you give people all the facts and they make up their own minds, the consequence is on them."

"That's shirking my duty."

"No. That's giving another person a choice. He—or she—might choose wrong, but you aren't responsible for the whole world, Caleb. Take care of your corner and the other parts I assign you, and then get the hell out of the way." She flipped the cover of the Stark folder closed. "You'll have your fax by five. I want a detailed ops report on my desk tomorrow."

"Will do." His apartment loomed before him, and Caleb pulled into the garage. "Thank you, Chief."

The line went dead. He stored the phone, picked up the envelope, and walked to the private elevator entry. The car opened on the sixth floor. Caleb strode down the corridor, stuck on Benton's admonition.

He'd given Fin a choice about Stark, but between them, he'd made the decisions. To keep her at bay, to protect her from the danger his life posed.

And, if he was truly honest, to protect himself.

Fin Borders flouted rules, defied conventions. She proudly made her living between respectability and a shadowy world of gaming that skated just past the edges. Without batting an eye, she blithely skimmed over pesky details like right and wrong. She stunned his senses, and a look from her could knock him sideways. His skin tingled at the thought of her.

She was braver than a hundred agents he knew. Willing to go to the wall for those she loved. He admired how she saw the world, and the world she helped him see. She barreled into trouble without a care. And faced the consequences for her decisions with the same forthrightness. The same determination.

Fin Borders was nothing he imagined in the woman of his heart, and the only one he wanted.

But, he decided, dismissing the gathering storm of advice, he knew himself. Until Stark was dealt with, he couldn't afford Fin or the complications of what might be between them.

He decided that later he'd apologize and explore what lay between them, drew them to one another. Later, after he'd processed his grief, after he'd completed his assignment. Satisfied with his plan, he turned the corner to his apartment and halted.

Fin stood on the threshold.

CHAPTER 27

Caleb made his way past her to the door. Close up, the brown eyes held a deadly gleam. Her jaw was set and firm, the dimple absent. Fitting the key into the door, he began to marshal his excuses. Grief, rage, sheer male stupidity.

"I didn't expect you."

Her eyes held him in the fluorescent glare of the hallway light. "You should have."

The weariness in her flat statement jabbed at his conscience. "Why?"

"Because you're not the only one in whatever this relationship is." She angled her head. "Can we go inside?"

Silently, he keyed open the door, held it wide for her to enter ahead of him. Once inside, he laid the envelope on the entryway table. After she said what she'd come to say, he'd read the report. And mourn his best friend. Alone.

Shrugging out of his jacket, he tossed it onto the sofa. He unknotted his tie, his back to her. It would be easier this way. "I know I was a jerk. I'm sorry for that." He gave her the opening, braced for the explosion.

"Tell me how I can help."

The quiet, solemn request spun him toward her. He searched her face and discovered a depth of emotion that shouldn't have surprised him, yet did. Kindness flowed over him in steady waves, and he found himself answering dully, "I don't know how to answer that."

She pressed a hand to his cheek, her thumb stroking the high plane. "Talk to me."

He shrugged again, this time in bewilderment. "I'm angry. So goddamned angry. At Stark for killing him. And at Eric." A hard laugh accompanied a shake of his head. "He had no business in the field. Ever. No right to get himself killed." Jerking away from her sympathy, Caleb cursed his candor. He wasn't mad at Eric. He was simply mad. But another vile wave rippled through him, catching him in the gut.

Fin watched as he marched into the kitchen. She followed and slipped onto a bar stool. On the other side of the counter, Caleb slammed two glasses onto the tiles and unearthed a bottle of whiskey. Without asking, he splashed liquid into both.

In two quick motions, his liquor disappeared, and he replaced it with a fresh pour. The harsh trail of the alcohol met his mood. "I don't know why I'm so mad." His free hand rubbed over his face. "I've known the truth for years. But God, it feels like he died today."

It would, Fin knew, feel like the same day, the same death over and over. For years. That knowledge had driven her to Mrs. F's car and across town. She'd taken shortcuts a man like Caleb wouldn't have learned about. Tracks that had cut across neighborhoods left fallow by neglect. She'd beaten him to his door, prepared.

Her glass untouched, Fin asked calmly, "Have you ever lost anyone before?"

Caleb took another drink, slower this time. "One other time. In the line of duty."

"Were you close?"

"No. Not really." He braced his elbows on the counter. "I respected John, had trained with him." Sniper fire at a drug raid had hit him. He'd been in the same outfit, but not his partner.

"Did you see him die?"

Wondering at her curiosity, he shook his head. "We were raiding a gang house. He'd taken the rear, I was leading a team through the front."

Fin lifted her glass, savored the heated glide. "My father shot my mother in front of me. I was ten."

"My God."

"Mom had been feeling sick, hadn't been able to take customers for a couple of days." Fin stood, wandered to the living area. To the mantel with his family photos. "My mother barely tolerated me most of the time. After she had me, she was incredibly careful about contraception." She picked up the silver frame, examined the family within. "Told me more than once that she had no interest in carrying another brat for the bastard."

Had she known any kindness in her first decade? he wondered, sad for the child, amazed by the woman. "Why in the world would she tell her daughter such a thing?"

"Because I didn't matter to her. Not really." She returned the photo and leaned against the mantel, her eyes clear. "I assume my parents got drunk one night and made me. I was a mistake, one always regretted not getting rid of."

"Fin."

She waved away the sympathy, the wounds too old to be tended. "But that weekend, she had the flu or something. Lay in bed, sick with a fever. We couldn't afford a doctor, and my father was MIA, so she dosed herself with tea and Nyquil." Hibiscus tea, she mused. She'd forgotten how her mother had loved the smell of flowers in her cup. "All weekend, I cooked soup for her, boiled the water for her tea. Sat by her bed and read her magazines to her."

The loveliest weekend she'd ever spent with her mother. "Dad got back Monday around dawn. I was sleeping in their bed, beside Mom. Her fever had gone down, but she'd been telling me a story and I forgot to leave."

Recalling the transcripts he'd pulled, Caleb forestalled her. "I've read the reports, Fin. I know."

Her smile broke his heart. "No, Caleb, you don't. I woke up because he was hauling her out of bed, demanding money. He'd come up short at his dealers and needed a hit." Screams and shouts and angry pleas. Then a gunshot, a bloom of red. "I watched my father murder my mother. She fell to the floor, and he just ran. Know what I thought?"

Throat dry with pity, he replied, "No. What?"

"That he didn't even care enough to kill me." Fin dipped her hands into her pockets, turned to face him fully. "For once in my life, she'd shown an interest in me, and he took her away. But once he'd killed her, he didn't bother to look at me or ask me not to call the police. I wasn't there to him. I was invisible."

His heart contracted at the bald, cool statement. And at the memory of turning away from her. "That's not what I was thinking, Fin." Leaden remorse smothered grief. "I see you."

"I know you do," Fin agreed, her tone brisk. "I've never met a man like you. Brilliant, yes, but you've got a slick side that I'd love to have as a partner at a hot table. Honor means something to you, and you take your obligations seriously."

Embarrassed, Caleb squirmed at the compliments. "So?"

"So, you won't believe you shouldn't have been able to save Eric. You won't accept that people are evil and will do what they want when they please. That a gun will snatch away the sweetest moment of your life, and you won't have anyone to tell for twenty years." Tears, unexpected, welled and spilled onto her cheeks. She brushed at the dampness, determined to finish.

"When Luke told you about Eric, I ached for you. Not simply because you lost your friend, but because you will beat yourself up for not being there, not saving him." She reached out her hand. He took it, drew him to her. Framing his face, she murmured, "You weren't supposed to save Eric, and you're not responsible for saving me, Caleb. I've been taking care of myself for a very long time. And I've done a hell of a job."

Shaken, moved, he conceded, "Yes, you have."

"Then believe these three things. One, we will stop Stark. You and me. Two, Eric's death should make you angry, not guilty. He died doing what he loved, and he needs you to finish this for him."

She said nothing more, prompting him as she'd intended. "And three?" he asked.

"Three is that you're not getting rid of me. Get drunk, get angry. I'm here. For as long as you need me. In any way you'll have me."

Their eyes met, held. His filled with questions, hers promising answers.

Which left him no choice but to lower his mouth to hers, to sink into the comfort he'd foolishly rejected. In the bright light of the early afternoon, he kissed her softly, an apology too intense to be spoken. Ebony curls spilled over his hands as he held her face still for his exploration. "I love your mouth," he murmured. "Each time I kiss you, I think that I could kiss you forever."

"Try." Her lips parted, inviting him inside. She'd thought the same, felt the same. Each time, he kissed with a single-minded focus that shattered, weakened her will.

Expecting the thrill of hot, of fast, she found instead leisurely and deliberate. In a breath, he filled her mouth, and, swirling inside her heart was more than she'd thought herself capable of holding. Quivering, her arms twined around his neck, and she gave herself to him.

Like an artist, his tongue painted every surface with long, slow sweeps. He tested the serrated edge of teeth, the warm moist cavern steeped in her exotic, unique flavors. Unhurried, he savored the agile dance as she tangled their mouths together, edging toward a dangerous precipice.

Not yet, he promised them both silently. *Not until we fall together.*

Because he could, Caleb swept her up, enjoying the flex of his muscles as he held her against his chest.

"I'm not a small woman," she protested, surfacing, and her arms tightened in faint apprehension. As proud as she was of her height and her body, she briefly wished to be as petite as Julia, as slim as Kell. Wriggling, she urged, "I can walk."

"I'm not a small man," Caleb retorted smugly. "I can carry you." It occurred to him, as he brought her to his bed, that he was compelled to carry her, to hold her precisely because she didn't need it. Wouldn't expect to be supported by any man.

Wouldn't expect to be cherished rather than seduced.

He set her on her feet by his bed, released her to draw down the simple navy spread, the crisp white sheets. Patiently, he brushed his mouth along her temple, traced the whorls of her ear. Smiled at her sigh as he nuzzled the spot where her jaw met her throat. The slender column of bronze trembled where he feasted on the thud of her pulse. He reveled in the way her skin heated beneath his lips.

Mesmerized, he experimented, stoking fire against the crest of her shoulders. Steel and satin, grit and a gracefulness to humble. Allowing himself to test the contrasts, he trailed a wet line across the hollows formed. "You taste of sunset, with a hint of sheet lightning. Unexpected, almost terrifying. Astonishingly beautiful."

Poetry, she thought dreamily, moved to trembling. No one had ever given her poetry. In the firm glide of his hands as he skimmed her waist, measuring. In the words breathed over her skin, tantalizing and seducing. She drifted into his arms, listened to the steady drum of his heartbeat.

Fin unbuttoned his shirt, dragged the tails free, and delighted as he quaked beneath her questing touch. A nip at the shadows carved into sinewy muscle at his chest. A long, slow streak of damp heat across the sculpted back. Salty, strong, powerful, he filled her senses and stole her breath. She circled around him, lathing the copper skin and glorying in his shudders of pleasure.

"I've never wanted anyone like this. Like you." Her flesh damp, her senses overwhelmed, she reached for him. "I want you."

"Hmm." Caleb gripped her wandering hands as her fingers nimbly released his belt. "Not yet. I intend to savor this."

In the liquid gold filtered by bamboo slats, her blouse disappeared over her head in a languid motion that left her standing in ivory silk trimmed in lace. Caleb dipped his head to stroke the taut curves, praising the satin skin. Deftly, he released the straining cups, caught the glorious mounds in his waiting palms.

Too slow, she thought, but spun with him lazily in the seduction. When his thumbs flitted over the pebble-hard nipples, she arched. Then his mouth covered her, and a whimper broke free.

"Caleb." A single word, a harsh demand.

"Not yet," he warned, his teeth grazing the high peak. Already hard, his knees nearly buckled as she cupped him. Bowing away from temptation, he cautioned hoarsely, "Oh, not yet."

Held enthralled by his marauding mouth, Fin plotted her revenge. She fumbled at his waist, her sure touch intentionally incendiary. Unable to help himself, he surged against her palm, cursing and praising.

Laughing darkly, she tracked the column of his throat with hot, biting kisses, with recipes for relief. And toppled him onto the welcoming mattress. Before he could adjust, she ranged over him, straddled the hard ridge of flesh. "Slow? Alright."

Fin dipped her head to take his mouth, a delicate invasion destroyed by the undulating rhythm of her hips. Bands of iron clamped along her thighs, pleading for speed. To torment, she ranged down the heaving chest, her mouth absorbing the full banquet. The tensed stomach arrowed by a thin black line. The flat waist and lean hips. Lost, she flowed lower, freed him.

Wet, delirious heat surrounded Caleb, and he broke. Gone were imaginings of languid lovemaking. Now, he craved the slick mating of mouths, the playful tussle as they tumbled across cool sheets.

Insistent, eager, he devoured the soft, dampened skin, the curve and dip of her.

Greedy, giving, she gorged on the friction of flesh to flesh, absorbed the thrill of strength yielding to pleasure.

He slipped inside her, overwhelmed them both. As he moved, both gave in to another level of lovemaking, where tender and frantic wound into a pliant generosity. Filling her, he skimmed kisses against her skin, soft promises he intended to keep. She wrapped herself around him, into him, allowing him inside, deeper, then deeper still.

Pleasure washed through, a flood of release that caught them both and swept them away. As they drifted toward exhaustion, he stayed inside, waiting for her eyes to flutter to his. "Fin."

"Hmm." Lassitude dragged her down, but she struggled to meet the intense look. "Yes?"

I love you. "Dream of me."

CHAPTER 28

Dusk settled, and Fin's eyes adjusted to the coming dark. Beside her, Caleb slept on his side, his left arm binding their bodies in a long, sensual line. Curve met angle, soft yielded to hard. One naked and, Fin noted sleepily, outrageously sexy thigh trapped her leg against him.

She propped herself up, gave herself the satisfaction of studying him. Such a beautiful man. Lean, muscular, and amazingly agile. Twice more, he'd driven her to madness, pleasured her into a torrent of release. And she'd returned the favor; his fevered groans and inventive suggestions still rang against her overly sensitized flesh. The last one had nearly toppled them off the bed.

Memory brought a naughty giggle to her throat. She held onto the effervescence of sound, to not wake him. But, unable to resist, she lightly stroked away a tiny frown marring his brow.

A tender smile curved her lips. Even in sleep, she

realized, he plotted. A mind like his wouldn't be content to rest, not when his mission remained undone. Grief over his fallen partner had stumbled him, but she had no doubt he'd already have a strategy when he surfaced. Stark faced a certain end, soon.

In that and in this bed, they'd built a partnership. Mutual trust, wary respect, a cautious affection.

And, if she accepted it, love.

Her heart jittered, pounded. Ties between women and men had several names. Lust, desire, chemistry. Love was the province of romantics. A foolish declaration designed to ease puritanical minds.

In thirty-four years, she'd nimbly evaded the trap of calling a healthy respect for sex by any other name. Until Caleb, she'd been content to slap clear labels onto her hungers and call a spade a spade. Until today, as they lay joined, sleep drawing her down.

As he'd asked, she'd dream of him. Only of him.

She shifted in his arms, tension shooting through her, paralyzing.

Sex had a nice beginning, and if done well, a terrific end. It took mere seconds to make the connection, to sense physical compatibility. Love required time to develop. And, from her jaundiced observations, lingered on, twisting your guts into knots and staggering your brain.

She'd loved four people in her life. Her mother had died scarcely returning her juvenile affections, and the other three had born the brunt of her carelessness.

Yet even as she dismissed the possibility, she thought of Kell and Luke. Of the gentle and solid affection, disagreements balanced by staunch, unshakable loyalty.

She and Caleb could have that, she thought. But at

what cost? Much better, she decided, to steep herself in what she clearly understood.

Curling her hand behind his head, she slicked her mouth across his. In sleep, he opened to her, his arm contracting in response. The kiss roused him, eyes wide, body rigid. Before he could form a coherent sentence, she slithered down, a journey punctuated by flicks of a sadistic tongue that found him rigid and pulsing. That drove him higher, harder. Vision dimmed and control fractured.

But even as he tried to gather the scattered pieces, she streaked up, brought him inside. His frantic hands captured the perfectly firm, perfectly creamy breasts. He fused his mouth to the delicate peaks, delirious as she rode him in abandoned response.

Overcome, they strained toward ecstasy, neither willing to fall into bliss without the other. In harmony, they thundered to completion, seamless, endless. Together.

"Will Mrs. Faraday be wondering where you are?" Caleb asked, drawing intricate patterns on the jut of her hip. His journey continued under the single sheet, grazed the delectable mounds tucked into him. One more area of her to be conquered, he thought, considering rash possibilities.

"No." Pillowed on his outstretched arm, Fin yawned lavishly. "I called before I headed over. Had to make sure the kids weren't coming home to an empty house."

"Very thoughtful of you. And farsighted."

Her fingertips danced over a tracery of veins. "I have my moments."

Caleb nuzzled her cheek. "Thank you."

With a throaty chuckle, she reminded him, "I enjoyed myself too. Several times. The gratitude is all mine." She gave a deliberately provocative wiggle and earned herself a light swat.

"Cut it out," he growled against her shoulder. "I'm trying to be serious." To ensure he could, he flipped her to face him, gently took her chin. Sorrow weighed on him, its burden eased. Shared. "Thank you for checking on me. For being here." He pressed his lips to hers in a kiss so piercingly sweet that it frightened him. Lifting his head, he added wryly, "When you forget to pay attention, you're remarkably kind."

"Oh, thanks." Fin wriggled free, reaching for her dignity and escape. It wasn't time for sappy declarations yet. Or for them to mean so much. "By the way, while you were napping, you received a fax." She held her breath, hoping the lure worked.

It did, better than she expected. Caleb jolted upwards, cotton pooling at his waist. "I forgot to tell you."

Fin clutched the sheet to her suddenly cool skin and sat up. She braced herself against the headboard—and the coming announcement. "Out with it."

"I spoke with Chief Benton this afternoon. It's time to force Stark to act." Climbing out of bed, he dressed while he explained, "The fax is a memo to me in my capacity as ADA and to Luke."

"Saying what?" Changing gears, Fin grappled over the side of the bed, certain she'd seen her shorts earlier. Her hand closed over heaps of cloth, some his, some hers. She tossed his shirt over her shoulder. As quickly as he, she shimmied into her discarded clothes. "And what can I do?"

Preoccupied by the sensuous movement, Caleb yanked

his mind from her to his plan. "The FBI intends to raid the Georgia Bank on Thursday and seize all assets and records. Funds will allegedly be frozen. I'm figuring the specter of losing everything should speed up their time line."

She was sure she'd been wearing shoes. In a crouch, she searched under the bed. A sandal peeked out from a wad of blankets. Hunting for the second distracted her from the jangle of uneasiness. Files and research had been a prelude to the main event—trapping Stark into revealing themselves. "We don't need speed. We need hyperdrive."

"Yes." Caleb hesitated, reluctant to lay out his full strategy. He knew she'd commit once he spoke it aloud.

Fin beat him to the punch. "If I tell Worley tomorrow, they'll have to act. Meet to decide their next move." The missing sandal had wedged behind the dresser. By the time she'd retrieved it, the spurt of panic had subsided. She'd worn a wire with the Albanian mob. Surely, she could bluff James Worley into hosting a meeting of Stark. From the carpeted floor, she buckled them into place. "Smart move. If they suspect a raid, they won't be willing to communicate by phone. They'll want a face-to-face."

"Exactly. Tomorrow, when you visit the bank, I'll attach a GPS tracker to his car. Luke and I can track him to their meeting, and with the records we've uncovered, we'll be able to take them into custody."

Neither mentioned the prints from Eric's killer, due in Hallden soon. "Does Chief Benton think you've got a strong case?"

"That's the beauty of RICO. Coconspirators carry the crimes of all their partners. Between the information

Luke has passed on and our efforts, they're looking at triple-digit counts." But he only craved one. Felony murder.

Fully dressed, they moved in tandem to the living room. Fin walked to the counter and picked up her purse. "Are you coming to the center?" she asked, her voice awkwardly polite. "Otherwise, I can brief everyone."

Caleb saw the play of nerves, felt them strumming through him. Which is why he plucked her free hand from her side and wrapped it in his. "I'll ride with you. You'll want to pack something more appropriate for tomorrow, but you should keep the Spitfire."

"Pack?" She tried for nonchalance and almost made it.

He decided not to smile in triumph. "Unless you want to wear the same shorts and handkerchief to meet Worley."

"I'm not wearing a handkerchief," she pouted, refusing to tug at the triangle of material. "Am I staying here tonight?"

This was a time for complete honesty—or as close as he could deal with. "I enjoy waking up with you, Fin. I'd like to do it tomorrow, if you don't mind."

"For the sex." Though it was a question, it emerged as a perfunctory statement.

He brought her hand to his lips, kissed the skipping pulse at her wrist. The speed, the uncertainty reassured him. "The sex is amazing, but so are your eyes." *So is your heart.* But it was too soon for that admission. "I'd be delighted to have both, but I'm willing to make a sacrifice."

Fin laughed, rested her head briefly on his shoulder. "I won't ask which one."

"Thank God," Caleb muttered as he ushered her into the hallway.

Tuesday morning brought a burst of summer rain. Fin struggled to put the top up on the antique car, which she'd fortuitously parked in the apartment building's private garage. Fumbling, she commanded her fingers to stop slipping on the controls. Waking up to Caleb had spun her system into chaos, a hectic diversion from what lay ahead.

And a constant, niggling worry of what lay between them.

Pushing her personal turmoil aside, she focused on the current situation—convincing Worley to convene Stark, using the fax secreted inside her bag to get it done. They hadn't planned to meet this morning, since all the monetary transfers had been completed, but she'd noted his schedule. Worley rarely ventured from the confines of his office except to dine.

The top shut, and she slipped into the car. In short order, she arrived at the bank. Today's outfit had been sneaked from Kell's closet. Though Fin normally eschewed power suits, during the past two weeks, she'd grown to appreciate their allure. Outfitted in a color Kell called hazelnut, she entered the bank.

Katie Meredith greeted her with a wide, warm smile and a quizzical gleam in her eye. "Ms. Borders. Mr. Worley didn't tell me to expect you."

"Spur-of-the-moment decision," Fin said, making certain her displeasure was clear. "Is he available?"

"I'll ring his office." Katie gestured to the waiting area. "Just a moment."

Soon, James Worley ambled through the bank. "Couldn't stay away, Ms. Borders?"

"Just checking on my investments." Fin permitted a glimmer of annoyed concern into her expression. "I'd like to discuss them with you."

Worley's bonhomie slipped for a second. Then, remembering he had an audience, he chortled. "My kind of customer. Watching your dollars work." He fastened onto her elbow, the hold tight. "Ms. Meredith, hold my calls."

In the capacious office, Fin settled into the wing chair opposite his desk. She waited patiently as he lowered himself into his chair, the friendly grin fading.

"An unexpected pleasure, Ms. Borders." Beneath his growing bulk, the chair gave a baleful squeak. "What brings you here?"

"When I asked you for help, you graciously overlooked my current environs," she began mildly.

"Living with the sheriff's girlfriend and being seen around town with the ADA are interesting choices for a woman of your interests," he conceded. "But I accepted your explanations and convinced my board you were a worthy risk."

The $750,000 she'd invested had eased their concerns considerably. A week of cautious movement, shifting funds from foreign accounts into pedestrian ones. Then, in the stroke of genius that had brought him to Stark's attention, the investments into small-cap companies or LLCs with flimsy operating agreements. Paid out in a matter of days as draws to partners or in declared dividends for longer-term investors.

She'd done her research, he gave her that. Knew before he told her that her holdings weren't worth the paper they'd been written on.

"You understand our process takes several days. For maximum benefit?" Discretion, a banker's hallmark, had been critical in recent days. Operation after operation had faltered, but none of Stark's more violently criminal ventures had fallen into his province. He was simply—and only—the banker. "Did you have another transfer?"

"Mr. Worley." Fin swallowed, as much to buy time as for effect. "James, I have news." Her voice quavered, then firmed. "Yesterday, I came into possession of this."

A single sheet landed on the surface of his desk. Worley saw only the seal, the words *Federal Bureau of Investigation*. Breath beginning to heave, he summoned the tai chi video he practiced weekly. Found the light that was his breath. "What . . . what is it?"

"The FBI has TGB under investigation, James." Prickly now, she added acid to her tone. "I've made a sizeable investment in this bank, and now, according to this"—she flicked the paper—"I run the risk of losing my investment. And coming to the attention of the FBI."

Florid color surged along his wide, fleshy neck. "Fin." At her arched brow, he babbled, "Ms. Borders, I can assure you I had no clue."

"That doesn't instill confidence."

"No, no. Of course it doesn't." The chair's squeak became a squeal as he turned to his computer. Columns of numbers in green glowed against a dark background. He scrolled through to a different screen. A running total of Stark's investments held on deposit in the bank. The number made him blanch.

"I acquired this fax at great personal risk, Mr. Worley." Brandishing the page, she insisted, "Read the memo."

Worley forced his eyes to rip away from the screen and scan the black lines of text. In reaction, color drained and his extremities numbed. A raid on the bank, his bank, on Thursday. Too soon to liquidate. Too quick to manufacture information. With the exception of the funds he'd siphoned off for Graves, the bulk of their deposits couldn't be accessed without raising shriller alarms. He was sunk.

"Dear Lord."

"Pray on your own time, Mr. Worley." Fin reclined against the supple leather. "I'd like to hear your plan for protecting my money."

His vision grayed. "Your money is in transit," he strangled out.

"In transit?" she repeated silkily, well aware that her funds had been funneled into the bank's reserves. "Really?"

"In order to release your funds prematurely, I'd have to get permission from the board. Given the large sums." Permission the bank's actual board would not grant. Nor would Stark.

"The very same sums that will be frozen by the federal government sometime in the next two days?" She bit out the query, her eyes flat and unsympathetic.

"Yes." Worley wanted to vomit. "I'm very sorry."

"I don't want your apologies. I'd like my money. Now."

He grimaced. "There is no money, Ms. Borders. I explained this last week."

"We both know your explanations are required by the FDIC and have absolutely nothing to do with our transactions. I hired you to do a job, Mr. Worley, and you appear to have failed. Miserably."

Testily, Worley shifted in his seat. "Listen here, Fin."

"Ms. Borders," she corrected, enjoying her tantrum. "And before you say something you'll regret, allow me to explain your one and only option. Before I leave this office, I expect to either receive my funds in full or to have another, equally profitable alternative presented to me. Are we understood?"

The Faraday land. The partnership with Graves. A clean break from Stark. Of course. He almost blurted out his idea, when he recalled his tenuous position. Before he offered them all an exit, he had to receive clearance.

"Ms. Borders, first of all, I apologize for my reaction. And I thank you for this information."

"You're forgiven, and you're welcome." She watched him expectantly. He'd nibbled the bait, but she needed him to bite. He didn't disappoint.

"I think we may have a mutually agreeable solution available." He stood, opened his office door. "I have a few calls to make."

"Make your calls, Worley." She crossed elegant legs and reached into her bag for a paperback. "I'll wait."

When James sulked back into his office, Fin met his glower with a level look. She held the upper hand, and they both knew it. With Caleb and Luke at her disposal, he could ill afford to incur her wrath.

"I've contacted my partner."

Fin closed her novel, prepared to listen. "You mean your board, don't you?"

"No, I have a business partner. A silent partner. And he has authorized me to extend a chance to participate in a lucrative land deal that we've been eyeing."

Bingo. "Surely you're not asking me to hand over any more money to you, Worley." She frowned with disdain, moved to stand. "Give me another alternative by this afternoon, or I'll be forced to use other means."

"Wait, wait." James shifted to block her, hands held out in supplication. "We don't need any money from you. In fact, with this deal, I'll be able to return your investment and increase it exponentially. But we do require one more contribution from you."

She didn't sit, but she didn't head for the door. "There are two ways to participate in real estate transactions, Worley. Either I bring the capital or I bring the land. I'm not giving you any more money, and I don't own any land."

"You don't, but Eliza Faraday does." Pressing her gently into the wing chair, he took a seat beside her, holding her in place. He had to tread lightly here. "I know that you and your friends have been named the trustees for the Metanoia Foundation."

"After her scare with the Griffin trial, she didn't want to be the sole trustee any longer. I don't see how this is relevant." Fin shrugged. "The only lands she owns are the Grove and the center's properties. Not exactly cash cows."

"The Grove is a drop in the bucket compared to the

rest of her holdings," Worley informed her. "That foundation owns the Metanoia Nature Preserve."

"The what?"

Excitement threaded his voice. "The preserve is a five-thousand-acre stretch from Hallden County up to Taylor. The Faraday family has owned the land for generations. In the seventies, her parents refused to sell it for development and converted its use to a nature preserve. They were tree-hugging kooks."

"I understood they were horticulturalists."

"That's the word." Frankly, he had never seen the appeal of greenery, unless it came as legal tender. "Anyway, they experimented with a plant that is now worth millions of dollars, in the right hands."

"And you think the right hands are yours?"

Clammy fingers closed over hers where they rested in her lap. "Our hands, Fin. Yours, mine, and my partner's. If you can convince her to sell the land to us, we have a line on a program that will pay us to harvest the plants and to generate an ongoing market for the plant's oils. Biofuels."

Fin honed in on a single phrase. "'A line on a program'? It's not guaranteed?"

Waving away the concern, he explained, "It's a government program, and I've already started the paperwork to let us apply. I've created another company to hold the land and a separate entity to develop the biofuels. That's what the plant produces. All we need to submit our application is proof of control of the land. But we do have a time constraint. Any day now, the court may issue an injunction against the program. We don't know when, but it's coming. Once we have the land, we can submit the application and beat the clock."

"How do you intend to pay for the purchase?" In a breath, Worley had confirmed all of their research, all of their speculation. One more piece of information would pull it all together. "Let's say I deliver the deeds and don't tell them about the magical plants. Kell will insist that Mrs. F be paid handsomely for selling her family's legacy. Who's supplying the capital? Not you." Tell me it's Stark, she thought. Say the name.

"My partner and I have access to capital. We'll offer Mrs. Faraday a top price for what is recorded as agricultural land in the middle of nowhere. No hardwoods worth logging. Just these strange little trees. Ms. Jameson won't be able to object to the number, and neither will she."

"Who is your partner, James? I'm not going into this deal blind." Say it. Tell me.

He leaned in, his voice a thread of sound, as though he was afraid of being overheard. Indeed, his eyes darted around before he spoke. "He's the former chief of police. Michael Graves."

Graves? The man who'd killed Clay Griffin and framed Mrs. F. The man who'd tipped Caleb off to Stark. An outcast, not the main kill. She fumbled for a response, thrown. "Your partner is a fugitive. You expect me to believe he's got the wherewithal to pull this off?"

James could feel her retreating. *What would a true Yakuza do?* Be bold. Intentional. "Graves and I are part of a larger organization. A group called Stark. Given your associates, I'm sure you've heard of them."

Relief sprinted through her. "Yes, I have. But I didn't realize you worked with them."

"I'm their banker." He bared his teeth in a smug,

brash smile. "Graves and I have decided to break away. Create our own enterprise. Stark has unwittingly agreed to fund our new venture."

"Won't aligning myself with you focus Stark's attention on me? Especially once they find out their money is gone?"

Graves had mentioned the same consequence to him. But Worley could only think of himself now. Fin Borders had made her choices, and if she joined them, Stark would indeed attack; Graves thought she'd make an excellent target while he and Worley collected their funds, unfortunately for her.

"Once we're in business, you won't have to worry that gorgeous head of yours about Stark. Just get me a resolution signed by you and the other trustees. I'll have the deeds couriered to you this afternoon, and I'll draw up partnership papers adding you to the company. We'll meet tonight for the exchange."

"On one condition," Fin said, standing again. "Graves must be here. I don't see him, and the deal is off."

"I'm not sure that will work," hedged Worley. Graves refused to come out of hiding, even to meet with him. "He's got significant reasons to remain hidden."

"And millions of reasons to meet my terms. No Graves, no deeds, Mr. Worley. Do we have a deal?" She held out her hand.

Reluctantly, gratefully, he clasped her palm. "Deal."

CHAPTER 29

"Stop fussing."

"Stop squirming," Caleb retorted. "If you'd stand still, I could finish."

Craning her neck, she tried to watch his hands as they splayed against her naked skin. For once, she was impervious to their seductive potential. "A wire is moronic. They'll be expecting me to wear one. Worley is already antsy. They find this, I'm dead."

The argument had raged for half an hour. During the battle, he'd managed to strip her out of the silky jacket and silkier shirt beneath. Without the enthralling consequences his libido had learned to expect. While she'd met with Worley, he'd trekked to the FBI's field office in Atlanta. Fast talking and a terse call from Division Chief Benton had supplied him with state-of-the-art gadgetry that did nothing to quell his racing heartbeat. "The mike is undetectable. Flesh-colored tape with a microtransmitter the size of a pinhead."

Currently affixed to the slope of her shoulder blade.

The technology was new, but the sensation wasn't. Butterflies with jagged, razor-tipped wings beat inside her stomach. Refusing to name it anxiety, she settled on aggravation. "Why put it on my back?" she groused. "I'll be sitting down. I could crush the transmitter if I turn the wrong way."

"The techs assured me you'd have to be hit with a sledgehammer to destroy the microphone," he returned reasonably. The fabric stretched over supple skin, adhering invisibly. "Besides, without it, you're not going."

"You can't stop me," she muttered mutinously. "I have an appointment."

"Without the wire, I'll cuff you to my bed."

"Bribes don't work," Fin taunted huskily. "But keep the offer open."

"This isn't a joke, Fin." Caleb tugged her bra strap into place, gave himself the respite of grazing his mouth against velvet flesh. "I have to keep you safe."

Delicious shivers chased anxiety, turning her into his waiting arms. But she resisted the urge to dive into passion, to kiss her worries into oblivion. "We've pushed them to the edge, Caleb. Boxed them in. Tonight, we'll get them." She stroked the frown lines forming around his mouth. "This is for Eric."

"I love you." The words rushed out, astounding them both. But he didn't step back. "I love you, Fin."

"Caleb." She whispered his name, searching for the truth of her response. "Caleb, I—"

"No." He kissed her, shutting off what she'd planned to say. Afraid to hear. Worshipful fingers traced the pale line between lace-covered breasts, lay over the thudding beat of her heart. Her life in his hands. "Wait until this is over."

"Why?" she asked steadily. The flicker of doubt in his eyes, in his demand, neatly slashed at her heart. "Why can't I answer you?"

Because if you say you love me, I won't let you out of this apartment. "I want what you say to be real. No adrenaline. No danger. Just you and me." Together. For a lifetime.

The refusal to hear her stung. Frustration smothered the hurt, though nothing could erase the wound completely. "You don't think I know what I feel?"

"Now isn't the time for this, Fin. Luke and the others will be here soon."

"You started it." She pushed his hand from her, eyes crackling with heat. "I'm a grown woman. I made my choices. However this turns out, Caleb, what I feel—or don't feel—are not illusions."

Before he could respond, she broke away and skated a look over him that flayed at his skin. "My eyes are wide open, and I know who and what you are. And exactly what you're not."

"Damn it, Fin." But the buzzer for his apartment sounded. *Perfect timing,* he thought, harassed. *Try to give a woman space before she breaks your heart, and wind up in a fight.* He jogged over to the door, jabbed at the release. Heard Luke's thanks. "Listen, Fin," he started, but the living room was empty.

"Fin?" He strode to the bedroom, only to find his door locked against him. Jiggling the knob, he demanded, "Open this door."

Only silence met his command. Then the doorbell chimed. "They're here," he shouted unnecessarily. "Come on, Fin. I'm sorry."

The bedroom door opened as the bell pealed a second

time. Fin came into the living room, met his imploring eyes with cool hauteur. "Aren't you going to get that?"

"They can wait." He couldn't. The woman he loved seemed to be slipping away from him. Already, the armor had shifted into place, and the distance became a canyon of misunderstanding. Hands lifted in truce, he started, "Obviously, I did this wrong."

A flick of her wrist cut him off. "Like you said, Caleb, we should wait until after tonight. If there's something to discuss then, we will." She pushed past him and answered the door. Kell, Julia, and Luke trooped inside, ending debate.

"Let's go to the dining room," Caleb invited, his temper barely restrained. "See what you've brought." Fighting to keep his emotions in check, he led them to the mahogany table, where Kell laid a file beside another folder carried in by Luke. Caleb noted the tab on Luke's folder. Tensed, he looked up at Luke. "You've gotten the ballistics report."

"We stopped by the sheriff's department on the way. They faxed the report to me just now."

"And?"

Luke flipped open the report. "The casing had a four-point match. Might not stand up in court, but the prints match Graves. As a law enforcement officer, he was in the system. He shot Eric Baldwin."

Forgetting her mad, Fin drew her hand along his arm, stiffened on the table. "Luke, does Graves own a twenty-two-caliber pistol?"

"When I got to Hallden, most of the sheriff's deputies carried a backup. Graves preferred a Saturday Night Special. Twenty-two caliber," Luke supplied. "It was missing when we searched his home. We find his gun, we can match it to the bullet. My guess is he'll have it on him tonight."

"What about the resolutions?" Knowing Caleb needed a moment, she turned to Kell. "I received the deeds before I headed over here. Are we all set?"

The second file opened, two signatures on the single sheet. "Julia and I have already signed. Mrs. Faraday did not. We've authorized you to negotiate a fair asking price." She pulled out another form. "This is a power of attorney. Gives you the right to immediately sign over the deeds."

"Are these genuine?"

Kell nodded. "Worley isn't stupid. He's done deals like this before, knows what to look for. I didn't want to risk faking any documents."

Aghast, Fin demanded, "But what if I have to sign it and the plan falls apart? She loses the land?"

"Give me some credit, Fin." Kell slid a final sheet across the table. "This is a conflicts of interest form. You'll sign this and swear to disclose any dealings you may have with interested partners. As you intend to become a party on both sides of the transaction to-night, I can move to have your vote annulled as in-valid." Handing her a pen, she added, "Without your vote, the resolution is invalid and the transaction was never authorized."

"Gotcha." Fin swooped her name on the power of at-torney and the conflicts of interest forms.

"Don't sign the resolution until you get the partner-ship agreements." Kell assembled the documents and returned them to the file. She examined her best friend, hunting for signs of nerves. "Are you ready?"

Fin didn't have a choice. Everything hinged on her

now. On getting Graves and Worley to describe their activities. On getting what Caleb needed to bring Stark down. "I've got one more task."

Fin left the table and Caleb followed, knowing what was to come. They hadn't discussed this with the rest of the team, the idea a flash of inspiration from Fin that left him queasy. But she'd convinced him, made him see the potential. Rather than wait for Worley to act, they'd move first.

"Julia, did you get the number for me?" Fin asked.

Reaching into her purse, Julia removed a slip of paper. "I have a friend on staff at the hospital. She was happy to give it to me. But I still don't understand why you wanted Dr. Hestor's cell number."

"Dr. Hestor is going to join our party tonight and bring along his friends." Without waiting for reaction, Fin typed in the number. The cell phone rang several times before the line was answered.

"Dr. Hestor," came the impatient greeting.

"Fin Borders." She closed her eyes, centering. "I have an invitation for you this time, Doctor."

"Another game of poker?" Hestor left the hospital corridor and entered a janitor's closet for privacy. "When you joined us last week, you left us with only the lint in our pockets."

"And helpful information on the Graves investigation."

"True." She'd warned them about the discovery of the knife in Graves's home, slim information, but more than had been released to the media. Ingrid had run a story the next day. "However," he continued, "our arrangement will require substantially better updates if we are to continue our détente."

"I'd rather not." Fin stretched her legs in front of her, gripped the phone tautly. "I'm calling to offer you a chance to recoup your losses and to forestall new ones."

"How is that?"

"One of your colleagues has made me an interesting proposal, and we're meeting tonight for final negotiations. I'd like to have you join us. See if you can counter it."

"Worley." Hestor had no trouble identifying the weasel as the culprit. "What has he told you?"

"More than you have, Doctor. According to Mr. Worley, I can bring valuable land to a pending deal he's cooked up. I assume Stark would like a chance to participate."

"What is Stark?" he asked carefully.

"Don't be coy, Dr. Hestor. I've done my research, listened at keyholes while the sheriff and the ADA fumble around for clues. We both know that your time is winding down, and I happen to know that the feds intend to freeze your assets. I also know who all of your members are. Amazing how easy it is to access bank records when the president isn't looking."

She dangled out the bluff, a last-minute gambit. If Hestor believed she actually had all their names and records, he'd have no choice but to show up and bring the rest. "Whoever makes me the best deal tonight will be able to avoid all the unpleasant collateral damage when the truth is revealed."

Hestor thought about the tools he'd bring. The way he'd dispense with Worley's corpulent body and the more refined death he planned for Fin. "What time and where?"

"Tut, tut, Doctor. Keep your phone on. I'll send you a

text message when I'm ready for you to join us, telling you when and where. You'll have fifteen minutes, so stay in town." She paused, feeling his rage vibrating over the phone. "If Mr. Worley fails to make an appearance or I meet any accidents, my friends in law enforcement will receive an early Christmas gift."

"Is that all?"

"Of course not," she derided. "I want to see every member of Stark. Tonight, you're adding a new member to your ranks. Bring the secret password and the whole club. Talk to you soon."

Disconnecting the call, she lifted her head and met four pairs of eyes bearing a range of expressions. "What?"

"Don't 'what?' us," Kell exploded. "You're sticking yourself inside a bank with the entire Legion of Doom?"

"I'm corralling them all together to make it easier for these guys to do their jobs." Nerves zinging, she hopped up from the sofa. "Caleb agreed with me. Worley is bringing Graves. Now, Hestor will bring the others. We've identified Ingrid Canton and Ernest King, but at least one other name is missing." In countless records, funds had been disbursed to the Stark members they'd identified, except for a sizeable chunk routed through twists and turns even the FBI hadn't been able to track. "Whoever the mastermind is behind Stark understands corporate law. Everyone else is traceable, but not the big fish."

"What makes you think he'll show up tonight?" Julia asked. "Twenty years of hiding. Why would he risk it?"

Caleb answered. "Billions are at stake, and Fin is the key. He'll show."

"I assume you've called in additional reinforcements," Luke asked, pulling out his own telephone. "I've assigned

Cheryl and Deputy Little, even deputized Curly to head communications. With men I'm pulling in from the field, I'll have six officers ready."

"Atlanta's FBI field office is sending nine agents," Caleb confirmed. "We'll have the bank covered, inside and out. And Fin will be miked the whole time." He linked Fin's hand to his, grateful when she didn't pull away. Pride and love filled him, and as soon as it was safe, he'd show her why she belonged with him.

"I'll show Curly how to monitor the radio," Luke added, "but I plan to be inside. You can lead the field."

Fin accepted the solid touch, the silent message. In this, at least, they were together. She'd take it. "Okay. Let's go."

CHAPTER 30

Old-fashioned gas lamps had been lit in the town
square, though their light drew its power from the city's
electrical grid. Still, the chrome-and-glass shapes fit
nicely with the centuries-old brick edifices, including
the Georgia Bank's. Fin stood at the modern plate-glass
door and awaited admission. When the door opened,
Julia would send a text message from Fin's phone, and
the final hand would be dealt.

At precisely 10:00 p.m., James Worley met her on the
steps, keys in hand. He caught sight of the slim briefcase and nodded approvingly. "Give me a moment to
deal with the alarms."

He keyed open the door and disengaged the high-tech
system that would summon the police in fifteen seconds. Emergency lights cast a faint glow around the
interior, shining onto empty teller stations glowing beneath locked doors.

"Come in, come in." He waved Fin inside, walked

briskly past the receptionist's desk toward his office. "This way."

Fin trailed him, noting that he hadn't bothered to re-engage the locks or the alarm. Caleb wouldn't have to leave his post inside the bank to reopen the locks. Confidence bolstered, she prodded, "I thought there would be three of us."

"Patience, Ms. Borders." He unlocked his office door, stepping aside for her to enter. Behind the oversized desk he favored, Michael Graves waited, feet propped on a stack of papers. "Chief Graves, Fin Borders."

"Mr. Graves and I are acquainted." Fin crossed to the leather chair she'd occupied for nearly two weeks and deliberately refused the hand Graves stuck out. Not masking her disgust, she flicked haughty eyes up to meet Worley's. "Your partner once caged me and my friends in a shop office after referring to me by several nasty names. I'd advise you to think wisely about the company you keep."

Infuriated by the slight, Graves kicked his boots off the desk, plunking them on the carpeted floor. Harlots, he'd called them. Jezebels sent to tempt men into mortal sin. Her in particular. But he'd have all the revenge he wanted once she signed over those papers in her briefcase. Until then, he could gnaw on a corner of humble pie. "I'd hoped you'd forgotten. My tongue and temper occasionally get away from me. Can't we let bygones be bygones?" he cajoled.

"For millions of dollars, I'm willing to overlook a myriad of behaviors," Fin said graciously. "Money makes excellent rose-colored glasses."

"Indeed it does." James hurried to sit next to Fin

without attempting to reclaim his rightful seat. Why quibble over places at the table when the feast mattered more? "Did you bring the papers?"

"As agreed." Drawing out the exercise, she casually released the catch, extracted a folder. "The resolution authorizing the sale and immediate transfer of the Metanoia Nature Preserve." She laid the pages on the desk. "Give me a name and a figure to fill in the blanks, and I'll be happy to sign."

"Excellent." James reached out to take a pen from his desk, but Graves beat him to it.

The pen flashed silver in his eager hand. "The corporate entity is Destination Realty. We think it best if everyone believes the new owners are developers. Fewer questions while we receive approval for our application."

"Shrewd." Fin accepted the pen and placed it on the sheets. "Which brings us to the matter of our partnership. The agreements, please."

"Here they are. All in order." James plucked a stack of papers from his in-box tray. "Had these drawn up this afternoon. As you can see, you'll be a twenty percent owner." He flipped through the pages. "I have thirty-five percent, and Michael has forty-five percent."

Fin gave him a stony glare. "We didn't discuss me coming in as a minority partner. Without my land contribution, you've got a shell company and a worthless application."

James winced, having expected her reaction. In fact, he'd warned Graves, who'd stood firm. It was his job to convince her to stay in the deal. "Michael and I conceived the idea, and we've done the legwork on the application. His contacts will get us in line for early consideration." A ball of nerves lodged in his throat. "He, um, we think a fifteen percent promote for me and twenty-five for him is fair."

"A forty percent promote?" Fin bent toward them, seizing the opening. Her gaze flattened, displeasure clear. "I don't see why filling out forms should qualify you to take almost half the corporation's profits. Not when I had to lie to Mrs. Faraday and the others to secure their cooperation. I've invested my relationships in this and all you did was read a grant application. Dangerous endeavor," she sneered. "Almost as hard as framing an old woman for murder."

"We've invested considerably more," Worley stammered out, seeing the rising flush of color on Graves's face. "Fin, please."

Fin saw Graves's reaction and revved up. "Forget it, Worley. Until you two put some real skin in the game, I don't see any reason to throw my lot in with a coward who hides out and lets his banker call the shots. A banker too stupid to cover his bets."

Graves's skin color deepened to beet red, lurching toward violet. For his part, Worley flapped his lips like a beached fish. A few more insults, Fin thought, should do it. "Show me you have a single pair between you, and maybe I'll consider not making my share fifty-five percent."

Rising, she shuffled her papers into the folder, swept up the file. "Until then, the deal is off. Good luck with Stark."

"Sit down!" Graves commanded angrily, his face resembling an underripe eggplant. "You sit your ass back down right now!" Enraged, he pounded on the desktop, sent pens flying. Pages jumped and skated across the slick surface.

Fin held her ground and gave a last push. "Am I supposed to be scared of you? Why? Because you wear a badge?" She patted the space where it used to reside. "Oh, yes. That's gone too, isn't it?"

"I killed Clay Griffin for this land." His meaty hand snatched at hers, grinding her bones together. "Hell, I've even killed a federal agent just for snooping around. Do you think I wouldn't kill you?"

Pain lanced down her arm and her eyes filled, clouding her vision. "You need me," she gasped as he crushed her fingers in his steely grip. "Kill me and what do you have?"

"Satisfaction," Graves retorted. "And your signature on multiple documents that you signed for James at the bank." With his free hand, he circled her neck, thinking about how easy snapping it would be. "We have your handwriting. We don't need you."

"Michael." Fascinated by the violent display, James tapped on the rigid arm. Though eager to see how far Graves would go, he gamely interjected, "If something happens to her, you'll draw attention to the deal. I'm sure she gets your point." Pleading with his eyes, he met Fin's watery gaze. "Don't you, Fin?"

Her airways rasped in desperate gulps. Purple spots danced before her eyes as she nodded her head as much as Graves's hold would allow. "Yes."

Graves released her throat and tossed her hand away. It pleased him to see her collapse into the chair like a broken doll. He flexed his hands, splayed them on the desk. He leered at her, amused at the turn of the tables. "Let that be a lesson. I'm in charge. Not him and not you. Do you understand?"

Certain the mike had picked up his confession, she weakly inclined her head. "Twenty percent."

"Twenty percent of nothing is a bad bargain, Ms. Borders," Hestor intoned. Striding into the office, followed by Ingrid and Ernest, he stopped beside the desk. "Given that Mr. Graves and Mr. Worley have nothing to trade you, I'm sure you'd like to reconsider their offer."

Worley scampered across the carpet, bumping into the towering bookcases that lined the far wall. Trapped, he turned and stammered, "Silas. What are you doing here? How did you get in?"

With an inclination of his head, he instructed Ernest to shut the door. *Now,* Fin thought, *we're all trapped.* "You were kind enough to leave the front door open, and Ms. Borders here extended the invitation."

From the corner of her eye, Fin saw Graves easing his hand toward the small of his back. "Dr. Hestor, I think Mr. Graves intends to shoot you."

Prepared, Hestor removed a shiny nine millimeter, ready to explode. "Lay your gun on the table, Michael. Slowly."

The snub-nosed pistol Fin recognized as a .22 was laid gingerly on the desk's blotter. "Ingrid, if you would?"

Ingrid Canton retrieved the gun, murmuring to Graves, "Should have kept running."

Weapon secured, Hestor beckoned to Worley. "James, stop cowering in the corner. This is a chat among colleagues. Take a seat on the couch. Michael, please join him." The men obeyed the orders without comment.

Hatred flamed in Graves's eyes as he passed Fin, his lips drawn into a snarl.

Ernest King, the former politician, stood guard at the door. He didn't appear to carry a weapon, but his bulk made escape difficult. Fin settled into her chair and waited.

"Ms. Borders, I think this is your meeting," Hestor said graciously. The gun glinted in his hand, but he took care not to aim the barrel in her direction.

Understanding the concession, Fin said, "I appreciate your attendance. But I only count three of you. Where's the man in charge?"

"For tonight's purposes, that would be me," Hestor asserted, his suspicion confirmed. As Judge Majors had guessed, Fin had been bluffing about knowing all of their identities. Majors's identity was still hidden. Would remain so. But Stark would perish in Worley's office tonight. "Our agreement was membership in Stark in exchange for the deeds to the preserve. I've brought Stark. Ingrid Canton. Ernest King. James Worley. And our former colleague, Michael Graves."

The calm admission tipped Fin off. Somewhere, she'd made an error. Hestor had no intention of letting any of them leave this office. A woman who made her living reading people could see murder in his flat, emotionless eyes. "How does joining your ranks work?"

"First, you are vetted. For necessary skills and humiliating peccadilloes. Like Ingrid here. Tell her what you did to earn your membership, dear."

The blond woman's face constricted in a mask of dislike, but she complied. "There is a tape of me. With my lover."

"Lovers," Hestor corrected with caustic delight. "Three

strapping young men who hadn't quite learned to shave. Eighth-graders, weren't they?" Before she could spit out her venom, he indicated Ernest King. "Our venerable politician made his political name by stuffing the ballot box. Paid off a clerk to register citizens in the grave-yard. Unfortunately, our Mr. King was cheap and the clerk threatened to tell. King joined Stark to protect his seat and to deal with his blackmailer. A fruitful partner-ship, wouldn't you agree, Ernest?"

The bluff older man didn't flinch. "Eighteen years of service to the citizens of Hallden County. No regrets."

"What about Graves?" Fin prompted, stalling. Where the hell was the cavalry? "How did you let such a wimp under your tent?"

Graves's growl ended abruptly when Ingrid aimed his own gun at his temple. She explained spitefully, "Graves was a pissant in the sheriff's department who liked to record other people's conversations. He also showed a predilection toward hookers and bondage. Very stimulating photos demonstrate his remarkable flexibility."

"And Worley's mistake was embezzlement." Fin met the shocked looks evenly. "People tend to stick with the same behaviors, good or bad. With Worley's gambling addiction and poor skills, he's been tapping your ac-counts to pay for his habit. If he's doing it now, odds are he did it before."

"Now for your secret, Ms. Borders." Hestor came closer, hovered. "You have the best secret of us all. Murder and theft. Leaving Louis Pippin's body to burn while you stole his money."

Unfazed, Fin retorted, "I don't know what you're talking about. Although I did see a report of an elderly woman given an overdose of barbiturates by a sloppy doctor. Take some of the pills yourself, Doc?"

The smash of his hand had pain bursting along her skin, her eye smarting. "I'm not an addict," he denounced brutally. "I am a physician."

Fin cradled her wounded face, the accusation a shot in the dark. One that had hit its mark. "Fine. You're entirely sane and sober." Lifting her head, she challenged, "But you haven't been in Hallden long enough to have rounded up this den of thieves. And how did any of you manage to gather the evidence against one another?" She shook her head, to clear it and to make her point. "I have records on you five, but there's a sixth person. The one who found you all. Who put you together."

She scanned the gathered, registered the varying degrees of fear. "Who is it? I'll sign over the deed to the person who tells me who is truly in charge."

Worley moved, a timid sway that could have been the result of nerves. But in the next second, a bullet careened from Hestor's gun and buried its lead in Worley's chest. Worley stumbled, listed, then rolled off the sofa onto the floor of his office. Dead.

The report of the gun hung over the room. Hestor aimed at Fin, ready to fire again. "The deeds. Now."

But Fin saw the slight movement in the window near the door. Timing their entry, she whacked the briefcase into Hestor's weapon and dove for the cover of the desk. Behind Ernest, Caleb burst into the room, a yellow FBI label emblazoned on his vest. "Get down!" he commanded. "Everyone down!" He aimed at Hestor, waving him against a wall.

Out of the corner of his eye, Caleb saw King move. "Luke!"

Luke barreled in behind him, tackling King as he tried to flee. King toppled over. Seeing no escape, Ingrid wisely complied, dropping Graves's pistol on the carpet. "Hold your positions!" Caleb yelled to the agents waiting outside the door.

In a flash, Graves dove for his pistol. He groped on the carpet and reared up, hammer cocked, aimed at Fin. "I'll kill her! Another step and I'll kill her." He dragged Fin from where she was hiding beneath the desk's overhang, then put the pistol at her temple. "Move back! Move back!"

The steel scraped against the bruise where Hestor had struck her. Fin struggled for air as Graves's arm closed on her windpipe again. Still, she scrabbled up with him as he forced her to her feet. "I want clear passage. I want to get out of here."

Caleb kept his weapon trained on Hestor, but he only had eyes for Fin. A vicious mark stained her face, and her eyes fluttered as she tried to stay conscious. "Don't hurt her, Graves. We can work something out."

"I was a goddamned cop, Matthews. I know when I'm being humored." To prove his point, he dug the barrel into the wound, and Fin whimpered. "This is real. I'll blow her brains all over this office unless you pull back."

On the floor, Luke straddled King, the fallen man inert. Placing his foot on the man's neck, he stood, slightly behind Caleb. "As a cop, you know we're not going to let you walk out of here. Besides, where would you go? Susanne left you and your assets are frozen. You've got nothing."

"I've got her." Reason bowed to panic. "And he's not going to let me hurt her," Graves retorted, ignoring

Luke as he focused on Caleb. "Worley told me about the two of you. Like the sheriff, you managed to get inside a Faraday girl's pants. How was the ride?"

Hold on, Fin. The prayer repeated in his head, a litany. "You may not have noticed, but I'm not one of your rookie cops. I'm FBI. Special Agent Matthews. So I know your gambit. Make me angry enough to drop my guard. Or scare me into making a mistake." He looked at Fin, her head lolling as oxygen dwindled. "First of all, if you don't give her some air, you'll be holding dead weight, which is harder to move."

Graves automatically eased his vise and Fin sucked in the air shakily. Her vision began to clear, sufficient to focus on Caleb. He was still speaking to Graves, telling him something about her.

"Sleeping with a woman doesn't mean much when you've been undercover for years. Don't mistake access for affection. Unlike Sheriff Calder here, I know the difference."

Fin stiffened, stricken. Which is why her eyes caught sight of Hestor as he grabbed for his gun. "Caleb!" The scream ripped from her raw throat as the scene played out.

Hestor dropped to the carpet and rolled toward Ingrid. A bullet ripped from his gun, and his shot flung the woman into the base of the couch, where she remained, immobile. Luke took advantage of the melee to aim at Hestor and fire. The doctor squeezed off another shot, which lodged in the ceiling as he fell.

Caleb held steady, eyes locked on Graves. Waiting for an opening. In the jumbled passage of seconds, he found it. Graves hauled Fin forward, surging for the door. The Glock jerked in Caleb's grip as he planted a single shot in Graves's shoulder. Graves flew back, releasing Fin, who caught herself on the corner of the desk.

Leaping the dead bodies, Caleb reached Graves before the man regrouped. A booted heel stomped into the bullet wound in his shoulder, but Graves's groan of agony did nothing to quiet Caleb's rage. He loomed over Graves. "I could have killed you," he told him softly. "For touching her, I could kill you. But you're going to prison, you son of a bitch. For every year you stole from Eric Baldwin. For every mark you put on Fin. Michael Graves, you are under arrest for the murder of Special Agent Eric Baldwin. For the murder of Clay Griffin. For the attempted murder of Findley Borders. And for any other crime I can think of." Heel slick with blood, he scrubbed it across the moaning man's heaving chest, then kicked him to roll him over. He manacled his wrists, wrenching harder than necessary. "You have the right to remain silent. Anything you say can and will be held against you. . . ."

CHAPTER 31

Julia wrapped a poultice around Fin's neck. "Ouch, Jules. This is cold," Fin complained.

"They have warmer pads at the hospital. Since you refuse to go, this is what you get." Julia secured the home remedy with a piece of tape, then checked on the ice pack lying against Fin's cheek. Tenderly, she stroked the black hair away from her friend's face, its skin mottled and bruised. "You should have been more careful."

Stretched out on the bed in their guest room, Fin couldn't help but agree. "Kell back yet?"

"No, she went with Caleb and Luke to the county jail. I think she regrets being a defense attorney for the first time. Kept muttering about who should prosecute Graves and King." Julia fiddled with the quilt she'd thrown over Fin. "She's worried about Luke. This is the first fatal shooting he's had since leaving Chicago."

"If he hadn't taken Hestor down, the man would have killed all of us." Fin shuddered as the fragments of the evening reeled through her. "Hestor murdered Worley and Canton. Would have taken out King, if he hadn't already collapsed."

"Heart attack." Julia had contacted the hospital and gotten an update. "Right now, he's touch and go."

A knock sounded at the door. It opened, and Eliza carried in a tray, steam rising from a sturdy ceramic bowl. "You'll eat something," she said without preamble.

"I'm not sick, Mrs. F. Just wounded in the line of duty." But Fin struggled to sit up, aided by Julia. Fluffy pillows pressed into her back, reminding her that she'd fallen against the edge of the desk. Hopefully, the aspirin Julia had given her would kick in soon. "I'll be fine."

"Don't placate me when I've seen a man's finger-prints on your throat," Eliza warned fiercely, gaze mist-ing. They wouldn't tell her how close Fin had come to dying, but she had her mother's intuition. Willing her hands steady, she traced the arrogant arch of Fin's brow. "Your eye is puffy and red. You need to see a doctor."

"I am a doctor," Julia reminded her dryly. "Other than being stubborn, which is a permanent affliction, she'll be good as new in a couple of days." She set her medical bag on the nightstand.

"Fin, eat your soup. I'll be back to check on you in an hour." Eliza stood and motioned to Julia. "Come along."

"Where are you going?" Fin demanded, annoyed at her reluctance to be alone. She'd seen death before. But standing in its cold, harsh center had shaken her. Her hand lifted to her throat, touching the bandage. "Stay for a while. I haven't finished eating."

Eliza bussed her forehead with a kiss. "You have a very anxious visitor. We'll leave you to it."

They passed Caleb hovering outside the door. "She'll mend," Julia soothed. "Don't let her talk too much. Which is probably a good idea on any day."

Caleb nodded, turned. Only to be stopped by Eliza.

"Caleb."

"Yes, ma'am."

"I owe you an apology." She took his hands, the ones that had saved her daughter's life. "Thank you. For keeping her safe."

He shrugged, strangled by failure. "If I'd done that, she wouldn't be lying in that bed."

"Don't be daft, boy." Eliza shook her head. "Fin is whole and here. Without you beside her, neither would be true." Remembering her own lost chances, ones she never discussed, she bent enough to advise, "I've made my share of mistakes, Caleb. Not accepting love is my dearest one. We rarely get another chance." With a gentle squeeze, she left him outside the cracked door.

Screwing up his courage, Caleb gave a light knock. Afraid she wouldn't answer, he entered without invitation. Fin lay propped against emerald pillows, a white breakfast tray balanced in her lap and white gauze taped around her bruised skin. Yards of jet-black hair tumbled in disarranged curls, flowing onto shoulders bare except for slender ivory straps. She looked glorious, but his eyes kept returning to the bandages.

Rage fisted his hands, a ball of fury stuck in his throat. "I should have killed him."

Fin set the tray aside and folded her hands in her lap. "Kill him and prove that you're as mean as Graves?"

"Maybe I am." He stared at her wounds. "He hurt you. Hit you."

"Strangled me a couple of times." Fin reached up to

the bandage on her face. "No, remember this one was from Hestor. When I called him a drug addict."

A shudder coursed through him as he recalled the sound. "I heard you provoking him, heard you moan." The memory propelled him across the floor to her side. "What were you thinking? We had Graves cold."

"But you still don't have the head of Stark. He's still out there. With Hestor, Canton, and Worley dead, and King on his deathbed, Graves is your only link."

Though the realization galled him, Caleb admitted, "So we'll get him to give us the name. Make a deal."

Fin's eyes narrowed. "How? By trading Eric's life for a reduction in sentence?" She'd been wrestling with the angles, the other plays she could have made. "If I hadn't let Graves grab me, you'd have been able to turn one of the others."

His hands closed over her shoulders, cautious of hidden bruises. But she would hear him. "Without you, we wouldn't have all the information we got about Stark. About Graves and Worley and the bank. No, we didn't lop off the head, but we will. And, for all intents and purposes, we destroyed them, Fin. You did that." He stroked her face where the skin was unmarred. Tomorrow, he would tell her about the message left at Hestor's, vowing revenge by the illusive head of Stark.

Tomorrow, he decided. For now, he had a more critical mission. "I'm proud of you. In awe of you. All of the agents listening in couldn't believe you weren't one of ours."

"I'm a good liar, Caleb." She grabbed his wrist, stilling his gentle touch. Her brain couldn't function when he unraveled her like that. "Will you head back to

Washington? I assume since your cover's been blown, you're out of a job at the Hallden DA's office."

"The DA called. He wants to see me in his office tomorrow. I doubt it's for hugs and kisses."

"Obviously, he hasn't sampled them."

"Luckily, I've got a day job."

The FBI. In Washington. "You planning to head home soon? To Washington?"

Caleb shrugged. "Depends on what Chief Benton says."

"She's a fool if she loses you. Only a fool would turn away a man as brilliant and passionate and committed as you are. A man whose loyalty survives the worst of tests, even death." She brought his hand to her lips, saying her good-byes. "You are the best man I've ever known, Caleb. And if you need me to tell her that, just drop me a line."

He brought his face to hers, eyes solid and bright. "I nearly lost you tonight."

"You saved my life. After the car crash, I'd say that makes us even."

"I helped with that, so I'm still up one." Leaning away, he reached into his back pocket. "You owe me."

When he dropped a deck of cards into her hands, Fin looked up, confused. "What's this?"

"A gamble. Shuffle."

Automatically, her hands removed the cards, then mixed them with a flourish. But her hands trembled, and she scattered the cards. Caleb helped gather those that had fallen, and she tried again. After a fourth pass, she handed them to him for a cut. "Here."

Caleb sliced the cards and restacked them, his heart

bumping in his chest. Earlier, he'd made a botch of this. "Deal."

"Any particular game?" she asked quietly. "Don't bet unless you know the game."

"You pick."

"Five card draw." She dealt the cards, asking, "What's your ante?"

He tipped her eyes up to his, his future hanging in the balance. "My heart. And, if that isn't enough, I'll throw in the rest of my life."

Startled, she let the cards flutter down, her nimble fingers useless. "That's a huge risk. You're putting a lot on the table."

"But think about what I could win." Cradling her damaged cheek, he explained, "A woman who is smarter and more courageous than anyone I've ever known. You're devoted to what you believe in. Who you believe in. Until you, I didn't realize how sexy sarcasm could be. And this face, this beautiful, fabulous face. You're willing to do what has to be done for those you love, and I will give anything to be one of those people."

Hope kindled, roared into flame, but Fin held her ace. "I tried to tell you today, but you didn't want to hear it."

"I didn't want to hear you tell me no." The admission was simple, eloquent. "I love you, Fin."

Fin steeled herself, taking her biggest gamble. "And I love you. If love means trusting a person with your life and believing your heart will be safe in his hands, then I've never loved another."

Dazed by the tide of love flooding through him, he drew her to him, kissing her as he would for the rest of their lives.

When they finally surfaced, he murmured against her lips, "Turn over the cards, Fin."

She did, and a wash of red stared up at her. "These are queens of hearts. All of them," she gasped, thinking of how many decks had to be lying around. Lifting her eyes to him, she glared lovingly. "You cheated."

Caleb shrugged. "Anything for you."

AUTHOR'S NOTE

Fin Borders returns to Hallden to face her past and, in the process, finds her heart. Telling the story of a woman who dances in the shadows is always a treat— and a challenge. But guided by her best friends, Kell Jameson and Julia Warner, and their surrogate mother, Eliza Faraday, there's hope.

Fin chases danger, and Caleb fights evil. So, of course, they must career into each other's lives as Stark's secrets are revealed. In the final chapter of this trilogy, Julia will face a threat to her image of herself and her very life. Stark has been crippled, but it has one last trick to play on the women of the Faraday Center. Please join me for their triumphant conclusion.

I eagerly welcome your comments and questions at www.selenamontgomery.com, by e-mail at selena_montgomery@hotmail.com, or by mail at:

P.O. Box 170352
Atlanta, Georgia 30317-0352

Happy Reading,
Selena